A NIGHT FULL OF STARS

A Siamese Love Story

A NIGHT FULL OF STARS

A Siamese Love Story

A novel by
V. Vinicchayakul
Translated by Lucy Srisuphapreeda

RIVER BOOKS

First published and distributed in 2024 by
River Books Press Co., Ltd
396/1 Maharaj Road, Phraborommaharajawang,
Bangkok 10200 Thailand
Tel: (66) 2 225-0139, 2 225-9574
Email: order@riverbooksbk.com
www.riverbooksbk.com

Editor: Narisa Chakrabongse
Production supervision: Suparat Sudcharoen
Design: Ruetairat Nanta

ISBN 978 616 451 080 7

Printed and bound in Thailand by Parbpim Co., Ltd

Contents

Translator's Preface

A *Night Full of Stars* is an award-winning novel by V. Vinicchayakul, one of Thailand's foremost novelists, and the author of over a hundred novels, many of which have been adapted for film and television. It is named after a song penned by King Prajadhipok, or Rama VII, the seventh king of the Chakri Dynasty and the last absolute monarch of Siam. The song has special meaning for Gade, a young woman from Phetchaburi, whose life is turned upside down after her marriage to Nart, a dashing young army officer, otherwise known as Colonel Phraya Wisetsingnart. The poignant and intriguing story of Gade's life takes place against the turbulent backdrop of Siam's Revolution of 1932, which transformed the country's system of governing from an absolute monarchy to a constitutional monarchy, ushering in a new era of social and political upheaval. Besides giving the reader a profound insight into the Thai way of life during this tumultuous period in Thailand's history, the novel's universal themes of love, loyalty, greed, anger, lust and jealousy will resonate with readers across cultural backgrounds.

I would like to thank V. Vinicchayakul, the novel's author, for her gift of this enthralling and heart-warming novel, which so impressed me that I was motivated to translate it into English in the hope that it will engage and inspire English-speaking readers as it has done Thai readers for over two decades.

Prologue

People slowly left the large pavilion after the first night's funeral prayers had been completed. The large number of people gradually diminished. A few left by taxi or bus, but most left in their own cars, some large and others small, until the last car had disappeared.

Two of the temple attendants switched off the last light in the pavilion and slid the metal gate shut before walking away together.

The great hall was left in shadows with only the dim rays of the waxing moon shining through the air vents onto the fine golden casket, the fresh flowers that decorated the room, and the large and small wreaths lined up tightly together. They all had a black bar across them with the name of a person of rank and status, who had sent the wreaths to pay their last respects.

An old lady dressed in Thai costume decorated with the Most Illustrious Order of Chulachomklao looked out from a framed photograph, with a half-length portrait. Her face, although wrinkled with age, still retained much of the beauty of her youth. Her eyes were penetrating and bold, and stared out of the picture as if they still had life in them and gazed upon their surroundings with undiminished interest.

The smell of incense wafted faintly through the hall, and the cold silence created an atmosphere quite different from outside. Dark shadows in the corners of the hall stretched out across the floor as time passed, creating strange shapes as if many thin bodies were welcoming the woman in the picture. The squeaky wooden floorboards and the sound of the wind gently blowing the branches on the windows sounded like whispers greeting the person who had just departed from this world and was about to step into the next.

If there was a spirit in there, it would probably have been drifting around the picture for the last time, recollecting the events that had taken place in her life before bidding farewell to everything without ever looking back.

1

The Young Woman from Ban Tha Hin

From the time she was born until she was sixteen years old, Gade felt that nothing in her life ever changed, apart from her body that had grown with age. Other than that, her life went on as usual year after year. As for her future, she could more or less see the examples from her mother and the other women around her in Phetchaburi province.

If anyone had asked her what she remembered most about the first sixteen years of her life, she would have answered without hesitation the orchards of Ban Tha Hin in the district of Na Phra Lan, her first home, the home where she had lived happily since the day she was born until the force of a storm in her life blew her far away never to return.

The morning sun shone on the spacious yard in front of the rural Thai-style houses on stilts with thatched roofs. There were two houses, a large one and a small one, connected by a wide veranda that reached all the way to the small kitchen behind the house, indicating the owner's wealthy status.

The several large mango trees that shaded the veranda were so full of fruit that their branches could hardly bear their weight. Beneath the house, small spry black chickens scratched in the dirt for insects. The courtyard was flattened dirt up to the garden furrow. Then beyond that were green bushes interspersed with several kinds of fruit trees, and tall dense bamboo clumps, which obscured the thatched roofs of the neighbouring houses from view.

The owner of the house was a tall, thin middle-aged man with yellow skin who wore only an old *jongkraben*, a long cloth wrapped around the waist and pulled up between the knees, with a cloth over his shoulder. His chewed betel nut incessantly, and he walked out of the house down the steps and into the garden as he did daily.

He turned to call someone in the house.

"Gade, bring the rice early today, and bring enough for Uncle Puan. He said he might come to see me later."

A young face with flawless ivory skin poked out of the window of the smaller house where his daughters slept and called out brightly.

"Today's a holiday. Mother wants me to go to the temple."

"Then tell Rern to bring me some instead. You're old enough that I shouldn't have to tell you."

With that he leapt over the furrow with agility and disappeared into the garden.

Gade's father was a hard worker in keeping with his Chinese ancestry, and he had worked tirelessly in his orchards until he had gained a status inferior to no one in the neighbourhood. The other houses were close enough to be within earshot if the residents called each other. All of them in the small community were related or knew each other and even further afield in Phetchaburi town, it seemed that everyone was connected in some way.

Whenever Gade thought of her father, she simply saw a tall thin man with yellow skin whose mouth was stained red from chewing betel, but her relatives said that when he was young, he was as handsome as a folk theatre hero.

Thinking of her mother, she pictured a plump woman with a cloth wrapped around her torso paired with the dark *jongkraben* that she usually wore. Her mother was fastidious about her dress, not sloppy like some of the villagers. Her short hair was regularly smoothed down with wax, and although her mouth was dark from chewing betel, she made sure never to have betel juice stains on her clothes, or on the floor around the spittoon. It was this same fastidiousness that made her renowned for cooking delicious dishes, both savoury and sweet, and whenever anyone had a party, they would regularly ask her to help with the cooking.

Gade ambled behind her mother along the small cart track that ran in front of their house to Phrip Phri Temple in the sun that was getting stronger by the minute. They passed villagers carrying baskets on their hips, who called out their usual greeting of asking each other where they were going. Her mother answered good-naturedly that she was taking alms to the temple because it was a holiday.

At sixteen years old, Gade was radiant like a flower that was starting to bloom. When people saw her for the first time, she was so striking they would have to ask whose daughter that pretty girl was. Of the four girls, everyone said the third daughter of Mee and Eeam had a combination of their best attributes. Her radiant creamy skin contrasted with those girls who worked outside in the sun, and she was slim like her father, not plump like her mother. She had her father's attractive slim mouth and round chin, and her mother's dark eyebrows and penetrating eyes.

Several of the young men in her village and the next had their eyes on her. Gade wasn't interested in any of them, and the more they tried to hang around and come to see her, the more she loathed them. She was irritated by all of them, no matter who they were, and would stay in the house, refusing to come out to greet them. Eeam went along with this and conspired to keep her out of their sight.

Almost all the women in her neighbourhood had married young. It could be said that within a year or two of cutting off their topknots, they were considered women*. Some were even married by the time they were only thirteen or fourteen years of age, so that their parents wouldn't have to worry about them anymore. If someone's daughter remained at home for too long, it was feared she might get into trouble and end up running away with a boy and bringing shame on her family. Or if she didn't get into trouble, she would end up a spinster and her parents would be ashamed that nobody wanted her.

Fortunately, or unfortunately, Gade was spared both of these predicaments. Being her mother's favourite daughter, her mother

---

* The topknot cutting ceremony was a rite of passage from childhood to adulthood with the topknot being a symbol of childhood.

refused to give her to any of the young men in the neighbourhood, or in other neighbourhoods further afield. She was hoping for a son-in-law whom she really liked. Because Eeam loved her third daughter best, she didn't make her do hard work like getting water or cutting firewood, which was the duty of her older sisters. Instead, she had Gade stay in the house to help take care of her younger sister and help with the cooking and the housework.

When Gade had passed the age for cutting off her topknot, apart from helping her father in the orchards, her mother had her help with the trading of some of the produce they grew to sell in the town, or to people who came to buy it directly. Therefore, the first thing Eeam had made her learn was to calculate the correct change. Even though she couldn't read and write, she was better at math than any of her sisters.

Mother and daughter walked a little longer and saw the temple chapel in the distance. Phrip Phri temple where her mother regularly made merit was close to her home. The abbot's name was Abbot Ward, and it was said that he was a distant relative of Gade's grandparents. Eeam's mother, Gade's grandmother, had been the abbot's attendant from when he was first ordained until her death, after which Gade's mother had taken on the role, and continued until he became the temple abbot, on account of his seniority.

Abbot Ward was so renowned for accurate fortune-telling that everyone in the neighbourhood talked about it, but he wouldn't tell anyone's fortune unless it was absolutely necessary. Eeam, like most people at that time, was a firm believer in horoscopes, and when she went to make merit, because she was the abbot's attendant and his relative, she succeeded in persuading him to predict her daughter's fate.

That day, after she had received the precepts, and was sitting discussing the merit-making ceremony that was coming up the next month, she steered the conversation towards knowing her daughter's fate once more. Eventually, either because he thought the time was right, or because he was fed up of being asked, the abbot agreed. Even after several decades, Gade could still picture the old abbot taking out a piece of paper painted black, and asking for the date and time of her birth before writing numbers in column after column with a clay pencil. He pursed his lips as if he was considering something before going to get an old book out of a cupboard and opening it carefully, because the paper was so old that it almost fell apart in his hands.

Then he gave the prediction in a hoarse, but steady voice:

"*Gade's fate is different from the rest of her family. She will be more fortunate than anyone else in the village, but she will also suffer because of both the merit and the karma she has made. Gade, I will warn you of two matters. First, you must learn to depend on yourself and not depend on others, since others will depend on you. Second, your husband will have a higher rank than anyone in the village. In the end, you will have rank and wealth, but your karma will come from fortune that is a curse. Whenever you have happiness, karma will suppress it, so that you can't attain it fully. Although you will be fortunate, you will suffer as a result, and although you will have a husband of high rank, you will suffer because of him. When you become aware of this, you must make merit and follow the precepts to reverse the old karma.*"

When he saw the alarm in Gade's face, his face softened and he comforted her.

"The important thing is never to give up. You are like a fish that has to swim against the current. If you leave it to fate, you'll have no way out. I've told many people their fortunes and I've never seen anyone's like yours."

Eeam listened and her face darkened. Her daughter would have a husband of high rank. This pleased her, but when the abbott said Gade would suffer, she became uneasy.

When she questioned him, the abbot refused to divulge any more.

'Gade will suffer because of her husband,' Eeam told herself after she had pondered the prediction.

She would have to be vigilant. If she was uneasy about someone, she wouldn't give her daughter to him and that would be the end of it. If she were to remain a spinster, what of it? She could take care of her parents when they were old.

Eeam had a younger brother, whom all the family was proud of, named Sot. He was a sergeant major in the army, whose military title and rank was Muen Reng Ngan Rob, but all the villagers respectfully called him Tan Muen for short. Eeam, as his older sister, courteously called her younger brother Por Muen.

Gade had seen 'Uncle Muen' since she was small. He wore a soldier's uniform that made him look more formal than the other villagers, except that he didn't wear shoes, since he was used to walking in bare feet because it was more comfortable. When he came to visit, 'Uncle Muen' didn't walk or come by cart like the rest of the villagers. Instead, he would arrive in a dignified manner, riding a big horse with several soldiers following behind him.

Greeting his sister, he would say, "I was passing this way, so I've stopped by for a drink of water. I'm in a hurry, so please don't go to any trouble on my account."

But every time, her parents would busy themselves setting out a mat on the veranda and finding betel, cigarettes and cold water to welcome him. If he arrived when it was almost mealtime, he would be persuaded to stay for a meal, and they would eat together on a mat on the veranda. During the meal, they would enjoy his conversation, since Muen always had stories from the town to tell them, which were exciting for people used to staying in the orchards and almost never getting to see the world outside.

Muen's house was also in Ban Tha Hin, some distance from Gade's house, so it wasn't convenient to visit him very often, except when there was an important event.

Gade had heard several months before that Muen's eldest son, Klai, had reached the age to be ordained as a monk that year, and his father had declared that his ordination was to be a grand occasion to which everyone in the village was to be invited. Naturally, all his relatives would be there to help out.

Gade became certain that the event was imminent when she heard her mother tell her father, "I'll need to go and stay there two or three days in advance. Por Muen says it will be a big party and a lot of townspeople will be going."

Gade and her sister were sitting close by and looked at their father inquisitively, so he answered, "I'm going on the Friday. If you want to go before, it's up to you."

"I'll take Gade with me. Rern can follow with you. Gade can help cook the rice and simmer the curry. It will be better if there are a few of us."

Since Gade hardly went anywhere, she couldn't help feeling excited about going to stay at her uncle's house. Besides, this was an important event, so she had to prepare her best outfit. Eeam went straight to Phrip Phri Temple for the gold jewellery that she'd left with the abbot for safekeeping and brought it home for her favourite daughter to wear.

Many decades later, when Gade had been to many grander parties, no event would ever be imprinted in her memory as indelibly as her cousin's ordination. Her excitement didn't begin at the party, however, but stirred within her from the first moment she stepped inside Muen's door. The atmosphere was bustling and people were scurrying from the yard, up to the veranda, and into the kitchen behind. On the washing line in the yard, cloth dyed with cumin, for making the ordination robe, was being checked to see if the colour had taken, and when it was found to be too pale, the women who were dying it sighed, "Oh no! We'll have to add more vinegar!"

Chan, her aunt, squatted down to add vinegar to the dye bucket, which was heaped with cumin and pounded, in order to make the dye thicker before putting the cloth back in. This time when she lifted it out, it was bright yellow and considered 'done'. Everyone heaved a sigh of relief as they hung the cloth in the sun so that it would be dry in time for the ordination day – another job done.

Chan's second son was cutting bunches of bananas from behind the house along with clusters of coconuts for curry. His helpers were a group of boys who carried the fruit to the kitchen to be put in the cooking. The sounds of chilli paste being pounded, coconuts being scraped, and sizzling as things were added to the pan, could be heard continuously, interspersed with the voices of the women in the kitchen. Meals had to be prepared for all the relatives who came to help every day as well as the special food for the ordination day. It was a mammoth task that required the assistance of almost all the women in the village. Meanwhile the children that had come with their parents ran around in the yard.

The men had less to do than the women, and since it wasn't often that they got to meet up with all their friends, they decided to have a good time. Some formed a group and gambled for small amounts of money in a leafy spot under the big trees in the yard.

Some older men, who didn't want to gamble played draughts on the veranda all day long, leaving the work inside and outside the kitchen to the women. Muen was a generous host and ordered his subordinates to bring fermented palm juice and rice wine for all the guests, but was careful that no one had too much.

Eeam had the job of cooking *panaeng* curry with chicken, and roasted curry, her specialty, while Gade was assigned to make desserts for the visitors from the town.

Muen told his older sister, "My boss is being kind enough to join us for Klai's ordination. We must make him welcome and provide meals and desserts especially for him. Oh, yes, can you make him *kanom krok*?"

Eeam's *kanom krok* was unlike the rest of the villagers', and she only made it for special occasions at the temple. Besides the soft sweet and delicate taste of the coconut pastry, Eeam's topping was made from finely chopped shrimp, stir-fried with garlic and pepper and garnished with coriander leaves to enhance the appetizing fragrance.

Sometimes, she made it with chopped chicken or chopped pork, but it was for the shrimp that she was renowned.

This time, since Eeam had to cook big pots of two different curries, she assigned Gade to make *kanom krok*.

"You make it instead. You've made it so many times you're an expert. You don't need me to supervise," Eeam told her confidently. "Make sure it's good. An important person is coming."

On the day of the ordination, Gade met that 'important person' for the first time.

When Friday evening arrived, Gade remembered that she had been sitting on the floor, her legs neatly folded to the side, with her parents and sister on the veranda, which was being used for the ordination ceremony that evening. It was then that she heard excited voices outside the house and the sound of the people who had been sitting next to the door above the stairs standing up. Something important was happening.

Someone shouted out, "Tan Muen's boss is here!"

One of the hosts unrolled the small mat that he had prepared and set it out especially for the honoured guest. Muen's daughter hurried to fetch a tray of betel and cigarettes and set them down close by. The other people sitting there moved back, leaving a space in the middle so that the new arrival could walk to his seat easily.

Several men in military uniforms walked up in an orderly file.

Gade heard her uncle say respectfully, "Please come upstairs, sir. We're most honoured that you've come."

Even though all the men wore similar looking uniforms, with just one look of her inexperienced seventeen-year-old eyes, Gade could tell who was the leader, just as the king of the elephants can be distinguished from the others, because of his dignity.

When she recalled her feelings when they first met, Gade remembered only the surprise she felt at seeing Muen's 'boss' because, in her mind, surely a person of such importance had to be considerably older than Muen in order to command such respect.

But the man who sat down on the mat that the host had prepared especially for him was quite young! Even though he was well past the age of ordination, he was far from old or even middle-aged. He was tall, even taller than Muen. His build was about the same, but he looked broader because his shoulders and his back were straight and dignified.

When Gade glanced quickly at his face, afraid to look him in the eye, she noticed his suntanned chin and cheeks and his smooth youthful skin that was not wrinkled like Muen's.

Then she heard a deep and dignified voice ask the host, "Is this your eldest son?"

Klai nervously placed his palms together and sat with his head bowed looking awkward. His father answered politely, "This is him, sir. He's old enough to be ordained, so he's going to be a monk for a year."

"That's good. When I was twenty, I was a monk at Bowonniwet Temple."

The soldiers that had been following him sat next to her father. She saw her father place his palms together and ask about the 'boss' in a whisper. The answer was whispered back, "His name's Major Luang Radaronayuth. He just moved here from Ratchaburi two or three months ago. He's the army base commander. He's not arrogant. He's kind and gracious to his subordinates. If he's invited to any occasion, he'll always attend."

"He's a major already? He looks young," her father whispered in awe.

"Some people are born lucky, Mee."

Eeam nudged her daughter, and when Gate turned to look at her, she whispered, "Go and help Aunt Chan bring the snacks for the boss, but don't take them to him yourself. Aunt Chan will do it."

Having seen all the young soldiers that followed the 'boss', Eeam was worried that her daughter would catch their eyes. By the time dinner was served it would be dark, so for now there were only the snacks that Gade had just finished making and had arranged nicely on a separate tray. Aunt Chan crawled to put the snacks in front of the 'boss' and sat on the floor with her legs to the side so that she might attend to him.

The leader of the ordination rites arrived, and everyone quieted down. They listened to him describe the virtue of mothers in carrying their children, giving birth to them and raising them, and explained how a son demonstrated his gratitude by being ordained. Everyone agreed that he spoke with such conviction that many an ordination candidate had been moved to tears, while the women became sentimental and had to dab their eyes with handkerchiefs. The sermon was long and lasted until after dark, so they needed to break every now and then, for people to stretch their legs and chat. Then the host brought out both sweet and savoury dishes for the guests, while the children went straight to the kitchen to help themselves.

Gade helped her mother take a tray of savoury dishes from the kitchen for her aunt to place in front of the 'boss'. It was at that moment that she heard him speak.

"Won't you join me, Muen?"

"Please go ahead, sir."

"I won't be able to eat all this by myself. Whoever made it will think I don't like it."

Muen smiled politely.

"I'm sure you'll like it, sir. My older sister made it. She used to work for a noble family and can cook Bangkok food."

"No wonder. I never thought I'd find *kanom krok* topped with shrimp in Phetchaburi. It tastes like what the aristocrats in Bangkok eat. Where's your sister? I'd like to see her and reward her."

Eeam crawled in front of him politely and the talkative Chan declared excitedly, "Eeam made the *panaeng* curry and the roasted curry, but her daughter Gade made the *kanom krok*."

"Well, in that case I must reward her daughter!" the 'boss' replied good-naturedly.

At once her aunt whispered to her, "He's giving you a whole *salung*. Go and get it."

Gade was afraid to look at him at first and crawled in front of him with her head bowed before glancing up to accept the money.

As soon as she looked up, she started. The gaze that looked down at her was penetrating and seared her eyes like a flash of lightning. The face that she had been afraid to look at was imprinted on her eyes and her heart from that moment on, even though at first, Gade didn't understand what her feelings were.

She felt that the 'boss' was gazing at her so intently that she had to lower her eyes and try to stop her hand from shaking as she took the money and placed her palms together before crawling away without looking at anyone.

Even several days after the ordination when Gade, her parents and her sister had gone back home and life had returned to normal, she knew intuitively that her life would never be the same again. Something new – Gade didn't know what – was targeting her stealthily.

If she'd had enough experience to discern what it was, she would have called it 'destiny'.

Gade recalled that she had had a strange feeling once again the next day during the ordination rites in the temple chapel which Muen's 'boss' attended as he had done the previous day. She was with a group of girls on the far side of the chapel wall from the 'boss', who was sitting alone, but whenever she glanced in his direction, she saw that he was staring at her and caught his eye, as if he had been watching her for a long time.

Gade began to feel hot and cold. She didn't understand what she had done wrong, or if there was something strange about her, which had made the most important person in the ceremony keep staring at her until she felt awkward and self-conscious.

Her older married sister, completely unaware of what was going on, asked her in a whisper, "What's the matter with you, Gade? You can't stop fidgeting."

"I've got pins and needles," Gade replied, startled and afraid she would look suspicious. "It's cramped and I can't stretch my legs."

"Then move over here," her sister said, believing her, and pushing her youngest sister out of the way. "How much space do you need for goodness' sake?"

Gade saw a way out and shuffled into the corner so that she was completely concealed behind her sisters. She breathed a sigh of relief, but, as she found out later, that was just the beginning.

The rain that year was heavier than usual and the villagers complained that it was too much. It had started to rain incessantly in June, and when the Buddhist lent began, it rained almost every day.

Eeam grumbled that the dried fish she had put out in the sun was getting mouldy and the mattresses, mosquito nets and blankets smelled musty. Whenever the sun came out, she and her two daughters would quickly lift the trays of dried fish out onto the veranda.

One afternoon, the sun was scorching and the leaves were motionless without a breeze, but as soon as the sun started to set, dark clouds filled half the sky before becoming heavy over the house, and the wind got up and blew the leaves all over the yard.

Rern hurried to take the fish back inside the kitchen, while Gade pulled the last piece of cloth from the washing line and brought it under the house, just as the first large droplets of rain began to fall. Then she rushed up the steps behind the house to avoid getting wet.

The rain poured down in torrents, and Rern pulled out the wooden strut that held the windows open and closed all the windows around the house. Gade tied her oldest breast cloth around her chest and behind her neck and went down the steps behind the house to place large jars around the house to collect clean rainwater for drinking.

Through the curtain of shimmering rain, Gade glimpsed the outlines of several towering shadows coming towards her, and she felt the ground tremor as the puddles on the ground splashed from the horses' hooves. Then Muen, who was leading the group, stopped his horse in front of the house.

Gade could only gaze in astonishment, forgetting the cold, while the rain soaked her clothes and made them cling to her skin.

Someone, who was riding beside Muen, jumped down from his horse with agility and dashed under the cover of the roof out of the rain. Those who followed behind, busied themselves tethering the horses to the pillars of the house out of the rain.

The same pair of penetrating eyes glanced towards Gade as if they had a special power to divine who was hiding behind the pillar in the darkness. Gade shivered, not because of the cold rain, but because of the power of those eyes, which chilled her from head to toe in a way she had never felt before. The feeling was neither anger, nor fear, but was more like embarrassment. She hugged her arms to her chest tightly, and turned to run up the steps behind the house, ignoring her uncle who called after her

"Gade! Is that you? Oh! She's run inside the house!"

Gade dashed inside shaking, from both the cold and another feeling she couldn't describe.

Mee came out to look at the commotion in front of the house. When he saw his daughter he asked, "Who is it?"

"Uncle Muen, Father."

With that she dashed across the veranda into the small house where she and her sister slept and shut the door tightly. Fortunately, her sister wasn't there to see her strange behaviour, since Gade was in no mood to explain anything. She had no intention of going out to greet the guests, but heard her mother calling her youngest daughter to help prepare a meal while asking, "Where's Gade gone?"

When Gade came to her senses, she found herself still hugging her chest and shivering with cold, the water dripping from her clothes onto the floor. She dried herself and quickly put on a blouse instead of the usual breast cloth, and a clean matching *jongkraben*, before combing her wet hair back.

Uncle Muen was sitting in her father's house across the terrace in the common room that was used as a living room in the day, and transformed by a mosquito net at night into a bedroom. The 'boss' had his back to him and the soldiers who accompanied him were sitting politely further away almost at the wall. The rain was still coming down in white sheets, but not as hard as before.

Gade was about to dart into the kitchen, which was behind the two houses, but the young major suddenly turned to look at her, as if he had eyes in the back of his head, causing her father and uncle also to turn towards her.

"Gade!" her father called "What's the matter? Why don't you come and pay respect to Uncle Muen?"

She crossed the veranda again and dropped to her knees with her palms together to pay respect to him and the 'boss', whom she dared not look at. She heard him chuckle softly, "After making my rounds, I thought I'd go back to the base this evening, but it started raining on the way. I carried on riding for a while, thinking it might stop, but then it came down so heavily I couldn't see in front of me."

Gade's father responded respectfully, "You're most welcome to stop here, sir. The rains have been heavy this year. By the look of it, I don't think it will be stopping any time soon."

"I don't want to impose on you, Mee," Muen chimed in.

Gade crawled away towards the kitchen without looking back and heard her father protest good-naturedly, "Of course you're not imposing. We're family. You talk as if we were strangers. I should be the one to apologize. I'm afraid we can only offer you simple food. I hope you don't mind."

"As for that..." Major Luang Radaronayuth broke in amiably. "Don't worry on my account. I came here to get out of the rain, and you've been kind enough to offer me a meal. I'm the one that should feel bad for putting you out. I can't thank you enough."

The food that day was nothing special, the sort of simple fare that they normally ate, but it was enjoyed by all the guests, particularly Khun Luang, who had a hearty appetite.

The meal consisted of Eeam's chilli paste, which was their mainstay, with raw vegetables to dip in it, including boiled young banana leaf and several other raw vegetables that grew around the house. But since there were several guests, more dishes were required, so Eeam had her daughters make fermented fish cakes by wrapping the fish in a banana leaf and roasting it until it was fragrant. Lastly, there was sour soup with mackerel made by Gade to counter the spiciness of the first two dishes.

The men ate until they were full, but the women didn't eat with them as Eeam made her daughters go inside when she noticed the young soldiers who accompanied the boss. Gade obeyed without hesitation. By the time the guests departed, the rain had stopped completely. Gade opened her bedroom window to let in the fresh air. Drops of water falling from the roof were caught in the moonlight. The dark blue sky was as clear as polished glass and the full moon looked down, shining its silver rays from above. The rainstorm that had passed left only the flooded furrows, which reflected the sparkling white moon, and the flipping splashing fish.

When she heard the clip clop of horses' hooves below, Gade peered down unthinkingly and noticed a horse had stopped in the yard. The rider looked up at the house and remained motionless as if he was looking for someone.

When Gade opened the window, the sound made him look up.

In the soft moonlight, Gade saw Khun Luang's handsome face smiling up at her as he caught sight of her oval face.

"Gade, dinner was delicious."

It was the first thing he said to her in a way she had never even dreamed of.

"When I have time, I'll be back for more."

Gade stood still and her hand, which had pushed open the window, remained motionless until the horse had galloped away after the others, the sound of its hooves fading as it disappeared down the winding cart road, leaving only a faint shadow in the moonlight.

"You're by yourself today, Por Muen. Are you on your way to somewhere?"

Eeam was not surprised to see her brother that evening, since Muen often stopped by on his way somewhere. After greeting him and inviting him to sit on the veranda, the customary tray of betel and cigarettes was brought out, and they started chatting as usual.

Muen didn't answer his elder sister at first because, from the moment he left the army camp in Phetchaburi town until the moment he arrived at Ban Tha Hin, he had been wondering how to raise the subject.

Before he could answer, Mee continued from his wife, "You can't be making the rounds because your boss isn't with you."

"No, he isn't," he replied and, seeing an opportunity to broach the topic, hastily continued, "Speaking of my boss, I really am fond of him. I haven't been with him long, but I feel as if I've known him for ages. He's so generous and kind to his subordinates, and he's not arrogant at all."

"That's just what I was thinking," agreed Eeam. Having no idea of her brother's hidden agenda, she continued praising him. "Last time he came, he gave me money for his meal and when I wouldn't take it, he insisted. He isn't at all intimidating. We can all relax when he's around."

"He never uses intimidation," her brother guaranteed. "If he wants something, he asks nicely so as to stay on good terms."

Muen's voice was suggestive because he was intentionally hinting, and Mee picked up on it.

"What does he want then, that you say he'll ask nicely for?"

Muen was silent for a moment and then asked casually, "Um, how old is Gade this year?"

Being asked about their daughter's age led Gade's parents to think of only one thing: marriage. Eeam stared at her brother, still not understanding.

"Seventeen, almost eighteen, Por Muen."

"She's practically a woman now. Both her older sisters are already married and she's still at home. Aren't you going to find her a husband?"

This time Mee got the hint and thought of the young soldiers who had accompanied the boss that day. He was afraid that one of them had taken a shine to his daughter and, having asked the boss to intervene, had sent Muen as an intermediary.

"No, we haven't found her a husband," Mee replied indifferently. He did not consider himself to be inferior to anyone and wasn't about to give his favourite daughter away without careful scrutiny.

He couldn't resist asking, "You're here as a go-between for one of your subordinates that came with you that day, are you?"

Muen looked worried while Eeam looked questioningly at him with sudden interest.

"Um..." he stuttered for the first time. "Not my subordinate...Oh, no, not at all..."

"Well, then who?"

Muen gazed at his sister and brother-in-law in silence for a moment before answering softly, "My boss told me to ask about Gade...I can tell he likes her..."

Their stunned silence made Muen continue hastily, "I didn't promise him anything. I said I'd ask you. He means to take care of her. A woman needs a husband. And a husband like him is better than one of the villagers."

If it had been any of the other villagers, they would have been full of respect for a noble military officer and would have gladly given their daughter to him, no matter if she was to be his principal wife or a minor wife, since the implication was that she would be taken care of for life. The status of both a principal wife and a minor wife were accepted by society, and mostly, they lived in the same house and divided the household duties between them. Some principal wives even found minor wives for their husbands.

It was Muen's duty to defer to Khun Luang, his commander, and he also respected him personally for his character, so he sided with his boss.

"As far as I'm aware, he's not married. He's a good man. He likes Gade and he wouldn't pursue her without your consent, so he asked me to talk to the two of you in case she's engaged to someone else. He would never force her."

Muen had rehearsed his words beforehand to make sure they were appropriate and not too biased towards his boss. If Gade's parents were happy for him to marry Gade, he would continue his plaudits towards him, but before he could, Mee cut in coolly.

"What does he want Gade to be his wife for? He's important enough. The town's full of young women."

"You seem to have forgotten what a beautiful daughter you have," Muen protested jovially. "Even in the town, I've never seen anyone to rival Gade. And she's a good housewife. He told me he liked her cooking. And as for her manners, you've taught her well. If he wants her to polish them, she's clever enough to learn."

Mee was speechless and began to get carried away with his thoughts. If his daughter was to be married, it was certainly better for her to be a the wife of a noble man than a local villager. She'd have status and be comfortable. He wouldn't have to worry about her.

He was about to give his consent, and was choosing his words carefully, so he wouldn't look overly keen, when his wife said casually, "Please tell him we appreciate his kindness to Gade, but she couldn't possibly accept such a fate."

Mee's jaw dropped as did his brother-in-law's, and both men asked almost at the same time, "Why ever not?"

Eeam was silent for a moment before replying as she considered how to put it.

"Two of my daughters are already married and Rern's still very childish. There's only Gade to help me. I'm not getting any younger and I want to keep her with us when we're old."

This excuse would have sufficed for any other young man who had come to ask for Gade's hand. He would have understood that the girl's parents were not satisfied with his qualifications, but had refused politely to prevent any bad feelings.

But now, when the young man was someone who was like a gift from heaven, Muen was left confused by this unexpected refusal. The only person who was more confused than Muen was Eeam's husband, who thought that this was a foolish reason. What's more, his wife had not even consulted him, so he barked back, "Eeam, are you crazy? A very important person has just asked for our daughter's hand, and you're not satisfied. What kind of divinity would satisfy you?"

Eeam scowled and replied sarcastically, "So? You want to give her to him on a plate!"

"Oh!" Mee countered forcefully. "I don't know who the heck I should save her for!"

"In that case, let her stay here with us. To look after us when we're old and feeble," Eeam answered emphatically.

Mee studied his wife's face in search of a clue, realising that she must have a hidden motive.

"What is it? Tell me. I've never heard you say anything like this before. Anyone else would gladly give their consent."

"I'm afraid..." Eeam replied hesitantly. "I'm afraid that if she has a partner with good fortune, she'll suffer as a consequence. That's what Abbot Ward said when he told her fortune."

When she mentioned the old abbot, whom everyone in the village respected, Mee fell silent. His wife had told him about the prediction before, and he didn't argue, owing to the respect he'd always had towards Abbot Ward.

"What did he say?" Muen asked curiously.

Eeam told him in as much detail as she could remember, recapping two or three times to make sure he understood, and Muen nodded with understanding and sympathy.

When he had digested the information, he ventured to say, with more foresight than the couple, "If you don't give your consent because of this, I understand, but you'll still have to find a husband for Gade."

"Why?" Eeam asked suddenly.

"Why? So I can tell my boss that she's engaged to someone else. Or he'll be insulted. If she's got someone else, he'll go off her anyway."

Ecam was silent as she hadn't thought of that. Mee looked at his wife in irritation.

"You'd better hurry up and find her a husband. Or you'll get Por Muen in trouble as well!"

Eeam's face fell and she looked at her brother questioningly. "How am I supposed to find someone at such short notice? What do you think, Por Muen? Is there anyone suitable?"

Muen rubbed his chin anxiously.

"How am I supposed to know? You'd better find someone from the village. Who was it that proposed to her?"

"There's Thom…" Eeam replied, "…and Rord, and Muean, but I don't like them. Thom's so lazy he'll end up a beggar, Rord's a bully and as for Muean, he hasn't been ordained yet…"

"You're finding fault with all of them," Mee retorted, seizing the opportunity to argue with his wife, since he was still annoyed with her. "You'd better find someone. No matter how stupid he is, you'll just have to put up with him."

Their discussion didn't go unnoticed by their youngest daughter. Rern hadn't paid much attention at first, but when she heard her sister's name, she took notice. The fifteen-year-old girl listened carefully to all the details from the other side of the wall and, when she was certain she'd got all the information, crept away, before running down the veranda steps to find Gade. Gade had been cutting banana leaves behind the house and was carrying them back when she saw her sister running towards her.

"Gade! Gade!"

Rern hurriedly grabbed her sister's arm and pulling her back inside the banana grove, excitedly told her all she'd heard. When she'd finished, the banana leaves fell from Gade's arms and she almost dropped the knife she was holding. Her knees grew weak and she had to sit on a tree stump. She could hardly believe her ears.

It was already a bolt from the blue that Muen's boss had asked her uncle to be a go-between in asking for her hand, but the fact that her mother had refused him and was planning to have her marry one of the villagers was a complete shock.

"Mother's going to have me marry Thom...?"

"Not yet," Rern corrected her. "I don't know which one. Thom... Rord...Muean...I don't know which one."

Gade bit her lip. She couldn't stand any of the three young men her sister had mentioned. If Gade had to marry one of those three, she would rather hold her breath and die.

"No way!" Gade heard herself say so angrily that Rern was alarmed.

"Which one?"

"All of them," Gade fumed.

She plunged the knife she was holding into a fallen tree stump lying on the ground to blow off steam, until the branches were strewn all around, and the thought occurred to her that she wished it had been the heads of those three men.

"You wait. If I'm forced to marry one of them, I'll stab his head."

Rern stared at her pretty older sister in alarm and burst out laughing.

"Then who will you marry? Uncle Muen's boss?"

"Quiet! Mother and Father will hear!"

Rern quickly fell silent and Gade told her forcefully, "If you hear anymore, let me know."

Gade was anxious for several days after that because she didn't know what would happen to her. There was one small comfort in that the parents of the three young men had not been to the house, and neither had they, which would have added to her despondency. Even so, Gade felt she could not afford to let her guard down and repeatedly warned her sister to be alert for any news. She lay down with her hand across her forehead trying to think of a way out if her parents tried to make her marry Thom, or Rord, or Muean. Meanwhile, her sister's words still rang in her ears.

"Mother and Father are afraid that if you have a partner with good fortune, you'll suffer as a consequence like the abbot predicted."

And what about a husband without so much as a shred of fortune, even in his fingertips, like any of those three? Did her parents really think she would be any better off?

Gade walked to the end of the bridge, which was a long wooden plank that went across Khlong Sai Gai behind the house, and sat on the end to bathe. Khlong Sai Gai was the name of the small canal, which was a subsidiary of the canal in Ban Tha Hin, and flowed from the orchards to the paddy fields behind them. Though it was small, it was clear and clean because it was always moving. Several coconut palms fringed the bank and leaned above the gently flowing water, in which they were reflected. At the canal mouth, Gade's father had stuck several bamboo poles close together to filter out waste matter.

Rern had been floating neck deep in the water, and when she noticed her sister, she pulled herself up onto the end of the bridge and shook the water from her hair.

"I'm going inside."

"Oh! Won't you stay and keep me company?" Gade asked.

"No," she retorted hastily. "You take too long bathing. I don't want to have to wait for you."

It was dusk and the air was getting cool. There was no moon and two or three stars gradually came out to shine against the dark blue sky. Gade bathed meticulously as she always did, scrubbing her body with ripe tamarind and squeezing kaffir lime juice onto her hair to wash it. When she had finished, she leaned back in the water to rinse her hair until she felt light and clean, and pulled herself up to sit on the bridge as before, letting the evening breeze dry her skin.

Hearing a rustling sound as if someone was stepping on the dry coconut palms that lay on the ground, Gade turned to look, thinking it was her sister coming back, but no –

Someone tall was silhouetted against the dusky sky and was moving closer. He hesitated and stopped before the bridge.

Gade gasped in shock and instinctively moved to jump in the water, but a deep voice called out gently.

"Gade! Don't be afraid. It's me."

Her heart almost stopped, either from shock, or because of something else that she couldn't yet identify, so all she could do was stand stiffly on the end of the plank.

Khun Luang stood still next to the bridge, only a few steps away, but he didn't move any closer. In the twilight, Gade could see his penetrating eyes staring at her.

Gade was unaware that, when she stepped out of the water to let the air dry her skin, her wet clothes clung to her firm and shapely figure, which was like a budding flower, and her smooth skin was radiant in the twilight. Her face was fresh and clean, and her natural beauty, the like of which he had never seen before, made other women, with their make-up and ornaments, look fake. Gade clutched the edge of the cloth tied around her chest with one hand and held the cloth she had brought to dry herself in the other to cover herself, but she knew that it didn't hide much. All she could do was to stand there feeling hot and cold.

"I didn't mean to startle you…I just wanted to see you. If I didn't come now, I don't know when I'll see you again."

Gade's voice trembled, "Wh…what do…you want to say to me, sir?"

"Don't call me sir," he protested softly. "I don't want to intimidate you, but I just want to hear for myself…"

Gade looked around her hurriedly, afraid that someone might see them.

"There's no one with me," he said as if he knew what she was thinking. "I came alone…I came to ask you, so I could be sure…Is it true that you don't want me to propose to you because you love someone else?"

Khun Luang must have heard the answer from Muen, but he hadn't given up and had found a way to talk to Gade directly.

Gade's thoughts turned to her parents. They were out that evening because Uncle Muen had sent someone to fetch them, as his eldest son was about to leave the monkhood and he needed their help with the merit-making ceremony to welcome him home.

Was it possible that Muen had found a pretext, because people didn't usually have a merit-making ceremony when their sons left the monkhood? Had he found an excuse to get her parents away, so that Khun Luang would be able to speak to Gade alone?

Gade knew that if she just nodded and went along with her parents excuse that she had someone else, Khun Luang would back off. She knew that he wouldn't force her. The fact that he had sent Muen as an intermediary, showed that he intended to do things properly. But, if she did that, would she be happy? She hesitated, not knowing what to say, until he repeated the question.

"Is it true? Is there someone else? Tell me straight. Don't be afraid. I want to hear it for myself...If there's someone else, I won't bother you anymore. You won't see me again."

Gade lowered her gaze, feeling embarrassed, but she couldn't bring herself to nod her head. Khun Luang waited. He wasn't in a hurry, and he wasn't the least bit annoyed that she didn't answer right away, because it gave him more time to look at her. The more he gazed at her, the more captivated he was. At last, Gade sat down on the end of the bridge as before and wrapped the dry cloth around her shoulders because she was feeling colder with every passing moment. She couldn't be sure if it was because of the cool evening breeze, or because of the alarm she felt at meeting him.

"There's no one else."

Gade overcame her embarrassment as much as she could, and continued softly, "My mother's worried about me...Abbot Ward told me my destiny...he said I'd suffer because of the good fortune of my husband...My mother's afraid..."

His voice revealed his confusion, and what sounded like relief.

"Is that all? You believe in destiny?"

Gade looked up at him puzzled as if to ask, "Don't you?"

Khun Luang stepped onto the bridge, stopping when he had almost reached the end, and knelt down. Now he was within touching distance, Gade sat tensed in alarm, but she was relieved that he was still smiling kindly. His teeth were straight and white, unlike the villagers, whose teeth were stained black from chewing betel.

"I believe in karma more than destiny. I believe that our happiness or our suffering is a result of our own actions."

Khun Luang was silent for a moment as if he was finding the right words, and then he continued quietly but firmly, "I respect Abbot Ward...and I've been to pay respects to him. I can't erase his prediction, but can I tell you something, Gade? And I'll tell your parents myself.

If I can marry you, I'll never leave you to suffer. All I ask of you is that you'll never leave me…Will you promise?"

Gade's heart beat faster like a boat being tossed about on a stormy sea, and she felt as if the plank she was sitting on was swaying. She looked down not knowing what to say. Khun Luang lifted her chin up, and when his strong hand touched her, she felt something like an electric shock. Her reaction made her push his hand away forcefully, but he caught her wrist tightly in his warm hand.

Khun Luang chuckled, "Don't push me away. You'll throw us both in the water!"

He let go of her wrist and did not touch her again, but he did not take his eyes off her.

"Did I startle you? I'm not toying with you. Ever since I saw you at Klai's ordination, I've been captivated by you. I never thought I'd meet the woman I want here. When I found out your parents had refused me, I couldn't eat or sleep for days."

Gade was embarrassed, but she felt strangely warm despite the cool evening breeze that caressed her skin. The moonless sky was like a big dark blanket dotted with sparkling stars and the trees around them were black silhouettes. The mangrove trees on the canal bank sparkled with the lights of fireflies. In fact, it was no different from other moonless nights, but, for Gade, it was the most beautiful night she had ever seen.

Khun Luang gazed at Gade intently, and said with a smile, "Or if you don't believe me, I'll swear an oath…I'll swear by the stars that I'll love you and I'll never leave you. If I ever leave you, may I suffer, and never be happy or prosper."

As shy as she was, Gade couldn't help laughing.

"What's funny?" Khun Luang asked.

"I've…I've never heard anyone swear by the stars," Gade answered shyly. "They usually swear by the Buddha…"

"I swear by the stars. Whenever I'm not with you, all you have to do is open the window and you'll remember my promise."

Gade had never heard such a thing. It sounded strange, but what was even stranger was that she understood, and with that understanding, she was deeply moved.

A light came on inside the house and brought Gade back to her senses. She jumped up and Khun Luang looked at her questioningly.

"Where are you going in such a hurry?"

"I can't stay any longer," she replied hastily.

Khun Luang glanced at the house and understood her anxiety, so he didn't hold her back. He led her from the bridge to the bank and turned to face her, blocking her with his hand, so that she couldn't walk past him, and asked gently, "When can I see you again?"

Gade shook her head.

"You can't. If my parents find out they'll punish me for meeting a man."

"Don't you care about me?" he replied, sounding a little hurt.

Gade shook her head again. Gade was already embarrassed and afraid. If her father came and saw, she didn't know how she could excuse herself. She pushed past Khun Luang and ran into the house without looking back, but she knew without seeing that Khun Luang was watching her until she was out of sight.

Not many days after that, Khun Luang Radaronayuth came to ask for Gade's hand himself. He had sufficient rank and honour that he did not need to ask an elder to come in his place. Having come to propose in person, and having assured them that he would never leave Gade to suffer, Mee and Eeam had no excuse with which to refuse him.

Eeam could only reply, "All I ask, sir, is that you do it properly according to tradition."

Mee was silent, but his silence indicated that he was in agreement.

Muen admitted that he had told Khun Luang about Abbot Ward's prediction. Although he was aware that his boss had met up with his pretty niece to discuss things, he thought it was best not to get her in trouble by telling her parents, and decided to ask about the bride price himself.

"He'll give you a generous bride price, and he'll find an auspicious day himself," Muen assured them, gladly assuming the role of the wedding organizer. "He wants the wedding to take place before the end of the rainy season."

The auspicious day that Khun Luang found was only a month

after the day that he proposed, and Gade hardly had time to prepare her wedding outfit and the belongings that she would have to take with her to the army base. It was during this period that Gade learned of the first 'difficulty' that would come by being Khun Luang Radaronayuth's wife.

That difficulty was transmitted to her via the wife of an officer under the command of her future husband. It was she who had been ordered to help the bride prepare for her wedding. Her name was Chalaem, a pretty name fit for a young woman from the capital, and her husband was a first lieutenant who had been posted to Phetchaburi around the same time as Khun Luang. Everyone stared at the plump, olive-skinned woman stepping down from the horse-drawn carriage that had brought her from the army base. Her jet-black hair was cut in a fashionable bob curled under at the nape of her neck, in stark contrast to the women in the village.

"I'm Chalaem, First Lieutenant Thongphoon's wife. He's under the command of Major Khun Luang Radaronayuth. Khun Luang asked me to help you choose your clothes, madam."

She spoke fluently as if they had known each other for ages. Gade composed herself and glanced at her sisters, who looked puzzled, so she was the one to reply.

Gade wasn't sure how to address her. All she could say was, "Uh… what clothes?"

"The clothes for your wedding, madam."

Gade soon realized that the words, "choose your clothes" meant that she was expected to dress differently and change her appearance if she was to be Khun Luang Radaronayuth's wife.

"These days, all the women wear sarongs, madam. I've worn one since I was a teenager. The last king liked women to wear sarongs, so all the women from good families wear them."

Gade understood that she would not be able to wear a *jongkraben* anymore. The real difficulty, however, had nothing to do with the clothes, but from something she had never imagined. When Gade offered her visitor the customary betel, Chalaem looked horrified.

"Oh, no! I simply can't!" she exclaimed in alarm. "Nowadays, people from good families and young ladies don't chew betel anymore! Only old people do that. The last king didn't chew betel, and neither does the present one. The people in the capital follow the king, so they don't chew betel now. If you chew it, you have to clean the stains off your teeth."

Gade looked up from the tray of betel and noticed that Chalaem's teeth were white without any betel stains. Gade couldn't imagine not chewing betel and felt sure she would get withdrawal symptoms if she stopped.

"Do I have to give up chewing betel, Chalaem?"

Chalaem looked smug again.

"Khun Luang doesn't touch it. He thinks it's smelly."

Suffice to say that this answer put a stop to any further questions.

Gade glanced at Chalaem's fashionable clothes; she realized that, as the wife of Khun Luang Radaronayuth, she wouldn't be able to wear a *jongkraben*, or chew betel ever again.

After Chalaem's second visit, Gade asked her younger sister to help her scrub her teeth until they were white, and she gave her all the patterned fabrics she had used for her *jongkraben* in return. Rern laughed as she scrubbed until her laughter turned into groans because her arm ached after scrubbing all day.

"If getting married is so much trouble, then I'd rather stay single.'

Gade couldn't help laughing and her thoughts inadvertently turned to the abbot's prediction. *This must be what he meant when he said I'd suffer because of my husband's fate. If I married someone in the village, my life would still be the same, day after day, year after year.* This was just the beginning. Where would Gade's life path turn next? She had no idea.

2
The Officer's Wife

Gade woke up before the rooster crowed. She looked out of the window, and saw that the sky was still full of stars, but she knew it was time to get up. Today was her wedding day.

Gade didn't know exactly what her parents had arranged, but she knew that for her wedding, there was to be no tray of betel carried in procession to her house as was customary, since Khun Luang had arranged for the ceremony to take place at his living quarters at the army base. Neither would there be the traditional barring the groom from approaching the bride with gates of gold chains, nor a Buddhist ceremony – only a water-pouring ceremony in the afternoon before the bride was presented to the groom on the wedding night.

When Gade thought of Khun Luang, she felt strangely uneasy because she hadn't seen him for three weeks. He had been to Bangkok on business, only returning two days before the wedding, and had been so busy with the preparations that he had not had time to see her. Finally, she would see him today. Thinking about it gave her butterflies.

Tonight, would be the first night she had ever been separated from her parents. She would not be staying with relatives, but in a place she had never been before. It was also the first time she had ever been alone with a man. Even though it was Khun Luang, she couldn't help feeling anxious.

For the past three weeks, Gade had not had time to worry about her future because there had been things to do from morning until night. She had had to enlist her relatives to help her sew new bed sheets and prepare new pillows and mosquito nets, which the groom had given her the money for. She had also had to sew her wedding outfit and clothes for after the wedding.

Chalaem had asked her relatives in Bangkok to send fabric for her wedding dress, and had helped Gade to sew it as soon as it arrived because there were only a few days left. It was the most beautiful blouse that Gade had ever seen. The style was simple like those Chalaem wore with a boat neck and cap sleeves, but it looked more elegant because it was made of delicate lace in a shade of dusky pink that Chalaem called "faded lotus". It was threaded through with pale gold yarn and the undershirt was the same colour. Her sarong was in a matching shade with gold brocade.

Gade crept out of the room, so as not to wake her sister, carrying a long cloth to wrap around herself in order to bathe on the veranda from a jar that her father had filled with water, so that on her wedding day she wouldn't have to go to the canal to bathe, as she usually did.

The sky was still dark like black velvet and the stars sparkled above the treetops. Gade had never paid much attention to the sun, the moon or the stars before, but now, for some inexplicable reason, whenever it was dark, Khun Luang's words echoed in her ears.

"Or if you don't believe me, I'll swear an oath…I'll swear by the stars that I'll love you and I'll never leave you."

Gade sat on a small stool and scooped water from the jar that Rern had sprinkled with fragrant jasmine flowers the night before. She poured water over herself and scrubbed more carefully than usual.

"I swear by the stars. Whenever I'm not with you, all you have to do is open the window and you'll remember my promise."

The sky began to lighten and the horizon began to sparkle with gold and silver rays, while the stars disappeared. Gade lifted her hand and studied the lines on her palm.

Then she glanced at her arms and down to her feet. Everything was still the same and nothing had changed. Nevertheless, she felt that her life would never be the same again,

The house in the army base was a teak building with a tiled roof. The area under the house, which was lifted on stilts, was higher than the Thai-style house that Gade lived in and you could walk under it easily without having to bend your head. The floor was covered in clean dry bricks, so it could be used as a sitting area. Wooden bars on the sides had hanging baskets of flowers. Two staircases led up to the house on either side, and met in the middle in front of the house. Upstairs had several large rooms, which looked spacious because all the large windows were open wide. Above the windows, carved fretwork panels let the breeze flow through.

That day, several young soldiers were busying themselves in the rooms helping to prepare for the wedding ceremony. The house was full of strangers and Gade clutched her sister's hand tightly. Her hands were getting colder every minute, but she felt better when she saw Chalaem coming down the steps and smiling sweetly.

She sat down on the floor and placed her palms together gracefully as usual, telling Gade smoothly, "Please come this way, madam. I've sealed off the back room, so no one can come in. Your clothes are pressed and hanging up inside."

Gade did not have time to think, and had no idea where Khun Luang was, so she just followed Chalaem into the back room with her relatives in tow. When she had finished getting dressed, Chalaem helped her do her hair. She had warned Gade not to cut her hair, but to let it grow into a bob like hers, and now she used hot tongues to curl it, complaining, "There's only time to curl it a little. If I curl it any more, your hair will burn."

The long oval mirror in an ebony frame that was handed to her reflected back a strange young woman with a shapely figure and creamy skin that glowed against the dusky pink lace blouse and sarong with gold brocade. Her pretty face looked radiant framed by shiny black hair that curled in waves above her forehead. She looked as elegant and as modern as Chalaem, except for the alarmed and anxious look in her black eyes, which warned her that, underneath the fashionable exterior, she was still the same as she had always been.

The pouring water ceremony was in the afternoon.

Gade realized that Khun Luang had been waiting for her and, when she looked up at him and saw him gazing at her with a delighted smile, her fear lessened. He was wearing his military uniform as usual, but Gade thought that on this particular day the 'groom' looked extraordinarily happy.

He whispered to her, "You look beautiful, Gade."

Gade blushed and was too shy to answer, or even look at him again.

Everything went by in a blur as Gade was led to sit on a low table with her legs to the side next to the groom. At that moment, her legs felt weak, unlike Khun Luang who appeared confident and poised. The water ceremony wasn't as long as she had expected because the groom's high rank meant there were only a few people more senior than him in the whole of Phetchaburi province who could therefore pour the water to bless the marriage. On the bride's side, there were only Gade's parents, because all her grandparents had passed away, and, since Muen was under Khun Luang's command, it would not have been appropriate for him to pour water from a conch shell on the couple.

Although she should have felt nothing but happiness, the water from the conch dripping down her forehead chilled her to the core. Each drop of water confirmed that she was being severed from her family's bosom completely, and would now be under the authority of the tall man with penetrating eyes who was sitting next to her. The butterflies that she had felt in her stomach since the early hours of the morning returned. Whether it was because of nerves, fatigue, or because she had hardly eaten all day, Gade felt weaker than she had ever felt before when she stepped down from the table and the ground seemed to give way beneath her.

She felt faint and everything went dark. Then lights flickered before her and she heard faint voices cry out in alarm before she was completely engulfed by darkness.

The sound of a gamelan in the area beneath the house drifted up into the back room where Gade was leaning with her back against a cushion on the wooden floor, and orange smelling salts filled her nostrils. Her sisters were sitting around her, but everyone else had left the room. Some of her relatives had already left, and only her parents and Muen were left to present her to the groom at the auspicious time.

She heard her eldest sister comforting her.

"I almost fainted on my wedding day, too."

"You've been sewing round the clock without eating or sleeping,"

Rern mumbled, holding her sister's hand and rubbing her shoulders comfortingly.

None of her relatives blamed her for fainting suddenly, and were relieved that she had not been hurt because the groom had caught her in time and carried her to the back room for the women to take care of until she came round. After that, Khun Luang saw the guests off and let the bride rest until it was time for her to be presented to him. The time passed slowly from dusk until darkness fell, and Gade fidgeted in her room until she felt achy all over. She wished she could go for a walk, but didn't dare, and Khun Luang didn't come to see her because he was waiting until the auspicious time for her to be presented to him. Finally, that time arrived.

The wedding chamber was Khun Luang's bedroom, and almost nothing was any different from how he had it normally, except for the jasmine flower garlands, made by the officers' wives, that hung on the bedposts. The large ebony bed was enveloped in a new white mosquito net that was parted to reveal a thick mattress with a clean white sheet pulled over it tightly and two pillows covered in matching white pillowcases.

Khun Luang was sitting on the end of the bed waiting when Gade's parents led her inside, and Gade sat on the floor and prostrated herself as her mother had taught her.

Her parents' speeches passed by her ears like the wind and she heard her mother's voice cracking a little at the end as she entrusted her daughter to her son-in-law, causing Gade to realize that she was still worried about her. Her eyes filled with tears before they began to roll down her cheeks and she hurriedly wiped them away before anyone could see.

Even if they had seen, having given their daughter away her parents could do nothing but walk out of the room, closing the door behind them, and leaving their daughter, and her future, in her husband's hands.

Gade's tears rolled down her cheeks, and no matter how much she tried, she couldn't stop them. Then she felt a strong warm hand stroke her from her shoulder to the middle of her back to comfort her.

"Why are you crying? There's nothing to feel sad about. Today's our special day."

Khun Luang was right. Gade managed to stop crying, telling herself that she had to stop being scared for no reason. Ever since she'd met Khun Luang, he'd always been kind to her. There was no need to be afraid.

"You weren't well. Are you feeling better?" her husband asked anxiously. "Your sister told me you were so busy sewing that you didn't have time to eat or sleep properly,"

Gade hesitated before answering, "I…I…don't know what happened. I just fainted."

"I know. You went pale and then you suddenly fainted. You had me worried. Are you alright now?"

"Yes, I'm fine," she stammered.

"I expect you were exhausted," he said, pulling her to her feet.

Khun Luang sat her down on the bed and moved away a little as if he understood that she was uncomfortable. The gamelan was still playing and Khun Luang raised his head to listen, smiling, "Listen to that song. Do you know it?"

Gade listened intently. The song was sweet and soothing, in harmony with the cool night. It was a song that she'd never heard before.

"No, I don't," she answered softly.

"It's called 'A night full of stars'. It was composed by the king. It's one of my favourites, so I had them play it for our wedding night."

It was the first time she'd ever heard the beautiful song. Even the name of which was melodic. Khun Luang sang along softly with the music from outside.

"Tonight's the night my heart delights in the moonlight,

Please come, my love, and sit with me as the breeze blows the scent of jasmine."

He had a good voice, and she listened in awe and wonder, mixed with amusement.

This feeling made Gade smile, and Khun Luang gazed at her face, which was beginning to brighten, asking with a smile, "Do you like the song, or are you laughing at my singing?

Gade was almost too shy to answer, but she forced herself to say,

"I like it."

She spoke softly, but she was bold enough to continue, "My mother sings well, and she tried to teach me to sing with accompaniment, but I could never do it."

"Really? How come your mother can sing with accompaniment? It's usually only in the palace, or the nobility that learns to do that."

"When she was a child, my mother lived in the house of a noble family. She stayed with them until she got married."

She was starting to get over her shyness, and spoke for longer as she became more comfortable.

"My mother's aunt was a lady-in-waiting to the governor's wife. She asked my grandmother to let her adopt my mother when she was a child, and, when my aunt died, my grandmother let her stay, and she didn't leave until she got married."

"Oh, I see!" the young man nodded, "She must have sung with the gamelan there."

"Yes, she has a good voice, and she can sing lots of songs."

Khun Luang lay back with his hands behind his head and relaxed as if he was talking to a friend, rather than his bride on his wedding night. Or perhaps he saw that Gade was young and, even though she wasn't charming and witty like the women in the capital, he found the innocent way she talked endearing.

Khun Luang gazed at her fondly, and was quiet for a moment before saying, "I never thought I'd meet my soulmate here, but as soon as I saw you, I knew you were the one. What about you?"

Gade was silent. His strong hand lifted her chin like the time they talked on the bridge, forcing Gade to look into his large dark eyes, before looking away. He held her in his arms gently but firmly until the fear that she had felt at first began to dissipate, leaving her with reticence, along with the feeling, which she couldn't erase for the next several years, that she and her husband were as far apart as the earth and the sky.

The sound of birds chirping outside woke Gade, and she sat up in bed with a start, even though she was still sleepy. The gold and silver rays of the sun shone in through the window above the bed, allowing her to see Khun Luang Radaronayuth's face only dimly. She remembered that for her he was no long Khun Luang, but simply Nart.

The night before, he had told her gently but firmly, "Please don't call me Khun Luang. It sounds distant. My name's Nart. You're my wife. Call me by my name."

When he slept, Khun Luang showed no trace of being a man of high rank, and looked like any other man. His handsome face was calm and peaceful as if he was having a good dream. Gade gazed at her husband for a moment, and she had the fleeting feeling that, right now, Nart was close to her, and there were no other people, duties or rank between them. It was the only time that they belonged to each other. Gade sighed and slowly moved away from him, being careful not to wake him, and parted the mosquito net as she stepped down from the bed.

The room was still strange; one day was not enough to make it more familiar. Gade carefully picked up the water jug to wash her face before lifting the latch on the door and stepping outside. Everything was quiet and obscured by darkness. The high-ceilinged room looked strangely empty, and all the windows were closed, so that the only light was the pale silver rays that shone in through the carved wooden air vents. That light became clearer when Gade opened the door to go downstairs to bathe.

She heard the sound of sweeping on the solid ground and, turning towards it, saw a dark-skinned man in his mid-thirties, wearing only a black *jongkraben*, sweeping leaves into a pile to use as compost. When he saw Gade, he put down his brush, squatted down and placed his palms together, raised above his head.

"I'm Khun Luang's servant, madam. My name is Man." His accent was different from the people of Phetchaburi and he sounded like a Bangkok native, the same as Nart.

Gade felt embarrassed and could only nod and walk away without speaking. A moment later, she noticed a plump, middle-aged woman with dark skin wearing a cloth wrapped around her chest and a dark *jongkraben* like a villager. She was carrying a basket, and a thin girl in a sleeveless loose blouse and a *jongkraben* was walking beside her. They both sat down on the ground and put their palms together respectfully when they saw Gade, without needing anyone to tell them who she was, and the woman introduced herself as Noei.

Her Phetchaburi accent put Gade at ease, so she questioned her and found out that she was the cook, and her daughter, who was with her, helped to clean the house and wash the dishes. Gade had decided that cooking should be her duty, so she asked what her husband usually ate, before entering the kitchen and cooking herself, leaving Noei to cook just the rice.

Man took a jug of water up for his boss, so he could wash his face in a bowl in his room upstairs before coming down for breakfast, which he usually ate before bathing, dressing and going to work. Gade didn't eat with her husband because she wasn't used to the Western-style plates set on the table, and Nart asked, "What about you? Aren't you eating with me?"

"You eat first," she answered, pushing his breakfast towards him attentively. "I'll eat later."

He didn't complain, and when he tasted his wife's breakfast said, "It tastes better than Noei's cooking." Gade was so happy that she almost forgot to eat all day. When Nart appeared in his uniform, ready to go down the stairs to work, Gade felt the gulf between them return.

In front of the servants, Gade's husband hardly spoke to her, except for a few words. He wasn't the type to flirt with his young wife, and Gade wasn't the type of girl to act coquettishly. She knew she was below him both in seniority and status, so she dared not be too familiar with him like her sisters had been with their husbands when they were newlyweds. Even though she felt that way, when her husband left for work with the young soldier who was his attendant in tow, Gade was alarmed at how empty the house seemed without him.

Three months flew by without Gade knowing where the time went. It was strange. Even though she had lived in the house in the army base for a while, she never felt at home, and the Thai-style house under the shade of the mango trees at Ban Tha Hin never left her thoughts, as if she still lived there.

Sometimes, she accidentally called him 'Khun Luang', until he said grinning, "Gade, you keep calling me that as if I was someone else."

The fresh-faced girl in a simple white blouse and a pale green sarong wrapped a duster around her finger and carefully wiped the dust from the carved wooden panels above the glass doors on the cabinet until all the dust had gone. After that, she set to work polishing the glass doors until they shone. She could have left this job to Noei's daughter, but noticing that her husband was particularly fond of that glass cabinet and didn't like anyone to touch it unnecessarily, Gade decided to dust it herself. The only things in the cabinet were books.

On the low shelves inside were books of varying sizes; some were bound in dark brown leather, others in green or gold fabric embroidered with gold. They were much more beautiful than the old parchment books that Gade had seen in the temple. When she had finished polishing the glass doors on the outside, she opened them to polish on the inside, and could not resist picking up one of the books.

The one she was holding in her hands had pictures of strangely dressed men and women, and Gade wished she could read it, but, as a village woman, she had not learned to read and write, since only boys had the opportunity to learn by going to the monastery. Even so, there were few who were interested in reading.

Of her relatives, only Klai, her Uncle Muen's son, could read and write well.

She was enjoying looking at the pictures when the sound of her husband's voice startled her.

"Are you reading?"

Gade hurriedly closed the book and turned around with a smile.

"You're home early. You came in so quietly I didn't hear you."

Nart passed her his hat to hang up, and glanced at the book she was holding.

"Ah! The king's work, *'Mathanapatha'*. What made you want to look at it?"

The name was so strange that she couldn't repeat it, and answered, "I like the pictures. I wish I could read it."

He looked at her kindly for a moment before asking, "Do you want to learn? I'll teach you."

Gade laughed shyly and answered, "Teach me? Isn't it too late? I've always wanted to learn, but I never knew where to start. That's how it is for girls."

Nart took another book out of the cabinet and went to sit on an armchair. Gade smiled before walking away to tell Man to bring him his snack and some tea. He opened the book that he'd taken from the cabinet and said, "I tell you what. I'll read you the king's work, *'Wenisawanich*'"

The name was even stranger than the previous one, and Gade felt a little despondent because it sounded as if it would be very difficult to read.

"What does it mean?"

"The king translated it from English."

"Can you speak English?" she asked in wonder.

He laughed, and answered, "I know a little. I learned it as a child when I lived in the palace with my father. He trained the royal guards. There was a teacher from England, whom he was close to, and he taught me English."

Gade was sitting on the floor next to her husband who sat on the armchair, and she leaned over to look at the book and asked him, "Can you read something to me in English? I want to know what it sounds like."

"Of course," he replied, touched by his young wife's enthusiasm.

He found the page he wanted and read softly in a deep voice.

"We should hold day with the Antipodes,

If you walk in the shadow of the sun."

Nart smiled and looked at her the way he had the first time they met, and told her, "If you walked outside at night, it would be daylight here at the same time as on the other side of the world."

He stopped reading and held his finger in the book to keep his place, gazing at Gade lovingly and saying softly, "Like when I have you near me."

His eyes reminded her of their wedding day, and, even though it had been three months ago, she couldn't help feeling weak in the knees whenever she looked back on it.

She answered him, shyly, "I don't know what you mean."

"Don't you?" he teased, lifting her chin up and gazing into her eyes. "If you're near me, even when it's night-time, I feel like it's daytime. It's because I'm happy when I'm with you. I've felt that way since the first moment I saw you."

Gade asked, "Is that why you kept staring at me?"

Nart laughed, "Everyone looks at a beautiful girl, but I didn't look at you just because you're beautiful. I must have known you were my soulmate."

His words were like a stream of water soaking dry ground, and Gade felt as if she was floating up to the ceiling.

"Do you want me to read to you some more?"

"Yes, please. I'd like that."

Even many years later, Gade never forgot the sound of her husband's voice as he read to her. Although she had never heard any poetry before, the poetry Nart read to her was like a flowing stream that carried her along with it.

It was late afternoon and a cool breeze blew under the house, where Gade had swept clean. She had set up a low bamboo table there, which she used as a work place, where she was shaded from the sun. Lately, she had been waking up feeling dizzy and sick. Because of this, the meals in the house had become the duty of the cook, since the smell of everything in the kitchen made Gade nauseous. But when she noticed that Nart was eating less, Gade forced herself to go in the kitchen and cook, but as soon as she had finished, she hurried outside to eat something sour or salty to alleviate her nausea.

In the months that followed, Gade found she wanted to eat sweet things. Even though Phetchaburi was renowned for sugar, Gade had never had a sweet tooth, and had always preferred sour tastes, until she became pregnant and wanted to eat palm sugar and sugarcane like never before.

"What are you doing, madam?"

The sound of Chalaem's high-pitched voice made Gade look up from the candy pots she had been making, which she was arranging in a line. Chalaem was standing in front of her smiling. She was carrying a small tray that held a white porcelain bowl with a lid on it, indicating that she had brought something for Gade as she usually did.

"Oh! Candy pots! Who are they for?"

She continued speaking without waiting for an answer.

"They're so cute! You're very artistic, madam, like the people in the palace."

"Have a seat," Gade smiled, inviting her to sit down, even though they were now close. "What have you brought?"

"Western-style roast chicken breast, madam," Chalaem answered as she placed the tray on the bamboo table beside Gade. "Lately, Khun Luang hasn't been eating much. He likes Western food, and you don't know how to cook it, madam."

Gade smiled without taking offense. Chalaem's polite manners and speech were sometimes interspersed with strange, almost negative comments as if she was warning Gade that she was falling short in her duties as a wife.

"I really can't. The smell of milk and butter makes me nauseous."

Chalaem's eyes wandered to Gade's stomach, which bulged under her thin clothes. She stared for a moment before looking up at Gade with a quizzical smile.

"I think it's a girl, don't you?"

"How can you tell?" Gade asked curiously.

"You want to eat sweet things, so it must be a girl," Chalaem answered confidently, before continuing regretfully, "It's a shame if your first child's not a boy. Khun Luang must want a boy. Fathers always want a boy to continue the family line."

"What about you, Chalaem? Do you want a son or a daughter?"

Chalaem's face fell when she heard Gade's question because she had been married for three years, and was still childless, even though she had visited many temples and shrines to 'ask for a child.'

"A boy, of course," she answered coldly, and stood up abruptly, picking up the tray as if she didn't wish to discuss the matter any further. "I'd better take this roast chicken to the kitchen. If I leave it here, it might get eaten by a dog."

She marched off to the kitchen scowling, leaving Gade looking at her back in confusion.

Gade had just finished making some sweets and putting them in a container before calling Noei's daughter to put them on the shelf. She walked out in front of the house to go up the steps inside when she saw her husband's horse-drawn carriage stop next to the steps.

Nart stepped down from the carriage looking happy.

"Gade!" he called.

Gade walked up to him more slowly than usual on her account of her heavy stomach.

"What is it?"

Nart grasped her arm and said, "Let's go upstairs to talk."

Gade slowly followed him up the steps and he handed her his hat to hang up as usual, but did not remove his jacket or his boots.

"I've got good news. I've been made a lieutenant colonel."

Gade's heart filled with joy.

"I'm happy...really happy for you."

Gade stopped abruptly when she saw Chalaem coming up the steps. Nobody knew where she had gone, and Gade assumed she had gone home. She was holding an empty tray, and was first to speak.

"I've made you Western-style roast chicken, sir. I know you haven't eaten Western food for a long time because your wife doesn't know how to cook it, and she hasn't been feeling well, either."

"Thank you so much," Gade's husband answered mildly. "We'll have it to celebrate."

Chalaem immediately pricked up her ears.

"Oh! What's the good news, sir?"

"Nart's been made a lieutenant colonel," Gade answered for her husband.

Chalaem's face fell as soon as she heard, instead of being pleased as she should have been, but a moment later she smiled, even though her eyes were not smiling.

"Oh! What good news, sir! Er, Thongphoon hasn't said anything," she said referring to her husband. "I wonder if he's been promoted, too."

"No, he hasn't. I expect he'll be promoted next year," Nart replied.

Chalaem's face fell even more. She glanced at Gade's happy face before laughing, and, even though she tried to sound joyful, her laughter sounded hollow and forced.

"If you're a lieutenant colonel, you must be a Khun Phra* now."

"Phra Narentharaksa," Nart answered and turned to tell his wife, "All my friends and subordinates are happy."

"I'm happy, too," Gade answered, stroking her stomach gently. "This child is bringing us good fortune."

"You're right," Nart smiled at her. "This is good fortune."

Other officers came in succession to congratulate him, along with government workers from the town, and, as Phra Narentharaksa's wife, Gade had to prepare meals for the visitors daily. Moving around was becoming difficult, and she wasn't as quick as before. This was one reason that she hoped the birth would come quickly.

Gade remembered clearly that the atmosphere that evening had not been any different from usual. She had retired to her room after preparing a meal for her husband and his subordinates, which they ate around the table together. After dinner, the men sat and chatted about work and other things until late. Suddenly there was the thud of boots coming up the steps, and the conversation ceased. Someone was talking quickly and was out of breath.

"There's been a fight between the army and the police, sir."

The sound of exclamations was followed by the sound of the men getting up and pushing their chairs loudly across the floor. Gade looked up in alarm and stood up, nodding to the girl sitting with her in the room and calling her to follow the men to the door.

The room outside was empty; the men had left in a hurry. Gade looked beyond the steps and saw the whole group of officers disappearing into the shadows. There was only the faint sound of orders being given, which became more muffled as they got further away, and of dogs barking as they passed by.

As Gade had anticipated, her husband did not return that night. All she heard was the sound of soldiers walking past the house every so often, and the sound of horse-drawn carriages going past time after time all through the night, telling her that something was amiss.

---

* The title Khun Luang was a rank equivalent to a British army captain and major. When an officer was promoted, he would gain the title Khun Phra, corresponding to lieutenant colonel and colonel, followed by the title Phraya, equal to major general and lieutenant general. These titles were abolished in 1942.

Nart did not return until evening, so he sent a soldier to ask Gade for food and a change of clothes, which made Gade anxious all day. The next day, he came home looking worried and there were dark circles under his eyes as if he hadn't slept all night.

After bathing, he told Gade, "Let me sleep a while...but don't let me sleep for more than an hour. I need to meet with the officers."

Gade felt her child kicking forcefully, as she did whenever she was tired or anxious. She tried not to think about feeling sick and slowly went outside to call Noei to prepare a meal for Nart. After he woke , he ate his meal with a little more vigour, but Gade could see that his face still showed signs of anxiety.

Gade waited until he was full and eating dessert before asking him hesitantly, "What's happening? Can you tell me?"

He stopped abruptly before answering gruffly, "Nothing much. A crook they caught two months ago escaped somewhere around the army base, and the police couldn't get inside. They asked my permission to search inside, so I let them, but they couldn't find the crook, and they thought we were hiding him. That's how it started."

Gade felt dismayed and asked, "And what about the fight?"

"The young policemen and soldiers were at a party, and, once they started drinking, they got into an argument, and started fighting. Then someone pulled a gun out, and when a police officer tried to stop him, he got shot and wounded."

Gade felt more alarmed. If a police officer had been wounded, it was serious.

"Oh, no!" Gade said, stroking her stomach. "What will you do?"

"I've ordered those soldiers to be put in jail. It's for the military court to decide on the punishment. They won't get away with it. They're all young and impulsive."

Gade breathed a sigh of relief.

"That's just as well. At least no one can blame you for taking sides."

Nart sighed and his face became more serious.

"I'm stuck between a rock and a hard place. My subordinates will say I'm being disloyal and not protecting them, but if I try to help get them off with a lighter sentence, I'll be accused of taking sides with the guilty party. The governor will have to inform the Interior Ministry, and the Interior Ministry will have to inform the Ministry of Defence. I'll have to take full responsibility."

"Bu…but…" Gade responded in the only way she could think of, "The guilty party is the one that should be punished. You didn't do anything wrong. How can you be punished?"

Nart smiled faintly, but his face remained serious.

"I'm their commander. I have to take responsibility for what they did...And for another thing…"

He sighed again.

"What worries me is that the governor's from an important family, and he's close to that police officer. I don't have those sort of connections. Whatever happens, I'll be held responsible. I'm not likely to get off lightly."

Gade woke up suddenly in the night when she felt a strange pain in the middle of her body, which came in waves. She turned to her husband out of habit and found the bed empty. That night he had gone to Nakhon Pathom province on business and would not be back until the following afternoon, but he had asked Noei and her daughter to stay with her.

Gade called the girl sleeping at the foot of her bed and stepped down from the bed with shaking legs, leaning on the girl for support as she went into the room that had been prepared for the birth and for lying by the fire afterwards*.

Noei woke up and shook off her sleepiness right away. From past experience, she knew just what to do, and called Man to go and fetch the midwife urgently. In the meantime, Gade tossed and turned until she was soaked with sweat, and the waves of pain that swept over her grew bigger and more frequent with every passing moment, showing no sign of letting up.

---

* Lying by the fire is a traditional practice for Thai women after childbirth. Although the practice is rooted in the superstitious belief that the fire will ward off evil spirits, the heat from the fire is believed to be helpful in shrinking the uterus more quickly.

Noei rolled a white sheet into a coil and tied it to the bedpost before helping Gade up to hold onto it with all her strength in order to alleviate the pain, so that she wouldn't writhe hysterically.

"The first time's always like this. It hurts a lot," she kept repeating. "It'll all be over soon."

Gade woke from a deep sleep several hours later. When she opened her eyes, she saw the pale rays of the morning sun shining inside the room and the fragrant smoke from the herbs being boiled filled her nostrils. The tranquillity of the room was like the clear sky after a storm.

The midwife was busy grinding ginger to apply to the tear, and when Gade groaned, she got up and walked over to where she was lying on the low bamboo table. She smiled, showing her black teeth and red mouth.

"It's a boy!"

She spoke with a Phetchaburi accent and had a kind manner.

"I'll bring him to show you. You stay lying down. You can't get up yet."

Although she was still sore, the pain disappeared completely when she set eyes on the tiny body wrapped in a white blanket in her arms. She tensed her arms and hardly dared to breathe as she carefully held the tiny body as if he was the most precious thing in her life.

My child, I can't believe how tiny you are, not like my sister's children that I've held. Your skin's red and wrinkled, and your little face is smaller than the round amulets they like to compare babies' faces to.

As she gazed down, the tiny baby opened his eyes, which were black and bright, even though they couldn't yet focus. His tiny pink mouth was smaller than her fingertip and he yawned like a little kitten. Gade smiled at her child through teary eyes, and her heart filled with love for him. She had never experienced anything with such intensity before.

The midwife chatted away.

"I didn't think he'd make it, madam. The umbilical cord was wrapped around him when he came out."

"What happened?" Gade cried.

"Yes," the midwife confirmed. "In the old days they would've put him in a pot and buried him because he wouldn't have survived, but I was careful. I unwrapped him and he was still breathing. You're lucky he survived. I've delivered hundreds of babies, and this is the first one like that who survived."

Gade held her son closer in alarm when she realized she had almost lost the most precious thing in her life.

"You must lie by the fire the whole time," the midwife cautioned. "You had a difficult birth. If you don't lie by the fire long enough, you'll get sepsis."

Up to that moment, Gade had still felt quite numb, but suddenly she became aware of the pain she felt all over until she could hardly move.

Suddenly Gade's thoughts turned to her husband.

"Where's Khun Phra?"

"He's outside. I'll go and fetch him."

With that, the woman left the room with an agility that belied her age, leaving Gade lying down with the child in her arms as before. A moment later, Nart entered the room wearing his army uniform as if he was getting ready to go to work. When he saw his wife lying down with the tiny baby, he sat on the low bamboo table and clasped her hand in his.

"How's our son?" he asked gently, and continued speaking without waiting for an answer. "He's as small as a kitten, but I'm happy...so happy to have a son."

Her husband's words revived her like holy water sprinkled on parched land, and she squeezed his hand with the little strength she had in response.

"I'm happy, too...Happy that he's alright. The midwife said he's the only one that survived... Nart, I'll take good care of him...the best..."

Nart reached over to stroke Gade's hair and gently touched his son's red skin.

"That's right. You'll have to be very careful with him. As he grows, he'll be as fit as any other child, but right now he's so small I daren't take him along."

"Take him along?" Gade asked in alarm. "Where are you going?"

Nart's face fell a little at the question, and he paused for a moment as if he was considering whether to tell her, but then he decided it was better to tell the truth.

"The order for me to move has come from the Ministry of Defence.

I am to take up a new position in Mark Keng. I have to report to the ministry first to take my orders. The journey from Bangkok to Mark Keng is difficult. You have to take the train, then a boat, and then walk through the Phaya Fai Rainforest as far as the Mekong River...Gade, I don't know how I can take you and our baby son."

The day Nart set out for Bangkok, it was foggy before it got light, and when Gade woke, all she could see was a thick white blanket of fog covering the whole area around the house. A cold mist blew in when she opened the door to go outside.

Gade entered the kitchen and set a fire before cooking the rice, steaming the eggs, frying the salted fish, and breaking the salted eggs that she had prepared for breakfast. By the time she had finished, it was light. She set aside some food to put in the monks' alms bowls as she always did, and when she had finished giving alms, she returned to the house. Everything was quiet and the dry leaves blew across the ground. Man, who usually swept the leaves, had gone on ahead several days earlier to take Nart's belongings to Bangkok.

Since giving birth, Gade had not slept in her bedroom. Firstly, because she was still sleeping in the room where she had been lying by the fire, and secondly so that her son's cries would not disturb his father, because he would cry almost incessantly and she hardly slept at all. What with taking care of her child, supervising the packing of things that had to be taken to Bangkok, and things that she would take back with her to Ban Tha Hin, she wasn't able to lie by the fire for a month as the midwife had insisted.

When she found out, she scolded, "Look at you, madam! You didn't listen to me! You got up from the fire after only a few days. You'll get sepsis and your uterus won't return to normal. Then you won't be able to have any more children."

Whenever she held her child's fragile form in her arms, she couldn't help being afraid that, at some point, the tiny life would slip away. And now her husband, who had been there to protect them, had to go far away. When she spoke of Mark Keng or Udon Thani province to her relatives, they shook their heads as if Nart was going to the ends of the earth.

Gade felt as if she was in a boat in the middle of a stormy sea and could not see the shore, but only a wall of dark clouds looming all around her. She heard the door upstairs being pushed open and was startled, so she quickly wiped away her tears and got up.

"Gade!" Nart called. "Where are you?"

"I'm here!"

Nart came down the steps, still wearing trousers and a cotton shirt, but he had washed his face.

"I wondered where you were. Are you making breakfast?"

"Yes, I've finished," Gade answered, trying to sound cheerful. "I'll bring it up for you."

Nart caught hold of her arm and gazed down at her fondly.

"There's no hurry. The train won't be leaving for over an hour. You've been working too hard. You look pale."

What he said was true. Her reflection in the mirror for the past few days had confirmed it. The woman who stared back at her each morning was a stranger with a dull complexion and sad eyes, and even though her figure was still full after giving birth, she lacked radiance. Her hair was pulled back, without being styled like before, her lips were dry and cracked, and there was no sparkle in her eyes like there used to be. Gade could hardly believe that it was the same beautiful young woman who had entered the house for the first time just over a year ago.

Nart led her upstairs to the room in the centre of the house. It was empty of belongings and all that was left was a table and chairs that belonged to the army. He sat on an old deckchair that was so shabby he had decided not to take it with him, and Gade sat on the floor at his feet.

"When will you go to Ban Tha Hin?" he asked gently.

"As soon as I come back from the railway station," Gade answered with her head bowed, stifling her apprehension.

"Good. You'll have your parents and your sister there," Nart said. "Then I won't need to worry too much about you. I really wish I could take you and the baby, but it's impossible."

Gade felt a lump in her throat and, before she knew it, she had laid her head on her husband's knee and was sobbing as if her heart would break. There had been many times when Gade had fought back tears and swallowed her pain because she didn't want to worry her husband, but, on the last day, the dam that had been holding her feelings back came crashing down.

"Gade...Gade…" Nart repeated, stroking her shoulders and back. "Don't cry. When I've got settled there, I'll come back and get you and Ned. It won't be long. Wait until he's a bit bigger. They say it's scorching hot there in summer, and cold in winter. It would be hard on you both. Don't cry. You'll make me worried."

They had discussed it several times, since the first time Nart had told her he would be moving to take up a new position. At first, they thought the three of them might go together, but Gade was afraid that the fragile little child would not survive the difficult journey. Never mind, Udon Thani, she dared not even take him to Bangkok.

Finally, Gade decided before her husband.

"Let me stay here. You go on ahead. Don't worry about me."

When she saw his disconsolate expression, her heart sank.

"And where will you go? This house belongs to the army. The person who takes my post will move in here. When I leave, so must you."

"I'll go back to live with my parents," Gade answered more sadly than before, but she remained resolute. "All my relatives are in Ban Tha Hin. They can help me take care of Ned. I'm not strong enough to make the journey yet."

Nart pondered for a while before assuring her, "When I get there, if it's not too hard, I'll send someone to fetch you."

This was a small drop of water on the dry land of Gade's heart, and all she could do was hope that it wouldn't be too long. By the time Ned was one, or two at the most, he should be fit enough to travel. It was this hope that gave her the strength to carry on and get ready to make the journey.

Another comfort for Gade was that one of her relatives was travelling with Nart under his command. Soon after Muen's son, Klai, had left the monkhood, he had joined the army like his father, and when Phra Narentharaksa was told of his new position, Muen asked if his son could accompany him. Muen had told his boss politely, "I'd like to go with you to Mark Keng, but I'm getting old and my health hasn't been so good this year, so I'd like to send Klai to serve you in my place, sir.

He's a fit young man, so he'll be of more use to you."

Gade knew that her cousin, who was only two years older than her, was hardworking and reliable, and she was relieved that Nart would have someone trustworthy working for him in a strange and remote place. Even so, when the time came for them to part, Gade couldn't contain her sadness any longer.

"Don't cry, Gade. It will be a bad omen for both of us," Nart warned again.

Gade quickly wiped away her tears. It was true. He was going far away and the journey was difficult. She didn't know what kind of sicknesses he would have to face, and she had heard that he would have to pass through the Phaya Fai Rainforest where many people had died. She forced herself to stop thinking about all the terrible things that could happen. Then she quickly moved away, so that he could stand up, and said in a trembling voice, "I'll go and get breakfast."

Nart got dressed quickly because he had a train to catch, and when Gade had prepared his breakfast, he stepped out of the bedroom looking handsome in his crisp army uniform, although his face was unusually downcast. He forced his breakfast down with difficulty and Gade brought the baby out of the bedroom lying on a small pillow. She had fed him and he was drowsy. His delicate skin showed the red blood running through his veins and his hair was thick and black because his head had not yet been shaved.

Nart took the clean white pillow from his wife's arms and looked down at his son who, by then, was fast asleep.

"Ned."

He spoke his son's name softly as if the small child could understand.

"You're the apple of your mother's eye. She chose to stay with you, so you'd live. Remember her love for you...and one day, we'll all be together again."

Gade's eyes were wet with tears and her vision was blurry, but the image of her husband holding the pillow with the tiny baby tightly to his chest, before returning him to his mother was one that never left her mind, day or night. It was like a lamp wick that sustained the flame of hope, and it did not die out for many years.

3
The Woman Named Nuathong

Lieutenant Colonel Phra Narentharaksa walked up the steps of the Ministry of Defence and was saluted by the soldiers on duty before going inside without being asked any questions.

Because of the rank on his shoulders, he was also saluted by several young soldiers that walked past him.

He went down the long dark corridors, lined with doors shut tight on both sides, and turned left and right until he came to a large long room with officers sitting at desks in rows. He went up to one desk and asked for the person he had come to meet.

"I'm Lieutenant Colonel Phra Narentharaksa, and I'm here to see Lieutenant Colonel Phra Ritdaeso."

The person of whom he spoke was sitting in a small office separated from the main room by a wooden and frosted glass partition. The afternoon sun shone orange rays through the long window and frosted glass air vents onto the smart and well-built officer who was bent over some papers at the large desk.

When he saw who was there, he jumped up and exclaimed happily, "Nart! I was just thinking about you! I didn't expect you to suddenly show up today!"

Nart shook his friend's hand before taking a seat on the chair in front of the desk. The ceiling fan whirred slowly casting dim shadows over the floor. Outside the window the pagoda and chapel roof of The Temple of the Emerald Buddha sparkled against the clear blue sky of the capital.

"I'm here to report to the ministry to take my orders, so I dropped by to see you."

His friend knew all about his transfer because the matter had been referred to him before it was sent up to the high-level commanders. He nodded sympathetically.

"The matter was sent from the Interior Ministry to the Ministry of Defence. You weren't to blame at all. This shouldn't have happened to you."

Nart laughed a little bitterly.

"I'm not upset. I'm a soldier. I have to go where my commander orders me."

Phra Ritdaeso sat on the edge of his chair and folded his arms. Compared to his guest, he was only of medium height, but there was something in his clean-cut dark face and his bold eyes that betrayed uncompromising determination.

"You mustn't think that way, Nart," he replied earnestly. "If it was just a matter of right and wrong, I wouldn't argue, but I know it's because, apart from being from an important family, that side is also close to the aristocracy. You're a commoner, so you don't have a say."

"You mean…" Nart picked up a glass paperweight and turned it back and forth. "You're saying it's because of the family he was born into."

"Definitely," his friend replied with conviction. "Everyone knows people are judged on the family they come from instead of on how good they are at their job, or their abilities. Take you, for instance. You've been smart since you were a cadet. If you'd been from an important family, you would have a comfortable position in Bangkok by now. You wouldn't have to be posted upcountry, or to out of the way places."

Nart raised his hand to stop him.

"Enough. There's no point saying any more. If anyone hears, you'll be kicked out of the ministry, too."

His friend sighed.

"The country's backwards, and it doesn't seem to be getting any better."

Nart grinned.

"Even after all these years, you're still grumbling about the country. I see your head's still filled with ideas of democracy."

Nart's friend didn't find it a laughing matter and continued earnestly, "Of course. My ideals haven't changed. You know as well as I do that Siam is the only country that still has an absolute monarchy. Other Asian countries don't have one anymore. Developed countries have democracy. If we want our country to be equal to civilized countries, we can't stay as we were in the days of King Uthong."

In other people's eyes, his friend was Lieutenant Colonel Phra Ritdaeso, the brilliant scholar who had been educated in France, but in Nart's eyes, he was just Det. They had hugged each other and played sports together, had been students in the same class from when they were young until they were grown up, and now they wore the same dashing army uniform together. Nothing had changed.

Whenever Det had lost his temper about something, Nart had been the one to calm him down. In the same way, whenever Nart was so calm as to be indifferent, Det would goad him into taking action. This had cemented their friendship, even though their duties had kept them apart for many years. Nart's silence made Det aware of his dissent, so he changed the subject.

"If I talk too much, I might put my foot in it, or at least make you uncomfortable. You've come to see me, after all. We should celebrate. How long can you stay in Bangkok?"

Nart was relieved that his friend had changed the subject.

"Not more than a month."

"Hey! That's plenty of time to get together with our friends. You can party to your heart's content. You've been upcountry so long you probably can't remember your way around."

Nart responded to his teasing with honesty.

"You're probably right. Last time I was here there were hardly any cars. Now there are plenty on the streets. They go so fast, I'm afraid they'll hit people walking on the pavement. Even in front of the ministry, you have to look left and right before crossing now. It's not like before."

"Did you bring your wife and child? You married a girl from Phetchaburi, didn't you?"

A shadow fell over Nart's face.

"I didn't bring them. Ned is still a new-born and he's not strong enough to travel, so I left them in Phetchaburi."

"She's gone back to live with her parents then, has she?" Det asked blithely and teased, "So now you're single again! Good for you! I can take you out on the town. You've been away too long. The women in Bangkok are much more beautiful than before, you know!"

Nart chuckled.

"I can see you're a ladies' man!"

Det laughed. The momentary tension eased and the atmosphere became friendly and relaxed.

"If you're not, what's the point of being a man?"

With humour and a hint of sarcasm, he continued, "When you're upcountry, you have to eat whatever grows there, but when you're in the capital, it would be a shame not to sample the delicacies."

Nart laughed without taking offense as his friend slapped him on the back.

"Anyway, you have to report to the commander soon, don't you? I'll get as many of our friends together as I can tonight, and on Sunday, you're invited to a big party at my house. Don't miss it. It's a housewarming party in my new home."

"A new house," Nart repeated. "Where?"

"Phraeng Sappasat Road. My father-in-law gave me some of his land, so I could build a house next to his. He just has one daughter, so he didn't want her to move far away."

"Which father-in-law?" Nart asked, grinning because he knew that his friend had been married since he was a young officer.

"My only father-in-law," Det chuckled bashfully. "My new wife's name is Malai. We had a big wedding. I finished with my first wife. She lives with her son. Don't forget, Nart. You have to come."

Lieutenant Colonel Phra Ritdaeso's house was situated on the land which Nart remembered had once belonged to Prince Sappasat Supakij because he had passed it often in his childhood. It was a two-storey compact modern wooden house with a fashionable red tiled gable roof, rather than a hip roof, which was seen as old-fashioned by people in Bangkok. It stood on the same plot as another large wooden house, which Nart guessed belonged to his friend's father-in-law. Nart didn't know the family of Phra Ritdaeso's wife. He only knew that her father was a wealthy man, who did not work for the government.

By the time Nart arrived, it was already dark, and the lawn and living room were filled with young men and women. The sweet sound of traditional Thai music could be heard coming from a string ensemble playing in a pavilion on the lawn, and a strip of coloured bunting was hung from the fence up to a blue and white porcelain jardiniere next to the steps leading into the living room.

The soldiers in their uniforms were striking as they congregated in groups on the lawn, and the women could be seen walking up and down and giggling in the living room inside the house. Phra Ritdaeso's wife was called Malai. Although she wasn't his first wife, she was considered to be his principal wife because of her beauty and her status as the daughter of a wealthy man. She was a perfect hostess, and when she saw Nart, she came out to greet him.

Then she left the men to socialize, while she went back inside the living room with her friends. Some of them had been invited because they were married to army officers and others were still single – all of them were beautifully dressed as if they were competing with one another. Malai understood only too well that as long as Siamese women in the 1920s could earn neither rank nor honour for themselves, they believed that: "A husband is a woman's crowning glory."

At this kind of party, it was certain that there would be plenty of young officers, and when Malai had sent out her invitations, she was amused to see that her friends almost fought over them. If you were lucky, you would get to be an officer's wife, and eventually, you would get the title "Khunying" if your husband became a general.

The darker the sky, the brighter the lights inside the house appeared. At that moment, a horse and carriage came to a stop in the street, and a figure stepped down and walked slowly through the open gate. It was a young woman with glowing skin and a shapely figure who was noticeable from a distance because of the way she was dressed. She wore a white silk sleeveless blouse with a large red rose clipped to the edge of the neck revealing ivory cleavage, paired with a deep red sarong.

Her jet-black hair was cut in a fashionable bob and curled above her forehead. She sauntered in elegantly and was not at all embarrassed that almost every pair of eyes in the party had turned towards her.

Her penetrating black eyes swept over the group of officers, a slight smile lighting up her oval face. When she came close enough to recognize the host, she pressed her palms together gracefully and said sweetly, "Forgive me for being a little late. I haven't been to your new house before, so I had to stop and ask for directions."

Lieutenant Colonel Phra Ritdaeso smiled as a man does when greeting a beautiful girl, but his smile did not show that he was particularly pleased to see her. He answered amicably, "Don't worry. Not all the guests have arrived yet."

She looked past the host to the officer who was standing behind him and was still smiling when she fixed her eyes on the new face that she hadn't seen before, before turning back to the host.

"There are so many guests that I haven't met all of them."

Taking the hint, the host introduced his friend with an amused expression.

"You're right. You haven't met my friend. Let me introduce Lieutenant Colonel Phra Narentharaksa. He's just moved from Phetchaburi and he's about to be posted in Udon Thani. As for this lovely young lady...This is Malai's friend, Nueang."

"It's Nuathong," she corrected him looking slightly askance. "You keep calling me by my old name. I changed my name ages ago."*

"You're right. I'm sorry," he hurriedly replied before adding, "Your new name suits you so much better than your old one."

Her luminous eyes met those of the newly-introduced officer and lit up before her bright red lips parted to reveal her even white teeth. She pressed her palms together and bowed her head gracefully and explained, "I went to school with Malai. We were close before she

---

* It is quite common for people in Thailand to change their given names, believing that a new name may result in improved fortune, thus increasing a person's confidence. 'Nueang' means 'often'or 'as usual' while 'Nuathong' means 'golden complexion'.

married, but now she's married, I don't get to see her as much. I know Khun Phra Rit, too."

Her smile was dazzling, and Nart caught his breath when he stared at her.

Nart answered, "I've been away from my friends for a long time. I hardly know anyone in Bangkok anymore. Even Det's wife. I've only just met her. I'm pleased to meet one of her friends."

Lieutenant Colonel Phra Ritdaeso slapped his friend gently on the back.

"You've got a whole month to party with your friends. Ah, here comes Malai."

Malai greeted her friend happily before leading her away by the hand.

Nart gazed after her, and she turned and caught his eye again before going up the steps with her friend. He turned back to his friend and heard him chuckling quietly.

Nart felt a little embarrassed, but his curiosity got the better of him, so he asked openly, "She's stunning. Who is she? Where's she from?"

Phra Ritdaeso replied nonchalantly, "Like I said, she's a friend of Malai's. As far as I know, she lives near Khlong Banglampu. Her father didn't work for the government. He was a clerk in a foreign department store. He must have been paid well because he could afford to send her to school with Malai, but both her parents are dead now."

"Is that so?" Nart murmured. "And who does she live with?"

He watched as the figure in the red and white outfit disappeared inside the living room and squeals of laughter emanated from the room.

"Malai said she lives with an old servant. She must be lonely without her parents. After all, she's still young."

Malai had once been to visit Nueang at her small house next to Khlong Ong Ang, where she had met her father, Arun, a good-looking and dapper man who always wore a Western-style suit in keeping with his job in a foreign department store. He never wore the white Raj style shirt with a purple *jongkraben* of civil servants, and his speech was so polished that he appeared almost boastful. He was disdainful of his neighbours and had a taste for expensive things that he couldn't afford. It seemed as if Nueang had followed in every step of her father's footsteps.

When they came out of the house, the women mingled with the group of men, and they sat at alternate seats at tables on the lawn instead of inside the house where it was cramped.

Instead of eating, Nuathong said to her friends in a loud voice, "Today's a special day. May I sing a song or two for our hosts?"

"Please do," the host encouraged and clapped his hands in support. "You're a fine singer. Let's give her a round of applause, everyone!"

The young woman who was now the centre of attention smiled beguilingly at the officers before nodding to the musicians, sitting down in front of the ensemble and whispering the name of the song she wanted.

Sitting demurely on the floor with her legs to the side, she tilted her head slightly and looked at the audience without making eye contact with anyone in particular. After a moment, she began to sing in a high sweet voice.

"I heard your lovely voice and fell in love
As if a phoenix had sung me a lullaby.
I woke from my slumber when I heard your voice
As if a spell had been cast over me."

In one verse, she looked up at the host's table as if by chance, and her eyes met Nart's for a moment before she looked away. Nuathong came back to her seat once she had finished and another officer, who happened to be sitting next to Nart, stood up to give her his seat next to the host.

"You sing very well," Nart complimented her sincerely. "Can you sing another song?"

She looked at him sideways and laughed, "Goodness! Won't you let me rest? My throat's dry from singing!"

After dinner, the Thai music ensemble continued to play. Everyone kept urging Nuathong to sing again, but this time, either because she thought it was inappropriate, or for some other reason, she refused and made excuses.

"I can't remember the words. There are only a few songs I remember the words to. We'll have to see which song I know the words to."

"How about 'The Mon Guest from Bang Khun Prom' Nart suggested, smiling as he caught her eye. "I like that song."

Before Nuathong could answer, someone else interrupted, "What about that song composed by the present king? 'A night full of stars'... It's a beautiful song."

The smile disappeared from Nart's face. Something – he didn't know what it was – stirred in his heart with such force it was as if something heavy had been hurled at him.

'A night full of stars', the song he had sung on his wedding night to the lovely young girl who was as innocent and pure as a lotus rising from the water. Images from the past, washed over him in waves – the young girl sitting on the bridge above the water when she had just finished bathing and drops of water clung to her soft cool skin, or the shy bride as innocent as the expression in her eyes. The last image was of the thin and fragile girl holding a tiny baby in her arms with tears running down her cheeks, the last picture he saw before the train pulled out of the station.

Nuathong noticed Nart's ashen face and sudden seriousness. Although she didn't know what had caused it, she knew that he did not want to play games with her anymore. Instead she asked him with a smile, "There are so many songs, I don't know what to sing. Can you help me decide?"

He answered quietly, almost curtly, "It's up to you. Any song is fine."

She hesitated before standing up, walking to the pavilion and telling the musicians to play 'The Mon Guest from Bang Khun Prom' to see what he would do if she picked the song that he had suggested. However, when she returned to the table, she was disappointed to hear from the host that his friend had gone home a few moments ago.

"Oh, it's you Nueang. You come to visit almost every day these days."

Malai greeted her with a mixture of amusement and puzzlement when she walked into the living room and saw her old friend sitting on the sofa. Since the day of the party, her friend had been diligent in coming to see her and had been three or four times already.

"I hope you're not getting fed up with me. I really mean it when I say that I'm so grateful you invited me to your housewarming party. I really appreciate your friendship…"

As she spoke, she took out a white linen handkerchief trimmed with lace and dabbed her eyes.

"You don't know how...scared...and lonely...I've felt since my father passed away, and then my mother. Every day I feel as if I'm all alone in the world."

Malai's heart softened when she saw her friend's obvious distress. She had both her parents, so she felt sorry for her orphaned friend. Malai reached over and squeezed her hand sympathetically. It was no easy matter for a girl in her early twenties to survive by herself without any family, especially when she had no livelihood to depend on and only a small inheritance, which would soon run out.

"Whenever you're lonely, you're welcome to visit," she told her as kindly as she could.

Nuathong was certain that Lieutenant Colonel Phra Narentharaksa would visit Malai's house often since he was only in the capital for a short time and would be sure to want to see as much of his friends as he could. If she was to meet the young man again, Malai would have to be the bridge. Even before her parents had passed away, Nuathong had sought a husband who would give her status, but those men she deemed good enough were either too far above her in their social standing, or were not serious and only wanted her as a minor wife or mistress.

Nuathong had missed her chance again and again until her parents passed away. The small amount of money that her parents had left her was almost gone because she had no job and didn't know how to earn money.

Lieutenant Colonel Phra Narentharaksa seemed to be the perfect answer.

As afternoon turned to evening, Malai saw that her friend made no move to leave, so she invited her to stay for dinner out of politeness.

Nuathong was clever enough to refuse, knowing that her host was unprepared, so she answered hesitantly, "Perhaps next time. This time I only meant to come and talk to you. I don't want to go home late."

She then asked, "Is there anything I can help with before I go? I don't know why, but today I feel like cooking. I'm fed up with cooking only for myself. It's more fun to cook for other people."

She knew that any housewife would appreciate help with the cooking and, as she expected, Malai accepted the offer gladly.

"That would be good. I could use some help. Today my husband's friends are coming for dinner and drinks. I have to prepare both sweet and savoury dishes. Help me think of what to cook."

"If you mean snacks to go with drinks, it would have to be spicy salads or stir fries, wouldn't it?"

"There should be a variety of dishes," Malai answered, unaware of her friend's ulterior motives. "Some people like spicy dishes like you said, but others plain ones. Khun Phra Naren, for one, doesn't like drinks with anything too spicy or sour. He prefers plain things such as garlic and pepper fried chicken or grilled beef."

Nuathong dropped her gaze, so that her friend wouldn't see the glint of satisfaction in her eyes beneath the long, curved lashes. She seemingly paid no attention to the name and didn't ask any questions, so that her friend would not suspect anything, replying casually, "That's not hard. I'll help you cook both before I go home. It makes me think of my father. He was good at cooking European-style grilled beef."

"Really?" Malai asked enthusiastically, still not suspecting anything because Nuathong was adamant that she would leave before her husband's friends arrived.

"Can you make it? Does it take long?"

Nuathong stood up with alacrity.

"You have to marinate the beef first to tenderise it. I know, some whiskey will do the trick. Can I go in the kitchen to see what meat you've got? Oh! And can you lend me a blouse and sarong? I don't want to get this outfit dirty."

She changed out of her pretty outfit and put on a plain blouse and a black sarong that her friend found for her. She calculated that it would take at least two hours before the food was finished and heard from the unsuspecting Malai that her husband and his friends would arrive at around seven, and would have drinks and snacks until about eight when they would be ready for dinner. It wasn't hard to act as if she was hurrying to finish the cooking while, in reality, she was deliberately taking her time. When the food was finished, Nuathong complained she was sticky from the heat of the grill, and asked if she could have a wash and change before going home. She took her time in front of the mirror until she heard the sound of deep voices downstairs, and smiled at her reflection with satisfaction before slowly walking downstairs.

Malai's husband was standing in the room downstairs with the young man who made her heart suddenly beat faster.

"Nueang! Oops, I mean Nuathong," he greeted her in puzzlement when he saw her. "I didn't know you were here. Have you come to see Malai?"

"Yes, I've been here since the afternoon."

The young woman greeted him respectfully along with Nart, and hid her joy, as she added, "Malai and I lost track of time, so she asked me to help her cook for you and your friends. Dinner's all ready. I was just about to go home."

After she had been so kind, it seemed only polite to invite her to stay for dinner, so he said, "Since you cooked it, why are you in such a hurry to go? You must stay and eat with us."

She turned to look at the other man, and when she saw that he did not try to coax her, but simply smiled amiably, she declined petulantly.

"I'd better not. I live alone. I'm scared to go home by myself late at night."

Phra Ritdaeso fell right into her trap, or at least had no other option but to say,

"Is that all? I'll have someone take you home."

"Well, in that case…" she stammered with feigned hesitation. "I'd be very grateful. In that case, would you excuse me while I help in the kitchen."

During this exchange, Nart hadn't spoken to Nuathong but she smiled at him again before disappearing downstairs into the kitchen.

Phra Ritdaeso didn't notice any of this, since he was a man who never paid attention to trivial things. He walked to the glass cabinet for a bottle of whiskey, which he carried back with a nod to his friend.

"Let's have a drink on the balcony. There's a nice breeze. We can sit and wait for the others to come."

Nart knew which of his peers were coming, so he asked about the junior officers whom he didn't know.

"There's someone I don't know if you remember. He came after us, but I've always said he was smart. He's a clever and convincing speaker."

Nart was amused.

"You talk as if we were going to watch a movie. I don't know who you mean."

"His name's Plaek Kettasangkha, Major Luang Phibun Songkhram. Do you remember him?"

Nart thought for a moment before shaking his head.

"I've invited him for drinks and dinner. Nothing formal."

Phra Ritdaeso looked back over his shoulder and chuckled as he waved and shouted, "Why, here he is! Your ears must be burning! I was just talking about you and here you are!"

Nart noticed a young officer walking up the steps to the living room. He removed his hat and saluted politely. His face was fresh and young and he smiled warmly.

"Do you have anything for me to do, sir?"

"No, no. I was just telling my friend here that you were coming for dinner."

The young major smiled showing his straight white teeth. Nart studied him unobtrusively and thought to himself that he was a fine figure of a man who must appeal to women. His clear, resonant voice fitted his modern demeanour. He looked at Nart respectfully and amiably, addressing him eagerly.

"I've heard your name, sir. Det talks about you often."

"It's a pity we won't see each other for more than a few more days," Nart answered smiling. "You're going abroad and I'm going upcountry."

Major Plaek looked at the older man sympathetically, but simply said, "I don't expect it will be for long. You might get to come back to

Bangkok. I'm sure the political situation in our country will get better. It won't stay like this."

He knew better than to say anymore, but Nart could sense with greater clarity something unsaid that he had felt when he first met his friend. He followed Phra Ritdaeso to the wide balcony at the side of the house where two or three of their friends were waiting. A servant was arranging snacks on a low table in the middle of some deckchairs supervised by Malai, who had not joined the party. Her young friend was behind the house, realizing that it would not be appropriate for her to come out yet.

At first, they chatted idly about nothing in particular until the conversation turned towards the subject that really interested them – politics. Nart sat listening quietly, or only gave short responses. He realized he'd been away from the capital for so long that he hardly had any idea of what they were talking about. The first day when he had met his friend at the Ministry of Defence, Nart had though that what Phra Ritdaeso had been saying was a personal, albeit somewhat radical, opinion, but after listening to his other friends, he realized that those weren't just his ideas. Nor were they likely to be the opinion of only one group of hot-headed officers.

There was an undercurrent of discontent in their conversation and their ideas that Nart had never heard or felt before. These days, people were complaining that the government had cut expenses and many departments had been dissolved causing job losses, even though the Ministry of Defence had hardly been affected.

Nart found such complaints puzzling. But their dissatisfaction didn't stop there. Next, they compared Siam to those more modern Western countries they had visited and discussed changes that nobody had thought of before.

"Other countries have all become republics. Look at France and now Russia. Tsar Nicholas has been overthrown. The power shouldn't be in the hands of just one person."

Nart felt something jar in his heart that made him uncomfortable, and excusing himself from the balcony on the pretext of going to the bathroom, he went to stand in the area under the house.

Although he had never been to Europe, Nart had been taught by a European who had come to provide military training, and he had learned English and French as a young boy because his father had sent him to live with the teacher in order to attend to him. For this reason, he was certain that his knowledge was not inferior to that of his friends who had had the opportunity to be educated on the other side of the world. The only thing he did not have was experience of living in a foreign country. But the word 'republic' made him feel so hot that he began to sweat without realizing. As he was pondering such thoughts, he heard someone behind him and, turning to look, saw Luang Phibun Songkhram, regarding him quizzically.

"I was stiff from sitting, so I came here to stretch my legs," Nart explained. "I'm not much of a conversationalist. I just listen."

The young major smiled and asked politely, "I noticed you were quiet. Was there something you disagreed with?"

"Not exactly. I have to confess that I've been away from Bangkok for so long that I couldn't really follow the conversation. It's only natural to have different viewpoints."

"I agree. People have different opinions. I admire my seniors because they genuinely love our country and want the best for it, and they're brave, too. They're well-educated and they know how developed Western countries are. They're our role models. It's not hard to see what will happen."

"We've known about Western progress since Rama IV's reign," Nart replied. "That's why King Mongkut opened the country to Europeans, so we wouldn't be colonized."

"The days of imperialism are over. We need to keep up with progress."

But before they could say any more, they were interrupted by a clear voice calling from the door behind them.

"Who's there? Come and help set the table! Oh, I'm sorry! I didn't know it was you!"

The speaker moved gracefully towards them with her hand on her chest and an expression of alarm mixed with embarrassment on her face.

Luang Phibun Songkhram glanced at Nart said softly, "Would you excuse me? It's almost time for dinner."

Nart gazed at the young woman coming towards him.

He observed her radiant creamy skin that contrasted with her jet-black wavy hair and her pretty red lips. Whether day or night, she was strikingly beautiful. Her yellow blouse trimmed with black and her black sarong complimented her complexion perfectly.

Before he could say anything, she looked at him reproachfully saying, "I've a bone to pick with you."

"What have I done?" he asked playfully, "to make a pretty girl like you angry? I must rectify it right away!"

She glared at him with blazing eyes.

"Don't you remember? That night I sang and you didn't listen."

"Is that all? I thought I'd done something terrible!" he teased.

Nart reflected that it was a pity that he had only a few days in Bangkok before he would have to part from her. He continued chatting attentively.

"A person would have to be crazy or drunk to not want to listen to you sing. Didn't you see that everyone in the party was listening to you?"

She looked away, pouting.

"I didn't see," she said sulkily. "I didn't see you listening at all."

"I was listening to every verse," Nart continued, "but my friend was leaving and he asked me to accompany him since we were going the same way. I couldn't stay until the end of the song because he was waiting, but I really wanted to."

Her taut expression gradually relaxed and a shy, but proud smile appeared in its place.

"In that case, I'm happy, but I know I'm not much of a singer."

"On the contrary, you're an enchanting singer."

They were interrupted by a servant bringing in a pile of plates followed by Malai.

Nuathong quickly changed her demeanour and smiled at her friend.

"I was just about to get the spoons and forks. They're in this drawer, aren't they?"

She moved away from the officer and walked over to the drawer casually as if she had just finished speaking to him. Nart quietly retreated from the room watched by Malai, and when she was sure he was out of earshot she asked, "What were you talking about?"

The young woman looked innocent, although her eyes were sparkling.

"Khun Phra Naren liked my singing."

Malai sighed as she knew her friend well and couldn't resist warning her, "Don't go getting ideas. It's just your singing he likes."

"What do you mean?" Nuathong asked.

"Khun Phra Naren has a wife and child."

Nuathong's face fell for a moment, but then she asked, "How do you know?"

Malai looked both annoyed and amused.

"Who do you think told me if it wasn't my husband? Do you have any more questions? Surely you're not going to ask who told him because Khun Phra Naren told him himself."

Nuathong pursed her lips and looked annoyed. She seemed to have forgotten all about getting the spoons and forks, leaving two servants to put the tablecloth on the table.

"Then why didn't he bring her to the party the other night?" she asked, reluctant to give up and believing there was still a ray of light at the end of the tunnel, albeit a dim one.

"His wife's just given birth in Phetchaburi, so he let her stay there for now. She's too weak to travel, so she's gone back to live with her parents."

Nuathong breathed a sigh of relief as if a window had been opened in a dark room to let the breeze in. Her short response revealed what she was thinking, even though she tried to hide it.

"His upcountry wife…"

After that, Nuathong did not say any more and busied herself preparing the table.

Malai, assuming that her friend had given up hope when she found out the young man was unavailable, didn't want to rub salt into the wound, and changed the subject.

Malai didn't realize that her words of warning had only served to fan the flames of her friend's hopes. His upcountry wife!

She had almost laughed out loud, but had restrained herself, so that Malai wouldn't think she was laughing at her. What meaning could that kind of wife have? When young noblemen went to work in the provinces, if they didn't take a wife with them from Bangkok, they would always find a local girl to accommodate them temporarily. Few ever married the girl, even though they would live together as husband and wife. Could such a woman really be considered his wife?

At dinner, Nuathong chatted cheerfully to the young officers with a bright smile, and sometimes she caught the eye of the man who was the target of her interest with a meaningful glance that only the two of them were aware of.

She was even more satisfied when it was time to go home because she got to ride in a horse-drawn carriage borrowed from Malai's father, and Lieutenant Colonel Phra Naren was riding with her to see her home. Everything proceeded so smoothly that no one could tell just how satisfied the young woman was.

The sound of the horses' hooves clip clopping mixed with the sound of wheels squeaking along the road as the carriage emerged from Phra Ritdaeso's front gate onto Phraeng Sappasat Road and then Asdang Road.

The carriage passed small rented houses and wooden terraced houses on one side of the road. In contrast to the silence and darkness of other areas, Asdang Road had electric street lamps and lanterns shining dimly at intervals. The shadows of people walking about as if there was a party going on could be seen, and the sound of singing and music wafted out. Several women dressed in bright colours and sleeveless low-cut blouses were sitting in rows outside the houses, their powdered white faces illuminated by the lights, and they laughed and called out to passers-by. All those entering and leaving the houses were men, and there were no other women around at all.

Nuathong looked away from the women, whom she knew were prostitutes, with unconcealed disdain.

"It's so horrible. I don't like coming this way," she said scornfully. "It's such a shame that there are places with green lanterns in this nice area."

She referred to brothels as 'places with green lanterns' since in those days, such places hung green lanterns in front as a sign.

"They must have just come here," Nart mused. "I didn't know about it, or I would have had the carriage go another way."

Nuathong became more cheerful as the carriage reached the main road in the silence and darkness of the night and the cool night breeze blew pleasantly. At one point, the carriage passed a group of drunks stumbling and shouting at the side of the road, and she moved closer to Nart until their knees touched.

She leaned against him and whispered shakily, "It's so scary. If you weren't with me...my heart would stop."

"They're just drunks. Don't worry."

"Horse-drawn carriages are so slow. If they see a woman, they can easily jump up. I dread to think what could happen."

Looking afraid, she continued, "I don't understand why Malai's father keeps a horse and carriage. Nobody uses them anymore. Cars are so much safer. If you weren't with me, I'd be really scared."

The fragrance of her powder and the warmth of her body as she leaned close to him, as if unintentionally, caught him unawares and the feelings that the presence of such a beautiful and enticing young woman aroused in him began to engulf him, even though he tried to suppress them.

Nuathong's home was in a narrow, flattened dirt street that ran between terraced houses, just wide enough for the horse-drawn carriage to park in front of the low hedge. The markings on the ground in front of her house showed that it had once been paved, but the paving stones had been broken until mostly dirt overgrown with weeds remained. Behind the house was Khlong Banglampu, and most of her neighbours lived in small cramped houses.

Nart stepped down first before helping the young woman and he felt her warm hand hold onto his for a moment before letting go.

She looked up at him and the moonlight illuminated her face as she said sadly, "This is where I live alone with an old servant. Since my parents passed away, I've had no one to turn to."

A few moments earlier, in the carriage, she had told him the sad story of how she had no one to depend on, and Nart's heart ached for her.

"If I come and visit you sometimes, would it bother you?"

She smiled sadly again, and replied simply, "Why would it bother me? I'd be very grateful, but I'm sure it would be hard for someone as important as you to find the time."

"I'm not busy at the moment. I'm just getting ready and waiting for my orders to leave."

Her face fell and her pretty black eyes became moist when she heard the word 'leave'.

"When are you leaving?"

"The beginning of next month."

"There isn't much time left...Just two weeks," she mused.

When Nart looked at her quizzically, she smiled.

"Oh, nothing. I was just thinking that you've been so kind to me. If you have any free time, I'd like to invite you for dinner."

Nart replied without hesitation, "Of course, I can find time to come."

Nuathong smiled again and put her palms together gracefully in farewell without saying anything more.

She pushed the gate open and stepped inside where her servant was holding a lamp for her.

Nart got back in the carriage and didn't see her turn and look at him again, the sad expression replaced with a satisfied smile, the smile of someone for whom victory was within reach.

❋❋❋❋❋

Nart stepped through the gate that the servant, a solemn woman in her fifties, opened for him. In a few strides he reached the three or four low steps that led onto the narrow veranda in front of the house before stepping inside.

Nuathong was waiting for him, naturally, and her face lit up with a radiant smile. She took his hat and hung it on a hook next to the door.

"Please come inside. I'm afraid my house is only small," she said modestly.

Inside was a large room with doors leading to one or two smaller rooms and all the windows were wide open with clean white net curtains shielding them from the neighbours' eyes.

The first thing Nart noticed was that the small house had hardly any furniture, and was clean and tidy unlike the houses of most ordinary Thais, which were usually messy and full of dust and cobwebs because they didn't want to throw anything away.

"Please have a seat," she offered, indicating the only furniture in the room.

It consisted of an attractive heart-shaped rattan suite, which had clearly been imported and, although not new, was in good condition. It looked fancy, unlike the house, and the young man mused that, in many of the noblemen's homes that he had been to, unless they were very wealthy or very modern, they did not have such fancy furniture but usually just a mat on the floor.

She smiled as if she divining his thoughts.

"People are always surprised that I have a suite. My father was given it by his foreign boss, the owner of S.A.B. department store, as a housewarming gift."

"Your father worked in that department store then, did he?"

"Yes, he worked there for many years," she answered proudly and glanced at the ebony glass cabinet with attractive spiral legs that stood against the wall, another piece of furniture that looked incongruously elegant in the small house. Nart noticed two or three crystal ornaments, which were clearly from Europe, arranged neatly in the cabinet.

"My father was close to his foreign boss, so he got a taste for Western ways. Take that crystal jug and bowl. It's from Belgium. Usually only wealthy people would buy something like that, but my father bought it for us to use. My mother and I always had nice things, better than our neighbours, when my father was still alive..."

Her face fell as she spoke the last sentence and her voice became shaky. She sighed and dabbed her eyes with a white handkerchief that she had sprayed with perfume.

"My father passed away too young...and my mother died just a year after. I was left alone with no one to protect me."

Nart found her vulnerability endearing and his heart was moved with compassion.

"Don't be upset. It was your parents' karma," he consoled her.

He took her arm and led her to the seat; she did not refuse. Now that she was certain that he felt the right degree of pity for her, she was careful not to allow the atmosphere to become clouded with sadness, and changed to a brighter tone.

"I'm ashamed for inviting you and making you listen to my sad story. We should talk about something more fun."

She smiled at Nart and added, "Please forgive me. I won't talk about it again."

She did mention her father again, however, when she helped her old servant to bring dinner to the table that was in the centre of the suite.

She told him with embarrassment mixed with pride, "I've prepared European food for you. Malai said you liked plain food, so I hope you'll find it palatable."

In fact, she had probed and pried until she found out that Phra Narentharaksa was partial to Western food, but why would she tell him that? The first dish was beef consommé, which she had ordered her old servant, who had been with her since she was a child, to simmer over the stove for several hours until it was tender, while she got dressed, before seasoning it herself later.

When Nart took a spoonful, he praised her with sincerity.

"This soup is delicious. Where did you learn to cook European food?"

"Because my father's boss was so keen on him, whenever he had a party, he would invite my father to help attend to his guests, so he learned to cook European food from his chef, and he passed it on to me."

She passed him a plate of freshly toasted bread, which her servant, Tieng, had just made.

"I used to make it for my father almost every week, but since he passed away...this is the first time I've made it."

After the soup, the main course was sautéed veal liver wrapped in bacon and fried until it was crispy, cut into bite sized pieces and served with steaming hot rice.

"Usually it's eaten by itself," she explained. "But we Thais would find it too greasy, so I'm serving it with rice. Europeans drink red wine with beef. Would you like a glass?"

She went to the cabinet and took out the bottle before picking up two glasses, which she had had her servant polish, and brought them to the table. Nuathong had prepared a vast amount of European food with no concern for the cost, and she opened the bottle of wine with equal nonchalance. She filled the young man's glass while she sat and watched him as if she had no idea that it would make him drunk. Her face was bright and her red lips smiled seductively like the sparkle in her eyes. The wine began to take effect and Nart refilled his glass and hers.

She took another sip and put down the glass, shaking her head.

"Oh, that's enough! I'm already starting to feel tipsy!" she exclaimed, even though she was still perfectly sober. Only her cheeks were a little flushed.

She kept refilling Nart's glass until he put his hand over the top.

"Don't!" he said laughing. "Are you trying to get me drunk?"

He asked in jest, but the question alarmed her, and she replied coldly, "I don't know what you're suggesting."

As the alcohol coursed through their veins, the night drew on and the sounds from the neighbouring houses got gradually quieter until all was silent except for the sound of banana leaves rustling in the breeze. The two of them began to get carried away by the silence and their proximity to each other. Dinner was long over, but Nart made no move to leave, until he finally said, "It's late. I'd better be getting back. Tomorrow, I have to go to the ministry."

Nuathong's heart sank and her face paled. She couldn't think how to delay him.

In a few days, he was going far away. What could she do in the few days left?

Nart had similar feelings. What if they went their separate ways and they never met again?

He only a few days left in the capital. After that, he would have to go almost to the farthest ends of the kingdom, and did not know when he would return. If he were to become entangled with this lovely woman, it would be impossible to find an outcome that would be satisfactory to both of them. Surely it was best to nip it in the bud, even though he regretted turning down her youth, beauty and eagerness. As he stood up, he noticed tears welling in her luminous eyes. His heart, that was already softening, melted like molten wax.

He opened his arms and enfolded her, caressing the soft warm body that leaned against him. She pretended to resist at first, and then yielded gladly. The wine in his veins, and the novelty of a beautiful young woman in his arms made him forget everything else.

Outside the window, the dew clung to the large leaves of the trees in the cool air.

Nart got up, pulled back the mosquito net, and walked to the window to open the curtains. He looked out into the darkness and was still for a moment. Drops of dew sparkled on the leaves outside the window in the moonlight, and a picture flashed into his mind of teardrops on the pale face of a young woman tightly clutching a small child in her fragile arms. She had not said anything as he had stepped onto the train, but when he turned to look at her for the last time, her face and tears had expressed her pain more clearly than any words.

He sighed without knowing and told himself that Gade and the child would be asleep in Ban Tha Hin. Gade would be cradling the child in her arms to protect him from the cold.

At least they were not alone and had Gade's parents and relatives around. Things were not too hard for them.

But what about this woman here? He turned to look at the body he could see dimly through the mosquito net. She was sleeping like a child, and didn't seem worried that when she awoke, the officer beside her might have run away. But had he the heart to do it? As he was thinking, and hesitating, she turned over and felt the emptiness beside her.

She sat up suddenly as if she'd been woken up by a bad dream. In a moment, she pulled back the mosquito net and tiptoed over to the young man who had his back to her. She wrapped her arms around him from behind and whispered, "I was startled...when I woke and didn't see you."

His hesitation left him and he turned around and held her in his arms, teasing, "Did you think I'd run away?"

Nuathong rested her head on his chest and held him tightly.

"You wouldn't have the heart to be so cruel to me."

Nart held her still for a moment until he heard her sobbing, so he lifted her chin and saw that her black eyes were filled with tears.

"Why are you crying?" he asked gently.

"I was thinking…" she sobbed. "If you don't really love me, I can't live any more. I'd rather die!"

Even though he knew she was just being emotional, he couldn't help feeling nervous.

"You think too much."

He held her close and feeling the fullness of her body was aroused once again.

"You're my wife now. If I leave you, I'm not a man."

Smiling through her tears, Nuathong closed the curtains before putting her arms around him and leading him back to the bed.

4
Feminine Wiles

Tieng, the old servant who had lived in the small house for many years, was so quiet and solemn that it was hard to know what she was thinking. She didn't utter a word or even look puzzled when she saw a man in the house because it wasn't the first time that it had happened.

When Nuathong came into the kitchen early that morning and ordered her to prepare breakfast for one more person, she reacted as if it were nothing out of the ordinary.

"Toast some bread. I'll boil the eggs myself," Nuathong ordered without offering any explanation. Breakfast was ready on the rattan table along with a steaming mug of coffee when Nart came out of the bedroom fully dressed.

Nuathong walked towards him, saying, "I didn't want to wake you, but you said you had to go to the ministry this morning. Breakfast is ready."

By the time he left the house, the sun was already overhead and orange rays were beating down on the courtyard in front of the house. Nuathong followed him to the door to see him off, pulling his arms tightly around her as she whispered, "Come and see me again tonight. I'll be waiting."

He went to the ministry and, after he had finished his business there, he went back to his relative's house, where he was staying, but he did not mention where he had been the previous night. Klai, who was also staying there, smiled and greeted him innocently, "Last night, I waited up until late, sir, but when you didn't return, I went to bed. Please accept my apologies."

Nart felt ashamed to look the young soldier in the face, even though he was of a lower rank, since Klai was his wife's cousin. "I stayed with a friend."

Klai did not suspect a thing because he knew that Nart had many friends, and they took turns to take him out almost every day. "Will you be having dinner here this evening, sir?"

"No," he replied and paused for a moment before finishing his sentence, "I'll be eating out. Please prepare a change of clothes or two for me."

Klai obeyed the order unquestioningly.

When evening came, Nart went to see his friends as usual, but kept what had happened to himself, without telling even his closest friend. That night, when he left Phra Ritdaeso's house, Nart hailed a carriage to take him to Banglamphu without any of his friends knowing.

❋❋❋❋❋

Lieutenant Colonel Phra Ritdaeso was speechless for a moment when his friend had finished telling him the story.

"I'll be leaving for Udon on the first Monday of this month. I'll tell all our friends. They'll find out sooner or later. I'm taking Nuathong."

When Phra Ritdaeso found his voice, he laughed rather nervously, not knowing what else to say, "You're a dark horse. You won Nueang's heart in just a few days. Are you seriously taking her to Udon?"

Nart nodded and answered confidently, "She's my wife now. I'll have to take her. It wouldn't be right to abandon her."

"And what about your wife in Phetchaburi? You said you'd have her join you in Udon later."

Nart was silent for a moment before replying hesitantly, "As for Gade...I'm not worried about her. She's got her family around, but if she comes to Udon, that's fine. Nuathong knows I already have a wife. I didn't hide it."

Phra Ritdaeso could tell from his friend's voice which woman he prioritized, and it didn't puzzle him at all when he pictured that seductive and beautiful young woman. Nor was he surprised as to why she had used her feminine wiles to ensnare his friend so tightly and so quickly.

Sergeant Klai felt as if a lightning bolt had struck him out of the clear blue sky, and he almost fell over in shock when, arriving at Hua Lamphong station, a young woman suddenly appeared. She was dressed in the style of a modern women from the capital, with a dark sarong and a blouse in a matching lighter shade. She was also wearing white stockings and elegant black shoes. She had a large number of belongings with her as if she was moving to live in a new place, and a strong looking old servant was walking closely behind her carrying large and small cases as well as laden baskets.

Phra Narentharaksa introduced the strange young woman to his cousin, whose house he had been staying in and who had taken him to the station.

"This is my other wife. Her name's Nuathong."

The man, Phra Prabribupai, was a police officer and he, along with the other officers who had come to see him off, stared at the young woman in shock. Those who already knew the whole story, looked indifferent and hid their smiles.

It was not until he heard the bell, signalling it was time for the train to leave the station, that Sergeant Klai hastened to carry the rest of the bags onto the train and check to make sure that nothing had been left on the platform. As he did so, he noticed that his boss helped the young woman onto the train attentively, revealing his infatuation. All Klai could do was to sigh quietly to himself.

❋❋❋❋❋

The pale blue sky was clear without any rain clouds unlike several days earlier, and the leaves on the trees that surrounded the house shook in the breeze, a sign that the cool season was approaching earlier than usual.

Gade finished feeding Ned, and put the soft little body down on the cloth hammock. Rocking it gently she sang a lullaby and watched his eyelids grow heavier until he fell sound asleep. Gade covered him with a blanket, and placed another above his small head that was covered in soft hair, to keep out the cold, before getting up from the room under the house and walking into the kitchen. Eeam was busy washing rice in a bowl, and Gade hurried in to help.

"Don't do that, Mother. You go and rest. I'll do it. You've only just recovered from a fever."

"I'm just cooking the rice. If I stay still, I'll feel even wearier," her mother replied weakly. Her eyes were still yellow from the fever, and she looked at her daughter gratefully.

"I must have caught a chill. This year will be colder than most."

Suddenly they heard footsteps running up the steps that led from the veranda to the kitchen and Rern came in, panting.

"Mother, Uncle Muen and Aunt Chan are here. They've brought a letter from Klai for Gade."

Gade almost dropped the rice pot when she heard the name, 'Klai', and her heart began to pound so hard that it almost came out of her chest. If there was news from Klai, there must be news from Nart. This gave her weakened spirit renewed vigour.

She had received one letter from her husband several months ago, telling her that he had arrived in Bangkok safely. After that, she had heard nothing. She could only guess that, about a month after that, her husband had travelled to Mark Keng, and that when he had got settled, he would send news. Gade ran from the kitchen to the room outside. Her father had not yet returned from the orchard. Since Muen was a close relative, he and his wife had already come in and sat down to wait, and he put his hand up to signal to Gade that she need not put down a mat for them.

"Don't go to any trouble, Gade. I've come to see Eeam. I heard she had a fever. And I've got a letter from Klai."

Gade pressed her palms together before taking the thick brown envelope from him with shaking hands, while Muen's wife, Chan, got up to look at her young nephew who was fast asleep in the hammock and exclaimed, "Aw! He's getting chubbier every day. He was like a tadpole at first! You've done a good job with him!"

Gade was too excited with the letter to answer her aunt, and with shaking hands she opened the envelope and pulled out the official looking white paper to read. At that moment she was able to put to use what Nart had taught her. Gade gradually put the vowels and consonants together and sounded out the words, her eyes blurred by tears.

Gade,

I've had Klai send you some money for your keep. I've arrived in Udon Thani, but I've been so busy with my work and my lodgings that I haven't had time to write. It's very hot during the day here, but it's really cold at night, so it's quite uncomfortable.

How's Ned? I expect he's getting stronger by now. I hope both you and he are well. I'm fine. I'll write again.

Nart

Gade hugged the letter to her chest and the tears she had held back for so long began to flow until her face was soaked. She tried to choke back her sobs as she looked past the curtain of tears at her aunt who was rocking her child gently and looking at her sympathetically. Her younger sister, who had joined the group and was sitting next to her mother, looked as if she was about to cry as well as she consoled her elder sister, "Don't cry, Gade. Nart isn't sick, is he?"

Gade wiped away the tears from her face and tried to calm herself as she turned to her uncle, "Nart said it's very hot there…" she began, trying to keep her voice as steady as she could, "but he's not sick. He's fine."

Muen nodded slowly.

"Klai told us the same thing in his letter. I've brought it with me. Do you want to read it?"

Gade took the other sheet of white paper and looked down to read the short message out loud for her mother and sister.

Dear Father and Mother,

I'm fine, so you don't need to worry about me. This place is much hotter than Phetchaburi, and much drier, but it's peaceful and there are no robbers. There is enough food to eat, so I'm not suffering from hunger. Now that the cool season is here, it's very cold at night.

My boss is fine. He gave me a letter for Gade and some money for her. When I have time, I'll write again.

From your son,
Klai

They were all quiet for a moment before Rern, being both talkative and observant, said, "Both Nart and Klai wrote very short messages as if they're holding something back."

Eeam reprimanded her at once, "Do you expect them to write a sermon?"

"It's good that they're both fine. We don't need to worry," her aunt added.

Muen excused both his former boss and his son, nodding to his niece and saying, "He means you can't take Ned there, just yet. I expect he wants to wait until he's a bit bigger."

"I expect so, Uncle."

Gade looked down to fold the letter and put it back in the envelope. Her heart, which had swelled to fill her chest just a moment ago, sank in disappointment.

Muen asked about his older sister's health, and she answered weakly, "It was just a chill. It happens when the cool season comes. Some sour curry made from katuri flowers will cure it."

Concern for her mother's health took Gade's mind off worrying about why she still had to remain at home. If her love for her husband was a stream, it was bursting its banks even more than the water that flowed during the rainy season, but she kept quiet as complaining would only have worried her parents and sister.

"Are you going to send news to Nart?" Muen offered, because he could read and write better than anyone else in Ban Tha Hin, since he had studied hard during his time in the monkhood.

"I'll write to Klai for you."

Gade's face lit up and she pressed her palms together.

"Thank you, Uncle. Please write that me and Ned are fine, and that he's growing strong. He should be able to go to Udon in a few months."

Muen looked at his niece sympathetically before nodding, "Good.

Tell him in advance. If there's a way, I expect he'll send someone to fetch you. I tell you what. I'll tell Klai to see if he can come home for a visit, and he can take you back with him on his return."

❋❋❋❋❋

The young sergeant stared at the big black letters that were as clear as the message they conveyed.

Dear Klai,

I got your letter. I'm glad to know you're well. If there's anything you need, write and let me know, so I can send it to you.

Your mother and I miss you. It would be good if you could take some time off to visit us, so you can take Gade and her child back with you to Lieutenant Colonel Nart, provided that he thinks it's suitable. Please give him my good wishes, and tell him Gade and the child are fine.

Father

Klai read and reread the letter two or three times, especially the second paragraph, and sighed. He put it back in the envelope. The low bamboo table he was sitting on to read the letter was under the neem tree between his lodgings and those of his boss. When he looked up, he could see the balcony on the side clearly, and through the bars of the balcony he could see someone dressed in a bright sarong and a matching blouse moving and shouting orders at Tieng incessantly.

There was the sound of a horse and carriage stopping in front of the house, so Klai stood up and went out to meet his boss as he usually did, but he was not as quick as 'madam' who ran down the steps smiling from afar. Klai tiptoed up the steps and saw Nuathong helping her husband out of his jacket and going to get him a flannel and a bowl of water, which she placed in front of him before kneeling down to wipe his arms attentively.

When Klai poked his head inside, she turned to look at him and snapped, "What are you doing here? Nobody called you."

Klai hesitated, but continued, "I've something to ask you, sir."

Nart sat up straight and put the flannel back in the silver bowl before asking kindly, "What is it, Klai? Come on up."

Nuathong sat down on another chair and glared at the young sergeant, grumbling, "I don't know what you want. Nart's just got home from work and you come to disturb him."

Klai ignored her and stepped forward to salute him before giving him the letter and sitting down on the floor.

"What is it?"

Nart scanned the letter quickly. When he read the second paragraph, he frowned a little and reread it without saying anything. Klai held his breath as he waited to see what his boss would say, and he noticed that Nart was silent as if he didn't know what to say.

Nuathong couldn't stand it, and asked, "Who's the letter from?"

Nart came back to his senses, folded the letter and put it back in the envelope, saying only, "It's nothing. Klai's father wrote me a letter."

The answer didn't satisfy her and she demanded, "Klai's father? Why? What does he need to write to you for? Can people upcountry write?"

She glared at Klai in derision until his cheeks burned.

"It's nothing," Nart repeated, and explained, "He wrote that he misses Klai, and wants him to go home and visit if he can get some time off. What do you say, Klai...?" He turned to Klai. "Do you want to go home? Is it necessary? Muen didn't say it was urgent."

The question was an answer in itself, showing that he didn't want Klai to take time off. Klai swallowed. "No, sir."

Clearly, Klai wasn't going home. Nart smiled faintly and said, "Write to your father that I still need you."

"Yes, sir."

"Is there anything else?"

Klai should have answered, 'No, sir,' and left, because Nuathong had let out several irritated sighs and was standing on the balcony with her arms on the rail, but instead he asked, "What shall I tell my father about Gade, sir?"

Nart was silent. He glanced at his wife, and she must have heard the name because she stood up straight and turned around, "Who's Gade?"

Neither of them answered. Nuathong marched over and pulled up a chair next to her husband. She craned her neck to look at the letter in his hand and, when she didn't see it because he had put it back in the envelope, asked again, "Who's Gade?"

Nart answered the young sergeant as if to end the conversation, "Just tell your father that you can't take any time off yet. As for the other matter...they don't need to come yet. When I'm ready, I'll write myself."

Klai felt his throat go dry and forced himself to answer, "Yes, sir."

So Nart's first wife and son had become 'the other matter.' Klai glanced at his boss and his eyes must have betrayed his disappointment because Nart added, "It's still difficult here and Ned's still small. If he got sick, it would be difficult."

His young wife put two and two together at once and muttered sarcastically, "Oh, is that all?" before turning to the young man and glaring at him accusingly. "What does Klai have to do with it? He's just your servant, isn't he?"

Klai's cheeks burned once more and the scorn in her voice was like a slap in the face.

His irritation made him forget himself, and he retorted, "I'm Gade's cousin. Gade is Lieutenant Colonel Nart's principal wife, madam"

Nart looked at Klai in shock, while Nuathong, after being dumbfounded for a moment, shrieked back, "What did you say? Who's the principal wife? Are you saying I'm the minor wife? How dare you!"

Klai was satisfied to hear her say it, but he answered politely, "No, madam, but strictly speaking, Gade and Lieutenant Colonel Nart were married two years ago in Phetchaburi..."

"You're crazy!" she interrupted. "What are you babbling about?"

Her cheeks burned crimson with anger and she looked at her husband.

"How can you let him say such things to me?" she sobbed as tears filled her eyes and rolled down her cheeks. "He thinks that because he's your relative he can be rude to me. Tell him...I won't stand for it."

Nart did what he thought was best at that moment and dismissed Klai with a wave, "Klai, go downstairs and don't come up again tonight."

Turning to his wife he said, "You quieten down, or the neighbours will hear."

The army camp was similar to the one at Phetchaburi in that there were several houses close together, and when someone in one house shouted, the people next door would hear for sure. Her husband's warning brought her to her senses because there was nothing Nuathong feared more than the other officers and their wives knowing that she was not Nart's principal wife. She stormed into the bedroom and sat down on the bed to cry, knowing that her husband would follow her inside, which indeed he did.

A moment later, Nuathong heard the door opening, so she threw herself face down on the bed and sobbed into the pillow as if her heart would break. His footsteps came closer and she felt his weight press down on the bed as he sat down beside her. He squeezed her shoulders gently, and she sobbed even louder.

"Don't…" he comforted as if he didn't know what to do. "Why are you making such a fuss about nothing?"

Nuathong lifted her head up from the pillow and turned to look at her husband, her eyes wet with tears.

"Of course I'll make a fuss when everyone is rude to me, even your servant."

Tears rolled down her cheeks, and her husband didn't know what to do, except console her, "It wasn't like that. Klai wasn't being rude to you. He's just a straight talker."

She sat up.

"A straight talker? How can you say that? He said his cousin was your principal wife. What does that make me? Everyone in this camp knows I'm your wife, and all of a sudden, another woman says she's your principal wife. Why wouldn't I be upset?"

The tears rolled down her cheeks again, but not enough to spoil her makeup, since she was always careful that her tears didn't make her unattractive.

"Now you're making a fuss!" her husband exclaimed in dismay. "Nobody said anything of the sort. You're still my wife. Gade didn't say she was coming. She's staying in Phetchaburi with her son."

Hearing the last sentence, she realized that her husband had not yet agreed for his other wife to come, and she was relieved. But there was no avoiding the fact that that woman was a danger to her. The young sergeant had said that his cousin was the principal wife because that upcountry woman had 'married' Nart. That meant he had asked her elders for her hand and had a wedding ceremony in the presence of others. He would not have made it up. In that case, Gade was the real Madam Narentharaksa and, even worse, she had a son as a golden chain to hook his heart.

When she came to Udon, Gade would certainly have an advantage over Nuathong. Even if her husband loved her more, a man like him would have to give some honour to Gade. The best way was to prevent that woman from coming anywhere near him.

Like a flash of lightning, an idea came into her mind. Nuathong became all smiles once again. Her tears had dried completely, leaving no sign that she had been crying her heart out just a few moments ago. She pulled his body on top of hers and hugged him tightly, knowing that there was nothing more to worry about.

Man, Nart's longtime servant, was sweeping the dust and leaves that were scattered on the dirt courtyard not far from the neem tree. When he noticed Klai dejectedly coming down from the house, Man, who knew everything that went on better than anyone, quickly swept the leaves into a pile before approaching him.

"What's up, Klai?" he asked sympathetically. "You look upset."

Klai sat down weakly on the bamboo table and nodded.

"Did you hear?"

"They could probably hear her up the river." Man threw the sweeping brush down and came closer to whisper, "You took that letter from Muen to the boss, didn't you?"

Klai nodded and felt a lump in his throat.

"When will he let Madam Gade and Ned come?"

This time, Klai shook his head and looked up at the house. Nuathong had stopped shouting. Just a moment ago she had run into the bedroom followed by Nart. Nobody knew what they had said. All they knew was that both of them were quiet now. The young sergeant could only sigh. Now they had made up, Gade wasn't likely to be coming to Udon Thani.

"He won't let her come," he replied and continued with a lump in his throat. "He won't let me take any time off. He said it isn't urgent."

"Listen, Klai," Man whispered gravely, moving closer to him. "I heard how she reacted. Klai, I'm worried. Now she knows you're Madam Gade's cousin."

"So what?"

Man looked serious. "You need to be careful."

"Why?"

"I don't know what she'll do," he said looking as grave as before, "but I'm old, and I've seen a lot. She's deceitful. She's afraid you'll bring Madam Gade to live with Khun Phra like before. Just be careful. She's marked you as her enemy."

*****

A thumping sound came from the bedroom, causing Nart to look up from the book he was reading with a quizzical expression.

He heard his wife cry out from inside the bedroom.

"Don't! Don't! The dust is blowing everywhere! Tieng! Enough!"

Nuathong emerged, choking from the dust and sneezing several times in succession, causing her husband to ask, "What is it?"

"I was lifting up the mattress to sweep all the dust from under it," she replied coughing. "There's so much dust...and the mattress is so heavy. Tieng and I can't lift it by ourselves. Go and get a man to help us, Tieng."

Tieng came out of the room and was about to go downstairs when Nuathong shouted after her, "Get Klai. Don't get Man. He works outside and his hands are dirty. He'll soil the mattress." She turned to her husband and explained, "At first, I was just going to sweep, but there's so much dust I need to turn up the mattress and take out the wooden planks on the bed frame to clean. Then I'll put it back, but it's so heavy we can't lift it by ourselves."

Her husband nodded and went back to his book.

Klai followed Tieng upstairs and stood in front of his boss politely. He appeared to be in a good mood because he greeted Klai cheerfully, "Klai, give us a hand, would you? Help Tieng lift the mattress onto the balcony to air, and take the wooden boards on the bed frame out. Lean them against the wall, and when they're finished, put them back."

Klai followed Tieng into the bedroom to help her lift the mattress onto the balcony. Then he took the wooden boards out and leaned them against the wall as instructed.

When he had finished, he left Tieng to sweep the room and was walking out of the room to go back down the steps in front of the house when he heard Nuathong ask her husband, "What time are you going to see the governor?"

"I need to go before the monks eat. They've invited monks to a merit-making ceremony. Have you made anything for me to take?"

"I made stir fried chilli and ginger with fried catfish this morning."

She called Klai and then called Tieng, who had finished sweeping and was dusting the wooden planks. "Klai, this is what I want you to do. By the time I come home, it will be evening. Make sure you put the mattress back on the bed before evening, but leave it out in the sun all day to air. And you, Tieng! I'm going to bathe now. You hurry up and finish your work and get ready."

"Yes, madam," Klai replied, relieved that Nuathong was not making snide remarks to him like she usually did.

Soon after, Nuathong and her servant servant left the army camp in a horse-drawn carriage.

*****

Late in the afternoon, the young man remembered the mattress that was airing on the balcony behind the house, so he hurried to lift it back onto the bed. He saw the wooden boards were still leaning against the wall, so he put them back on the bed frame and lifted the mattress on top. His task was completed. When he came down from the house, he felt hot from exerting himself, so he went to the well behind the house and scooped water into a container to wash himself and cool down.

After that, he was walking towards the bamboo table when he was startled by the sound of Nuathong screeching.

"It's really not here! It's really disappeared!"

Klai couldn't imagine what she was making such a fuss about. He looked out and saw the horse-drawn carriage going towards the stables on the other side of the road in front of the house, indicating that the boss had returned. Something must have happened. A moment later, he heard the boss calling his name.

"Klai! Klai! Where are you? Come up here!"

Without knowing the reason, Klai quickly belted up his black trousers more tightly and with only a cloth over his shoulder, panted up the stairs. His boss came out of the bedroom with an uncomfortable expression on his face. Klai did not see Nuathong, but he heard her shouting at Tieng inside the bedroom.

"Oh, you make me so angry! Find it! You're just as useless as ever! Why are you looking for it over there? Look for it over here!"

Phra Narentharaksa looked at the young sergeant with a grave expression that made him nervous.

"Klai, Nuathong left a diamond necklace on the dressing table stool. Have you seen it?"

Klai was shocked, even though he couldn't understand what was happening, and replied immediately, "No, I haven't, sir."

Nuathong shot out from the doorway at once, her face full of anger, and spluttered, "Klai, you went in my bedroom this afternoon, didn't you? It had to be you! Don't deny it! The mattress is back on the bed. You had to have lifted it."

Klai was confused because she had ordered him to do it. Why did she think he'd deny it? He replied truthfully. "Yes, madam. You told me to put the mattress back on the bed, so I did."

"Just as I thought," she retorted in triumph and asked him, "And you didn't see the diamond necklace that I left on the dressing table stool in front of the mirror?"

"No, I didn't, madam."

"How could you not have seen it?" she shouted at him. "Anyone that walked past would have seen it. If you went inside the bedroom, you must have seen it."

Nuathong's anger made the young sergeant's heart sink, but he insisted, "I didn't see it, madam. After I put the wooden boards back, I lifted the mattress on top and came out of the room. I didn't look at anything else."

Nart interrupted, "Are you sure you left it on the dressing table stool?"

Nuathong wrung her hands in irritation. "Of course, I'm sure. I put it there because I planned to wear it, and then I went to bathe, but I was in such a hurry I forgot all about it, and I didn't remember it until I was in the city. If nobody had taken it, it would still be there in front of the mirror…"

She sounded as if she was going to cry and slumped down on a chair. "I am really upset. I was afraid of losing it. You gave it to me before we left Bangkok. Where can I find another one? It was twenty-five carats."

Nart stood up and put his arm around her shoulder comfortingly, in contrast to her agitation. "Don't worry. I guarantee it hasn't been stolen. It's probably around here somewhere. Keep looking for a while. It'll turn up."

Nuathong turned on the young sergeant again, "When we were out, how many times did you go inside my bedroom?"

"Just once, madam."

"And were you alone, or did you bring someone with you? Was Man with you?" she persisted.

Klai was growing more uncomfortable. "I was alone, madam. Man didn't come inside the house."

"And did you see anyone come inside the house?"

"No, madam."

"In that case. You were the only one that went inside my bedroom... Do you admit it?" she accused pointing at him.

Nart looked from one to the other and interrupted, "Why are you shouting at Klai? He's telling the truth. He brought the mattress inside like you told him to. Of course, he didn't see the necklace. He wasn't looking, or maybe the necklace wasn't there."

Nuathong bit her lip and turned her face away, her eyes flashing. "And where else would it be? Tieng left the house at the same time as I did, and came back at the same time. You can ask her. Tieng! You saw where I left the diamond necklace, didn't you?"

Tieng was sitting politely on the floor. She bowed her head and answered, almost in a whisper, "Yes, madam."

"Did you steal my diamond necklace?" she demanded. "If you stole it, return it right now. or I'll whip you."

Tieng bowed her head even lower. "I didn't steal it, madam. I wouldn't dare."

Nart interceded, "Tieng's been with you for over ten years. She's not a thief, and Klai's trustworthy. As for Man, he's never been inside the house. He would never come inside without permission."

Nuathong covered her face with her hands and sobbed. "Then where can it be? I'm so upset!"

"Let's have another look for it."

Nart led her back inside the bedroom followed by Tieng while Klai crept back down the steps in trepidation.

Klai walked down the steps of the house in confusion, not knowing what to do.

Nuathong's questions showed that she suspected him more than Tieng. That was no surprise, since Tieng was her servant and she had it in for him anyway. It was only natural that she would blame him for any little thing that happened. Man was clumsily carrying a hoe in one hand and a bunch of bananas in the other, presumably bringing them to Tieng to make a dessert for the boss. When he saw Klai, the older man came over to him.

"What's going on? I could hear her shouting from the hut."

Klai told him the story with an anxious expression while Man listened, open mouthed and almost dropped his hoe. "Oh, heaven help us!" He exclaimed. "This is serious!"

"I don't think anybody took it," Klai declared, trying to calm himself. "She must have left it somewhere. It's bound to turn up."

Before Man could answer, he heard his boss calling him.

"Man! Come upstairs!"

"Coming, sir," Man replied before running up the steps.

Klai looked up anxiously and heard the same questions that he had been asked followed by Man's adamant reply, "I didn't come in here at all, sir."

After a while, Man came down the steps dripping with sweat and grumbling to himself before walking under the house and back to his hut without even turning round to look at Klai.

Soon after, it was rumoured that Nart would either be promoted or transferred to Bangkok.

5
Apart

Word spread throughout the town that Lieutenant Colonel Phra Narentharaksa had been promoted in rank and position. No one was more excited than Nuathong. At the same time, the shadow of a major obstacle towered over her. Now his attention would probably turn to his wife and child in Phetchaburi. It wouldn't be out of place if he sent Klai to fetch Gade and bring her to live with them. They might live together in the same house, just as countless noblemen in both Bangkok and the provinces lived with more than one wife.

When that woman arrived, who would be the principal wife then? Of course, it would have to be her because she was the mother of his son. That child would give his mother status. And where would that leave Nuathong?

"Nart, I still haven't found my diamond necklace."

The young woman changed tactics from being angry and upset to looking depressed.

"Haven't you found it yet?" he asked, puzzled, since he had forgotten all about it.

"No, I've looked everywhere," she sighed. "I'm afraid it's been stolen."

"Who could have stolen it? No outsiders have been in the house."

She looked at him askance and muttered casually, "It must have been someone in the house. Someone with claws under white gloves."

"You mean Klai?" he replied in irritation. "Why would you think it was him?"

It was because Nuathong was well aware of his position as Gade's cousin that she was impatient to get rid of him.

"Like I said, he has claws under white gloves. If you don't believe me, let me have someone search his room. Will you let me?"

Nart was silent for a moment before answering, "It wouldn't be fair to him."

She lifted her chin and declared resolutely, "If we don't find anything, I won't mention it again and I'll let it go, but if I'm willing to let it go, you should be willing to let his room be searched, okay?"

Klai's room was in a small shack behind the house that was simply built. The walls were bamboo, there was a flattened dirt floor and a thatched roof. The kitchen was open at the front and the sides to let the smoke out. Klai's room was small and contained a bamboo table and a chest on a bamboo shelf above the ground, which Klai had made himself.

On hot nights, he would sleep on the bamboo table under the neem tree outside.

Today, Klai had just returned from visiting his friend at the army base and they had talked and laughed about the opportunity to accompany the boss to Bangkok in a few days' time. He was walking back cheerily along the grass path behind the house when, as he approached, he noticed Nuathong standing in front of his hut with her hands on her hips. Man was standing behind her looking pale.

Her face was taut and as soon as she saw Klai she blurted out, "I've turned the house upside down searching for my diamond necklace and I still haven't found it, so Tieng's come to search your room. You come and look."

Klai could hardly believe his ears and his face felt hot, but the discipline of his training enabled him to maintain his composure. A loud rustling came from the room when she stepped inside, followed by Klai, and he saw Tieng bending down in front of the bed. She shook the pillow and then stretched up to pull down the calico mosquito net that was hung above the table in order to shake it.

"Have you found it?" Nuathong screeched.

Tieng turned around and the ray of light that came in through the window shone on her pale face that was dripping with beads of sweat as if she was about to faint.

"No, madam," she answered, her voice trembling.

Nuathong glared at her and shouted, "What have you been doing, you, blundering old fool?"

The old woman darted over to the chest as Klai stood watching calmly. He wasn't afraid because he knew that the diamond necklace couldn't possibly be in his room. Instead, it was Man whose face belied his obvious anxiety.

Tieng knelt down to open the bamboo chest. Inside were two or three of Klai's shirts, washed and folded, along with a small number of necessary items, such as traditional medicine and small tools. In a corner of the chest was a small drawstring purse that he kept his money in.

With shaking hands, Tieng picked up the purse and put her hand inside to pick up a few silver coins. She let them fall from her hands and all that was left was something that sparkled as the light hit it in the palm of her hand.

Man groaned as if he was about to faint, "The diamond necklace!"

Klai felt as if the ground beneath him had given way and he was spinning like a top. He had never fainted before, but now he blacked out for a second and a moment later he was soaked in sweat. How it could have miraculously appeared in his purse he did not know, but he was certain that, two days earlier, when he had put his pay inside, it definitely wasn't there. Nuathong snatched the piece of jewellery from her servant's hand and turned to Klai with a triumphant expression.

"See! It's here. Man's a witness. I caught you red-handed. You stole my necklace and hid it."

What she said after that Klai did not hear. His ears were ringing and his vision of the room was blurry like he was underwater. All that he saw clearly was the diamond necklace in her white hand. The hand that held his fate!

There was no point in denying it or making excuses when there was both evidence and witnesses, but, even so, Klai would not admit his guilt when he knew full well that he was innocent. He decided that he would accept the punishment, no matter how harsh, but the one thing he refused to do was confess.

To his boss, whom he still respected, all he said in a trembling voice was, "I don't know who put it there."

"You're a liar!"

It wasn't Nart that blurted out this accusation, but Nuathong who was seething with fury. Nart did not say a word, but he sighed. The evidence was a chain around the young sergeant's neck, despite many things that made Nart reluctant to believe that Klai could have done such a terrible thing. It was unlikely that Klai had given in to sudden temptation because his family were not poor, and if he'd needed money, he could have asked them and they would have sent him some.

The situation indicated that there must have been another reason behind his actions.

As his commander, Nart considered the matter carefully because he didn't want to punish Klai in accordance with army regulations and ruin Klai's record. Nart couldn't help thinking that it might have been another servant who had taken it and got cold feet about it, so he had tried to frame Klai to escape punishment. With this in mind, he ordered Klai to go back to his room and stay there.

His wife asked in annoyance, "Why don't you send him to jail? He should be put in the prison on the base. Why are you letting him off?"

"I don't want to cause a scandal. It will look like I can't even control my own subordinate. Everyone will lose faith in me."

Confronted with such a reason, Nuathong fell silent because she couldn't think of counter argument.

The two others under suspicion were Man and Tieng.

Nart could not believe that it was Man because he knew Man well and knew that he was not a thief. Man had worked for him for years, so how could he not have known what he was like? Moreover, on the day the necklace went missing, Man had not set foot inside the house. Or could it have been Tieng?

When he mentioned it to his wife, she cried, "What? There's no way it was her! She's been with me forever. She sees my jewellery every day and when I leave it lying around, she always picks it up for me."

Nart questioned them both, but he didn't get anything out of them.

Man was adamant that he had seen nothing and Tieng denied it with trembling lips. After pondering the matter, he came to a decision.

Sergeant Klai stood to attention before his commander. Although he was calm, his face belied his misery.

"Klai, there's a heavy punishment for what you did," Nart said gravely, but he continued in a kinder tone. "If I press charges, your record will be ruined and I don't want to do that. And you're Gade's cousin, after all."

Klai's heart ached until he could hardly stand it and he opened his mouth to ask something, but stopped.

"Your good deeds and the wrong you did cancel each other out, so I'm going to have you transferred from here. I'm sending you home. It's the best I can do."

Klai slumped down on the bamboo table in front of his hut and was silent for a moment before he found the strength to speak.

"I have to go back to Phetchaburi. The boss won't keep me anymore."

Man took the banana leaft cigarette from behind his ear and stroked it contemplatively. He sighed and said, "You're a good man and an honest one. It's a shame you have to leave. I'm sorry for you, but not as sorry as I am for someone else."

Klai was confused and asked, "What do you mean?"

Man sighed again. "When you're gone, there'll be no one left as a bridge between Mark Keng and Phetchaburi."

Klai was even more confused and wondered what his relatives in Phetchaburi had to do with it. "Phetchaburi? Do you mean Gade? What does she have to do with it?"

"If you're not here, who will go to fetch Gade? She and Ned are waiting in vain."

"Not in vain, surely. I expect the lieutenant colonel will send for them eventually."

Man shook his head wearily. "Even if he wants to send for her, who could he send? Gade's still young. She wouldn't travel alone overnight with a man unless he were a relative like you."

It was true, Klai thought and became even more dejected.

"That's why I said when you leave, Gade and her son won't get to see his father. His wife here won't allow it."

Things suddenly became clear. Klai stared at Man in shock.

"You mean…"

Man reached over and covered Klai's mouth with his hand and glanced left and right as if he was afraid someone would hear.

"I may be a servant, but I'm not stupid, but I daren't say anymore. If the mistress hears, she'll stuff my mouth with ripe coconut."

Klai was sweating, but he contained himself, even though his blood was boiling.

"I'll tell the lieutenant colonel…"

Man shook his head in the manner of someone who had lived a long time.

"The master is only good at fighting. He's no match for a woman's wiles. Do you think he'd listen to you instead of that wife of his? Look how much he loved Gade. He's even forgotten her."

"You're right." Klai was lost for words.

They both pitied Gade and the child from the bottom of their hearts.

❋❋❋❋❋

Gade held her son in her arms and sat on the end of the bridge. When he saw the water, he squealed and wriggled because he wanted to go and splash in the clear cool water of Khlong Sai Gai.

"Keep still! You'll fall in!" Gade scolded him before bending down to immerse him in the water to wash him clean before rubbing him with cumin. The sultry summer evening breeze blew and, although the sun had gone down, the air was still warm. This year, as soon as the cool season had ended, the hot summer began and it was so scorching that Gade had to bathe her son several times a day. This evening, she planned to bathe him and powder him with clay before putting him to bed.

The little boy was soaking wet. He laughed and splashed the water with his chubby hands, calling her to come in, "Mommy...Mommy... water...water."

The drops of water that clung to his clean skin brightened Gade's spirits and made her want to go in the water with him.

"Gade! Gade!" Rern cried in the distance as she ran towards her sister looking excited.

"Gade, Klai's come home! Let me hold the baby…"

The name 'Klai' almost made her drop the child and she handed him to her sister with shaking hands. As Ned was lifted out of the water, he cried out in protest.

If Klai had come home, it could only mean one thing, and that was that Nart had sent him to collect her and Ned to take them to Mark Keng.

"Stop that! You're not going back in!" Rern scolded her nephew and he stopped crying at once.

When she went up the stairs to the veranda, the eyes of everyone turned to look at her.

"Klai, you came without telling us! This is a surprise!" Gade greeted him happily.

Klai smiled at his cousin in return, and she wasn't sure if she had imagined it, but she his smile seemed forced. When she looked at him, she noticed he was no longer fit and muscular, but had grown thin and weak as if he'd just recovered from an illness.

She asked him questioningly, "You've lost weight. Have you been ill?"

He didn't make eye contact and answered reluctantly, "I don't know what it was. I've been recovering in Bangkok for a month."

Gade thought of her husband and became anxious. "It must be terrible in Mark Keng. Has Khun Luang...er...Khun Phra been sick, too?"

Klai felt a lump in his throat and swallowed with difficulty. "No… no. He's fine."

"Even if he's fine, it must still difficult there," Eeam remarked, thinking of her esteemed son-in-law, "if even Klai couldn't take it."

Klai didn't know what to say. He alone knew that the boss was 'fine', even 'finer' than anybody here could imagine.

If he told them one thing, it would be a chain leading to another, which would eventually force him to reveal that which he wanted to hide, so Klai decided it was best not to say anything at all. After that, the questions turned to other topics and Klai answered with caution and thought before answering each question. Nobody suspected anything, thinking that he was simply exhausted from his illness, and so was answering weakly without his former vigour

Nobody knew that inside the young sergeant's chest, his heart was on fire. The more he looked at his young nephew with his freshly powdered skin, whom his youngest cousin was holding in her arms as she brought him back from the bridge, the heavier his heart became.

"Let's have a look at him. He's really grown!" he said to Rern with forced cheeriness.

Ned showed no sign of being afraid of the stranger, as he was used to relatives coming to visit and picking him up. The little boy looked up at him with big clear eyes as if he was wondering who he was. Klai held him for a moment and sighed. He wanted to say what he was thinking, but he didn't dare. All he could do was avoid it by talking about something else. "How old is he now? He must be at least one."

"He's already two!" Rern answered. "We all helped look after him until he got chubby. He's easy to handle now. He eats and sleeps well. Not like before. He was such a handful that Gade lost weight!"

Klai looked at Rern fondly. Although he'd seen her since she was a child, she had changed a lot in the past two years and was now a beautiful young woman with flawless skin and a shapely figure. He couldn't help thinking that if she was dressed in fashionable clothes, she would be a match for any of the women he had seen in Bangkok. When he thought of the women in Bangkok, he looked at Gade, who was smiling at her son, and his heart sank.

Although she was more radiant than when she had just given birth and had got her figure back, when she looked at Klai, there was an anxious expression in her eyes, which he knew was because she was waiting for news of her husband. What in the world was he going to tell her without hurting her feelings? As he was thinking, his Uncle Mee, spoke up as if he had read his mind.

"Klai, has Khun Phra sent you to fetch Gade and the little one to take them to Mark Keng?"

Although he had anticipated the question, he couldn't help being alarmed.

He forced himself to recite the answer he had prepared, which he had already told to his parents. "Not yet, Uncle. The lieutenant colonel...er...transferred me back to the army base here like before."

There were puzzled exclamations from his aunt, uncle and cousins, and Eeam declared at once, "Then Khun Phra must be moving back here. If that's the case, I'm glad…"

What would he tell them now? Klai forced himself to make eye contact.

"Er...not yet, Aunt," he repeated. "Not yet…"

Klai's mother explained the situation as she understood it. "Klai was sick, so the lieutenant colonel was kind enough to send him home. Is that it, son?"

"Yes," he replied without the strength to explain any more.

"I expect he'll be moving back as well, before too long," Mee said hopefully. "Is that right, Klai?"

"I er...I er…" Klai found it hard to find the words. "I don't know."

All the time, Gade had been waiting in anticipation, and now her heart, which had swelled at first, sank little by little.

"Did Nart send any news for me?"

Klai breathed more easily. "He's written you a letter. He didn't give me any money to give you, but he left some money with his friend in Bangkok. Did you get it?"

"Yes, I got it a while ago."

Gade took the letter in the white envelope as if it was something of great value. Money had no meaning for her. It was the news from her husband that she cared about, but the letter in the envelope had only a short message.

Gade,

I'm fine here. I asked my friend to give you the money at the army base. It will be quicker and more convenient that way. Spend it carefully.

I hope you and the child are well. Don't worry about me. I'll send more money later.

Nart

Everyone was watching her in anticipation of some news, but she calmly put the letter back in the envelope.

"Khun Phra is fine. He said not to worry."

Mee sighed, while Eeam asked about the details. "Did he say when he would be sending someone to fetch you?"

Klai held his breath and breathed a sigh of relief when Gade replied, "No, Mother. He didn't say."

Chan, who was naturally more outspoken than the others, and who was not reticent about asking, on account of being Klai's mother, spun around and demanded, "What's going on, Klai? His son's old enough to walk now and his father still hasn't sent for him. What's the problem?"

The directness of the question made everyone fall silent. Every eye was on Klai and he couldn't avoid answering. "It's dry and desolate there," he said after a long pause. "He doesn't want Gade and Ned to endure it, since he's still so young."

"If it's so difficult, how come he can stand it?" Rern asked. "Who's taking care of him?"

Eeam spun around to glare at her and snapped, "Think before you speak!"

Rern fell silent at once, while Gade's heart sank and she looked at Klai pleadingly for an answer.

When Klai caught her eye, he knew he couldn't tell her. Even if it was wrong of him, he had to hide the truth from her. "He's got Man to take care of him. He's fine."

"But I thought you said it was difficult there," Rern persisted.

"It would be difficult for Gade and Ned, but Khun Phra is a soldier, so it's not difficult for him."

Only Klai knew how hard it was for him to answer. Even if the others, especially Gade's parents, were astute enough to suspect the truth, they kept their lips sealed and didn't ask any more questions in front of their children and grandchildren. The conversation turned to other matters, such as Klai's journey and his work. Nobody mentioned Nart again.

Even so, Klai noticed that, since that day, Gade's face was downcast and her manner was solemn.

❋❋❋❋❋

Since she had moved out two years before, Gade had only set foot inside the army base twice within the last six months. Both times were to collect the money her husband had sent for her through an officer friend who was posted there.

Gade asked her younger sister to go with her when they reached the town, since their father who had travelled with them had other things to attend to. The weather that morning was cool and the grass was still wet with dew. That morning, Gade had set out before it was light in order to reach the home of her husband's friend before he went to work. As she walked up the steps of his house, the major, who had known Gade since she got married, greeted her cheerfully. "You're early. Please come on up."

Gade put her palms together respectfully, not considering herself to be superior because of her husband's higher rank. He hurried inside to take the money that Nart had left for his wife and excused himself, "Khun Phra sent it to the ministry, so it was a bit slow this time. Count it to make sure it's all there."

"That won't be necessary, Khun Luang," Gade replied politely. "I'm sure it's all there. Have you heard any news from Khun Phra?"

"I heard he's going to be transferred back to Bangkok, but I haven't had a chance to see him. When I went to Bangkok this time, he hadn't arrived yet."

A ray of hope arose in Gade's heart and, even though there wasn't any more news, her heart felt light and swelled with joy. Gade said goodbye to the major and went to the entrance gate of the army base. The sun got hotter and the sisters quickened their pace in order to meet their father at the market in time to catch the bus home.

Gade could not have guessed that, due to his greater experience of life, even one lived in Phetchaburi, Mee had figured out what was going on some time ago – in fact since the previous year when his son-in-law didn't show any sign of being eager to fetch his wife and child. He remembered that after his nephew returned to the base here, he had tried to ask him about his son-in-law, but he had become uncomfortable and refused to divulge anything as if he was afraid of letting the cat out of the bag.

"He's fine, Uncle. He's not sick, but...it's difficult there."

That was all he would say. If nothing was wrong, why would he be so awkward just to annoy them? Both Muen and his wife tried to get the truth out of him, but Klai refused to say anything until they gave up. Although they were close relatives, it was only natural that they were not as concerned about the matter as Gade's parents.

When a man could live serenely in such a dry and desolate place so far from his family for over a year, it could only mean one thing. He had a new woman taking care of him, someone who pleased him so much that he didn't give his former wife a second thought.

Mee recalled the abbot's prediction. It was a sign that he had not been mistaken in predicting Gade's fate.

"Although you will have a husband of high rank, you will suffer because of him. When you become aware of this, you must make merit and follow the precepts to reduce the old karma."

Mee remembered too how Eeam had tried to avert their beautiful daughter's fate by preventing her from marrying a man of high rank, and he couldn't help feeling guilty for having quietly endorsed the match in order to gain status.

If Gade had married a local villager, by now she would have been comfortable. Her husband would have owned paddy fields and plantations, and he would not have abandoned his wife and left his child fatherless.

❋❋❋❋❋

For several months after that, since hearing the news that Nart would be moving to Bangkok, Gade's heart was full of hope. Soon Nart would come to collect them in Phetchaburi and the three of them would never need to be separated again. But her hope gradually faded with the weather that signalled the changing seasons. The rains of the monsoon season were replaced by a breeze that shook the leaves and chilled her skin, until now it was almost the end of the cool season.

Gade looked at her son, who was lying comfortably on his side with his leg across a pillow. By the light of the lantern that shone dimly inside the room, she could see that his eyes were wide open and he showed no sign of drowsiness.

"Go to sleep," Gade whispered as she stroked his hair. "Why aren't you sleepy tonight?"

"I want to play," he said brightly. He was talkative for a child of two and a half.

"You've been playing all day. You played at your aunt's house, didn't you? Wasn't that enough?"

"Mother…" he called, clutching his young mother's slender arm in his chubby hand. "Where's my father?"

Her arms that were about to hug him became limp, the words feeling like a sharp stab to her heart. She hadn't expected such a small child to ask that question.

"Mother," he persisted. "Where's my father?"

Where was his father? Gade asked herself the same question every day. Where was Nart? Until today, there had been no news from Bangkok, only silence. Gade wiped away the tears that had spontaneously started to flow and answered hoarsely, "Your father's in Bangkok…"

"Where?"

"Bangkok…" She didn't know how to explain,, so she asked, "Why are you asking about your father?"

He thought for a moment before answering, "Juk said I don't have a father."

Gade was startled and bent down to hold him tightly.

"That's not true...It's not true."

"You do have a father. Your father is Khun Phra...Phra Narentharaksa...Remember that. Your father isn't from Phetchaburi.

He's from the capital. He's a soldier there. He wants us to stay here because you're still young and it's a long way. When you're older, he'll come and fetch us and we'll go and live with him."

Gade didn't know how much of what she had said Ned understood. She hugged him comfortingly and sang to him until his eyes grew drowsy, his body became limp and, at last, he fell asleep. She pulled away and tucked the mosquito net in tightly. When she was sure that he was sleeping soundly and would not wake up, she crept out of the room in the small house and walked outside to the veranda where a lantern was lit.

Gade's parents sat on the raised floor of the large house which had a veranda in the centre. They had finished dinner and the two of them were talking quietly to each other because their youngest daughter had gone to spend the night with her eldest sister. Gade sat quietly on the floor for a moment before she decided to bring up the subject without beating about the bush.

"My son's old enough to know what's going on. Today he asked me where his father was. He knows other children have fathers, but he doesn't."

Although she had been determined to be resolute, her voice faltered at the end.

Mee looked at his wife, but she turned to spread limestone paste on a betel leaf, so as to avoid making eye contact with him. In fact, the topic they had been discussing just a moment earlier was none other than the one on everyone's lips and involved their noble son-in-law who had left his wife and child alone for several years.

"I heard a rumour that Khun Phra has abandoned me. Has anybody asked about it?"

Mee was silent, while Eeam answered evasively, "No."

"Mother, don't hide it from me. I know that the more time passes, the more they gossip. It's understandable. Khun Phra returned to Bangkok several months ago, and he hasn't come to Phetchaburi. That's why they're gossiping."

Eeam sighed dejectedly. She pitied her daughter, but worried that if she admitted it, Gade would be even more devastated. As someone who had lived a reasonably long time, Eeam knew without a doubt that her son-in-law had changed. If he had remained faithful to his wife, then why had he not come to collect her?

But what could she do, except console her?

"Don't think too much. If it's meant to be, Khun Phra will come for you eventually."

Eeam's words did not make her feel better.

"Do you expect me to wait like this for months or even years? Ned's growing up. He's the son of a lieutenant colonel, after all. Do you expect me to leave him fatherless?"

"No, but what are you going to do?" Mee spoke up for the first time. "What can a woman do? The fate of a married woman depends on her husband."

Gade pursed her lips. She felt as if she had been cornered.

"I've done nothing wrong. Do you expect me to accept my fate because my husband abandoned me? Well, I won't!"

"Who says he's abandoned you?" Mee countered.

"Khun Phra hasn't abandoned you. He still sends you money. It's almost time for him to send more, isn't it?"

"I don't care about the money," Gade sobbed. "I can survive by myself, but what about Ned? He can't live like me. If Khun Phra doesn't take care of me, I don't mind, but he should take care of our son. If he doesn't come to find me, I'll go and find him myself!"

Her parents looked at each other in shock and exclaimed together, "How?"

"Don't we have any relatives in Bangkok?"

Mee shook his head dejectedly.

"No. All my relatives have lived here since I was born. When I was young, I went there to be a soldier, but that was decades ago."

Gade turned to her mother, who shook her head.

"I don't. I've only been there a few times."

Gade's quest stopped abruptly before it had even started.

❋❋❋❋❋

The small bridge was where Gade used to bathe with several others in the village, but now whenever she set foot on it, she felt hot and cold as if she had a fever. The scent of the evening breeze along with the shadows of the trees all around her reminded her of a time, several years before, when someone's shadow had fallen on the bridge on an evening like this one. That person's steadfast words were still as clear in her memory as if they had been spoken only yesterday.

"Or if you don't believe me, I'll swear an oath…I'll swear by the stars that I'll love you and I'll never leave you. If I ever leave you, may I suffer, and never be happy or prosper."

Gade remembered that, in spite of her shyness, she had burst out laughing.

"What's funny?" Khun Luang had asked.

"I've…I've never seen anyone swear by the stars," Gade had answered shyly. *"They usually swear by the Buddha…"*

"I swear by the stars. Whenever I'm not with you, all you have to do is open the window and you'll remember my promise."

If Gade had let those strange words go in one ear and out the other, and had not taken them to heart, understood them, and been moved by them, her tears would not be glistening on her cheeks in the starlight tonight.

The gossip about Gade and her noble husband which at first had been a mere whisper gradually turned into a subject that was discussed openly. All her relatives were of the opinion that her husband had finished with her. Even though none of them had seen Nart in the capital, the fact that they knew he had moved back to Bangkok several months ago and had not sent any news to his wife, except for sending money for his son occasionally, was confirmation.

"At least he hasn't abandoned his son," Muen reasoned, since he still had a great deal of respect for his past commander.

"This kind of thing depends on karma. You stayed together until your good karma ran out."

Gade remained silent and stayed inside the house to avoid her relatives' questions as much as she could, since the pity she saw in their eyes embittered her more than anything else. Nobody, apart from Eeam, knew that beneath her solemn demeanour, Gade had no intention of 'leaving things to fate' like everyone thought.

Nevertheless she was somewhat relieved when another matter of importance made her relatives forget to question her for quite a while. That matter was Muen's marriage proposal to his youngest niece, Rern, on behalf of his son Klai. Mee and Eeam were glad to have their nephew as their son-in-law coming to live with them.

Muen built a house for his son that was connected to his in-laws' by a veranda, and a grand wedding ceremony was arranged. On the day of the wedding, Gade, as the bride's elder sister, diligently took care of the refreshments instead of her mother, who was no longer as fit as before. She almost had no time to come out of the kitchen to join the wedding party, emerging only when all the refreshments were finished. She received compliments from the guests and smiled, hiding her exhaustion.

One of those who praised Gade's fermented rice noodles with curry paste was Thongpheng, the richest man in the village, who was usually too arrogant to attend the villagers' parties unless they were really important.

"I've eaten fermented rice noodles with curry paste in a lot of places, and I've never tasted curry paste as smooth as Gade's."

Gade paid no attention to Thongpheng's comments until a few days later when her aunt, Chan, came to see Mee and Eeam, looking excited and a little embarrassed.

"Thongpheng asked me to tell you he wants to propose to Gade. He wants to put her in charge of his household, and he'll give her the rights to all his money and property. She'll be second to no one in the village."

Thongpheng asking Gade to be his principal wife was something that Mee and Eeam had never dreamed of, so they were taken aback and did not know how to answer.

They discussed the matter for several days without reaching any conclusion, so, in the end, they told Gade to decide for herself. Gade's answer was, "No. I don't want to remarry while Nart's still alive."

"If you don't want to remarry, I won't force you, but if you're waiting for Khun Phra, then where is he? There's still no sign of him coming back."

"He'll definitely come back, Mother. His wife and son are here," Gade answered resolutely. Her resolve was not rooted in confidence, but in the hope that sustained her heart.

"It was wrong of me to let you marry him," Mee confessed dejectedly. "If I'd have let you marry someone in the village, you'd have a house full of children by now, and you wouldn't have to put up with all this gossip."

When Gade heard her parents speak in that way, she realised that circumstances were closing in on her and she could no longer continue waiting indefinitely.

Gade tried to muster her resolve and spoke with determination, although her voice faltered.

"I think, Mother...I won't wait. I'll go to Bangkok to find Nart. Help me think, Mother. Even though we don't have any relatives there, when people from Phetchaburi go to Bangkok, where do they stay? There must be someone we can depend on."

Mee and Eeam looked at each other trying to think until finally Eeam spoke, hesitatingly at first. "There's...the house of the old governor's daughter."

"The governor? The Chao Khun you used to live with when you were a girl?"

"Yes. He was from Phetchaburi. When anyone from Phetchaburi went to Bangkok, they could stay in his house. He never minded."

A ray of hope glimmered in Gade's heart.

"Can I go there, Mother? Where is his house?"

"I remember it's near Din Sor Road. His daughter's title is Chao Chom*...Khun Chom Amphan. I've known her since I was a child. She's very kind and hospitable, just like her father was."

---

* Chao Chom is a title that was held by royal wives who were born as commoners.

That was the first time that Gade had heard the name, 'Chao Chom Amphan.' At the time, she had no idea how it would completely transform her life.

So this is Bangkok!

This was her first thought when she stepped down from the train at Bangkok Noi Station. Even though it was only a small wooden station, for someone who had never been there before, it seemed grand and exciting. Everywhere groups of people were waiting to meet passengers, and there was the sound of excited chatter, or shouts telling people to make way for goods that were being carried through. Gade was excited and disoriented, but she held onto her mother's arm tightly.

"We're finally here, Mother! Are you alright?"

Klai, who had come with them because he knew the capital better than anyone else, told Gade and her mother, "They call this Thonburi. We're not in Bangkok, yet."

"Oh!" Gade exclaimed, feeling embarrassed by her lack of knowledge. "I thought we'd arrived. Aren't we there yet?"

There was nothing else for Gade to do but follow Klai, who was supporting Eeam on his arm, her arms full of the gifts she had brought from Phetchaburi and a bag of clothes over her shoulder, until they reached the pier. Gade saw a large waterway stretching before her, framed by the clear blue sky. On the other side, further away, were rows of trees interspersed with houses. Standing out was the gleaming roof of a temple, which seemed more magnificent than any she had ever seen. It was only later that she found out that it was the renowned Grand Palace. The vastness of the water under the wide sky made Gade feel tiny so she forced herself to swallow her fear and step onto the paddle boat. As if in a dream, she heard her mother saying, "When we get to Tha Phra Chan, would you hail a rickshaw to take us to Din Sor Road? I can remember the way from there."

From the pier known as Tha Phra Chan, Klai hailed two rickshaws that were pulled by Chinese men. Eeam and Gade sat in one, while he sat in the other and told the men in Chinese where to go. Gade wondered how she would have made it this far without Klai to guide them. It would have been difficult enough just getting to Bangkok Noi Station, let alone Chao Chom Amphan's house.

The rickshaws sped along the roads, and Gade saw that on the left side of Phra Chan Road was a towering wall with boundary stones along the length of the road. The size of the place intimidated her and she had to look away to the right to rest her eyes, but there were magnificent temples along that side of the road as well.

At the time, Gade did not recognize a single place, but she pondered that in Bangkok everything was huge.

"Mother," Gade whispered, feeling like a child again. "Do you know what that temple is?"

"Mahathat Temple," Eeam replied knowingly, even though she didn't really know that much more than Gade. "On the other side is Bowon Temple." When they had passed Phra Chan Road, they came to a large open field that was known as Thung Phra Mehru. The rickshaw turned left and they passed numerous buildings and stores, until they finally came to the biggest street that Gade had ever seen in her life. It was so vast and devoid of people that Gade felt afraid because all she could see were trees on both sides of the road. She later learned that this was the biggest street in Bangkok and it was called Ratchadamnoen, or King's procession, Avenue.

The rickshaws slowed and pulled into the side of the street, which was lined with a hedge of hibiscus up to the crossroads. Here detached houses alternated with small single-storey terraces. Eeam told the Chinese men to pull the rickshaws into a small flattened dirt street where grass grew sparsely and, when she glimpsed the roof of a two-storey house peeking through the hibiscus hedge, she told her daughter, "We've arrived."

Eeam had told Gade about Chao Chom Amphan before they left Phetchaburi, but the woman that Gade now placed her palms together in front of was nothing like what she had imagined. Her mother had told her that Chao Chom Amphan was the daughter of the governor of Phetchaburi and had been given the title 'Chao Chom' during the reign of Rama V, since she had been one of the last to have that title. As it was now the reign of Rama VII, Gade had assumed that she would be elderly, or at least as old as her mother. However, the woman sitting on a chair on the wide veranda in front of the house was still beautiful. She had creamy yellow skin, an oval face and naturally wavy jet-black hair cut in a neck-length bob. As far as Gade could see, she was well-proportioned, and neither too fat nor too thin.

The only thing that indicated her life experience was the wise expression in her eyes that was unlike a naive and innocent young girl's.

That day, the weather was hot and Chao Chom looked as if she had just taken a bath, since there was still a trace of powder on her skin and she appeared cool and comfortable. She wore a pale green strip of cloth around her chest paired with a purple sarong. Gade had never seen any woman wear such colours before, not even the fashionable Chalaem.

Gade later learned that Khun Chom dressed in colours in accordance with the days of the week as she had done when she had served in the palace, and that the colours she had worn that day were those for Tuesday.

"Eeam, is that you?" she said in surprise and her voice sounded sweet and melodic. The first sentence was spoken in a Bangkok accent, but those that followed had a Phetchaburi lilt.

"I haven't seen you for over ten years. You've grown plump."

Eeam sat on the cool patterned tile floor with her legs folded to one side, and Gade noticed that when she was in front of her old boss, her manner changed and she became calm and composed.

"I've only just had a chance to come and pay my respects, madam," her mother answered politely, and turned to Gade. "I've brought my daughter to see you."

"Your daughter? Let me look at her."

Gade looked up and met Khun Chom's eyes, which had a kindly expression in them.

"I have four daughters. This is the third one. Her name's Gade."

"She's a fine-looking girl. She could be from Bangkok."

The compliment made Gade forget her shyness.

"What are you doing in Bangkok? Would you like to stay at my house?"

Khun Chom got straight to the point, indicating that she was used to people coming to see her for the same reason.

"Yes, madam. My daughter wants to find her…" Eeam paused before continuing. "My son-in-law lives in Bangkok, but he hasn't been in touch, so my daughter's come to find him."

Khun Chom looked at Gade again.

"You're already married, are you? You look too young to be married. What does your husband do? Bangkok's very big. You have to know where he lives, or you'll never find him."

Gade's heart sank when she heard the words, 'Bangkok's very big'. Just travelling along two or three streets by rickshaw had left her dazed. Was Bangkok even bigger than this?

"He's a soldier, madam," Gade forced herself to say, trying not to be discouraged.

"A soldier? Then he's under the Ministry of Defence. What a pity it isn't the Ministry of the Interior. I have relatives there. What's his name and rank?"

"His name's Lieutenant Colonel Phra Narentharaksa, madam."

Chao Chom Amphan looked puzzled.

"He's a lieutenant colonel? Then he's a high-ranking officer. It's strange that I've never heard the name before...Phra Narentharaksa…"

Eeam looked disappointed, but answered resolutely, "I don't know anyone else in Bangkok. You're the only one I can turn to. Please let Gade stay with you until she finds her husband. He hasn't been in contact for several years. His son can already speak and he's never seen his father."

Khun Chom's eyes filled with sympathy and the puzzled expression disappeared.

"Rest assured, she can stay here. You don't need to worry. I'll have someone find a room for her, but as for finding her husband, it's going to take a while. We can't just go looking for him blindly. We're going to have to do some investigating before we can track him down."

6
Moving Slowly

Gade awoke to the melodic crowing of a rooster as she usually did, except that the smell and atmosphere in the room were different from her home, so she reminded herself, "Oh! Khun Chom's house!"

Over the three or four days that Gade had spent in Chao Chom Amphan's house, she had gradually adapted and her confusion from the first day faded. She pulled back the mosquito net and quietly stepped out, but when she moved, the person sleeping under the mosquito net next to hers, called out huskily, "Are you awake, Gade?"

"Yes, Grandmother."

She heard an old person's cough, and an old lady stepped out from the mosquito net.

"Don't go, yet. Can you help me? I've got a stomach ache. Would you dissolve some medicine for me? Oh, where's my balm to rub on my stomach? I'm getting forgetful in my old age. Don't mind me."

Gade rubbed balm on the old lady's stomach for her. The water in the hot water jug was cold since it had been standing all night, so Gade hurried from the room and walked out of the house to ask for hot water from the kitchen, where she found the cook lighting a fire to make breakfast with two or three helpers. When she came back, Gade dissolved the medicine in hot water and handed it to the thin white-haired old lady. When Gade saw that she was feeling better, she helped her to the bathroom. By the time she had finished, and Gade had washed her face and cleaned her teeth, the night had been replaced by gold and silver rays across the sky.

The room that Gade was staying in was a downstairs room behind the house, separated from the servants' quarters. The owner of the room, whom everyone called 'Nai Khim', was Khun Chom's old wet nurse.

Because 'Nai Khim' had known Eeam since she had served the governor of Phetchaburi, Gade called her 'Grandmother'.

Nai Sap was responsible for all the housekeeping from the meals, the laundry, and the cleaning to the bookkeeping. Everything had to be inspected by her, so everyone in the house was afraid of her. When Gade walked across the courtyard, smoke was already emanating from the kitchen, and the smell of boiling rice and freshly fried fish were carried on the morning breeze. The sky was brightening with yellow rays and a flock of cawing crows came flying swiftly out of their nests.

Nai Sap's voice reached her ears before anyone else's.

"The sun's already up and you've only just come. A lazy person's good for nothing."

Gade was startled. She wasn't sure who Nai Sap was talking to, but from the first moment Gade met her, she felt that her manner was cold towards her. Gade tried to think if she might have done something to offend the middle-aged woman, but she couldn't come up with anything. Nai Sap emerged from the kitchen. She was a thin woman who reminded Gade of a wooden board because both her face and her body appeared flat. Her black hair was oiled and her skin was sallow as if she was sickly. There was nothing striking about Nai Sap's appearance except for her eyes, which never looked at anyone directly, but darted from side to side. If they weren't darting to the left, they were darting to the right, and when she spoke, she was always looking sideways.

When she noticed Gade, her eyes started darting left and right, so Gade greeted her first.

"Is there anything for me to do?"

Nai Sap looked askance in her usual way and spoke in a derisive tone.

"It's too late now! Everything's done. It's almost time for Khun Chom to offer food to the monks."

Gade's face flushed hot. Nai Sap spoke as if Gade was being lazy when every day she had got up before her, and had been helping out with the housework without ceasing as all the servants knew. When she had finished speaking, Nai Sap hurried out to meet Khun Chom Amphan who was just coming down from the house with a young woman who had come to visit her the previous evening and had stayed the night.

Her manner was quiet and at first glance, she appeared solemn. Only her eyes showed an anxiety that contrasted with her calm demeanour. She looked towards Gade, who was walking away and frowned slightly, asking, "Who's that? I haven't seen her here before."

"Oh, her name's Gade, madam. She's the daughter of one of the governor's old servants from when he lived in Phetchaburi. Her mother brought her here..." She lowered her voice and whispered scornfully, "She married someone from Bangkok, but he left her."

Gade gazed up at Khun Chom's house with the same admiration she had felt the first time she saw it. Nai Khim explained that, at the end of Rama V's reign, Khun Chom had moved out of the palace along with the other royal consorts. At first, she had lived with her father, but he had died soon after, and his assets had been divided amongst his children. Khun Chom had inherited a plot of land on Din Sor Road, so she had built a house there with her brother.

The house had been designed and built by a European. It was a modern style two-storey brick house with two or three low wide steps leading up to a spacious wide veranda before turning on the left side into an open room below. There were doors leading to several rooms and a large staircase leading upstairs.

All the large doors and windows were made of polished teak, and when they were open, they let in the breeze and lit up the pale-yellow room. The furniture was mainly European but a mother-of-pearl inlaid cabinet of the type popular in the reign of Rama V displayed Chinese blue and white porcelain.

Khun Chom's usual place for relaxing was a wide upstairs balcony under the roof where it was pleasantly breezy. The floor was made of wide wooden planks polished with wax until they shone. There Khun Chom would sit on a square cotton mattress on a large soft Persian carpet. A low round bamboo table next to her held various utensils. When close relatives came to see her, they knew they would always find her there on the balcony.

When Gade crawled towards her that day, she found that Khun Chom was not alone, but had been joined by the young woman she had seen that morning. They were sitting slightly apart and chatting softly but fell still when they noticed Gade. The young woman moved away slightly and the way she looked at Gade made her feel as if she was intruding, but she didn't know what else to do since Khun Chom had asked a servant to fetch her.

Gade bent forward and placed her palms together in front of Khun Chom as she always did, asking, "Did you ask for me, madam?"

"Yes, Gade," Khun Chom answered brightly and introduced her to the young woman. "This is Gade who I told you about."

Gade placed her palms together before the young woman, but felt embarrassed when she not only did not return the gesture, but looked at her out of the corner of her eye and turned away. Her expression was cold and unwelcoming. She was dressed elegantly, her hair was permed in a wave and cut in a bob, her skin was white with powder, and she wore a silk sarong with a gold belt and a gold chain with a diamond pendant. Gade could see that she was wealthy, but her expression was strangely dry and lifeless as if she was so engrossed in her own thoughts that she paid no attention to those around her.

"Surai is my sister-in-law," Khun Chom said by way of introduction. "She has lots of friends, so she might know someone who knows your husband. Gade's husband's a soldier."

"I doubt I'd know him."

It was a flat refusal from the outset.

"My friends are only married to officers. They wouldn't know any sergeants."

Gade realized that she considered herself superior to everyone around her, but Khun Chom, used to her sister-in-law, took no offence and answered good-naturedly, "It's because you know lots of important people that I'm asking you. Gade's husband's a lieutenant colonel. What's his name, Gade?"

"Lieutenant Colonel Phra Narentharaksa, madam," Gade answered immediately, since it was a name that had been in her thoughts from morning until night for many years. Surai looked a little surprised, but her expression remained as cold as before.

"I've never heard of him."

"He was posted to Udon Thani...that's right, isn't it, Gade?" she asked to be sure.

When Gade nodded, she continued, "but she heard that he's been moved back to Bangkok. If you see your friends whose husbands are lieutenant colonels, would you ask them? They'd probably know him."

"There are lots of departments in the military," Surai remarked indifferently.

"Even if they're in different departments, surely lieutenant colonels know each other," Khun Chom persisted. "What's the name of your friend, Surai? It's Malai, isn't it? You told me she's invited you to a party at her house, didn't you? Why don't you ask her husband? Tell her I asked."

Surai looked a little annoyed, but she held her irritation in check out of deference to Khun Chom.

"Yes, Malai's invited me to a party to celebrate her husband's promotion. He's been made a colonel and he's been promoted from Khun Phra to Phraya, but I don't want to go."

"Oh, why ever not?"

"I don't know what to tell my friends," she said bitterly. "I don't want them to ask what Chat's doing now. I don't know how to answer. This...writing of his. If he worked for the government, at least he'd be a clerk, but this..."

"Now, Surai," Khun Chom warned.

By then, Gade realized she should excuse herself. The matter the two older women was discussing was not something they would want a third party to hear. Gade placed her palms together and said that she was going down to help Nai Khim supervise the young servants making sweets.

❋❋❋❋❋

Khun Chom Amphan was never idle and did not let a day slip by without doing something useful. There was a total of around twenty servants in the house, both those who lived in and those who lived outside. All of them had different duties, since the friends and relatives of Khun Chom commissioned her to make keepsakes, such as perfumes and powders in small containers, to give out at important events. In addition, they made snacks and sweetmeats for special occasions.

This was something that Nai Khim greatly admired about her.

"Khun Chom's a hard worker. She's not idle like other aristocrats. They just waste money. If you want to impress her, help out with the work. Don't just sit and watch. The more you increase her profits, the more she'll love you."

In actual fact, Gade did not intend to depend on Khun Chom's charity for long. She thought she would stay for only a few days in order to find out where Nart lived. Gade missed her home and her little boy so much that her heart ached and when she saw the birds flying back to their nests in the evening, she could not hold back her tears. Nevertheless, she heeded Nai Khim's words and resolved to repay Khun Chom's kindness by helping out to the best of her ability.

In the afternoons, Khun Chom liked to have a snack with hot Chinese tea, so Gade took the opportunity to ask Nai Khim for a small earthenware stove in order to make *kanom krok* for Khun Chom to try.

"My mother told me she learned to make *kanom krok* in the governor's residence. Have you ever made it?"

"I haven't made it for ages. If you want to make it, go and find the stove in the room under the house."

Khun Chom Amphan's house was surrounded by a hibiscus hedge on three sides, while the fourth side bordered a wide canal, which ran into Khlong Lot, or Khlong Mahan Temple, as it was called by the locals. The water was clear because it was always flowing, and the people living next to it used it for bathing, as well as washing clothes and utensils.

On the other side of the canal was a teak house painted pale turquoise, which still looked new. It had been built by skilled craftsmen and it was connected to Khun Chom's land by a small bridge across the canal. Gade had been told by others in the house that it belonged to Khun Chom's younger brother.

Surai lived there, but she she kept herself to herself and never came outside to walk on the lawn. All the windows were tightly shut as if no one lived there. Sometimes, Gade heard a child crying inside the house and now and again she saw servants walking to and fro.

It was dusk and a cool breeze was blowing pleasantly. Gade sat on the canal bank and let her mind drift. It did not drift far, however, and soon came to the matter that was still unresolved. Before she came, Gade had expected that, when she arrived in Bangkok, she would soon find out about her husband's whereabouts, but in actual fact, the capital was too vast for a woman on her own like Gade to go searching for an officer named Lieutenant Colonel Phra Narentharaksa.

Almost every day, Gade went for a walk along the road outside Khun Chom's house. Some days, she walked as far as the Giant Swing, and other days she walked in the other direction to Phra Sumeru Road, which went around the city wall. She passed large and small wooden houses and terraced houses and would look inside in case she saw a soldier in uniform whom she could muster the courage to ask.

Once she did ask one, but all he said was, "No, I don't know him."

When Gade thought of Khun Chom's kindness, she felt a lump in her throat. Besides providing her with food and a place to stay, she was also trying to find out about Nart from her friends and relatives, not only her sister-in-law, who had answered curtly, "I don't know him."

The cawing of the crows flying back to their nests in the tall coconut palms on the other side of the canal punctured her reverie. It was getting late and back home everyone would be together, except for one person – Ned's mother.

Tears fell onto the back of Gade's hand and she hurriedly brushed them off her cheeks. Suddenly she heard a child's voice, and thought for a moment that it was her son's until she realized it was coming from beneath the betel palms on the other side of the canal.

She smiled when she saw a small boy of no more than two, bending down to pick up the green and red nuts, putting them in his mouth and spitting them out, all the while chattering away innocently to himself.

As she sat watching, Gade noticed him moving closer and closer to the edge of the bank, since he was so preoccupied with picking up betel nuts that he didn't look around him. Just as Gade was about to shout out a warning, the little boy's foot slipped on the muddy bank and he fell into the canal, letting out an alarmed shriek.

Without a second thought, Gade jumped into the canal, and the next thing she knew she was pulling the little boy up onto the bank in the nick of time. She held onto him as he hugged her neck tightly and sobbed in dismay. In actual fact, the canal only came up to an adult's chest, but for a small child who couldn't swim, it was life threatening.

Gade climbed up onto the opposite bank holding the sobbing child, and ran inside the two-storey wooden house, crying out, "Is anyone home? A child fell in the water!"

The kitchen door opened and a young girl dressed in a servant's clothes came rushing out breathlessly.

"Oh, no! Cheng fell in the water!" she cried when she saw them, understanding the situation right away.

"I just turned my back for a second and you fell in the water!"

Gade recognized her, remembering that she had often seen her crossing the bridge into Khun Chom's house, so she said, "It's alright, Suk. Take him for a wash and get him dry, or he'll catch a cold."

Gade tried to pass Cheng to his nanny, but he wouldn't have it and wriggled away from her, shouting. The nanny looked as if she was about to cry and said to Gade, "Would you mind carrying him inside the house, madam. I'll wash him."

Gade carried him after her up the stairs behind the house into a downstairs room, which was dark because all the window shutters were closed. Only dim white, red and blue rays shone through the air vents onto the polished wooden floor, and she noticed that the furniture was ebony inlaid with mother-of-pearl inlay like in Khun Chom's house.

The bathroom was under the stairs that led to the upper floor. It was in Western style with clean white tiles covering the entire room. In the corner was a blue and white porcelain bowl filled up with clean water. Gade told the nanny to fetch hot water to mix in, as she was afraid Cheng would catch a cold.

The nanny asked Gade to hold onto the boy while she rinsed him with water and scrubbed his muddy arms and legs. He was quite a handful, wriggling and shouting in protest until Gade was wet through. She noticed a graze all the way down his shin where he must have scraped it on the rocks when he slid into the water.

"Suk, go and get some antiseptic. I'll put it on for him."

Suk hurried out of the bathroom and Gade followed, taking a large towel to wrap him in and gently rubbing him dry, being careful not to touch the graze. Her tender touch made his sobs subside. When she gazed at the little boy's face, she noticed that his skin was fair, his eyes were large and black and his nose was sharp. Cheng was a good-looking boy and, even though he wasn't the same as Ned, he was the same age, which endeared him to her, and she hugged him tight. She heard the door open and a light came on. Gade assumed the nanny had returned, so she didn't turn around, but all of a sudden, the little boy looked past her and jumped out of her arms into the outstretched arms of the person who had come in.

"Hey, son! You've had a wash, but you're still not dressed, are you?"

At the sound of the deep and unfamiliar voice, Gade turned around.

When Gade saw the young man who was holding Cheng, she knew at once that he was Khun Chom Amphan's younger brother, because he looked very much like her, and she could tell from his face that he couldn't have been more than thirty.

He was dressed in a Raj patterned shirt, but instead of the purple *jongkraben* that civil servants wore, his trousers were dark silk. He started a little when he saw Gade and his eyes showed a puzzled expression, so Gade slowly stood up and explained, "Your little boy's just had a wash. The nanny's gone to get his clothes."

He continued to stare at Gade until she felt embarrassed, and realizing this, he explained. "Excuse me for asking, but I've never seen you before. You're not new here, are you?", indicating that he was observant enough to realize from Gade's manner and appearance that she was not a new servant.

"No," Gade replied softly. "I'm staying in that house...with Khun Chom."

Before he could ask her anything else, the nanny came in, panting, and when she saw the young man, she looked startled.

"I'm sorry, sir. I didn't know you'd come back...I…"

She gave the antiseptic to Gade, so Gade said, "Would you mind putting him down and I'll put some antiseptic on for him."

His father raised his eyebrows and asked, "What happened?"

"I fell in the water," the little boy, who had stopped crying, answered cheerfully and pointed to the graze on his shin. "Here! I'm hurt!"

"You fell in the water?" he exclaimed and glared at the nanny. "What water? What were you doing, Suk, that he fell in the water?"

The nanny's face grew pale.

"I...I was boiling the rice for him...in the kitchen, sir. The cook wasn't there...She's gone to the market…"

"And what about the others?" he asked, naming each one. "Where's Choy? And Pan? And what about my wife? I come home and the house is empty."

"She's gone to stay at the house in Thonburi, sir," Suk answered hurriedly, her voice trembling. "She took Choy with her, and Pan's gone with the cook, sir."

The young man passed Cheng to Gade and he continued loudly and irritably.

"That's a fine thing. When I'm not here, everyone goes out and my son falls in the water. Who saw it? Is he badly hurt?"

He picked up his son again and felt his forehead with the back of his hand, complaining, "Just as I thought. He's got a temperature. He'll need medicine. Suk, go and get medicine. Get my Western medicine, not that herbal stuff. And bring him some rice...Have something to eat, son, and then have your medicine."

The gentle way he spoke to his son suddenly brought a lump to Gade's throat, and she thought of another boy's father.

Khun Chom Amphan stared at her younger brother when he had finished speaking. She sighed as she explained to him, "There's no point being angry with your wife. Surai was hurt that you didn't come home for days, so she's gone to stay with her parents. She didn't think her son would fall in the water. She was just being impulsive."

The young man, who was sitting in front of her on the floor of the upstairs balcony, shuffled irritably.

He pouted petulantly before grumbling, "I know she's sulking...If she's not sulking, she's criticizing other people. She's so touchy, she's never happy."

"And what woman can be happy if her husband never comes home?" Khun Chom retorted.

"I wasn't out partying," he reasoned weakly. "I don't work at the ministry with regular hours. There are no regular hours in newspaper work."

When her brother mentioned his work, Khun Chom suddenly felt uncomfortable. It was such a pity. Chat had been given many opportunities in that he'd had the chance to study in France for several years. Even though he hadn't graduated, he had gained enough knowledge from living abroad to have got a decent job working for the government and then working his way up to a respectable position. Khun Chom could not imagine what her brother had been thinking when he decided to write for a newspaper, translating articles from French, and writing articles about politics. Some of his articles were so radical that their relatives were upset and asked him to tone it down, but to no avail. Her main concern was that his earnings were irregular and sometimes non-existent. In fact, he relied on her to cover his expenses.

Khun Chom took advantage of the opportunity of having him alone to warn him. Even though she knew he wouldn't listen, she believed it was her duty to correct him.

"I heard you wrote about the rebellion again. When I read it, it made me uneasy. It sounded like you were accusing Prince Boworadet of planning a revolution.* How can you accuse him of such a thing? I can assure you he'd never betray the king."

The young man laughed as if he didn't think it was a serious matter. In truth, it was his way of evading telling the truth to whoever he was talking to. His long oval handsome face, sparkling eyes, and smiling lips that parted to reveal straight white teeth looked bright and innocent, which always endeared him to his older sister, even though she was annoyed with him.

"I didn't mention any of the princes by name, but people are talking about it for a reason. Prince Boworadet objected in parliament when they refused to increase the salary of ninety-one officers."

"And what of it?" Khun Chom persisted. Her answer indicated that she had been following the news. "He resigned from the Ministry of Defence last year. The matter's finished, but people are still talking about it. I don't feel right about it, I tell you. There's been so much awful news this year, I don't know what is true anymore."

"I didn't know you listened to rumours."

"Oh, honestly!" Khun Chom scolded. Even though she knew he was teasing her, she couldn't help feeling irritated. "There are so many rumours flying around and when I opened the paper, it seemed my own brother was spreading them. How do you expect me to keep quiet about it?"

Chat bowed his head remorsefully before saying, "There are some things you can't talk about. It's awkward. Our country's backwards. We respect people based on their birth. How's that right? How can you choose what you're born as?"

This wasn't the first time they had discussed such matters, so Khun Chom answered, "If Siam's as backwards as you say, you wouldn't have it so easy. In the old days, you'd have been executed."

Her brother listened politely and didn't argue, but Khun Chom could tell that her words had gone in one ear and out the other, and

---

* Prince Boworadet was a grandson of King Mongkut, and a son of Prince Naret. During the reign of Rama VII, he was the Minister of Defence when the Prime Minister did not approve a salary raise for military officers, so he took responsibility by resigning. At the time there were rumours of a 'revolution', which was later secretly carried out by the 'People's Party'.

In the Revolution of 1932, Prince Boworadet joined the 'People's Party', but by 1933, he realized that the democratic principles set by the People's Party were not being adhered to, so he staged a coup against the government, which failed, and fled to Indochina. He later returned to Thailand where he spent his remaining years in Hua Hin until his death in 1953 at the age of seventy-six.

he hadn't taken any notice. At the same time, she noticed him looking through the rails of the balcony into the courtyard below at a tall slim figure walking out of the kitchen and carrying a tray of something into the house.

When his sister had finished speaking, he asked, "Who's that girl? All I know is that she's staying with you. She doesn't look like a servant, but she doesn't sound as if she's from Bangkok."

Khun Chom realized who he was talking about as she glimpsed Gade disappearing inside the house.

"You mean Gade? She's from Phetchaburi. Her mother used to live at the governor's residence. You wouldn't know her. She wasn't born then. She's come to find her...Oh! I almost forgot…"

Khun Chom leaned forward, pleased to change the subject because the other matter had annoyed her.

"Her husband's an officer. He moved from the provinces to Bangkok and she hasn't heard from him, so she's come to look for him. You have a lot of friends in the military. Have you ever heard…"

Khun Chom had no way of knowing what the other was thinking, so she didn't hear him exclaim in his head, 'She's already married?'

"...the name Lieutenant Colonel Phra Narentharaksa?"

Chat collected his thoughts in time and answered, "No, I've never heard of him. Why doesn't his wife go and ask at the Ministry of Defence?"

"She doesn't want to go there alone. And for another thing, I don't want her to cause a scene. It's better to ask people we know. Then she can go to him directly."

"Alright," he answered agreeably. "I'll ask around. If he's a lieutenant colonel, there must be people who know him."

The door to the balcony opened, and Khun Chom looked at her brother and said, "Here are some refreshments. Won't you stay and have a bite to eat before you go?"

Khun Chom was so busy looking at the servant holding the tray of Chinese tea and snacks that she didn't notice her brother staring at the young woman who had crawled onto the balcony in front of her. Her servant, Pin, was holding a teapot and small cups.

She greeted her cheerfully, "Your ears must be burning, Gade! I was just talking about you. I wanted to thank you for saving my nephew when he fell in the water. His father's just told me about it."

Gade put the tray down and placed her palms together, bowing her head, to greet the young man, and when she looked up, she noticed that he was staring at her. He looked at her again out of the corner of his eye, although she was unaware of it. The more he gazed at her lovely face, looking down as she arranged Khun Chom's refreshments, the smooth skin and the sad black eyes, the more he was moved by her beauty, which was like the moon veiled behind clouds.

He was so mesmerized that his sister needed to cough a warning, and she asked, "Oh, is there *kanom krok* today? I haven't eaten this for ages! Did you make it, Gade?"

"Yes, madam."

Chat didn't normally eat dessert, feeling that those that Khun Chom usually served were too sweet, but he found the soft white *kanom krok* with a savoury topping, of fresh red shrimp stir fried with garlic and pepper and garnished with coriander, very palatable.

Khun Chom took the opportunity to mention Gade's husband once again, in order to remind her brother that Gade was a married woman.

"Gade is the principal wife. Khun Phra Naren hasn't left her. He still sends money home. It's just that she doesn't know where he is. If you ask your friends about him, they can be reunited."

She could see full well that Madam Narentharaksa was still young and beautiful with a figure so shapely that it was impossible to tell that she had already had a child. Her manners and speech were as polite and gentle as any Bangkok woman, and it was not hard to see why a high-ranking officer like her husband would choose her to be his principal wife.

"I'll ask around. We'll probably find out within a few days."

In order to conceal his true feelings, he changed the subject. "I'm worried about my son. I want to bring him to you during the day."

Khun Chom was well aware of the situation in her younger brother's home. She also knew that whenever her sister-in-law was angry with her husband, which was almost every day, she would leave her son and her home to go and stay with her parents, who were always ready to indulge her.

"I was going to ask you to bring him here," she replied. "Let his nanny bring him here every day."

Chat took the opportunity to speak to Gade. "When my son comes here, can you help look after him, Gade?"

His voice was normal, as if he was just concerned for his son, but he alone knew that he meant much more than that.

*****

Chat left his sister's house in the afternoon, and hailed a cab to take him to the printers. Upstairs was the office of the newspaper that he regularly wrote articles for.

Chat enjoyed the freedom of this kind of work, preferring it to sitting at a desk all day shuffling papers for the government.

Besides this, he enjoyed exchanging opinions with his co-workers about politics and important individuals, which he found more agreeable than taking orders from the director of a department or ministry, which would have bored him even more than shuffling papers.

Even though his earnings were small and irregular, unlike a government worker's salary, he wasn't at all bothered by it.

He walked up the stairs and found everyone sitting around a table. When they saw him, they called out to greet him.

"Why are you late today? Eat first and then you can tell us!" one of them called.

"Sorry. I was at my sister's house. I don't go to see her very often, so I didn't like to rush off."

"On the first of next month, Phra Ritdaeso's having a big party at his house to celebrate his promotion. He's been made a lieutenant colonel Phraya now."

"Phraya who?"Chat asked, remembering his sister's request.

"Phraya Thepakanee. He asked me to invite all of you. He wants it in the news."

Everyone nodded and Chat asked nonchalantly, "Do any of you

know Lieutenant Colonel Phra Narentharaksa who's just moved to Bangkok from Udon Thani?"

They were quiet for a moment before one of them exclaimed, "Oh, he's also been made a Phraya now! Colonel Phraya...er...let me think... Oh, I remember! Phraya Wisetsingnart. He's friends with Phraya Thepakanee."

Chat turned to face him.

"Are you sure?"

"Yes, I'm sure," he replied confidently. "He's a deft one. He snapped up the position of Phraya in Bangkok, and he might move to Khorat soon. I met him at a party once. His wife's a knockout!"

Chat's heart beat faster.

"Where did you see his wife?"

"He brought her to that party. She's like a movie star and was dripping with gold. Her name's Khunying Nuathong."

❋❋❋❋❋

Colonel Phraya Wisetsingnart stood on the balcony of his large house surveying the grounds. The lower floor was stuccoed brick, while upstairs was solid teak. It was built in so-called 'colonial' style with a rectangular ground plan and imposing balconies that wrapped around the house both upstairs and downstairs, making it look open and inviting.

The evening breeze blew gentrly around him as if he was standing outside, except that he was shaded from the sun by the wide roof. Nart took a deep breath and filled his lungs contentedly.

He was feeling like someone who had achieved success in everything he had dreamed of – honour and rank, reputation, wealth and status. He peered down onto the wide oval lawn surrounded by a gravel path. In the centre of the lawn, there was a pond with yellow and purple lotus flowers floating on the surface of the water. The gardeners were mowing the grass around the edges of the pond and neatly trimming the hedges around the lawn in preparation for the party in a few days' time. As Nart was watching the gardeners working, he noticed a shiny black car turn into the gate and gradually come to a stop in front of the house.

Two servants hurried out to meet the young woman in the car. White stocking clad legs in bright red shoes emerged from the car first, followed by a shapely figure in a red and white blouse and a bright red sarong. Diamond earrings and the diamond necklace around her neck sparkled, even though it was daytime and she had only been out to the shops.

When she looked up and saw her husband on the balcony, Nuathong gave a wide smile.

Phraya Wisetsingnat smiled back at her and leaving the balcony, walked into the bedroom. A moment later, his wife entered the room.

"Oh! Are you going out?"

"Yes. You're back late. I've been waiting for the car."

She walked towards him and put her head on his shoulder and enfolded him in her arms.

"Are you going to Ratchawong? Can I come too?" she cajoled.

"I'm not going to Ratchawong. I'm just going to Det's house."

"I can drop you off at Det's house, then go to Ratchawong with Malai, and pick you up on the way back," she coaxed. "I don't want to stay at home by myself. I'll be lonely."

"You can go and see Malai, but you shouldn't hang out with some of those friends of yours. When you gamble with them, you lose a lot of money. I don't like it."

"Oh, I just have a little flutter now and again," she replied playfully. "But I never play for much. The rent for this place is already two or three thousand."

Colonel Phraya Wisetsingnart did not own the house, even though he and his wife lived there proudly. His higher rank and the society he kept in Bangkok made it hard for him to turn down the luxurious lifestyle that he now enjoyed, which was in complete contrast to the simple life he had experienced in Udon Thani. Moreover, his wife had embraced their new lifestyle wholeheartedly.

Fortunately, his salary was enough to keep his wife in the manner that she desired, and in a few days' time, they would be hosting a party to jointly celebrate Nart's promotion to Colonel Phraya and the former Phra Ritdaeso's promotion to Phraya Thepakanee.

Although they were as comfortable as they could be, Phraya Wisetsingnart prudently reminded his wife, "I know my salary has increased, but everything's more expensive in Bangkok than in Udon. You shouldn't spend money wastefully, especially not on playing cards. Go easy on that."

Nuathong didn't think it was a big deal. In fact, she thought it was trivial and told him, "Everyone thinks we're from upcountry because we've just moved to Bangkok. I need to make friends, and if I don't play cards, I won't get to know anyone. I don't play for much money."

The new friends with whom Nuathong had become close since moving to Bangkok was a group of women who played cards together. All of them were the wives of high-ranking government workers or prominent wealthy men, who did little else from day to day but feed off their husbands' wealth. For relaxation there was nothing better than a set of playing cards and a pile of money, along with snacks galore. Indeed, they could play all night long until the next morning without getting tired.

Nart was puzzled at how quickly Nuathong had acquired a taste for gambling. In fact, he felt that she was becoming addicted to it. She said she had been to someone's house where they had been playing cards, and told him that she would try her hand for the first time. But it seemed to him that she had played before, and after that she played almost every week, until now she played almost every day.

Nart was alarmed at the amount of money she sometimes lost, and could not ignore it.

"Last time you lost a hundred baht. Are you saying that's not much money?"

She wasn't bothered and answered brightly, "You win some, you lose some. I'm always careful. I've got back everything I lost, and I made a profit."

Her clever answer ended the matter amicably, and a moment later, she took her husband by the arm and led him back to the car, which she had just got out of less than half an hour earlier, in order to go and meet their friends.

That day, Colonel Phraya Thepakanee had invited several friends to his home, but they looked tense as if they had business to discuss, rather than enjoying a social visit.

Nuathong whispered to his wife to invite her to go for Chinese food in Ratchawong, and she answered, "Good idea. I've been wanting to invite Surai. She doesn't go out much."

"Surai?" she asked, frowning, and then cried, "Oh, Surai! The one that got married before anyone else. What happened to her?"

Malai knew full well that Surai's marriage was an unhappy one, but she did not want to gossip, so she answered evasively, "She has a son now. She lives in Din Sor Road. Tell the driver to drive slowly. I'm afraid I don't remember the way in. He'll have to park outside and we'll walk in."

Nuathong grumbled when the driver pulled up at the side of the main road. She and Malai had to walk across a long wooden bridge above the surface of the narrow street, which led to the front of Surai's house.

"It's too far! What a nuisance!" she exclaimed, bending down to look at the high heel of one of her brand-new red leather shoes as if she had never had to walk before. "Can't we let the driver go and fetch her? We can wait in the car."

"If you do that, she'll never come out," Malai warned. "She'll think you're looking down on her."

Nuathong pursed her lips and opened her umbrella to protect her delicate skin from the strong sun. She ordered the driver to ring the bell when they arrived.

"Tell the servant that Khunying Wisetsingnart and Khunying Thepakanee are here to see Surai. Tell her to hurry up and open the gate. We're dying from the heat."

She sounded important, so the servant hastily opened the door. When she stepped inside the gate, Nuathong's sharp eyes noticed nothing that indicated privation. It was a beautiful and tidy house, but she still managed to find fault with it.

"How can Surai stand it with all the windows shut?"

Malai did not answer and walked up the stone steps onto the narrow veranda in front of the house before going inside to the living room. The servants opened the shutters to let the light in, and almost at once, a man and woman appeared at the door. Malai put her palms together to greet her friend's husband and smiled at her friend before telling him politely, "I've come to see Surai. I haven't seen her for ages. Are you both well?"

Chat returned the gesture and smiled cheerfully, giving no sign that just a moment earlier he and his wife had been arguing heatedly.

"Yes, we're both well. And yourself?"

"Fine, thank you." She indicated her friend with her palm. "This is a friend of mine and Malai's...Nuathong. She's the wife of Chao Khun Wisetsingnart. Surai, you haven't seen Nuathong for ages. You haven't forgotten her, have you?"

"Malai said that you were Khun Chom Amphan's brother," she said in a confident manner. "When I was little, I remember Khun Chom used to order from the catalogue of my father's department store."

She said "my father's department store" with a straight face, leading him to believe that her father was the owner of the most expensive department store in the capital.

Surai looked at her friend in annoyance.

"Your father was a clerk there. I remember, Nueang."

Nuathong's face flushed red in anger.

"I changed my name ages ago," she retorted when she had collected herself. "And my father earned a good salary."

She turned to Surai's husband. He was both annoyed and amused, but then he suddenly remembered something that he'd forgotten all about. This glamorous young woman was Khunying Wisetsingnart!

Wisetsingnart. The new title of Lieutenant Colonel Phra Narentharaksa!

Sensing the tension that had arisen, Malai quickly changed the subject.

"We've come to invite Surai for noodles in Ratchawong. You don't mind, do you, Chat?"

"No, I..."

"I'm not going," Surai retorted, ignoring her husband. "Thanks for inviting me, but you'll have to excuse me. I'm not feeling well."

"Perhaps Ratchawong's not fancy enough for her. She can come to the party at my house instead. It will be a big party, Surai. Malai, you've invited Surai and Chat, haven't you? You will come won't you, Chat?"

Surai didn't answer and turned to go. Chat felt the same way as his wife for once, and wanted to shut the door in her face. He was about to refuse when he remembered his sister's request, and realized that it would be a good opportunity to meet Colonel Phraya Wisetsingnart.

"Yes. Thank you," he answered in contrast to what he was thinking, but he couldn't resist putting her in her place, "I expect you'll send an invitation. I wouldn't go to someone's party if they didn't know the right etiquette."

Nuathong bit her lip when she realized she'd been corrected. Malai, who was standing next to her, feeling hot and cold, quickly defended her.

"I sent an invitation to Surai a while ago, and I told her a month ago. It's a party to celebrate our husbands' promotions. We're having it at Chao Khun Wisetsingnart's house...Oh, yes, Surai said that in Khun Chom's house, they're well known for making keepsakes and sweetmeats, so I asked her to help. I don't know if she's done anything about it, yet."

"Er, I don't know if she's let my sister know. It's best if you go to her house yourself. It's right next to my house."

As soon as they had walked down the steps that led to the gate, Nuathong said angrily,

"I'll wait in the car." Nuathong took a handkerchief out of her white leather bag and dabbed her face. "It's hot. If you're going, you can go alone."

Malai had no other option than to say, "In that case, I'll leave it for another day because if I go to see Khun Chom I might be there a while, and we have to go to Ratchawong."

❋❋❋❋❋

"Sap!" Chao Chom Amphan called her trusted housekeeper up to see her after the guest who had been visiting all morning had gone home.

"Yes, madam," Nai Sap answered respectfully, kneeling before her.

"Khunying Malai has just left. She's asked us to make keepsakes and sweetmeats for a party to celebrate the promotion of her husband, Phraya Thepakanee and his friend. It's on the first of next month."

Nai Sap put her hand on her chest.

"Oh, good heavens! That's in six days' time and she's just told us. How are we going to get everything ready in time?"

"Exactly," Khun Chom replied. She shook her head in irritation as she continued, "She asked Surai over a month ago, and my sister-in-law has been so busy arguing with her husband that she forgot to tell me. It's a good job Malai came to tell me. Otherwise, they would have been without sweetmeats at the party."

Nai Sap looked worried, but she didn't say any more when she found out it was Surai, realizing that, since Surai was her sister-in-law, Khun Chom was bound to make allowances.

"And what are we to do, madam? Did you refuse her?"

"I hadn't the heart to refuse. It wasn't her fault. When I told her I didn't know a thing about it, Khunying Malai looked most upset."

Khun Chom turned to the round bamboo tray of utensils next to her and picked up a piece of paper with her notes.

"The desserts we have to make are *ja mongkut* and *thong ake.* You'll need to prepare enough for a hundred people. The sweetmeat should be something we don't need to prepare in advance. It can be made at the party."

"What would that be, madam?"

Khun Chom looked past her housekeeper at the young woman who had just crawled inside and was sitting on the floor, and smiled.

"Gade, I'd like your help. You were asking what sweetmeat, Sap? *Kanom krok* would be just the thing! You can make it fresh and steaming hot at the party. It will be fun, don't you think, Gade?"

Nai Sap looked at her sideways until her pupils disappeared inside her head.

"*Kanom krok* is a sweetmeat for commoners, madam. Don't you think it should be something classier?"

Nai Sap felt that she was close enough to Khun Chom to disagree with her, and it was only natural for her to feel jealous when Gade won her approval. Khun Chom was aware of this and glanced at her sternly before replying coldly,

"Gade's *kanom krok* uses a recipe from the palace. My mother taught it to the people in the governor's residence. Don't talk about things you know nothing about, Sap, or you'll make a fool of yourself."

Nai Sap's face fell and she was silent.

"Gade," Khun Chom said, turning to face her. "On the first of the month, I'll need your help supervising the girls in the house to make *kanom krok* at the party...If I remember rightly, it's at the house of Phraya Wisetsingnart. I don't know him and I'm not going myself, so I'll need you to be in charge of the girls who are making the sweetmeats. You'll need to dress well. You mustn't look scruffy, or it will reflect badly on me. If you don't have an outfit, I'll find you one."

Gade placed her palms together before her.

"Thank you, madam."

"There's no need to thank me," Khun Chom chuckled softly. "I'm asking for your help. This is a soldiers' party, so you might see your husband there."

Gade got goosebumps in anticipation, and realized that this was Khun Chom's way of helping her to find her husband. After hearing no news for so long, she was about to give up and return to Phetchaburi because she missed her son so much.

"Yes, madam."

Nai Sap glared at Gade resentfully. Gade felt that no matter what she did, Nai Sap was always displeased with her, but she tried not to take offense for Khun Chom's sake, and out of her own necessity. This time was no exception, and when Nai Sap went into the kitchen, she began to make a fuss. In actual fact, this party was no bigger than other parties she had prepared for, but if she was involved, Nai Sap wanted to make sure everybody knew it was a matter of importance.

"Oh, you girls will like this party, I'm sure! There'll be lots of soldiers for you to flirt with," she told the servant girls sarcastically, but Gade didn't answer.

"Are you sure, Chat?" Chao Chom Amphan exclaimed when she heard her brother's story about the husband of the young woman who was staying with her. She considered his words carefully before concluding, "Then Gade's the principal wife. She had a proper wedding and the guests were witnesses."

Chat had never seen Gade's husband, but he envisaged him as an older man who was always infatuated with new young women. Gade could not depend on such a man. Perhaps she would be better off with a man who had finished with his first wife and was ready to begin a new life with her. He communicated only half of this to his sister.

"I expect Chao Khun Wisetsingnart's an old man who wants a young wife to look after him. He's probably bored of his old wife and wants a new one. Gade can't expect much from him."

Khun Chom looked at him disapprovingly.

"He wouldn't be that cruel to his son. He still sends money home."

That was true. Gade had a son. Chat had almost forgotten, since she was still so young that it was hard to believe she had a child. He tried probing a little.

"What if he really is that cruel and he wants to finish with her? What would Gade do?"

"What would Gade do?" Khun Chom repeated. "She would go back to live with her parents and siblings in Phetchaburi. She couldn't stay here by herself."

She was unaware that her answer had lit a fire inside the young man who didn't say a word, not daring to reveal what he was thinking, because he knew that his sister would disapprove and give him a lecture.

It was Gade's first time inside Khun Chom's bedroom. It was open like what Gade called a 'Western room'. There were long French windows almost all the way around the room, but the lower half of the windows were slotted to allow the air to circulate, even when it was very hot. Her bed was ebony with delicately crafted pale pink and blue mother-of-pearl inlay in the shape of swans and lotus with a small pearl cupboard at the bedhead. The wardrobe and dressing table were also made of ebony with European-style spiral legs, fashionable during the reign of Rama V. Everything had been polished until it shone and and indicated that she had been used to living in grandeur.

Khun Chom was sitting on the bed when Gade crawled inside and placed her palms together. She took the blouse and sarong that were folded next to her and gave them to Gade.

"This blouse and sarong of mine are still new. I'm giving them to you. Have them altered so the style's up to date and they'll be suitable for you to wear at the party."

Gade took the clothes with trembling hands, noticing that they were made of lace and were probably very expensive because they were soft to the touch, not coarse like the lace sold in the markets. The blouse was pale green, the colour of jasmine stems, unlike the colour of any lace she had seen before, while the sarong was a little darker than the blouse with silver brocade flowers and silver trim. It was even more beautiful than the faded lotus outfit she had worn on her wedding day.

Gade was too happy to speak and held the clothes to her chest, while Nai Khim laughed kindly, "Look at Gade! She looks like she's been struck dumb!"

Gade came to her senses and placed her palms together before Khun Chom with a lump in her throat in gratitude for her kindness.

"It's so kind of you, I don't know what to say…"

Her eyes filled with tears until she couldn't see the sympathetic and anxious expression on Khun Chom's face clearly, but Nai Khim was astute enough to notice and sighed. The old wet nurse had heard all about Gade's husband and his new wife from Khun Chom. From her years of experience, she and Khun Chom were sure that the life course of the young girl from Phetchaburi would not be as smooth as she hoped, but in their wisdom, they did not share their thoughts with Gade. They both agreed that when Gade met her husband again, Phraya Wisetsingnart should see his wife looking as beautiful as possible in order to restore their relationship more easily, even if it could not go back to how it was.

Nai Khim brought the matter to a close, saying, "Khun Chom is so kind to everyone. You just keep on working hard and being honest and she'll be happy. I tell you what, you go and try on that outfit, so we'll be able to adjust it in time for the party."

When Gade had crawled out of the room and Nai Khim was sure she was out of earshot, she whispered to Khun Chom, "Do you think it will work, madam?"

Khun Chom smiled.

"I think so. When Gade's all dressed up, she can rival any girl in Bangkok, and when her husband sees her, he'll be sorry."

"That's how men are. No matter how much they love their first wife, if they meet someone prettier, they soon fall in love, especially soldiers. They say they all like beautiful women, don't they?"

"I don't know!" Khun Chom laughed. "I've never been married to a soldier!"

"Oh, you can laugh," Nai Khim sighed. "I don't like all this competing to be the principal wife. In your father's day, this would never have happened. Your mother made sure his minor wives knew their place. They were afraid of her."

"Gade's still too young for a minor wife to be afraid of her," Khun Chom replied sympathetically, having seen such situations before. "Chat said his new wife's cocky. She won't back down easily."

Then she added, "Before she goes to the party, send Gade to see me and I'll give her some jewellery to wear. The clothes alone won't be enough. She'll need some gold and diamonds to make her look splendid, so when her husband sees her, he'll realize she's fit to be his principal wife. After all, he's a Phraya now. He doesn't want anyone looking down on his wife."

"Yes, madam," replied Nai Khim, but she couldn't resist asking, "Which ones are you going to let her wear?"

"Go and close the bedroom door."

She got down from the bed and went to the low ebony cupboard with mother-of-pearl inlay next to the bedhead, taking out a set of keys from her waistband.

Khun Chom took one of the metal boxes from the top shelf and unlocked it with another key before opening the lid. Even though Nai Khim was accustomed to seeing her jewels, she couldn't help craning her neck to stare. Inside the box lined with red velvet, faded with the passing of time, were several compartments for different kinds of jewellery, and the gems sparkled and glistened.

"Gade will be supervising the *kanom krok.* She should wear a ring or two on her fingers."

Khun Chom was enjoying choosing the jewellery and picked up one thing after another for her old wet nurse to admire.

"What about emeralds? They'll match her green blouse. Green and red will be too flashy...or what about a bracelet? An arm bracelet will be too showy."

"Green to match her outfit would look nice, but don't let her wear the whole set of emeralds. It would be too much. I haven't seen it for a long time."

Chao Chom Amphan's beautiful face looked a little sad as she recalled the past that had long since gone and would never return.

"The set that the king gave me? I still have it. I haven't worn it for many years. Occasionally I get it out to polish. It's a shame I don't have a niece to give it to."

As she spoke, she took out the other metal box and opened it.

There were only three pieces of jewellery in it.

The first was a dark green Russian emerald necklace. The large rectangular emerald was surrounded by sparkling diamonds with two smaller emeralds on either side, and small emeralds alternating with diamonds along the length of the necklace; two emerald and diamond bracelets completed the set. Khun Chom's eyes had a dreamy expression when she touched the set that was special to her before she closed the lid and put it back. Then she turned to Nai Khim and smiled.

"I got carried away and lost track of time. I'll choose something now and give it to Gade before she goes to the party."

She opened the first box again and took out a pair of emerald earrings and an emerald pendant.

"Nowadays people prefer small jewels. My mother bought me these earrings when I was sixteen. They should be just right. And this emerald pendant will match her blouse. Oh! What about this ring? Do you think it's too big?"

Nai Khim took the ring which had a large diamond surrounded by smaller diamonds and said, "These diamonds are just the right size, but they're a bit dull. They need a polish to make them sparkle."

"I'll polish it myself. I don't want anyone to see. On the day of the party, call Gade to put it on and she can return it as soon as she gets back. The fewer people that see it the better."

Nai Sap's eyes nearly bulged out of her head when she saw Gade come down the front steps of the house ready to get in the car to go to the party. The servant girls, who were sitting in front of the house, all whispered to each other.

"Doesn't she look pretty? She's even prettier than Surai."

"She's really pretty. Much prettier."

The pale green blouse complemented her skin perfectly and contrasted with her black eyes and shiny back hair that was pulled up into an elegant bun. Khun Chom had lightly powdered her face and the high heels she wore with white stockings gave her added height. Most importantly, the sparkling emeralds and diamonds made Nai Sap reel.

Nai Khim hobbled out to see her off and remarked so that everyone could hear, "Gade's not a servant like you thought. Her husband's an officer, and now he's a Phraya. Someone as elegant and beautiful as Gade is destined to become a woman of status."

The last words made Nai Sap fall silent and all she could do was gaze in the direction of the car as it drove slowly out of the gate.

Chat arrived at the house of Phraya Wisetsingnart with Surai in her father's car.

When he had asked her to borrow her father's car, the first thing she had said was, "Why don't you ask to borrow your sister's car? She isn't going to the party, is she?"

Chao Chom Amphan's plan was a secret, so he had only told her half the truth.

"She needs it, so I can't borrow it."

"So I'll have to go grovelling to my father to ask for his car," Surai sighed loudly. "If he asks me why my husband can't afford a car, I won't know what to say."

"Tell him the truth that he let his daughter marry a man without a car. He knew that before we got married."

Inside the old but elegant car, the husband and wife sat ignoring each other, staring pointedly out of their respective windows the entire way.

The grounds of the house were extensive and it was clear that it had been decorated for a party. Along the fence were coloured lights that had not yet been switched on and there were palm trees and yellow betel trees along the edge of the lawn, which had a pond with a fountain in the middle. The mist from the fountain sparkled against the evening sky.

Chairs and tables were arranged in groups on the lawn and small booths had been arranged in different spots for guests to help themselves to snacks to take the edge off their hunger before it was time for the main course. Most of the guests had not arrived yet, and only the host's servants and close friends were there, helping to get everything ready. There was a platform on one side for Thai stringed instruments, and the musicians were lifting their instruments onto it.

The first thing Surai said when she stepped down from the car was, "I thought people had no money nowadays because they're out of work, but Nueang's showing off like she's wealthy. How odd."

"Then your friend Nueang must be wealthy," he retorted.

"No she's not. She's just a commoner."

"Well, Chao Khun Wiset must be wealthy. He's not out of work."

Chat had never met Colonel Wisetsingnart, but he expected him to be middle-aged at least, and perhaps bald with a belly, his skin leathery and wrinkled from all those years upcountry. He would, no doubt, still have a twinkle in his eye, having been a womanizer since his youth, and he likely had two or three more pretty young minor wives to attend to him in addition to the attractive young wife that he took to parties. But when he walked up to greet the host, who had just walked down the marble steps, he was shocked to realize that he had been completely mistaken.

The man in the dashing uniform, who commanded the respect of everyone, looked young and handsome, and his eyes smiled along with his lips. When Chat had collected himself, he put his palms together and bowed his head.

"Chat, Surai," he greeted them in a voice that was both friendly and authoritative. "Please thank Khun Chom for her kindness in helping out with this party. I know it was short notice."

Chat had regained his composure.

"You're most welcome," he answered with equal politeness, feeling strangely uneasy when he thought of the young woman who was on her way. "Er...have you tried the sweetmeats, yet?"

It was a strange question, considering they had only just met, but Phraya Wisetsingnart did not look surprised.

"No, not yet. I expect they'll bring some up to the house soon. Make yourselves at home. Surai..." he smiled at the young woman at Chat's side, "if you want to see Nuathong, you might have to wait. My wife hasn't come down yet."

Surai forced a smile. Colonel Phraya Wisetsingnart's manner and the way he talked about his wife led her to compare him with her own husband, and her dissatisfaction showed clearly on her face. This resulted in her blurting out, when they were out of the host's earshot on the lawn, "We don't have honour or rank, so he didn't invite us in the house. We have to stay outside."

"He probably doesn't know my father was a Phraya," Chat whispered in irritation. "If you're going to find fault with the hosts, you'd better go home. There's no point staying if you're going to be miserable."

Surai replied angrily, "Fine. I didn't want to come in the first place. If I wasn't friends with Nueang, you wouldn't have been invited."

"Don't talk rubbish! I'm Khun Chom Amphan's brother. Of course, I'd have been invited."

Surai saw her father's car was parked outside the fence and suddenly stormed off leaving her husband behind. She got in the car and, taking a lace handkerchief out of her small leather purse to wipe her tears, ordered the driver, "Take me home. To my home, not Chat's."

"Where did Surai go? I saw her suddenly walk out the gate," Malai asked Chat quizzically, and he answered with a nonchalant smile.

"I expect she left something at home. She'll probably be back soon."

Having fended off her curiosity, he paid no more attention to his wife's friend, and looked for his sister's car expectantly. An old van had brought the ingredients and utensils for making the sweetmeats ahead of time, and Tieng had set them up at the station on the edge of the lawn. After a while, Khun Chom's car followed. The young woman in the pale green outfit caught everyone's attention the moment she stepped down from the car.

The hostess had still not finished getting ready, which was a boon for Khun Chom's plan, and Chat hastily told Malai, "My sister's representative is here. She's come to supervise the girls who are making *kanom krok*. They're going to make it hot and fresh and take it to Chao Khun in the house."

Malai looked at the lovely young woman walking towards them and wondered how the beautiful girl with the sweet face was related to Khun Chom. Her clothes and the jewels that sparkled against her smooth skin indicated that she was not a commoner. She thought she'd seen her before, and when she bowed her head and put her palms together, Malai, impressed by her manner, returned the gesture with equal politeness.

"Come with me," she said warmly. "I've set everything up for you under the trees. I hope you'll come and eat with us later."

"Thank you," Gade replied graciously.

Malai wanted Chat to introduce them, but he said instead, "Chao Khun is in the house?"

"I expect he is," Malai answered, not understanding his remark. "My husband's in the house, too. The guests will probably be here soon."

Chat looked at Gade quizzically and Gade looked back at him as if to say she didn't know what to do, and was waiting for him to tell her. He suddenly realized Gade didn't know that her husband was the host. He could take her inside the house to meet Phraya Wisetsingnart, and he knew he ought to, but for a reason he could not explain, he was reluctant to let this beautiful girl slip away. Even though she had no idea of his feelings for her, Chat wanted to prolong the time spent with her as long as he could, even if it was only by a few minutes.

"Go and supervise the girls making the sweetmeats," he said quietly, so that only the two of them could hear.

Gade was puzzled.

"I haven't met the host yet, Chat. I should really pay my respects to him first."

"Er…" the young man faltered and hurriedly replied, "Wait a while. He hasn't come out yet."

The girls who had come with Gade began the work that she had carefully taught them. The batter that they had prepared ahead of time was poured into the small wells in the earthenware stoves and soon after, there was a pleasing aroma of chopped prawns stir fried with garlic and pepper. Gade arranged the *kanom krok* garnished with coriander on the porcelain plates from Europe that Malai had placed on a silver tray for the host and his important guests. As Gade arranged the sweetmeats, her mind drifted back to the event that seemed so long ago, even though it had only been a few years.

At Klai's ordination, her relatives had all got together. Young and old had fun together, were full of food, joy and merit, and Gade's life had been changed forever.

Someone had stepped inside the house, and everyone had been in awe. He was tall and dignified with broad shoulders and a straight back. His face was tanned from the sun and his voice was deep.

"I never thought I'd find kanom krok topped with shrimp in Phetchaburi. It tastes like what the aristocrats in Bangkok eat... I'd like to see her and reward her."

And that reward had changed her life, in a way that none of her relatives or even she herself could ever have imagined, until Gade was not sure if that reward had been a blessing or a curse. The servants took the tray of sweetmeats to the host, and a few moments later, Gade was invited to meet him.

Gade looked for Chao Chom Amphan's younger brother to go with her, but she couldn't see him in the crowd of guests that had filled the lawn. The yellow evening sun had set. The sky was lit up by the light of the full moon and the first star appeared shining in the sky. The string ensemble played Thai music in harmony with the atmosphere and made Gade start for a moment.

"Tonight's the night my heart delights in the moonlight,

Please come, my love, and sit with me as the breeze blows the scent of jasmine."

Gade felt her ears ringing, and her eyes went blurry for a moment.

A night full of stars..

The song from her wedding night. Nart had liked to sing it softly when he was in a good mood with nothing to do. Since he had left for Udon Thani, Gade had not heard the song again. Was it a good omen that she was going to find her beloved husband, so the gods had given her this song to let her know, so that she wouldn't be too overwhelmed with happiness?

Her eyes filled with tears and blurred her vision of the steps going up to the house, but she forced herself to walk carefully up each step into the living room.

Gade saw several men sitting down. They were all wearing uniforms like the one that Nart had worn. She felt her knees go weak and fell to her knees with her palms together, but dared not look up at any of them.

A young woman walked towards her and helped her up, saying cheerfully, "Come this way. Khun Chom's sweetmeats are so delicious that Chao Khun wants to know who made them so he can give you a reward."

Gade looked up and the lights that illuminated the room fell on the figure of a man who stood up the moment she looked up at him. He was tall and dignified with broad shoulders and a straight back, and his skin was tanned from the sun. His eyes pierced her soul as they had pierced the soul of the seventeen-year-old girl from Phetchaburi the first time they had met.

"Gade...Is it you?" Colonel Phraya Wisetsingnart blurted out as if he couldn't believe his eyes when he caught sight of the young woman in the pale green outfit. At the same time, the stylish woman who had been sitting next to him also stood up.

7
When Love is Shunned

"Gade..." Phraya Wisetsingnart repeated his former wife's name in amazement. "Is it really you? Am I hallucinating?"

He went towards her and caught her instinctively, without thinking about anyone else in the room, particularly his present wife. He had not forgotten her, but whenever he thought of his wife in Phetchaburi his memory was of the last time he saw her – the thin, pale girl who had just recovered from a fever, holding a baby as tiny as a kitten in her arms. The image of his radiant bride on their wedding day had faded from his memory.

Now that beautiful girl in a stunning outfit was holding onto him tightly with her face buried in his chest, sobbing in his arms.

"Gade..." Phraya Wisetsingnart repeated again in confusion. "Don't cry...Tell me what you're doing here."

Gade remembered the white linen handkerchief that Nai Khim had tucked into her waistband before she left, as if she knew she would need it, and wiped the tears from her face. She collected herself before answering in a trembling voice, "Nart...I've found you at last. I searched for you everywhere."

At that moment, she felt someone else come up close to her husband and tug the sleeve of his shirt, followed by the high-pitched screech of a woman's voice, "What's going on? Who is this woman?"

That voice was like a lightning bolt and Gade drew back from her husband's arms, startled. At the same time, she saw the radiant, but furious face of a strange woman standing next to Nart and forcefully tugging on the sleeve of his shirt. Her eyes were as fierce as a tiger about to rip into its prey.

Gade felt the hairs on the nape of her neck stand up and her arms and legs turned to ice. She instinctively knew who the woman was without needing any explanation.

"Nart…" Gade heard herself ask, "And who is this woman?"

Phraya Wisetsingnart released his former wife from his arms and turned to his new wife hesitatingly. Out of the corner of his eye, he could tell from his friends' behaviour that they realized what was going on. When none of his friends said anything, Nart thought desperately how he could resolve the matter calmly.

He decided to reply to Nuathong first.

"Darling, I told you about Gade, didn't I? She's the one from Phetchaburi." Then he turned to Gade. "Gade, this is Nuathong...She's been taking care of me since I lived in Udon. It's time you met her."

Gade's heart began to beat erratically like a dry leaf tossed by a gust of wind the moment she heard her husband call the other woman 'darling'. She closed her eyes and opened them again to make sure she was not hallucinating.

"Nart…" Gade heard a voice coming from her throat, so dry it was sore. "Do you have another wife?"

Nuathong lifted her chin and looked Gade up and down from head to toe. On the one hand she told herself to accept the situation, but on the other hand she was astonished that Nart's upcountry wife was more beautiful than any high-society girl she had ever seen, and the only thing that indicated she was not from Bangkok was her accent, so she replied boldly, "Yes, I'm Nart's wife. We've been together for several years. Everyone in Bangkok knows."

Gade forced herself to stand up straight. She refused to faint or cry and make a scene in front of this woman. The suffering she had endured for all these years had become a shield to protect her bruised heart from any more pain, so Gade asked her husband, "Is this true? In that case, what am I?"

"You're my wife and the mother of my son. Nothing has changed. Nuathong is also my wife and she takes good care of me. If you care about me, you'll try to get along with her without being jealous."

Nuathong lifted her chin once more. Her husband's answer made her feel that she had the upper hand. Yes! He would never leave her for someone else. He might feel sorry for his former wife, but it was Nuathong he loved, so she spoke up, "You know me well enough to know I'm not the jealous sort. All I ask is that she doesn't bully me, because we're equals. There isn't a principal wife and a minor wife."

Equals? This woman considered herself Gade's equal? Gade looked her in the face. She was as flashy as a chorus girl. Gade had no idea that Nart liked this kind of woman, so she replied, "We can't be equals. Nart's married to me, so I'm the principal wife. If you're also Nart's wife, then you're the minor wife."

"How dare you!" Nuathong screamed, causing everyone in the room to start.

"Keep it down! You're making a scene!" Nart warned her.

Nuathong's wrath had reached boiling point. Her voice became louder until everyone in the room was uncomfortable. Phraya Thepakanee glanced at his wife, motioning her to intervene, so she did.

"Nuathong…" she said soothingly, shaking her gently to warn her. "Don't lose your temper. The guests outside will hear. Our most important guests will be here soon."

Nuathong spun around and retorted, "And what do you expect me to do? This woman suddenly shows up and claims to be Nart's wife when I've been living with him for several years. He finished with her ages ago. Everyone knows that. Now he's been promoted, she claims to be his wife!"

The men started to leave the room, not wanting to get involved and in order to prevent the other guests from entering. Nart didn't know what to do and finally said :

"Please don't cause a scene in front of the guests. There are important people coming."

Nuathong gave Gade a look full of hatred before calmly but threateningly telling her husband, "I'll come out to greet the guests with you. I won't stand for her coming too. No matter what, I won't stand for it. Everyone knows I'm your wife. You don't want to humiliate me, do you?"

Malai took advantage of the opportunity to put a stop to the drama.

"You can discuss this later. Today's an important day. Let's not spoil it. Please."

All this time, Gade didn't say a word, but kept her eyes and her heart fixed on her husband's face.

"Nuathong, don't make a scene and embarrass me, please. Khunying Malai's right. Gade, go and wait upstairs. I'll have Man take you to sit in the back room and I'll meet with you later."

Lieutenant Colonel Phibun Songkhram hurriedly entered the room and said in a low voice, "Chao Khun Siraja Daeso, the Army Chief of Staff's here, sir."

The name was of such importance that Gade saw her husband leave the room immediately, paying no attention to the matter that was still unresolved. Malai tugged on her friend's arm imploringly and whispered, "Stop pouting and come and greet the guests."

Nuathong glared at Gade with such malice that the hairs on the back of her neck stood up, since she had never seen such a menacing look in anyone's eyes before. Then she turned on her heel and stamped out of the room, not forgetting to turn around as she reached the door.

"Man! Clear the table now! Remember, don't show your face!"

She directed the last remark at Gade and slammed the door behind her. Man came to his senses and picked up the tray, telling Gade in a trembling voice, "Come this way, madam. I'll show you downstairs. There'll be no one to disturb you there."

Gade stood frozen to the spot as if she had been turned to stone, and the cold spread from her heart to her fingertips.

"Man…" Gade tried unsuccessfully to stop her voice from shaking. "Man, has Khun Phra been with his new wife for long?"

Man's legs felt weak and he sat down on the floor with his legs to the side.

"Yes, madam."

Tears might have flooded her heart, but her eyes were strangely dry without a single tear.

"Since when?"

"Er...Come inside, madam," Man implored. "Don't stay here. Nuathong will see you and she'll be angry. Whatever you want to know, I'll tell you, but please come inside."

He called two or three young men to clear the table and hurried to open the door to the back room for Gade. Man sat on the floor in front of the chair, upon which Gade sank down. Gade's legs felt so weak that, if there had been no chair, she would have sat down on the floor.

Her voice trembled so much that she hardly recognized it.

"Tell me, Man. How long has Khun Phra been with this woman? Why didn't anyone tell me?"

Man had a good memory and he told her everything in detail, so that Gade knew the whole story within the next ten minutes. She found herself looking around her as if she had just woken from a dream. She was in a house that she had never been in before. It was a new world and everyone was alien to her. But the strangest thing of all was that the head of this house was a stranger called Colonel Phraya Wisetsingnart! Her Nart had disappeared without a trace the moment he left the railway station in Phetchaburi.

The music from the lawn in front of the house wafted into the silence of the backroom, and the singer's voice cut through her heart. How could she not feel betrayed when the song was 'A night full of stars', the song that Nart had sung to her on their wedding night?

"Bees flit and fly to jasmine blooms,
But I am many miles removed.
Their sweet perfume calls me back home."

Gade wanted to put her fingers in her ears. It was natural for bees, when they went away from one flower, to move to another, but Gade did not want to believe that Nart was among them.

Man observed her manner uneasily and finally, he asked, "Would you like something to eat, madam? I'll bring you something on a tray."

Gade shook her head. Her throat was dry and, although her stomach was empty, she felt bloated with pain.

"I can't eat anything," she replied frankly and, not knowing what else to ask, inquired, "When can I leave this room?"

Man looked at Gade sympathetically, and replied awkwardly, "Er...um...Chao Khun said for you to wait here."

Gade sighed. The title sounded strange to her.

"Chao Khun…" she repeated softly. "It sounds like you're talking about someone else. I don't know who that person is. I'm used to hearing Khun Phra. If I'm really his wife, then why do I have to hide?"

Man avoided eye contact and the expression on his face revealed his uneasiness.

"I don't want to hide. I want to see for myself what Nart's doing."

With that, Gade stood up, leaving Man unable to stop her, and walked out of the room.

Outside the door were three or four narrow concrete steps leading down to a small path made of large paving stones that went between the house and the bright red hibiscus hedge.

Gade followed the empty path to the corner of the house where she stopped and looked out onto the lawn.

The lawn was lit up with lamps, and the lights from the room in front of the house illuminated men and women moving about and having a good time in the middle of a Thai string ensemble. Gade caught sight of a couple among them and started. She felt a lump in her throat and her eyes welled with tears.

Nart and that woman!

A strange pain strangled her heart, her knees buckled and she had to lean against the side of the house. The ground seemed to sway, so she closed her eyes and shook her head, but when she opened her eyes again the ground was still rolling like waves until she dared not walk forward in case she fell.

"Khunying…"

She heard Man calling anxiously from behind her, making her jump, so she forced herself to turn around. Man dropped to his knees and looked behind him.

"This man has been looking for you, madam."

It was Chat. Her eyes were so blurry that she didn't see him at first, and only recognized him when he walked forward and was standing right next to her. He sounded worried.

"You've been gone for ages. I was worried, so I came to look for you. Hey, what's wrong?"

Gade moved away before Chat reached out to touch her without thinking.

"Nothing," she answered quietly, trying to compose herself. "Why were you looking for me?"

Gade had almost forgotten why she had come and suddenly remembered the sweetmeats that Khun Chom had assigned her to make.

"I'm so sorry! I completely forgot about the *kanom krok...*"

"It's not about that," Chat answered.

The lamps from the lawn illuminated the sorrowful and disappointed expression on her pale face and Chat was filled with pity. He had guessed that when she met her husband, there would be no easy solution.

"Have you met Chao Khun Wisetsingart?" he asked, knowing the answer already. "What did he say?"

Gade's lips began to tremble again.

"What did he say?" she repeated. Her heart began to pound again. "Nart didn't say a word. He made me hide away in a room, while he went out to greet his guests with his minor wife...You probably don't know…"

Before they had time to say anything more, a middle-aged woman in servant's clothes came hurrying towards them, calling Man in a husky voice.

"Man, hurry up! Chao Khun is asking for you...He says…"

She started when she saw Gade and stared at her strangely, making her uncomfortable.

"Er...I know, Tieng," Man replied hurriedly, turning to look at Gade as he said, "Please come upstairs, madam."

Gade turned back to the lawn and saw that Nart was no longer there. He must have gone inside the house and asked Man to fetch her.

The moment she had been waiting for had arrived.

The place that Tieng took her to meet the owner of the house was not the living room, but a balcony behind the house, which had large patterned tiles on the floor and a wooden railing entwined with pink and red Rangoon jasmine, shielding it from the eyes of the people in the house. A lamp shone on a white wooden chair, where Gade's husband was sitting.

Gade didn't realize that Chat had followed her and was standing behind her unseen in the shadows of the climbing jasmine, so that the couple could talk freely.

Colonel Wisetsingnart stared at his wife, from whom he had been separated for more than two years, with a feeling that was hard to describe. It was a mixture of gladness, puzzlement and awkwardness. He stared at her naturally wavy hair framing her perfect face. In her elegant clothes, she looked even more stunning than when he had first set eyes on her. When she began to kneel down as she used to do in respect for her husband, he quickly stood up and took both her arms to lead her to a chair.

"Gade, come and sit next to me...and tell me why you're in Bangkok. I had no idea I'd see you here."

Everything he said was true, especially the last part.

Yes! Nart, had not thought for a moment he would see his former wife, especially since his new life in the capital was so enthralling. He had a new position in the ministry, a new rank, and a new circle of friends as well as his old ones. Every day flew by in a whirl.

If he thought of his wife in Phetchaburi, he told himself, "I'm sending her money, so she's alright. When I'm free, I'll go and see her."

But yet another day passed without him ever being free. Who would have thought that such a country girl would have found him in the capital?

Gade tried to hold back her tears, telling herself that there was no point in crying.

"I…I'm staying with Chao Chom Amphan. My mother knows her."

Although she tried to speak with control, she couldn't help her voice from shaking.

"I haven't heard any news from you for over a year. Everyone thought you'd left me, but I didn't believe them. I knew you wouldn't leave me and Ned, but...but...nobody told me…"

Nart held his breath awkwardly and interrupted, "Didn't you get the money I sent you? I send you money every three months."

"I got it."

"Well then, how can you say you haven't heard from me?"

Gade looked at him reprovingly.

"I wanted to know if you were alright...I wanted to know when you'd send someone to fetch me and our son like you said you would before you left Phetchaburi...if Mark Keng wasn't too difficult. You said you'd send someone to fetch us."

Nart's face fell when his wife spoke of the past, but he answered calmly.

"Udon was difficult. You and Ned wouldn't have coped there. It wasn't easy like Phetchaburi. Didn't Klai tell you about it?"

She felt a stab of pain when she remembered Klai's silence. Even Rern, who had since become his wife, could not get a word out of him. Tonight, Gade understood Klai's silence for the first time. His love and sympathy for his cousin, added to his respect for Nart, had forced him to keep what he knew to himself. Revealing the truth would only have caused harm to both parties.

Gade's pain and resentment made her face her husband head on.

"No, Klai didn't tell me anything except that you were well. No one else told me anything. I didn't understand why, but now I know."

Nart looked away, and the look of shame on his face made Gade stop. He tried to avoid talking about his new wife, who by now was busy greeting the guests.

"You're staying with Khun Chom Amphan…" he said, recalling what she had told him. "Why are you staying in Bangkok? Why aren't you taking care of our son?"

If Gade had had a sharper tongue, she would have answered angrily.

"I told you I came to look for you. I haven't heard from you for over a year."

Gade's voice was no longer shaking, but was steady. She couldn't believe that while she had been desperately searching for him, he had been living in luxury only a few streets away, so busy enjoying his new life that he had not given his wife and child a second thought.

"Our son can talk now. He's been asking for you. He asked why he didn't have a father like other children, so I told him you lived far away."

Colonel Phraya Wisetsingnart felt hot from head to toe.

Hearing about his 'son' stirred feelings in him that he had never experienced before because the word 'son' had until now brought to mind a tiny wrinkled baby that cried like a kitten.

"Ned..." He said his son's name with a lump in his throat. "How old is he now? Is he walking?"

"He's three." When Gade spoke of her son, her throat tightened, but she forced herself to continue. "He's been talking since before he was one. Now he's as big as a boy of four or five. He's clever and he understands everything."

"Did you bring him to stay with Khun Chom Amphan?" he asked excitedly.

"I left him at home."

"Oh!" Nart cried in disappointment. "Why did you leave him? He's only three."

His reproving tone was like a slap in the face. Gade had been in Bangkok for only a few weeks and Nart accused her of leaving their son, when he had been gone for three years. Gade's voice became curt without her realizing, even though she had never spoken curtly to her husband before.

"My parents and Rern are taking care of him. I'm already imposing on Khun Chom. She was helping me find you, but there was no news. If I'd known where you were, I would have come to see you from the start, and I would have brought our son to see you."

Nart was silent and looked ashamed. Before he could say anything else, Nuathong burst out of the door onto the balcony and snapped, "The guests are leaving. You should come and see them off. Other things can wait."

Gade could not be sure if it was because Nart thought what she said was important, or because he thought she was important, but he jumped up at once.

"Really? Who's leaving?"

"Lots of people," she replied, giving Gade a dirty look. "Come and see them off and stop dithering."

Gade stared at her in disbelief. When she had lived with Nart in Phetchaburi, she had never even dreamed of ordering him about.

"Wait here," he turned to tell her, before striding out from the balcony. Nuathong glared at her in open hostility before turning on her heel and following him out. Gade stood up, having a good mind to go after them, but restrained herself. Although it was Nart's house, and even though Gade was the principal wife, she had only just arrived, so it wouldn't have been proper for her to walk around as if it were her own home.

There was a rustling from behind the Rangoon jasmine, followed by someone calling her name softly, "Gade...er...Khunying."

Of course! Gade suddenly remembered Chat and hurried down the stairs at the side of the balcony before seeing a man's figure stepping out of the shadows. The lamp shone on his face, revealing his anxious expression.

"Please call me by my name like before, Chat. I still…" She tried to find the right words and felt a lump in her throat. "I still don't know who I am."

Chat looked at her sympathetically.

"It will be fine…" he answered hurriedly, not having been given an opportunity to say anything other than words of comfort. "Don't be upset. From what I can see, Chao Khun isn't heartless. He still cares about his son, so that's...er...good."

Gade bit her lip and the pain she felt was replaced with confusion.

"Chat, are you going home, yet?" Gade asked, not knowing what else to say. "I don't know...if I should go...or stay. I don't see how I can stay here with that woman."

"True," the young man agreed. "If you were staying under the same roof as her, I'd be worried...er...I mean your husband would be worried. I'm not going, yet. I'll wait."

The last couple to leave was Phraya Thepakanee and Khunying Malai. He looked serious, as if he was hiding his unease about something, while she looked obviously uncomfortable. Phraya Wisetsingnart, however, maintained his composure and acted as if nothing had happened.

"I'll see you tomorrow evening. I won't forget."

In the end, Chat was the only guest left. Gade walked down from the balcony. She stood on the edge of the lawn watching the cars go out through the gate and looked at the lawn, which was quiet and empty except for the servants who were clearing up. All the musicians had left and the coloured lights had been put away. Only the dim rays of the moon shone on the grass.

"Gade," she heard Chat calling her softly, causing her to turn around to look at him. She did not know how long he had been standing there.

"Are you going back to Khun Chom's house, or are you staying here tonight?"

Gade felt a lump in her throat as she turned to look at the beautiful house. She looked up at an upstairs room, where the lights were still on, and knew who it belonged to.

"How can I stay here?" she asked a moment after, and her voice trembled with bitterness. "I haven't been given permission."

As soon as she had spoken, her husband walked back from seeing his friend off and walked back across the lawn to where the two of them were standing. The shadows helped to hide his expression as he peered at Chat. When he spoke, his voice was normal.

"Gade, are you going back, or will you stay here tonight?"

It wasn't only Gade who pursed her lips on hearing the question. It also jarred on Chat. Why did he have to ask her? Why didn't he say, 'Gade, I'm so glad I've found you. Don't go back tonight. You can stay here.'?

He was gratified when he heard her answer back coolly, "It's up to you. Do you want me to go back to stay with Khun Chom, or will you let me stay here? Whatever you think is proper."

Phraya Wisetsingnart was silent and reproached himself for giving her an opportunity to answer back. If he brought another woman to live in the same house, as his principal wife, Nuathong would never allow it, even though she herself had simply moved in with him. But could he call her his minor wife when she had never had a principal wife to compare herself to? It had been wrong of him not to tell her of her status since the beginning, but now, she had been with him the longest, while his first wife had only lived with him for a short time and then they had separated.

"I think…" he finally said with difficulty, "You've been staying with Khun Chom for a while. It wouldn't be right for me to suddenly bring you here. Go back for now and I'll go and ask her permission to bring you here."

The tears that had dried now welled up in Gade's eyes once more, and she asked at once, "How long do you expect me to wait? Days? Months? Years?"

He frowned and looked at Chat who stared back at him coolly.

"Perhaps tomorrow. No, I'm busy. The day after I'm not free. The day after. In three days' time, I'll go to see Khun Chom to thank her for helping you."

That was it. There was nothing more to say. After being separated from Gade for three years, he was in no hurry to bring her back to live with him when he saw her again. It showed how fragile the bond between them had become. Gade faced him head on as if she was imprinting his face in her memory for the last time. She placed her palms together to say goodbye.

"If you're so busy, please don't go to any trouble. Now I've seen you and I know you're alright, I can go back to Phetchaburi to be with my son."

Phraya Wisetsingnart started and was silent. Even Chat was surprised as he had not expected Gade to be so resolute.

"Gade, why do you have to be sarcastic? I said I'd come and fetch you. Don't make mountains out of molehills."

Sarcastic? Making mountains out of molehills? These were the accusations he welcomed her back with after she had searched for him so desperately, while the other woman, was simply warned not to make a scene. Chat couldn't help staring at him in disapproval and he felt himself getting so angry he couldn't contain himself, so he excused himself by saying he would wait in the car.

Gade bowed her head and took her husband's reproof without arguing.

"It's up to you," she repeated. "I'm sorry for the trouble I've caused you."

He frowned again in annoyance.

"If you're going to be sarcastic, then there's no point in talking. You should at least remember that this is a special day for me and my friend to celebrate our promotions and our titles of Phraya."

"Yes, I know," she answered. The bitterness she felt turned to blandness. "It's a special day for you. Now you've been promoted, all I can do is admire you from afar. I won't impose on you. You're out of my reach."

Phraya Wisetsingnart turned his face away. His anger could not bury his shame, and he answered gently, "I haven't forgotten that I'm your husband. You're my wife and the mother of my son..."

He suddenly thought of a way to ease the tension.

"I tell you what. Why don't you go and fetch our son from Phetchaburi? I haven't seen him since he was a tiny baby. Bring him to me. I want to see him."

When she heard her husband speak of their son, her throat tightened and her eyes welled with tears.

"Nart," she called him by his name and it felt strange. "Won't you come to Phetchaburi with me?"

He glanced around him as if to indicate his many responsibilities.

"I can't go anywhere at the moment. I've got so much work to do. It's better for you to go."

"And you want me and our son to stay here…do you?" she asked, "Or do you want us to stay with Khun Chom like I do now?"

He frowned again as if she was asking about trivial details, but he knew, in truth, that if he brought Gade and their son to live under the same roof, it would be no easy matter, at least at first.

"Bring him to see me first. Let's not talk about the details yet. I want to see him."

Downstairs, the doors had been locked and the lights were turned off. Colonel Phraya Wisetsingnart walked lightly up the stairs in contrast to the heaviness in his heart, since he expected his second wife to be sulking and ready to pick a fight when he entered the bedroom.

But when he opened the bedroom door, he was surprised. Nuathong was sitting in front of the dressing table. She had finished bathing and was wearing a low cut thin white silk nightshirt trimmed with lace and a sarong. She had dusted her arms and shoulders with talcum powder and was fragrant with the scent of European perfume. When she saw her husband enter the bedroom, she hurriedly stood up and took him a towel and a change of clothes.

"Do you want to bathe? It will make you feel fresher."

When she said that with her usual smile, he breathed a sigh of relief.

"Good idea."

As soon as the bathroom door had been closed, Nuathong turned to her old servant and nodded for her to leave. She came away from the door and whispered, "Remember, Tieng. If that woman comes here when Chao Khun isn't home, don't let her in. Throw her out."

"I won't let her in, madam."

"Don't worry about anything. I'll deal with Chao Khun myself. You can go."

When Tieng had left the room, Nuathong paused for a moment and prepared herself for the scene that she would stage when her husband came out of the bathroom.

She had been extremely disturbed by the evening's events. In fact, when she had set eyes on her husband's first wife, she had been so shocked she had almost fainted.

She knew Gade had an advantage as his first wife, and with a son as a chain to bind him to her. If she were to claim her status as 'Khunying', even her husband would not be able to refuse her, but Nuathong knew his weakness for her wiles. If she were to defeat his first wife, it would be with her artfulness and nothing else.

When Nart emerged from the bathroom feeling fresher and more cheerful, he was met with a simpering display from his young wife. She knelt down and hugged his knees, and sobbed, "Please forgive me. I'm so sorry if I made you angry. It was only because I love you and I don't want to lose you. We've been through so much together and no one has ever come between us. Then she comes along and tries to tear us apart. I'd rather die than be separated from you!"

He had expected that she would sulk and cry as she had done earlier, but now that the opposite had happened, he was relieved. Along with relief, his heart softened and he was touched by her sincere apology, realizing that she had behaved that way because of her love for him. He made his voice reproachful, but so gently that she knew he wasn't really angry.

"Don't do it again. Stand up. No one can tear us apart. You overreacted."

Nuathong let her husband lift her up and she took advantage of the opportunity to put her arms around him and lay her head on his broad chest.

"If I didn't love you so much, I wouldn't be so upset. I'm just so afraid. If your first wife throws me out of the house, where will I go? I have no parents and I'm all alone in the world? What will I do?"

She began to sob and buried her face in his chest as if she was wiping her non-existent tears on his shirt.

"Who can tell me what to do? There's nothing to be afraid of," he reproached her and added, "Gade's not mean. You don't have to be afraid."

These last words showed the bond between them had not been completely severed. Nuathong hid her anger with difficulty. If Gade had been a piece of cloth or a piece of paper, she would have ripped her in two.

He might bring her to live under the same roof. Plenty of noblemen had a principal wife and a minor wife in the same house, but Nuathong saw the danger if 'that woman' brought her son into the house.

It was a pity that she had not been able to give him a child.

"Now you've given me your word, I'm relieved. Are you coming to bed? You've been taking care of guests all evening, so you must be tired. Let me massage you. Nothing else matters as long as I know you still love me."

She wrapped her arms around him and led him to the bed where the mosquito net was already hung. She turned off the lamp, leaving only the moonlight shining in through the window. And in that moment her charms ensnared him so tightly that he didn't give his first wife another thought all night long.

"And what will Gade do?" Chao Chom Amphan asked her brother, after he had told her the whole story in detail. She was disappointed, even though she had anticipated that there would be no easy solution to Gade's dilemma. Now, when things had turned out as she had feared, she felt downhearted.

"In the car on the way back, Gade told me she was going back to Phetchaburi."

"Going back to fetch her son, or going back for good?" she asked as if she were trying to guess what Gade was thinking.

Chat was sitting in front of his sister on the upstairs balcony. He picked up a small tube of her lipstick and twirled it open and shut, in agitation.

"I don't know. I think she might...she might go back for good. She was pretty upset about her husband."

"I sympathize with her. He didn't desert her, but it's as if he deserted her. He's obviously infatuated with his new wife," Khun Chom answered and continued in the manner of someone with more experience, "But, nevertheless, I don't want her to take offense and split up with him. What good will come of her going back to Phetchaburi?"

Chat lowered his gaze and hid his frustration with difficulty.

"Gade's still young. If she splits up with him now, she'll still be able to find a new husband who will really love her and not abandon her."

Khun Chom looked at him disapprovingly, and her voice was reproachful.

"What a strange thing to say! Who could be better than her husband?"

Chat was silent. He could not answer, 'Me, of course. I'm better,' because, apart from his family name, he did not have even half of her husband's other qualifications.

"At least she has her parents there," he said, finding words to mask his true feelings. "If she stays in the same house as his new wife, she'll be in for a rough time. That woman's got a nerve. Gade won't be able to stand her."

"It depends on her husband. If he's a good man, he won't allow his minor wife to bully his principal wife."

Chat couldn't contain himself any longer.

"Men soon forget their old flames when they find a new one. If you saw him, you'd understand. He's not old like I thought. He's good-looking and charming. Men like that are always unfaithful."

A shadow appeared at the door and Khun Chom turned to look. When she saw who it was, she called out to her cheerfully, "I was just talking about you and here you are! I was telling Chat I'm worried about you."

Gade crawled in to see her as she always did. Chat watched her every move, just as Chao Chom Amphan watched his every move, although he was unaware of it.

Today, Gade was dressed in her usual manner, in a plain white blouse and a sarong that was neither old nor new. Her face was free from makeup and looked a little pale, but in Chat's eyes, she was as beautiful as the moon behind the clouds.

Gade had no idea of Chat's feelings for her. She placed her palms together before Chao Chom Amphan as usual and carefully unwrapped the cloth with the jewellery that she had worn the previous day.

"I've brought it back, madam. Last night I got back late and I saw you were already in bed, so I gave it to Nai Khim to keep. This morning, she told me to return it to you myself."

"Thank you, Gade."

She took the cloth package and placed it next to her casually before getting straight to the point.

"Chat's been here since this morning, so he's told me everything. What are you going to do?"

It wasn't only Khun Chom who was wondering what she should do. Gade had lain awake all night wondering the same thing. Now she tried to answer as honestly as she could, since she had grown to respect Khun Chom almost as much as her own mother.

"I think I'll go back to Phetchaburi."

"You'll go back to fetch your son, or you'll go back for good?"

Chat listened intently for her answer.

If she went home, it would mean her relationship with her husband was over, and she would be free to start a new life with someone else without anyone blaming her. Gade was silent for a moment before she decided to answer the question truthfully. At this moment, there was no one she trusted more than Chao Chom Amphan, and she believed that her brother was also trustworthy.

"I don't know what to do. I'm undecided. On the one hand, I want my son to have a father, but on the other hand, I don't want to live with Khun Phra...I mean...Chao Khun."

She was still unfamiliar with his new title.

"...and suffer more. Now he's got a new wife, he isn't the same anymore. I don't want to live in misery with him."

Chao Chom Amphan was unperturbed by this dilemma. She had lived in a place full of women who had experienced the same kind of suffering. Every day, there would be rumours of which consort was 'in', which meant she had gained the king's favour, while others who had previously been favoured were now 'out'. Some, like Chao Chom, accepted their changing circumstances with equanimity, realizing that change was a part of life, and that it was impossible to expect the most illustrious man in the land to be true to only one woman.

So she answered Gade as a woman who was used to traditional Thai ways.

"Gade, as soon as a man has gone down the steps of his home, he's not the same anymore. It's men's nature. Your Chao Khun is no different from all the other men in Siam. But another way, in which I'm sure he's like other men, is that he won't desert you, especially if you have a child. You can trust me on that."

Gade bowed her head and swallowed her tears. They won't desert their children? Was this the only redeeming quality that men had? Was this enough to compensate for everything else? What about the love, faithfulness and loyalty that they had shared in Phetchaburi? What had happened to those things? Did they no longer have any meaning for her and Nart?

"He won't desert us. He's been sending money for the past few years, so I'm sure he'll continue to send it."

She answered bitterly with a throat as dry as her heart.

"My relatives said he wouldn't come back, and now I've seen for myself I know it's true. He doesn't want me anymore. That's why I want to go home. Ned and I can live with my parents. It's better than the humiliation of staying here. I can only depend on my husband for money, and nothing else. What's the point in staying together?"

"I'll tell you. I was just saying to Chat that no good will come of you going back to Phetchaburi. Don't take offense. Don't forget that you're not the girl from Phetchaburi anymore. You're Khunying Wisetsingnart…"

Chat couldn't help but blurt, "And what about his new wife?"

Khun Chom's reproving look told him she was displeased with his interruption, so he was silent at once.

"That woman is not a Khunying because Gade is the woman he married. I will refer to Gade as Khunying Wisetsingnart, and soon everyone else will as well. You just see if they don't."

When she spoke with such finality, he knew better than to argue with her.

"For another thing, if you don't separate from Chao Khun, your son will be known as the son of Phraya Wisetsingnart, and in the future, he'll get to be an officer like his father. Why would you take away your son's opportunities?"

Khun Chom's words were like an arrow hitting a target, and Gade's heart, which had been hardened by her anger and disappointment, was softened and her eyes welled with tears.

She placed her palms together before Chao Chom Amphan in response. She did not need to say any more except to answer, "Chao Khun said he would come to see you the day after tomorrow. The next day, I'll go to Phetchaburi to bring my son to his father."

Colonel Phraya Wisetsingnart walked up the steps of the Ministry of Defence with a solemn look on his face. He had been feeling out of sorts from the moment he woke up until he arrived at the ministry, and even Nuathong's cajoling had not improved his mood. There were two main reasons for his discontent. The first was that he had an important meeting with the Deputy Minister of Defence, and the second was that he had an uncomfortable feeling about some of his close friends.

Nart was in the habit of meeting his friends at a Chinese restaurant called 'Laow' in Yaowarat, or at Norasing coffee shop for social get-togethers after work. But lately on several occasions Nart had noticed that many of his friends had been meeting in their homes and he hadn't been invited. He wasn't offended at being left out, but he had a nagging suspicion that something was going on, which he did not know about. Although he had no evidence, he suspected that his friends were planning something major, but he could not bring himself to believe that one of his closest friends, like Colonel Thepakanee, would do something momentous without consulting him.

Nart believed that his friend Colonel Thepakanee was quite capable and bold enough, since Det had been presumptuous since his youth, but now that he had matured and reached a high rank, surely, he would not do anything foolish without talking it over first.

If he had, Nart would have dissuaded him. He sighed, pushing the thoughts that were bothering him from his mind, as he walked to the office of the Deputy Minister of Defence, Prince Alongkot.

The matter that he had called Nart to discuss was something that Nart had vaguely heard about, which was that he was to be appointed to a new position in Nakhon Ratchasima in a month's time.

"I know you've only been in Bangkok for a few months, but going to Khorat isn't bad."

This was how he congratulated him. He called him by his name, since he had known him since he was a boy and knew his father well.

"It's fitting that you should go there, Nart" he remarked, slapping Nart on the back.

"I don't want to lose you, but you're still young and there are more prospects of promotion if you go to Khorat. Here in Bangkok, all the top positions are taken, so it's hard to make progress."

Nart wasn't worried that he had to go upcountry. Nakhon Ratchasima was a big city in the Northeast where he knew almost everyone. It was like going home, and on top of that, there were opportunities for promotion.

Life in the capital was comfortable, but the cost of living was high. All his salary was spent on his rent, his household expenses, and his social expenses, the latter shockingly high. If he moved upcountry, this would no longer be a problem.

His thoughts turned to Nuathong. She would probably make a fuss at first because she enjoyed her city life, or perhaps, he could leave her here to start with and have her join him later.

"I'm going to Bang Khun Phrom Palace tonight," Prince Alongkot remarked. "Come with me."

This meant that he was meeting Prince Paribatra Sukhumbandhu, the Interior Minister, who was highly respected by everyone. It was an indication that Nart had found favour with him, and he gladly accepted the invitation.

*****

Later, Nart remembered that the day had begun like any other, and everything in the capital was peaceful as usual with no sign of danger. There were no soldiers, or even whispers of a 'revolution'. The news about it had gone quiet for months and the country's leaders had breathed a sigh of relief, thinking that it had been nothing more than a rumour. The king had gone to Klai Kangwon Palace in Hua Hin with several top military officers and his courtiers.

The stillness was like the calm before a storm, and Nart had never imagined that the lightning would strike so suddenly. Indeed, he had been so preoccupied with telling his wife about his transfer to Nakhon Ratchasima that he hadn't given a second thought to his friend whom he hadn't seen since the previous day.

"What? We've only just got here, and now you're telling me we have to leave Bangkok and go upcountry again! What did you do wrong to get transferred?"

"It's not bad news, It's good news," he told her patiently. "I'm supposed to be posted upcountry."

Nuathong turned her face away angrily.

"But it's so hard in the Northeast. It's so hot in summer and so cold in winter...How can you say it's good news? It's like living in hell."

He frowned and his irritation began to show in his voice.

"I tell you what. I'll go on ahead of you and you can stay in Bangkok until you decide you want to join me. I understand if you don't want to go."

Nuathong looked at him askance and pouted.

"How can I let you go alone? You might find a new wife there and I'll be left abandoned."

She spoke without thinking and didn't realize the truth of what she had said.

But that truth was like a blow that hit Phraya Wisetsingnart straight in the heart.

Left abandoned!

Tomorrow, he was going to meet Gade to sort things out, but now his fate had changed again and he would have to leave once more.

It seemed that destiny was not going to bring him and Gade together again.

Colonel Phraya Wisetsingnart appeared at Chao Chom's house in the evening on the day of their appointment. Khun Chom showed him respect by meeting him in the living room. He looked around the elegant room and the European decor reminded him of Rama V's reign, of which he had only a vague recollection because he had been just a boy.

But Khun Chom was even more surprising. Nart had never seen her before and only knew that she had been a royal consort of Rama V, so he expected her to be considerably older than himself, but when he saw her, he was shocked to find that she was still a beautiful woman, not the intimidating old lady of his imagination.

But as soon as he heard her speak, he was filled with respect for her.

"I'm most grateful that you've been so kind as to let Gade stay with you. I didn't know she was in Bangkok. I thought she was still in Phetchaburi."

"Gade's like my relative. She can stay with me as long as she likes, of course, but the fact is she's not alone. She has a husband and son. If she stays with me for too long, people will start gossiping that she's not doing her duty as a wife. After all, you're a man of high rank. I'll leave it to you to decide what to do."

And she turned to call her housekeeper.

"Sap, go and fetch Gade. Tell her Chao Khun is here to see her."

Nai Sap was sitting in the room staring at Nart without taking her eyes off him in excitement and surprise. She really wanted to go and gossip with the other servants, but when she heard her instructions, she crawled out of the room.

Since the day Khun Chom had ordered everyone in the house to call Gade 'Khunying', Sap had felt awkward about it. She was too resentful to submit, but too afraid to be defiant, so she awkwardly told the young woman outside, "She's asked for you...er...Khunying."

Gade tried to compose herself, but her hands and feet felt cold when she entered the living room. Her husband and Chao Chom Amphan were sitting on chairs, and Gade curtsied as she had always done. She looked past the lady who had been so kind to her to the man who she was no longer sure whether to call 'husband' or 'former husband'.

"Please have a seat, Khunying," Khun Chom said, smiling encouragingly. "Chao Khun has come to see you. I'll let you two talk to each other by yourselves. Please come up and tell me what you decide on."

When they were alone together, Phraya Wisetsingnart looked at his estranged wife in contemplation and asked her carefully, "How much does Khun Chom know?"

"She knows everything," Gade answered truthfully.

"So you told her everything, did you?" Phraya Wiestsingnart had not intended to find fault with her, but his tone of voice was harsh all the same.

Gade stared into his eyes, and her resentment returned.

"It isn't a secret, is it? Everyone knows what you've been doing in Bangkok. I was the only one who didn't know. Everyone at the army base in Phetchaburi knew. Whenever I went to collect the money, nobody would tell me where you were."

"Don't bring the army base into it. I didn't do anything that bad. I never missed sending you money, so I knew you were alright."

Gade stared at her husband in shock, after the shock of two days ago.

"Alright?" she repeated bitterly. "Everyone in Ban Tha Hin said the same thing...that you had deserted me, that you wouldn't be coming back, and that I should find a new husband, so I wouldn't be taken advantage of. I was the only one who didn't believe them. I came to look for you when I didn't have a clue how I'd find you…"

"What did you say? he interrupted, forgetting himself. "Your relatives have found you a new husband, have they?"

"I didn't say that. I said they told me to find a new husband, so I wouldn't be taken advantage of."

"And this new husband they've got their eyes on. Who is he?"

Her husband's voice was getting angrier and Gade wished she hadn't brought the subject up, since she hadn't intended to discuss it.

"If I remarried, it would probably be to a farmer, so that nobody could accuse me of trying to rise above my station."

Her voice began to shake, even though she had meant to stop her voice from trembling.

"Is that so? A farmer? I thought it was someone from a noble family. More noble than mine."

His voice was tinged with sarcasm and Gade was confused.

"What do you mean? I don't understand."

Phraya Wisetsingnart smiled mockingly.

"You ought to understand. You just said you're still young and you might be taken advantage of. Even in the country, you were lucky enough to find an officer for a husband. Now you're in the capital, you should find a new husband from a more noble family than your old husband. Then your relatives won't need to worry."

"I'm not a man who can keep finding new lovers. They say as soon as a man goes down the steps of his home, he isn't the same anymore. Now I've seen for myself that it's true."

Nart was silent and did not have an answer. Gade collected herself. To continue arguing was pointless, so she swallowed her bitterness and said quietly, "I don't want to argue with you. I'll ask you again. Where do you want me and Ned to live? If you want to finish with me, then I'll go back to Ban Tha Him like before. Tell me."

"You talk as if I'm throwing you out," he accused angrily. "Yes,

I think you should go back home because you've been away from our son for so long, and even though Khun Chom said she's happy for you to stay with her, you shouldn't impose on her. And for another thing, her brother lives right next door. Even though he's married, he's still a young man, so you should keep your distance."

The last sentence was like a needle in her heart.

"You mean Chat? Is that who you meant when you said a husband from a noble family?" she exclaimed. The idea had never entered her head, and if she had heard it from someone else, she would have been angry, but hearing it from her husband made her realize he really believed it.

"How can you accuse Khun Chom's brother of such a thing?" Gade retorted and became suddenly vexed again.

Phraya Wisetsingnart came to his senses, realizing that the more they argued, the less likely they would be to resolve the matter.

"Alright. There's no need to bring anyone else into it. I didn't come here to argue with you. I just wanted to tell you...that you should go back to Phetchaburi to fetch Ned. He's growing up and I haven't seen him."

Gade looked away and bit her lip as she tried to restrain herself from blurting out.

"Bring him here as soon as you can, because I have to move to Khorat in a month."

Gade spun around suddenly and her heart sank.

"Move to Khorat?" she repeated in disbelief and her heart began to race. "You're going again? I didn't think…"

"In a month," he repeated. "Bring Ned to see me before I go to Khorat. We'll talk about other matters later."

'Other matters' meant how he was going to deal with Gade and Nuathong as smoothly as possible, but until now he had no idea of how he was going to do it. Nart saw clearly that there would be trouble if both wives lived in the same house in Khorat. At the same time, there could only be one Khunying Wisetsingnart in the army base at Nakhon Ratchasima. There was no way that Nuathong would accept being second, and as for Gade, he could tell that she would not be willing to stay hidden away while another woman superseded her.

If he let her go back to live with her relatives in Ban Tha Hin, there would be another problem. Gade was still young, and her parents could easily assume he had finished with her and find her another husband, but he was not willing to allow that to happen, since she was still his wife. And for another thing, how could he allow his son to be raised by a farmer?

Or he could let Gade continue to live under Khun Chom's protection. He could provide the money for her to rent a house, or build her own house close by, so as not to impose on her too much. That seemed like a better option than either taking her to Khorat, or letting her return to Phetchaburi.

Except there was one problem, and that was Khun Chom's handsome younger brother, who might prove to be a thorn in his side.

8
The Starless Night

It was the night of June 23rd, 1932.

Colonel Phraya Wisetsingnart met his visitor in his office and gave an order not to be disturbed. His visitor was Police Lieutenant Colonel Phra Prabribupai, a relative and a trusted friend, whom Nart called Nop. The matter that they needed to discuss in private was something that could not be heard by a third party. What the police officer told him made Nart feel as if the storm that had been brewing had turned into a sudden lightning strike.

"When will they do it?"

"In the next few days. The leaders, as far as I know, are three Colonels: Phraya Songsuradet, Phraya Pahonphonphayuhasena, and Phraya Ritakanae. Under them is Luang Phibun Songkhram, and ..."

He paused for a moment before continuing carefully, "the minister, Phraya Thepakanee."

His answer made Nart feel as if the floor had given way beneath him.

"You mean Det has joined them?"

The police officer was silent, but his taut expression confirmed it more than any answer. Nart inhaled deeply and felt as shaken as if a storm was rocking his chest. He foresaw two possible scenarios. If the large tree that had stood steadfast and spread out its branches for the past hundred and fifty years, since Bangkok had been established, could withstand the storm until it died down, his friends would be sent to the gallows as 'traitors'. But if the storm, which Det had helped to create, succeeded in toppling the tree that had protected all the lives in the forest, his friends would be safe and would be successfully rewriting a new chapter of history. But what would the cost of toppling that tree be? Pictures of the bloodbath that had followed the French revolution flashed through his mind and chilled him to the bone.

"Nop," Nart said. "I'll go and see Det tonight and find out everything."

Nop raised his hand to stop him.

"Please listen to me. I don't agree. First of all, on what grounds will you stop Chao Khun Thepakanee? He's not acting alone. He's part of a group and has been with them from the start and helped with the planning. They won't listen to you. And for another thing, it's a secret. If it leaks, heads will roll. You're not supposed to know about it. If you know, you'll be in danger. I'm worried. That's why I'm warning you."

His stark warning silenced Nart for a moment as he weighed up the situation, but he finally answered resolutely, "My best friend's on one side and my sovereign, whom I honour, is on the other. I can't not do anything. If I plead with Det and he doesn't listen, I'm willing to die, but I won't tell him who told me. I won't get you into trouble. If he starts to relent, I might ask someone else to talk to him. If the minister agrees to give up, the others are bound to follow. We can soften the blow."

The police officer shook his head.

"I can't imagine who you'd ask."

"Colonel Phraya Si Sitthisongkhram. Is he on their side?"

"I don't think so. Are you going to ask him?"

"I can't think of anyone else, but…" Nart glanced at the grandfather clock that stood in the room. "I'll go to see Det tonight. If he's not home, I'll wait for him."

The conversation ended and the police lieutenant colonel went home with a heavy heart. He knew Nart well enough to realize that it was futile to try to stop him, since Nart made decisions based on reason and, once he had made up his mind, there was no changing it.

Gade arrived at her husband's house just after nine o'clock that night two hours later than planned as it had taken her a while to find it, being unfamiliar with the Bangkok streets. Rern stepped down from the cab and passed her nephew, who was fast asleep in her arms, to her sister. Klai helped carry the gifts from Phetchaburi and put them down in front of the large front gate, peeking inside through a crack.

"Gosh! Why is his house so big? Is this an army house?" he blurted out as he caught sight of a bell rope and pulled it. A moment later, a servant appeared from behind a smaller gate next to the large one, and looked at the three of them in puzzlement.

Klai greeted him politely.

"Hello. Would you tell Chao Khun Wisetsingnart that his relatives from Phetchaburi have brought his son to see him?"

"Wait here."

They waited until they became restless, and Rern became worried when she felt the cold mist from the breeze on her skin. Dark clouds were moving in, signalling it was about to rain.

"What shall we do, Gade? It's going to rain. I'm afraid Ned will catch a cold."

Gade was also worried, and she began to wonder if something had happened to make Nart ignore them.

"Perhaps he's not in," Klai ventured.

He rang the bell again and a moment later, Tieng appeared at the gate. Her expression was as unfriendly as ever but she did not look surprised to see Klai.

"Tieng," he greeted her, feeling glad to see someone he knew and forgetting his past mistrust of her. "Do you remember me? It's Klai. I've brought Chao Khun's son to see his father. Can we come in? It's going to rain."

Tieng looked uncomfortable for a moment before answering curtly, "No, you can't. Go home."

Tieng was about to shut the door, but Klai was quicker and pushed his way inside. Rern was just as quick and forced her way in angrily. Only Gade stood outside the gate with her son in her arms, telling herself not to be hasty. She would not push her way in without Nart's permission. Rern was more impatient than her sister and marched inside the fence ahead of her husband, ignoring Tieng's protests, only stopping suddenly when she heard someone scream, "Who's that? Who dares come into this house?"

She looked up and when she saw a young woman at the top of the steps, her angry face illuminated in the light, Rern put two and two together at once.

"Oh, it's Chao Khun's minor wife!"

She then retorted without restraint, "I'm Khunying Wisetsingnart's sister. I've brought Chao Khun's son to pay respect to his father."

Nuathong was momentarily startled when she heard the equally fierce retort, and her anger flared up.

"I'm Khunying Wisetsingnart. Everyone knows it. I don't have any upcountry relatives. Hey! Lue! Man! Where are you? Throw these intruders out!"

Klai breathlessly caught hold of his wife's arm when he saw her about to leap up the steps to lunge at Nuathong, so he told her, "Chao Khun told Gade to bring his son to see him."

"Get out!" she screamed. "Get out all of you! Do you think Chao Khun would allow you to set foot inside this house after he kicked you out in Udon? You've got a nerve to show your face again!"

"I'm not leaving until I see Chao Khun. You know full well who it was that framed me, so I had to leave the army base. I've never stolen or lied. May the one that did it be cursed!" Klai shouted back.

From behind the shadows, Man looked on in alarm and his shock turned to pity for 'Khunying Gade'. He prayed that Chao Khun, who had just left the house, would return in time to see what was going on, but he knew he would not be home until late, when his wife would simper and fawn all over him, hiding her tracks completely. He knew if anyone told Chao Khun the truth, Nuathong would dismiss them immediately.

It began to rain, so Man grabbed a paper umbrella and ran across the lawn and out through the small gate to find 'Khunying Gade', out of concern for her and the young boy.

"Stay out of the rain, madam. You'll get wet."

The paper umbrella wasn't much use in heavy rain, but it was better than nothing, so Gade took it to shield the little boy, and spoke to Man in a trembling voice, "Thank you, Man. Tell Klai and my sister to come back. I don't want to set foot in this house again."

Man's face fell and he answered hesitatingly, "Chao Khun's not home. If he knew you'd brought the boy, he'd let you in."

Gade just nodded and said no more. The rain was coming down

more heavily and Gade shielded her son with the umbrella, not caring if she got wet herself. She hoped that Man would think that the drops of water on her face were raindrops and not tears as they actually were.

In the rest of Bangkok, the night of June 23rd, 1932, passed without anyone knowing that something had happened to set it apart from other quiet nights. No one except for one group of people, who knew that it was a matter of life and death. The next day, they put their 'top secret' plan into action and sent soldiers to ambush those military officers who were not on their side.

That night, Colonel Phraya Wisetsingnart's misgivings became stronger with every passing hour. At each of his friend's houses, he was met with the same answer.

"Chao Khun is not back yet, sir."

Or, "He's just left, sir."

There was nothing unusual about an officer coming home late or staying out talking at a friend's house all night, but what was strange was that all of his friends had gone out at the same time and nobody knew where they were. Little did Nart know that, while he had been calling on all his friends, his own home was the target of an ambush. The group was led by a lieutenant, and reached his home only moments after Gade had left.

Having found no information, Nart decided to return home filled with a sense of foreboding that was hard to describe. The next morning, he intended to find Colonel Phraya Thepakanee and talk it out with him.

Looking down the road, he noticed a car outside the home of Major General Phraya Sena Songkhram, the commander of the Royal Guards, so he instructed his driver to stop, thinking that he must have been suspicious about the matter his relative had told him about.

The car stopped a short distance from the gate and when Nart got out of the car and walked to the gate, he glimpsed the house owner moving inside the fence, so he called to him.

"Chao Khun!"

"Who's there?" Phraya Sena Songkhram asked suspiciously. "You're early."

"It's me, sir. Wisetsingnart."

"Oh, Chao Khun!" he exclaimed and hurried closer, calling out to his servant to open the gate. "Come in."

Nart did not notice a group of people who had just arrived and were hiding behind a large tree on the opposite side of the road, since he had his back to them.

"I was about to go to the base. I thought…"

He stopped short when he looked past his visitor and saw the officers, who had appeared from behind the tree, push their way inside the gate as if they were going to attack him.

"What's going on?"

Nart spun around and recognized the man in front as First Lieutenant Khun Sri Sorakorn, whom he had met at Colonel Phraya Thepakanee's house.

Instinctively, Nart moved in front of Phraya Sena Songkhram, using himself as a shield, and shouted, "Stop right there!"

In the heat of the moment, the order was meaningless. First Lieutenant Khun Sri Sorakorn had been ordered to guard Phraya Sena Songkhram's house since the previous night, but because of a misunderstanding, he had been guarding the wrong house on the same street all night long, until he saw Colonel Phraya Wisetsingnart arriving, and realized his mistake. The young lieutenant had burst inside impatiently and when they saw that the two opponents were high-ranking officers, one of the group fired a gunshot.

The gunshot reverberated in the silence of the early morning all along the road.

The sound of that gunshot pierced Phraya Wisetsingnart to the soul, not only because he saw the Royal Guard Commander fall to the ground, but also because it signalled that, in that instant, a new chapter in the pages of history had begun, a chapter stained with the blood of Major General Phraya Sena Songkhram.

In the early hours of the morning on Friday 24th June 1932 almost no one in Bangkok realized that a revolution had taken place.The first troops to charge into the Royal Plaza were from the navy, led by two young officers, Lieutenant Luang Nava Wichit and Lieutenant Luang Sangwon Yutthakit. The small group of young army and naval officers had boldly carried out a surprise attack. Many of the troops deployed that day had, in fact, thought that they were carrying out their normal duties, because their commanders did not reveal the truth until everything was out in the open. A handful of people attacked like a flash of lightning and seized the heart of the city, intercepting the royal family and high-ranking officers by the power of their guns.

Colonel Phraya Walaphanusit, the commander of the Palace Guards, was one of the first high ranking officers to be detained in the Ananta Samakhom Throne Hall, and the atmosphere became increasingly tense until not even the coup leaders knew how it would end.

Gade awoke with a start that morning, feeling that something strange had happened, although she had no idea what it might be. She heard Nai Khim talking to several people outside the room, and her tone of voice was excited and anxious. The old wet nurse shakily came into the room, calling Gade by the title that Chao Chom Amphan had instructed everyone to use.

"Khunying!" she called from outside the mosquito net. "Are you awake? Something's happened!"

Gade pulled back the mosquito net in alarm and the dim light that came in through the window fell on the old lady's pale face as she caught hold of Gade's arm with trembling hands.

"What's happened, Nai Khim?" Gade asked, holding onto Nai Khim to calm her. Her thoughts first turned to Chao Chom Amphan and she asked in alarm, "Has something happened to Khun Chom? Is she alright?"

"No...Not in the house. They're saying there's been a revolution. There are soldiers all along Ratchadamnoen Avenue..."

It was the first time that Gade had seen Nai Khim panicking.

"The cook was on her way to the market and she was halfway there when she ran back to tell Sap. Sap wouldn't listen and ran upstairs to tell Khun Chom. I don't know what's going on! I feel faint."

Gade quickly found smelling salts and held them under the old nurse's nose before helping her out of the room. Although the word revolution sounded frightening, Gade was less alarmed than the others because it seemed to be a matter that was far from her, and she couldn't imagine how it might affect Khun Chom's household.

When she came out into the courtyard, she saw all the servants standing in groups, looking more puzzled than alarmed. Nai Sap's voice rose above the whispers of all the others as she shouted, "Where's the announcement? If it's true, bring me one of those fliers. Oh, you've got one, have you? Bring it here!"

When she turned and saw Gade and Nai Khim, she ignored them and looked the other way, but she continued to speak loudly so that everyone could hear.

"I'll take it upstairs myself. What's this? It's all crumpled! What have you done to it?"

Nai Khim raised a hand to stop her.

"Wait a minute. Let's talk first. There's no need to alarm her...Our house is all women. Has anyone told Chat, yet? Then if anything happens, at least we'll have him to protect us."

Nai Khim was thinking of incidents in the past when property was the first thing that needed to be protected, so it was important to have men around. Nai Sap looked at her askance until her eyes disappeared into their sockets as usual, and answered harshly, "There aren't any robbers. This piece of paper here...is the announcement of the revolution. I'm going to take it to her. She's waiting."

As Nai Sap hurried up the stairs, Gade realized that she had a duty and a responsibility to be informed about what was going on, so she said to Nai Khim, "Let me just wash my face, and I'll go upstairs. Someone help Nai Khim upstairs."

A moment later, Gade came down again and found Chao Chom Amphan sitting on a chair in the living room. The windows were shut and the room was dark and stuffy.

A dim light shone through the air vent onto her face, which looked as pale and lifeless as a waxwork, causing Gade's heart to sink because she had never seen such a look of panic and despair on Khun Chom's face before.

A piece of paper lay on the floor at her feet, and when Gade knelt down, she spoke softly without looking at her.

"Read it, Khunying."

Although she didn't understand much, Gade bent down to read it carefully.

The first page made her so confused that she looked up at Khun Chom questioningly, but she remained as still as a statue, so Gade forced herself to continue reading. As she read, her heart, which was already thumping, beat faster and faster until it was like a hammer pounding in her head.

People's Party Announcement

Fellow citizens,

When the king was crowned, some citizens hoped that he would rule fairly, but this did not happen. The king continued to be above the law and appointed his ignorant relatives and sycophants to important positions without listening to the people...

Gade's eyes began to glaze over and the room started to spin, but she forced herself to continue reading.

Citizens should know that our country belongs to the people and not to the king as he would have us believe. It was the people's ancestors that helped to maintain our country's independence and save it from our enemies...

The government has dismissed countless employees, while graduates and discharged soldiers are without work and have been left to fend for themselves. This has happened because the king is above the law. He has forced low level government workers, sergeants and clerks out of their jobs without any pension.

Therefore, both soldiers and civilians, who were aware of our government's evil actions, joined together to establish the People's Party, and seized the king's power from him.

The People's Party has informed the king of our demands. If the king selfishly refuses or ignores our demands to reduce his power, he will be considered a traitor to the nation, and it will be necessary for our country to become a democracy, which means that the head of state will be a commoner appointed by the House of Representatives, who will hold the position for a limited time. In this way, the people can trust that they will be taken care of in the best way. Everyone will have work because our country is abundant. When we take back the money that the aristocrats have accumulated at the expense of the people, our country's prosperity will be restored.

Fellow citizens, we implore you to help the People's Party to make this happen...Do not obstruct the People's Party in any way...

Gade stopped reading, unable to continue to the last line. Her hands were shaking so much that she had to put the leaflet down. Although Gade knew little about politics, and the closest she had been to anyone in the palace was to Chao Chom Amphan, she realized that the words on this piece of paper spoke of a revolution and, whether it was successful or not, she was shaken.

Gade asked hoarsely, "Who are they, who call themselves the People's Party?"

"As far as I know, they're soldiers."

"Soldiers?" Which soldier it was did not matter as much as the only soldier in Gade's life: Nart.

Gade put her hand to her chest and felt as if her heart was about to stop.

"Is Nart one of them?"

The expression on Chao Chom Amphan's face told her that such a thought had only just occurred to her as well. This time, she looked at Gade with compassion, as if she understood what she was feeling.

"I don't know. I'm waiting for news from Chat. I've sent for him. Why is he not coming?"

Gade clenched her fists and inhaled deeply to dispel the giddiness she was feeling.

"Nart can't be one of them," Gade reassured herself. "He's loyal to the king."

Gade hoped that, even though his faithfulness to her had diminished, his loyalty towards the king remained unchanged.

Later that morning, people began spilling outside onto both sides of Ratchadamnoen Avenue, under the tamarind trees, to watch the tanks and army vehicles moving down the street.

Their faces were excited and they talked animatedly, not realizing how tense the situation was for both those who had seized power and for those from whom power had been taken. Most of the people in Bangkok felt that it was a matter that did not concern them, and they were just spectators at an unheard of and sensational event whose outcome was still unknown.

Chao Chom Amphan listened attentively for news. She maintained her composure, even though she was anxious for the royal family, whom she knew, as well as her relatives who worked for the government. She tried to contact her siblings as much as she was able to and, by evening, there was news.

The People's Party had seized Ananta Samakhom Throne Hall and Parutsakawan Palace as their headquarters, and all the royal ministers were being held hostage in the Throne Hall. Even Suan Sunandha, where there were only women in charge, was under siege.

Nai Sap seemed to know what was happening better than anyone. As soon as the event had happened, she started behaving like a soldier, and went out to find news from her friends and relatives. That evening, she reported back.

"It's a matter of life and death, madam. It won't end easily."

"I know, Sap."

Khun Chom maintained her composure with difficulty.

"There are soldiers all over the city. It's no joke."

Nai Sap's reports alarmed her, and the news that Prince Paribatra Sukumbandhu was being held hostage almost made her faint.

"Bang Khun Prom Palace…" she began in disbelief. "I can't believe their audacity."

"They're saying he's being held hostage in Ananta Samakhom Throne Hall, madam."

"That's not all, madam. They also stormed Varadis Palace and took Prince Damrong hostage, and I heard Prince Naris was there, so they took him as well. They might take them to Ananta Samakhom Throne Hall."

Nai Khim, having taken some medicine, had recovered enough to exclaim, "How could they do it? Where were the police and the other nobles? Why didn't they stop them?"

"Oh, Nai Khim! Do you think they would let them get away? They're holding everyone who's not on their side. Who knows if they're still alive?"

Gade put her hand to her chest in alarm, feeling as if her heart had stopped beating.

Only last night, when she had returned home with Ned, she had told herself resolutely that she and Nart were finished, and there was no point in remaining in Bangkok. In a few days' time, she had planned to say goodbye to Khun Chom and take her son back to Phetchaburi. But no matter how much she had been hurt, the bond Gade felt for Nart remained unbroken.

Despite her alarm, Chao Chom Amphan was composed enough to notice Gade's pale face, and realized she was worried for her husband, so she asked at once, "Sap, have you heard anything about Chao Khun Wisetsingnart?"

Nai Sap glanced at Gade and replied a little curtly, "No, madam. You'd better ask Chat."

When she heard her brother's name, she remembered she had been waiting for him.

"You're right. Where is he? Why hasn't he come home? I'm worried about him. Sap, send someone to wait at his house. As soon as he returns, tell him to come and see me. Tell him not to have dinner. He can eat here."

Chat did not go home until late the next morning.

When he returned, Khun Chom's servant, who had been waiting for him all night, asked him to come to her house right away.

"Nobody's dead, yet. If they can come to a peaceful agreement, then everyone will be safe. Don't be overly alarmed. Everything will work out."

"How will it work out?" his sister retorted.

"Chao Khun Pahon has asked Lieutenant Commander Luang Suphachalasai to take the letter from the People's Party to the king, asking him to return to Bangkok. If he agrees, then the constitution will be changed and no blood will need to be shed."

"Chao Khun Pahonphonphayuhasena!" Chao Chom Amphan exclaimed. "So Phot's the leader of the rebellion, is he?"

Chat frowned and his voice showed his disapproval, even though he tried to sound polite.

"Please don't use the word rebellion. It sounds harsh. They're not rebels. They're just trying to make Siam civilized like other countries."

Chao Chom's expression became tense and she asked coldly, "Then what should I call those who are holding the royal family, and anyone who disagrees with them, at gunpoint?"

"Call them the People's Party," Chat answered calmly. "There won't be any violence. Nobody wants unnecessary bloodshed."

Khun Chom turned her face away in disapproval.

"And what if the king refuses to submit to them? Will they retreat as if nothing has happened to avoid bloodshed like you say?"

Chat ignored the sarcasm in her voice.

"If he refuses, then the People's Party will choose another royal to be king."

He could tell by Khun Chom's expression that she was holding her tongue with difficulty.

Gade was sitting on the floor listening to the conversation attentively, while keeping an eye on the two small boys who were playing in the courtyard below under the nanny's supervision. By now, Chao Chom Amphan considered Gade to be like one of the family. It was to Gade she confided her innermost thoughts, rather than her sister-in-law.

It wasn't surprising that she and Surai had grown apart as Surai had been staying at her father's house indefinitely, since the day she had fallen out with her husband at Phraya Wisetsingnart's party, and had left her son with the nanny. Khun Chom had consequently brought her nephew to live with her and, since Gade's son was also there, it was natural for the two boys to play together.

"Khun Luang Pradit asked those of us who work for the newspaper to understand the People's Party's motives, and not to oppose them without knowing the facts, so we obliged."

"Who's Luang Pradit?"

"Luang Pradit Manutham. He used to be called Pridi Panomyong. Have you heard of him? He studied Law in France. He's one of the leaders of the People's Party. He's really smart."

"If he's a lawyer, your father-in-law would know him for sure, Chat. I don't feel comfortable about it. I didn't think things would get so out of hand. I hear that anyone in the police or the army who disagrees with them is being held hostage."

"The People's Party will try to make sure that no one gets hurt. That's all I can tell you."

Khun Chom sighed, realizing it was futile to ask her brother any more questions.

It was obvious that Chat agreed with the People's Party wholeheartedly, and that if they discussed the matter further, they would fall out.

"Have any of our relatives been affected? Can you find out? I've been trying to contact them since yesterday, but nobody can tell me anything."

Chat felt relieved that she had changed the subject.

"I don't think so. None of our relatives are soldiers or police. Work in the ministries should continue as usual."

Chao Chom Amphan glanced at Gade.

"And what about Chao Khun Wisetsingnart? Which side is he on?"

Chat looked into Gade's luminous dark eyes and saw their anxious expression.

"He isn't on the People's Party's side, and his name wasn't on the list of the officers being held hostage, but you never know. He might join the People's Party later because he's friends with Colonel Phraya Thepakanee, and Phraya Thepakanee's the right-hand man of Phraya Songsuradet."

"How can we find out which side he's on? At a critical time like this, he can't stay neutral, can he? If he's not with them, then he must be against them."

"As far as I know, he's not in charge of any troops in Bangkok, and he's about to move to Khorat. He won't have much to do with it."

Chat glanced at Gade again, and said sarcastically, "A lucky fellow like him will be alright. After all, his best friend's in the People's Party. He might be promoted if he plays his cards right."

His words made both Gade and Chao Chom Amphan uncomfortable. Chat's sister gave him a warning glance, as she realized why he was being sarcastic. Gade was unaware of the reason, and assumed that he thought Nart had joined his friends in order to gain promotion. Gade felt that it would have been rude to contradict him, after he had been so kind to her, so she found a way to excuse herself.

"Your son's playing downstairs. I'll bring him up to see you."

Khun Chom nodded and watched the slim figure crawl out from the balcony until she was out of earshot before she spoke to her brother in a low but stern voice

"Don't make it so obvious, Chat. I'm warning you. She's a married woman with a child, and she's a Khunying and the wife of a Phraya. She isn't a commoner, you know. If she finds out, she'll lose all respect for you. And her mother will be upset with me. She brought her here for me to look after. You're being selfish, and we all stand to lose."

❋❋❋❋❋

Colonel Phraya Wisetsingnart was taken up the stairs behind the Ananta Samakhom Throne Hall by army majors and captains who watched him closely. He noticed that the Royal Standard that used to fly at the top of the flagpole had been taken down, and that the royal palace had been turned into the rebel's headquarters, where soldiers of all ranks were milling about.

He had to sit and wait for a while before the door to the room was opened, and an army major with a serious expression invited him inside curtly.

"Come in, sir."

It was, in fact, an order, so the Lieutenant Colonel stepped inside without delay.

Three or four officers were in the room, but Nart only had eyes for the person giving orders. When he saw Nart, he signalled for the other officers to go outside, leaving the two of them alone together.

Phraya Thepakanee spoke first.

"We did it!"

Nart didn't answer and waited to see what his friend would say next. He had an answer in mind, but there was no point in speaking first.

"I'm sorry, Nart, for not telling you before, but if we hadn't succeeded, we might have been executed, so I had to take the risk by myself. But now, I need a friend like you. There are lots of things you can help me with. Don't be offended that I didn't tell you from the start."

Colonel Phraya Wisetsingnart's response was to regard him coldly.

"It's not finished, yet. And you haven't succeeded yet."

Colonel Phraya Thepakanee frowned and his expression indicated his disappointment and disapproval.

"You misunderstand. We have all the important people now. Even the soldiers that command the troops are in our hands. Don't you see? We've already succeeded."

Phraya Thepakanee assumed that his friend was beginning to soften his stance, so he continued, "We can't go wrong. Now the Three Tigers in charge of Bangkok are Chao Khun Pahon, Chao Khun Song and Chao Khun Ritakanee. There's no need to worry."

Nart held his breath when he heard different names to the previous Three Tigers. Before today the so-called Three Tigers, who had been educated in Europe, were Phraya Pahonphonpayuhasena, Phraya Songsuradet and Colonel Phraya Si Sitthisongkhram. It was the latter who Nart was closest to, and for whom he had the most respect.

"Don't you have Phraya Si Sitthisongkhram?"

The expression on Phraya Thepakanee's face indicated his displeasure and he continued as if he hadn't heard the question.

"Let's get back to the heart of the matter. Like I told you, we've succeeded, my friend. One of the things the leaders have assigned me to do is to give a chance to those who agree with us to put their names, addresses and occupations on a list, along with a promise to help us, and they'll be given membership of the People's Party. Lots of people want to join, but you were the first person I thought of. There are important jobs I want you to be given. The history of Siam has been changed, and a bright future lies before us, one which we were willing to risk our lives for. This is a good opportunity for you."

Nart knew that he would face this predicament, but Phraya Thepakanee was unaware that his friend had already decided on his answer, and that his heart had turned to ice since the moment he saw the bleeding body of Phraya Sena Songkhram. He also didn't know that his answer might be the end of their lifelong friendship.

"I was at the house of Chao Khun Sena Songkhram at Sri Yan this morning when he was shot."

A look of discomfort passed across Phraya Thepakanee's face.

"I'm afraid it was unavoidable. I'm sorry. I didn't want any bloodshed. But he was only injured, not killed, which was a relief."

"Yes. Khunying Sena Songkhram's a brave lady. She shot at those who were trying to capture him. I was the one who told Khun Sri Sorakorn to move back from Chao Khun because he agreed to go with them. If he hadn't moved back, there would have been a bloodbath."

"You did the right thing, Nart," he said, reaching out to pat him on the shoulder.

Nart moved away and answered, "Det, you say you've succeeded, but your idea of success is different from mine. I don't believe that something that began with killing will end peacefully. I can't push that aside."

Phraya Thepakanee's eyes flashed.

"You think we won't succeed, so you don't want to join us."

"I believe you've succeeded. You've got all the important people of Siam in your hands, both the royal family and the armed forces. The king won't allow blood to be spilled by bringing in troops that are still loyal to him to fight to the end with you. But I don't believe democracy can be achieved in this way."

The blood rushed to Phraya Thepakanee's cheeks and his eyes burned with fury, but Nart held his gaze calmly.

"Why?" he growled. "If you don't have a better reason than that, then you'll be..."

"I've got three reasons. In a democracy, the power belongs to the people, not to the military, but what you've done, the people know nothing about. That's the first reason. The second is that the military is supposed to protect the nation, but you've betrayed it. And the third is that power gained too quickly won't be shared fairly."

Phraya Thepakanee thumped the table with his fist.

"Enough!"

Nart continued as if he hadn't heard.

"In another year or two, reconsider what an upcountry soldier like me, who's never been to Europe, said."

Phraya Thepakanee pointed at him, his hands shaking with anger.

"I said enough! Or you'll be the first to be accused of treason!"

Phraya Wisetsingnart's voice remained calm.

"I've nothing more to say. Thank you for wanting to promote me with you. We're friends and we both mean well, but we have different opinions. It's up to you what you accuse me of, but if I don't tell you what I think, then I'm not being honest with you. You can be angry with me, or stop being friends with me, but I'll never bear you any ill will."

His words dampened the flames of Phraya Thepakanee's anger and he soon regained his composure, although his eyes were cold.

"Fine," he said tersely. "I'll have to have you detained with Chao Khun Phichai Channarong and the others you mentioned just now, but because you're my friend and you were straight with me, and you didn't try to gain favour with your friends who are going to be promoted, I won't tell anyone what you said, for your safety. Do you have anything else to say?"

"There is one thing…"

"Go on."

"If you succeed, and I'm punished, I'll accept the punishment, but If I'm not punished, and I'm transferred instead, can I go to Khorat like I'd planned to?"

Phraya Thepakanee nodded, hardly needing to think about it.

"Yes, but you won't be able to come back to Bangkok."

Phraya Wisetsingnart nodded, his face solemn, as he looked at his friend like he was saying goodbye for the last time.

"Thank you."

On the evening of 23rd June 1932 the rebels were confident that they had succeeded when all twelve ministers met with them at Ananta Samakhom Palace.

After the meeting at Ananta Samakhom Palace, the rebels announced that they had taken power from the king, so all government matters that had previously been reported to the king were to be reported to the military government, and all government workers were to continue their work as usual.

Two months later, Nart found out what had happened in Hua Hin from Major General Phraya Anuphap Traiphop, Commander of the Third Army in Nakhon Ratchasima, who had been there when the incident happened. Phraya Anuphap Traiphop had been given an order from the king, delivered by the Minister of Defence, to fly to Nakhon Ratchasima and take troops from the Third Army Area to Kaeng Koi or Phachi and join with troops from the Fourth Army in Nakhon Sawan.

But the plane did not come to meet him, indicating that the king disagreed with resisting the rebels who had taken over in Bangkok, so that afternoon, Phraya Anuphap decided to take the train to Bangkok. However, when he got to Phetchaburi, he passed Prince Purachatra's carriage, and was ordered to return to Hua Hin because it was too late for him to go to Khorat, since the train had been taken over by the rebels.

The king had three choices.

To seek asylum in another country.

To return to Bangkok in order to negotiate with the rebels.

Or to assemble troops from the provinces who were loyal to the king, most of whom knew nothing about the coup that had taken place in Bangkok, in order to surround the capital, since some army units there might have been hesitant about which side to join and would have joined the king's side.

Finally, the king chose the second option: To return to Bangkok.

"I cannot sit on a bloodstained throne."

This was the explanation he gave to his nephew, Prince Chula Chakrabongse, two months later. Another reason was that when he asked Queen Rambhai Barni what they should do, she gave the same answer as her mother, Princess Abha Barni, which was, *"It is better to die with honour and truth."*

The king wrote, *"Both the Queen and her mother should be honoured for the bravery they have shown, because we all know that, even if we go to Bangkok willingly, we may be killed. These women are brave enough to be willing to die rather than lose their honour, and I agree with them."*

While Gade was worried, her sister was even more anxious about her. In truth, Rern was not affected by the political situation at all, aside from the fact that her husband, Klai, had warned her that he would have to hurry back to the army base in Phetchaburi. He reassured her that even though the train was not an option, they could go by boat.

Rern said to her sister anxiously, "Come home, Gade. I'm afraid to stay in Bangkok. What if they start fighting? Come home. It's safe there."

"If you want to go back, go home with Klai," Gade answered simply, without showing any alarm. "I must stay here."

She knew that if she showed her anxiety, she would worry her sister even more. Rern looked as if she was going to cry.

"Why do you want to stay? Are you worried about Chao Khun? His wife will take care of him."

Although she knew her sister was upset on her behalf, Gade felt a stab of pain in her heart, and decided to say as little about Nart as possible.

"I think it's best if I stay. You go home. Don't worry about me."

Rern looked at her pleadingly, but she didn't say anything more except to let out several long sighs.

"Can I take Ned back? I'll be worried about him if he stays here. He's still so little. What if something happens? You've no one you can depend on apart from Khun Chom and she's a woman."

Gade's heart sank because she did not want to be separated from her son, but she knew that her sister was right. How could Nart protect his son when Gade didn't even know what his fate would be?

"Alright. Take Ned back first. As soon as I know what's happening here, I'll follow."

Klai Kangwon Palace
25th June 1932

Dear government leaders,

From the letter you sent to the Secretariat, I have learned that the military has asked me to return to Bangkok as a constitutional king. For the stability of the kingdom and to avoid bloodshed, and also to avoid causing a riot, and because I believe in becoming a constitutional monarchy, I agree to be a puppet in order to oversee a smooth transition in government because if I do not agree, the world will not accept this new government, which will cause many difficulties. As you are aware, I am an invalid, I do not have an heir, and I will not remain in office for long, because I do not harbour ambition above my status and ability to support our nation's progress.

Sincerely,
Prajadhipok

On the night of Sunday 26th June 1932 King Prajadhipok returned to Bangkok by train, arriving at Chitralada Station at one o'clock in the morning, having refused to return by the 'Sukhothai' warship, which the rebels had provided.

Chat had been anxiously walking up and down close to the station since ten o'clock at night, and his legs ached, but he would not give up waiting for the king. Even though it was not his duty, his reporter's soul was not willing to pass up this opportunity. The atmosphere was quiet and subdued, and even when the royal carriage pulled up to the platform there was no commotion. Among the people that he saw was a man of around thirty years old who prostrated himself before the king as he walked past, and Chat was moved to see tears on the king's face. Although Chat wholeheartedly agreed with the main aim of the People's Party, which was that Thailand should have democracy, and he felt relieved that the king had returned to Bangkok peacefully without a civil war as many had feared, he could not explain why he returned to the newspaper office from Chitralada Station with a heavy heart.

He did not know that the sad atmosphere of that night would haunt him in his dreams for many years after King Prajadhipok had abdicated until his death.

On the 27th of June 1932 King Prajadhipok signed a temporary charter.

The next day, six hostages were released. All had to sign an oath that they would *"refrain from doing anything by word or deed that would jeopardise the People's Party,"* and that if they broke their oath they would be *"punished as the People's Party deems appropriate."*

❋❋❋❋❋

Two or three days later, Colonel Phraya Wisetsingnart was released along with other high-ranking officers.

"Everything is in order," was all he was told.

He did not have a chance to meet with Colonel Phraya Thepakanee, and nor did he wish to, since there was now a deep chasm between them.

The man sitting in front of Colonel Phraya Wisetsingnart was about forty years old, and polite but serious. Everyone knew him as a quiet man, and those close to him also knew that he was clever, determined and sincere. It was because of this last quality that Nart, a friend and junior who had been close to him since their youth, told Colonel Phraya Si Sitthisongkhram the whole story.

"Det and I haven't had a chance to speak to each other since that day, but he kept his word. The order has come for me to go to Khorat. I've come to say goodbye."

"I wish you happiness and success, Nart."

"Someone like me can't hope for success like some people, but I'll definitely be happy. Going to Khorat's like going home."

"I'm glad you know yourself well."

"On that day…" Nart meant the 24th of June. "Where were you when you weren't taken hostage?"

With a slight smile, he answered, "I came close. That day I didn't go to work. Around three in the afternoon, an armoured tank came into the First Field Artillery Regiment right opposite this house, and a captain got out and called across the canal that there had been an order to take me. Someone in my house was quick and shouted back that I was out. Then my children realizing something was amiss, ran upstairs to tell me, so I changed my clothes and went down the steps behind the house and cut across the garden to Khlong Prom Prachakorn and escaped."

"Who was it that came to take you?"

"I was told it was Captain Surajit Charuseranee, but I didn't see him. When he realized I wasn't home, he left."

"And where did you go?"

"I went to Phot's house near the Bangsue Cement Factory."

He meant Phraya Pahonphonphayuhasena, the leader of the rebels, and Nart was stunned for a moment.

"But you didn't join the People's Party."

"I don't agree."

Phraya Wisetsingnart didn't need to ask for an explanation because this answer was clear enough, so he changed the subject.

"Do you know the details of the charter that the king is signing?"

"I've read it."

"There are some parts that I'm uncomfortable about. We want the power to be in the hands of the people, but why are there two types of members of parliament in the House of Representatives, instead of only representatives elected directly by the people? The People's Party has the right to appoint seventy-one members of parliament, and will only allow all members of parliament to be elected by the people on the condition that over half of the country's citizens have completed elementary education, which will not be for at least ten years. Where did that condition come from?"

Phraya Si Sitthisongkhram answered ruefully, "It came with this new charter, after the People's Party had seized power."

"They used to say that the aristocrats were clinging to their power and refusing to share it with the people by claiming the people were not ready for democracy, but after the People's Party said they were ready, now they're saying we have to wait at least ten years before they're ready. When will that be?"

They were both silent for a moment knowing he did not really expect an answer. Phraya Si Sitthisongkhram asked, "Who wrote the charter?"

"I understand it was Luang Prasit Manutham, but the People's Party approved it. It wasn't the idea of just one person."

He got up and patted his friend on the shoulder, telling him quietly "Keep calm and see what happens, Nart. It's not over yet. It's only just begun."

That afternoon, it was hot and humid as if it was going to rain. Gade had bathed and changed into fresh clothes before giving Chao Chom Amphan's nephew a bath. Then she powdered him and put a mat down for him to nap downstairs, where all the windows were open for the air to circulate, before singing him to sleep as she usually did every afternoon.

Chao Chom Amphan was not at home. Although she hadn't planned to go out, she had had to go to her sister-in-law's house because Surai's parents were upset about her threats to finish with her husband and had asked Khun Chom to intervene to find a solution.

Nai Sap had gone with Khun Chom, and Nai Khim was lying down in her room. All the other servants were behind the house, so Gade did not notice someone come onto the downstairs balcony as she was singing the little boy to sleep. Suddenly she became aware of someone standing behind her, so she turned and her heart almost stopped beating.

Nart was standing on the balcony outside the door. They gazed at each other without speaking for a moment before Nart turned to the sleeping boy, and his face lit up as he asked, "Is that our son?"

He didn't know that his words had reopened the wound in Gade's heart, after she had thought there was no room for any more pain. He still had no idea what his son looked like.

"No," she replied, shakily. "This is Chat's son, Cheng."

The excitement in his eyes dimmed, and he turned away from the little boy coldly.

"And where's our son? I still haven't seen him."

Why hadn't he seen him? Didn't he know that Gade had stood holding him in the rain in front of his house while his minor wife had screamed at them not to set foot inside the house? Had nobody told him?

"He's gone back to Ban Tha Hin with his aunt."

"You send your son to Phetchaburi, while you stay here with someone else's son. Is that it?"

His words jarred so much that Gade felt a surge of anger.

"I'm depending on Khun Chom's kindness. When she's not home, the least I can do is babysit her nephew."

He sensed the coldness in Gade's voice, but before he could say anything else, she continued, "I sent our son back to Phetchaburi because I was afraid he wouldn't be safe in Bangkok. I'm going to follow as soon as I know...there's nothing to worry about...here."

Their eyes met again. He sat on a chair feeling uncomfortable, while she sat on the floor feeling hurt, but too proud to cry. When Nart looked at Gade, his heart was moved. He knew he had hurt her and that there was nothing he could do to assuage his guilt.

"I came to tell you…" he hesitated. "To tell you...I'm moving to Khorat...I leave the day after tomorrow."

If Gade had not been sitting on the floor already, she might have collapsed. Her throat felt too dry for words.

"This time...it's different from last time. I don't feel that I did anything wrong, or that I failed in my duties, but I don't know if I'll be able to come back to Bangkok. It will be many years before I can come back."

His words made her feel numb and she forced herself to sit upright.

"Gade, I want to take you, but...there are still many things I'm not sure about…"

Nart meant the political situation, but Gade had no way of knowing that, and assumed he was talking about his second wife and whether she would allow it.

With this assumption, her resentment rose up again.

"Please don't worry. If you don't want me to go, I'll go back to my family in Ban Tha Hin."

"I didn't say I don't want you to go. I won't forget you…"

He stopped, ashamed, before continuing, "...and Ned. I tell you what. Let's wait until everything's settled down, and then I'll send someone to bring you to Khorat."

He had forgotten that he had said the same thing before he left Phetchaburi, and he didn't realize that his words cut like a knife. Gade looked up at him, her eyes blazing.

"You expect me to wait again?"

"Let's not talk about that. I don't have much time. I came here because I want to know how you're going to live when I've gone to Khorat. You ought not to stay with Khun Chom Amphan for too long. She isn't your relative, and, even though you're married with a child, you're still young…"

He paused without mentioning Khun Chom Amphan's good-looking younger brother, but Gade understood what he meant.

"If you go back to Phetchaburi, your family won't want you to stay alone. If they persuade you to remarry, what will you do? They have someone in mind, don't they?"

"If you think I'm going to remarry, I can tell you straight that I've never even thought about it."

"Don't make promises that you don't know if you'll be able to keep. You're still young. If something happens to me, what will you do without anyone to protect you?"

At once, Nart realized he had put his foot in it again when Gade answered piercingly, "You forget. I lived alone with Ned in Ban Tha Him for years. No one dared to harass me. I'm a mother and I have to take care of my son the best I can, not selfishly find a new lover."

"Good," he said, feeling relieved. "I trust you to stay faithful."

After he said it, he realized he had given her another opportunity to react, but it was too late to take his words back. Gade looked him in the face and answered coldly, but without sarcasm and with a frankness that cut to his soul, "Yes, because I'm the mother of

Phraya Wisetsingnart's son. I'll never ruin my son's name by being unfaithful."

At first, he felt annoyed, but then he realized that she regarded the bond between them as still intact.

"It would ruin his parents' reputations, not his. What about his father's reputation? Aren't you worried about that?"

Gade started and the blood rushed to her face.

"Mine's already ruined…" she answered softly.

Nart leant towards her and Gade began to move away, but she was not quick enough and his hand touched her chin and lifted her face.

"That's not true, Gade. I'm still your husband. Even though you didn't say it, I appreciate that you still care about my reputation."

Gade felt almost the same as she had felt the first time they had been alone together. She had almost forgotten that feeling. But only a minute later, Nart straightened himself up when he heard the sound of footsteps and the swish of a sarong coming closer, and Gade moved away in alarm.

"Who's there? Oh, it's Chao Khun Wiset!"

Chao Chom Amphan did not realize that she had spoiled the mood and when she entered the room and saw them, she looked surprised.

"Am I interrupting?" she asked, smiling.

Colonel Phraya Wisetsingnart stood up and paid respect to her, before answering politely, "I stopped by to see Gade. I was about to leave."

Gade moved towards Cheng, who was sleeping soundly, in order to carry him to another room, but Khun Chom nodded to Nai Sap as a signal for her to do it instead.

"How are things with you, Chao Khun? I was worried when I heard the news. No one can tell me anything. The situation's very worrying."

"Everything's in order," Gade's husband answered, so as not to worry her. "I'm leaving for Khorat the day after tomorrow, so I came to say goodbye."

"I wish you all the best and a safe journey," Khun Chom replied, beginning to worry about Gade. "I'll take care of Gade. Don't worry. When you're ready, let me know and I'll have someone take her to you."

"I was just saying to Gade that Phetchaburi is too far away for her to stay and it will be hard for me to contact her, but if she stays here in Bangkok, she's a grown woman and I don't want to impose on you…"

Khun Chom understood more than he thought she did.

She had just returned from her sister-in-law's house, certain that Chat and Surai's marriage was over. Whether they divorced or simply lived in separate houses, her obstinate brother had no intention of reconciling with Surai, and it was clear that Surai no longer cared for him.

Now that Chat was single, it was no longer appropriate for a beautiful young woman like Khunying Wisetsingnart to stay so close to him like sugar near an ant. Khun Chom saw immediately that the best solution was for the sugar to live separately, so that the owner of the sugar would be able to visit, as she could tell that the officer still cared about his wife.

As long as Gade still lived with her, it would be difficult for Chao Khun to visit, since her house was full of women, and staying the night would have been out of the question for such a high-ranking officer.

"I tell you what, Chao Khun," she suggested calmly after a moment's consideration. "While Gade's waiting to go to Khorat, I think it would be best for her to make her home in Bangkok, and find a house of her own. Even though you're going to Khorat, I don't expect you'll stay there until you die. One day, you're sure to return to Bangkok, so Gade should have a house of her own."

She looked at both of them and, seeing that neither objected, she continued, "Bring some of your relatives here, and I'll find you a place to live, Gade. You can buy some land on which to build a house and plant a garden. You can do it yourself, or rent out the land, so that you have some extra income, and whenever you're ready, you can go to live with Chao Khun. While you're waiting, you can raise your son here and send him to a good school. What do the two of you say?"

Gade bowed her head and placed her palms together to thank Chao Chom Amphan, and when she raised her head and looked at her husband, his face showed his approval.

On 3rd July 1932 Prince Paribatra Sukhumbandhu left Ananta Samakhom Throne Hall, where he was being held, and returned to Bang Khun Prom Palace under the surveillance of Major Luang Amnuay Songkhram and his party. The next day, he was taken, along with Princess Nabhabhorn Prabha and all the members of his family, out of the country by train from Chitralada Station to Penang.

Later, he lived in Bandung, Indonesia, until his death, and never set foot in his homeland again.

9

When the River Runs Backwards

Colonel Phraya Wisetsingnart asked his wife gravely, "Nuathong, what did the house owner say when you asked for the rent money back?"

Nuathong had been out of sorts since the change in the system of government. She didn't care about how it had affected the country, only its impact on her.

Her husband's friends had been promoted, while he was being sent off to Nakhon Ratchasima because he refused to side with them. What was so difficult about it? Didn't he know how much she hated living upcountry?

When she heard the question, she retorted, "Why would she agree to give us the money back? You know how stingy she is. She told me we'd rented it for a year, so we have to pay the year's rent, whether we live here or not..."

"Can't you find a compromise, like finding someone else to rent it for her? The rent's high, and we ought to save money."

Nuathong frowned as she often did when she heard the word 'money'.

"Don't talk to me about money. I've got a Phraya for a husband, and yet I have to scrimp and save. It's embarrassing!"

"If we can't understand each other, then we'd better not talk!" he answered and pointed towards the door, so she stormed out.

Then he heard her shouting at the servants as usual, so he had to get up and shut the door before returning to his work with a weariness that was hard to describe. He opened the household budget ledger and looked at it in confusion. There had been no extra household expenses, but Nuathong had been spending more money each month.

Impatiently, he rang the bell to call for a servant to fetch Man.

When Man knelt down in front of him, he got straight to the point.

"Man, you've been recording my expenses for me. Have you recorded everything?"

"Yes, sir," his old servant answered confidently.

"Tell me the truth, Man. How often does Nuathong play cards?"

Man swallowed with difficulty.

"She goes every day, sir. As soon as you've left the house she goes."

Phraya Wisetsingnart was shocked. His anxiety prevented him from asking any more questions. The only solution he could think of to pull her away from this vice was to take her to Khorat.

He waved his hand for Man to leave and was surprised when he hesitated.

"Is there something, Man? Tell me what it is," he asked in irritation. "Why are you dithering?"

Man summoned up the courage to ask a question for the first time, after always being the one to answer.

"Have you seen your son yet, sir?"

"Who?" he asked, still preoccupied with the problem of his wife.

"Ned, sir. Khunying brought him to the house the other night."

Phraya Wisetsingnart thought he had misunderstood and looked at Man quizzically for an explanation. Man hesitated.

"The night of the revolution, sir. Not long after you left, Khunying brought your son to the house. Sergeant Klai and her sister, Rern, were with her.

Understanding began to dawn on him and he asked angrily, "Why wasn't I told about it? Did Gade meet Nuathong?"

"Khunying was holding your son outside the gate, sir. Sergeant Klai and Rern came inside the gate, but Nuathong saw them and wouldn't let them into the house."

"What did you say?"

"It's true, sir, I swear. After that, Khunying went home...It was raining, you see, sir. She didn't want the boy to get wet. I gave her an umbrella, so she took it and left."

He listened in shock. Gade had brought their son to see him, but they were met with rudeness from the other woman who was in charge of their home. In spite of everything, Gade had not said a word about it when he went to see her.

"Man, I won't take you with me to Khorat. You're getting too old to work for me."

Man was dumbfounded and looked at his boss in alarm because he didn't know if this meant he had been fired.

"Am I fired? Please…"

"Did I say that? You're jumping to conclusions."

Man was silent when he heard the irritation in his voice.

"I'd like you to look after Gade. I don't want her to stay alone with our son and only a few female relatives. I'd like you to be there to help keep an eye on them for me."

The older man's face lit up.

"Yes, sir."

Nart relaxed a little, but urged, "If you see anything amiss, let me know at once. I don't trust anyone else but you. I know you're loyal to Khunying and to Ned."

❋❋❋❋❋

Chao Chom Amphan quickly found some land for Gade, and put the deeds in front of her, explaining, "This plot is suitable. It's a fruit plantation, so the land's fertile and you'll be able to grow things on it. It's reasonable, too. Three rai for two hundred baht. You'll be able to buy more in the future."

"Where is it?"

"At Bang Pho, near Rama VI Bridge. It's not far from here. You can just hop on a boat and it will bring you to Phra Athit Pier."

Everything worked out so much more easily than she had expected with the help of her kind protectress. Gade felt that for the past few months, even when there was lots to do, everything was completed smoothly with her help. The new house was a simple single-storey building on stilts with a tiled hip roof of the sort that was popular in those days. It was not extravagant like Phraya Wisetsingnart's house, but it was more than adequate for the young woman, whom the villagers who lived in the surrounding plantations referred to as 'Khunying Wiset'.

The best thing about it was that Gade now had a home of her own in Bangkok, and her son would have the opportunity to go to the same school that his father had been to, a school with a very good reputation. Moreover, the atmosphere in the surrounding plantations made her feel that Ban Tha Hin was not that far away.

Gade wrote to her husband, telling him about the house and Ned, without expecting a reply, but soon after she received one.

Dear Gade,

I'm glad that by now, you will have had a merit-making ceremony for your new home, and I'm glad to know that you and our son are well. Please remind Man to take good care of Ned, since he's still too young to go to school and is probably naughty, and we don't want him to fall in the water.

Khun Chom has been very kind. It would be proper for you to visit her sometimes, but don't go too often. After all, you have your own home now, and you're a woman alone, so you're vulnerable. I'm glad your sister comes to stay with you often. It would be good if Klai could be transferred to Bangkok. I'll see what I can do.

Can you send me a picture of Ned? I still haven't seen him.

Gade finished reading the letter aloud and glanced up at her sister, whose sharp eyes were regarding her quizzically.

"What did Chao Khun mean when he said not to visit Khun Chom too often? It sounds strange."

Gade folded the letter and put it back in the envelope before sighing, "Oh, it's nothing. He's worried about Khun Chom's brother. I don't know what he was thinking. I don't want to know."

Rern had seen the way Chat looked at Gade and had her suspicions, but she decided to keep them to herself.

"I heard he's finished with his wife."

"I guess so. I'm not interested."

"Has he been to visit you?"

"What? Even when I was staying with Khun Chom, I hardly saw him. Why would he come here?"

No sooner had she spoken when Suk, the former nanny of Chat's son who no longer worked for him and now lived with Gade as Ned's nanny, crawled inside.

"Khunying, the master..." she said, still referring to Chat as she used to, "asked me to tell you he's here to see you, madam."

Rern looked at her sister as if to say, 'What do we do now?'

"Suk, tell him I'll be out in a moment. Don't forget to give him a drink of water."

When Suk had crawled out of the room, Gade whispered to her sister sternly, "Wait ten minutes and if he's still here, bring Ned in."

Rern agreed, adding, "We were just talking about him and here he is."

Chat sat on a wooden chair that was part of a matching set with a table, and looked around him at the clean and tidy room with satisfaction.

A clean white net curtain was blowing in the breeze, and he looked out at the green vegetation surrounding the house, noticing a scarlet-backed flowerpecker perch on the branch of a mango tree outside the window before flying away. A rustling sound at the door made him turn around and his heart beat faster with anticipation as he stood up. Gade walked calmly into the room and placed her palms together to greet him.

"Please have a seat and make yourself at home."

Chat hardly heard a word she said because he was so preoccupied with gazing at her. The more he looked at her, the more he was stirred by her.

"I've only just had time to visit. This is a nice house. You must be happy here, Gade."

He called her by her name out of habit, and also because he couldn't bring himself to call her in accordance with her husband's rank.

"I'm fine, thank you," Gade replied as concisely as possible.

She noticed that he did not call her by her title, as Chao Chom Amphan had reminded everyone to, and was puzzled. In order to shorten the duration of his visit, she asked, "What has Khun Chom asked you to see me about?"

Chat was silent for a moment before answering, "She didn't ask me to see you...It's just that...I wanted to see your new house...to make sure you're alright. You're a woman alone with a small child, and I was worried."

The tenderness in his voice made his feelings so obvious that even Gade could not mistake them. Moreover his feelings were written all over his face. She answered gently, so as not to hurt his feelings or sour their relationship, but she did not give him any reason to hope.

"I'm not alone with my child. I have my sister with me. And for another thing, Chao Khun has left his servant with me. If there were only women and children here, he'd be worried."

Knowing that her husband had left for Khorat and taken that woman with him, Chat had assumed that the relationship between him and his principal wife was over.

"Chao Khun…" he said hoarsely, "did that, did he?"

"Yes."

A photograph of Colonel Phraya Wisetsingnart hung by itself on the wall between two windows, and Chat suddenly noticed it. The eyes of the man in the picture stared at him as if to warn him, 'This is my house and my wife. You're an outsider with no business here. You should leave.'

At that moment, Rern, who had been timing his visit, came inside holding her nephew's hand, and said cheerfully, "Ned wanted to see you...Oh, I'm sorry! I didn't know you had company!"

Gade picked up the little figure that ran towards her. He had just had a wash and was freshly powdered. The whiteness of the powder contrasted with his black eyes and red lips. Everyone said he looked like his mother, but when he climbed up on her knee, the way he looked at Chat reminded him of Phraya Wisetsingnart.

Chat sighed and hardly heard Gade say, "Ned, this is your friend's father. Do you remember him?"

Although he was shy at first, when he learned that Chat was his friend's father, he placed his palms together obediently.

Chat couldn't even force a smile and stood up.

"It's time I was going."

Gade said nothing, and stood up to walk him to the door, asking Rern to accompany him to the gate as was customary.

Rern returned a moment later, smiling with relief.

"At least Chao Khun doesn't have any children with that woman.

As soon as he sees Ned, he'll be smitten. He's so handsome all the neighbours say you can tell he's from a noble family."

Gade beamed with pride at her sister's compliment and said, "Chao Khun asked about him in his letter. Tomorrow, I'm going to take him to have his picture taken, so I can send a photograph to his father. Do you want to come?"

Rern happily accepted, and added with a smile, "Why are you only having his picture taken? Send him a picture of you holding him."

When Gade hesitated, Rern insisted, "It will remind him of both you and Ned. If that woman rips it in two, she'll be ripping his son's picture, and he won't stand for that, you can be sure."

Gade couldn't help laughing at Rern's joy in her plan.

"Oh, Rern! You're still as sassy as you've always been!"

*****

The photograph reached Colonel Phraya Wisetsingnart at the end of the month. As soon as he pulled the photograph out of the envelope and saw the large picture, his heart quickened. The young woman in the picture was pretty and slim, and she was wearing a short-sleeved lace blouse with a sarong just above her ankles, paired with tasteful jewellery. She was sitting on a chair with one hand resting on the arm of the chair and the other around the waist of the three-year-old boy who was sitting on her lap.

The little boy looked clean and tidy in a short-sleeved pastel coloured shirt and black shorts, and he was wearing shoes and socks. His hair was neatly combed and he was looking straight at the camera with no sign of shyness, his expression was bold and curious. Nart felt as if he was staring straight at him with interest and curiosity because he had never seen him before.

Is this my son, Ned? he exclaimed to himself.

He was no longer the skinny baby he had left in Phetchaburi three years ago, but had grown into a healthy little boy, and the chubbiness of his arms and legs indicated that he had been well looked after. He was the spitting image of his mother, and it was clear that he would grow up to be handsome. The more he looked at him, the more he felt that when he grew up, he would look fine in an army officer cadet's uniform.

Phraya Wisetsingnart rang the bell to call for the officer outside his office, and instructed him, "Take this into town and have it put in a silver frame with a stand. Get it done today."

Nuathong had been out of sorts since she had accompanied her husband to Nakhon Ratchasima because the only entertainment she could find was with the wives of a few other officers. Hearing someone moving in the next room which was both a study and a sitting room, she realized that her husband was back, and lowered the voice with which she had been berating her servant.

She put on a cheerful face and walked inside, asking brightly, "You came in so quietly, I didn't hear you come in."

She stopped when her husband turned from the ebony cabinet where he kept his books and other valuable items that he had brought with him from Bangkok. The photograph in the shiny new silver frame stood on a shelf, and Nuathong noticed it immediately.

"Who's that picture of?"

Phraya Wisetsingnart didn't answer the question that was more of an exclamation.

"Why were you shouting at your servant? I could hear you from outside."

Nuathong didn't pay any attention to her husband's question either. She was staring at the picture in the cabinet. When she realized who it was, jealousy rose up in her until she could hardly contain herself.

"Good heavens!" she cried as if she had seen something dreadful. "Why have you put your old wife's picture up?"

Nart frowned and gave her a warning glance, so she quietened down sulkily.

"If anyone sees, it won't look good. Everyone knows I'm your only wife."

"Everyone knows," he said, almost adding that everyone knew who Khunying Wisetsingnart was.

"In that case, throw...er...put it away. I don't understand," she continued, "why you have to put that picture there when you've finished with her, or are you trying to tell me that you're going to bring her here? I won't stand for it."

"Don't worry. Gade won't come."

"At least she's not that bold. And do you still care about her? Is that why you put her picture up to humiliate me?"

His weariness with her made him feel as if something was stuck in his throat, so he answered harshly, "Gade's the mother of my son. Don't forget that."

His answer touched a nerve and she shrieked back at him, "And is it...my fault that I don't have a child?"

Only a few days after the picture had seared her eyes, an accident happened.

When Phraya Wisetsingnart returned home, Tieng reported nervously that one of the servants, a local girl, had been sweeping behind the cabinet and had clumsily knocked the picture on the floor, causing the glass to shatter and cut through the middle of the picture like a knife. When the incident happened, Nuathong was not home, but when she returned, she made a show of anger in front of her husband.

She had fired the servant at once and told her husband angrily, "Khammee's so clumsy and careless! I'm fed up with her!"

"If you knew she was careless, why did you ask her to sweep this room? You know I keep valuable things here."

Nuathong did not give up.

"Everything's inside the cabinet. I thought it would be safe. I used to let her wash the dishes, but she broke so many glasses I decided to have her sweep instead, which turned out to be even worse."

She pretended not to notice the picture, even when her husband bent down sadly to pick it up. How could he put the picture up now when it had a big slash in the middle?

At last, she'd got rid of that picture. It was she who had picked up the pieces of broken glass and slashed the picture. She had wanted to slash it more, but was afraid he would suspect, so she left it at just one slash.

As soon as her husband had left the room, she called Tieng in and gave her some money.

"Give this to Khammee and tell her to leave at once without saying goodbye to Chao Khun."

She couldn't help noticing that Tieng, whose face was normally indifferent, looked uneasy.

"What is it? Do you want Chao Khun to find out it was you who bumped into her and pushed the picture onto the floor?"

Tieng sighed and asked, "Don't you think he suspects us?"

"What?" she hissed so that no one else could hear. "What proof does he have? You're getting impertinent. I'll fire you, too, if you're not careful. If you dare tell anyone, you're dead, do you hear? I won't stand for traitors!"

Tieng was silent, but Nuathong continued to rant at the old servant.

"Why would I stand for Chao Khun putting up a picture of his old wife? The only reason he put it up was because he's besotted with his son. If it wasn't for him, he wouldn't care a jot about her."

Chao Chom Amphan was weighed down with various concerns, but when Nai Sap came to tell her that Khunying Wisetsingnart had come to see her, she cheered up visibly.

Gade had come to visit the woman she admired with gifts of the best fruits picked from her orchard, and palm sugar desserts, which she was sure her nephew would like.

"What's all this you've brought with you?" Khun Chom asked when she saw all the gifts. "It looks as if you want me to set up shop."

Gade smiled and asked about Khun Chom's nephew and the other people she knew, and they chatted for a while about this and that fbefore Khun Chom asked about Phraya Wisetsingnart.

"Chao Khun wrote to me asking for another picture of me and our son. He didn't say what had happened to the first one I sent."

"It must have got damaged," Chao Chom Amphan guessed, having a good understanding of such matters. "You should send him a dozen to put up all over the house, and we'll see if they all get damaged, too."

Then she burst out laughing, causing Gade to laugh too, even though she was uneasy about the matter.

"What did he say about his son? I'll bet he was besotted with him.

He's such a handsome boy. Everyone says so."

"He said he's grown so much he can hardly recognize him, and he said when he's old enough he'll get him into Suan Kulap School, but…" Gade's voice became softer, "he didn't say when he would come to visit."

The beautiful older woman looked at Gade with understanding and sympathy.

"It won't be long. Send another picture, and keep sending him news about his son to keep in touch."

Chao Chom noticed Gade's cheeks turn pink, but a moment later they paled again.

"I don't expect him to come back. He gave me money for a house and land to plant an orchard, and now I can earn enough money from selling the fruits to live off. I want to give my son the best life possible. That's all I wish for."

This was Gade's intention. Love was something from long ago that she had buried in the past, and the sadness that remained was just a reminder not to make the same mistake twice. Her happiness would lie in seeing her son grow up. Ned would grow up as was proper for the son of Phraya Wisetsingnart. He would go to a good school and become an officer like his father, according to his father's wishes and Gade's dream.

Khun Chom looked at the young woman in front of her with compassion. She probably understood Gade far better than Gade understood herself.

"No, Khunying. I wasn't trying to set you up with false hopes. I meant that you shouldn't give up and let what's rightfully yours slip away. Most women make a fuss when their husbands are unfaithful, complaining that the other woman has come between them, but I want you to have a different perspective."

When she saw Gade look up at her with a puzzled expression, she smiled and explained, "Think of it this way. It's you that needs to come between Chao Khun and that woman. Why would you let him slip away when he's your husband and the father of your son? Ned needs a father, so you should hold onto your position as Khunying Wisetsingnart. Don't refuse to be reconciled with him and let her take your place. Everyone knows who you are."

"But she's his wife now. He never…"

"Oh, don't take offense…" Chao Chom interrupted. "Now he's an officer of high rank, you can't expect him to come crawling back. He's too proud for that, but I can tell he's relenting. That's why I told you not to reject his goodwill. Swallow your pride and choose the option that will yield the best outcome."

She laughed before continuing, "If one day women become Phrayas, without having to depend on their husbands, I won't blame you if you divorce him and gain a high rank for yourself!"

Although Gade loved Chao Chom Amphan, she dared not visit her too often because of her husband's warning, and the way Chat had been towards her was still causing her some anxiety. Even so, despite coming just once a month and not staying very long, Gade could not help but meet Chat.

When she saw him for the first time after he had been to her house, she was so shocked that she exclaimed, "Are you sick, Chat? You've lost so much weight!"

"It's nothing," he answered, and although he knew there was no deep meaning behind her words, he was pleased that she cared enough to ask. "I'm a news reporter, and this year, there's always something to report. I never know what's going to happen."

"What IS going to happen?" Khun Chom asked with a mixture of sarcasm and concern.

"Lots of things. There are all sorts of rumours flying around. I can't separate truth from fiction."

Chao Chom Amphan looked uneasy, feeling that the country was not as peaceful as it should have been. He knew that her disquiet and sadness was due to huge changes in the lives of many of those she had known since she was young. Many of the royals, whom she had always been loyal to, had been expelled from their palaces and sent to live in exile indefinitely.

"I'm starting to feel that I don't want to stay in Bangkok anymore. I might go to Phetchaburi. We still have relatives there."

Chat began to feel uneasy.

"And what about this house? There are lots of people living here. How can you leave the house empty?"

"I'll take some of them with me, and whoever I can't take care of can go back to their parents' homes. The house will be alright. You live right next door. Keep an eye on it for me."

And she returned to the previous topic.

"You're the same as everyone else, Chat. Don't think I'm old and outdated. Listen to some of the things I warn you about. The political situation might be different, but people's hearts have been the same since the beginning of time. Power is tempting and people have always fought over it. And how will the power be shared equally? Have you thought about that?"

Gade listened to Chao Chom Amphan in alarm. At first, she had been like many Bangkok people, who felt that the political situation did not concern them and that the conflict was between a certain group of people, who were far above them. Ordinary people's lives, whether difficult or comfortable previously, would continue as before.

But now, she began to feel that the events of the 24th of June 1932 had caused her to become separated from those she loved. Nart had been forced to leave again and she didn't know when she would see him next, and in another two or three months, the woman who had been so kind to her, and on whom she depended for emotional support, was leaving for Phetchaburi, and didn't say when she would be back.

Even so, life for Gade had in many ways improved. She loved her new house and felt that her life had more financial security. For one thing, all the land consisted of fertile orchards and provided her with a good and constant source of income. She also planned to rent out some of the land to a charcoal factory, instead of letting it go to waste.

For another thing, when Gade's relatives from Phetchaburi found out she had her own home in Bangkok, it became a meeting place for them whenever any of them came to the city. As time went on, they would send their sons to stay with her so that they could go to school, and their daughters to help out and learn housekeeping from Khunying Gade, rather than staying in Phetchaburi with nothing to do. So Gade's home was full of life and not isolated as it had been at first.

The labour of these relatives enabled Gade to increase her income in many ways. Besides rambutans, mangosteen and prunes, she could also sell flowers for making perfumes and traditional medicines, thereby providing for her relatives, without needing to touch the money that Nart sent her each month. It was her intention to save all the money that Nart sent her for Ned's education, so that he could become an officer like his father, whether he paid for his son or not.

Another blessing was Man, Nart's old servant. Not long after he had come to live with Gade, Man, who had never married, fell in love with Juan, a wealthy young widow whose family owned a nearby orchard. Gade was pleased for him and assumed the responsibility of paying the bride price to the woman's family, and he proudly took charge of his wife's orchard.

Man was a good man and was kind to the woman's son, who was not yet ten, and worked hard in the orchard. Nor did he drink or smoke, which pleased his wife very much.

Gade was afraid that his wife's family might look down on him because he had no wealth of his own, so she advised him to carry himself with dignity on account of closeness to Colonel Phraya Wisetsingnart. He was also able to read and write, and was familiar with the etiquette of those of high rank, unlike other villagers.

Man followed her advice wholeheartedly and his wife's relatives were full of respect for him. Indeed, he became highly regarded in the neighbourhood and Gade's influence grew accordingly. Nobody dared to harass her, even though she was a woman without a husband to protect her.

The rainy season of 1933 commenced in June as it always did.

Rern had come to visit her sister as she did every two months or so. Although Klai could have been transferred to a post in Bangkok, he decided to remain in Phetchaburi because his father was getting old and he had to take care of both his own and his wife's plantations.

"Klai didn't ask to be transferred, and mother and father don't mind because you've got plenty of relatives staying with you, so they don't need to worry. It's not as if you're all alone like you were at first."

"I feel at home here now," Gade insisted, so that her sister wouldn't worry. "Especially now, since most of the neighbours are Juan's relatives. They respect Man, and now they respect me, too."

The rainy season passed and in October the sky became clear and blue again and the evenings got cooler, indicating that the cool season was coming. One night that Gade could never forget, the moon was almost full and shone its rays through the mosquito net onto the white mattress where Ned was lying with his eyes wide open. She decided to sing him a lullaby to help him sleep.

"Dear Moon, please grant me rice and curry and a copper ring."

"Mother," Ned interrupted. "I don't want that song."

"Then what song do you want?" Gade asked, hugging him.

"I want you to sing the moonlight song."

Ned meant the song *'A Night Full of Stars'* because it began, *'Tonight's the night my heart delights in the moonlight.'* Sometimes, when she wasn't feeling emotional, Gade would sing it to him, but she could never forget that she had first heard the song on her wedding night.

Nor had she forgotten the words of the one who sang it to her, when he swore by the stars that he would love her forever, even though he had clearly forgotten.

Ned noticed his mother's face was sad and reached up to hug her.

"Mommy," he said as he sometimes called her, "Why are you crying?"

Gade hugged him and kissed his soft cheeks that smelled of talcum powder.

"I'm not crying. I'm trying to think of the words. I'm afraid I can't remember. Go to sleep and I'll sing you the cuckoo song instead."

"No, I want the moonlight song."

Gade relented and, laying him down gently and fanning him, she sang the song he asked for.

"Tonight's the night my heart delights in the moonlight,

Please come, my love, and sit with me as the breeze blows the scent of jasmine."

The white flowers of the night jasmine that had been planted next to the fence, close to the window, were in bloom and their fragrance was carried inside on the breeze. Gade's voice began to break as she sang.

"The night jasmine, although not bright, has sweet perfume,
Just as kindness and character are much sweeter than pleasing looks."

Gade paused before the final verse as she always did because she could not bring herself to sing the part that Nart had once sung to her.

"Bees flit and fly to jasmine blooms,
But I am many miles removed.
Their sweet perfume calls me back home."

Little did she know that her sweet voice floated outside the window and could be heard clearly in the silence of the night as it reached the ears of someone who was standing right outside the window. That someone listened intently and a smile appeared on his face, which had been solemn when he had first entered the gate outside the house. Now the moonlight shone its silver rays onto the broad figure of Colonel Phraya Wisetsingnart.

Man had been the one to lead his former boss inside the gate of Khunying Wisetsingnart's house. Bright lanterns that were hung on the gate shone onto the courtyard in front of the house, where several people were selecting fruit. A few dogs ran out from under the house, but when they recognized who it was, they didn't bark and were chased back.

"Where's Khunying, Suk?" he asked Ned's nanny, who was now the housekeeper and took care of Gade's young relatives.

"She's inside the house, Man," she replied, looking past him at the dashing man in the officer's uniform with a mixture of curiosity and excitement. When she recognized his face from the picture that hung in the living room, she hurriedly got down from the bamboo table and sat on the floor to prostrate herself.

"She's putting Ned to bed. She'll be down in a minute."

Phraya Wisetsingnart looked around him and noticed a boy of about twelve or thirteen and four or five teenage girls. All of them had fresh faces and were simply dressed, but looked clean and tidy, so he knew they were not servants. There were also female servants ranging in age from their teens to middle age, but there wasn't a single man among them.

The single-storey house with the hip roof, as far as he could see in the lamplight, wasn't that big, but it looked imposing and well maintained. The area under the house was used for storage, but it was tidy and didn't look messy.

"Please come up, sir," Man urged politely.

Then he turned to Suk.

"Suk, go and tell Khunying that Chao Khun is here."

"I won't come in yet," Phraya Wisetsingnart responded, concealing his awkwardness by asking, "What are you doing?"

"I'm selecting fruit for the merchants to take to the market in the morning, sir," she replied respectfully and hurried away.

As far as he could see, the house was in good condition and all of Gade's relatives were hard at work, indicating that she managed them well. Moreover, she clearly knew how to supplement her income, which did not surprise him because, since he had known her in Phetchaburi, she had always been a hard worker.

The scent of night jasmine had enticed him to walk in the direction the fragrance was coming from, and he had stopped outside the window unintentionally, seeing that there was no light, when he heard a sweet clear voice singing.

"*The night jasmine, although not bright, has sweet perfume,*
Just as kindness and character are much sweeter than pleasing looks."

A smile appeared on his face. If Gade had not forgotten this song, she could not have forgotten who had sung it to her the first time on her wedding night.

The dogs that had been chased back under the house, did not recognize the scent of the stranger who had been standing there for so long, and began to bark. The sound of dogs barking, as if they had seen an intruder, aroused Gade's suspicions and she got up from the bed and went to the window. She called out sharply when she saw the shadow beneath the window, recognizing that it was the figure of a man.

"Who is it? What are you doing here?"

Gade was not afraid of a robber, if she had him cornered, because she was able to protect herself. Nart had taught her how to use a gun, and she had also asked Klai to show her, but she had never had to face this situation before.

But when that person standing outside looked up at her, she felt as if the ground beneath her had opened up and she had to hold onto the window frame.

The door that had been ajar was pushed open and Suk knelt down and told her hesitatingly, "Khunying, Chao Khun is here."

Ned was about to fall asleep, but when he heard his nanny, he sat up and asked, "Who's here, Mother?"

Gade collected herself and pulled open the mosquito net to lie her son back down, and answered shakily, "It's nothing. I'm just going outside. You lie down and Suk will keep you company."

Ned sat up again and insisted on going with her.

"No, Mother. I want to go with you."

If she had refused, it would have taken a long time to get him settled back down again, so she decided to pick him up from the bed, telling Suk, "Invite him inside. I'll be down in a minute."

The meeting between the two of them in the living room was awkward, and they were polite but cool.

Nart was standing and did not sit down. He looked around the attractively decorated room, similar to his home when he was an officer in Phetchaburi. When he saw his picture hanging on the wall, an old picture of him when he had been Lieutenant Colonel Phra Narentharaksa, he was satisfied that Gade still cared for him. But when she entered the room, accompanied by the nanny who was holding the hand of the four-year-old boy, he could sense that things would not be as easy as he had thought.

"Gade, how are you?" he asked, hardly knowing what he was saying.

Gade knelt down and pulled her son close, as if she was paying respect to an elder relative rather than her husband, answering simply, "I'm fine, thank you."

When he didn't say anything else, neither did she, and she waited patiently until he could stand it no longer.

"Sit on a chair, Gade, so we can talk."

When she sat down, she chose a chair far away from him and lifted her son onto her lap. The nanny left the three of them sitting alone together in silence.

Ned was the one to ease the tension, without realizing it. He regarded the stranger with large innocent eyes, and his quick mind immediately recognized that he was the man in the photograph, whom his mother had told him was his father for as long as he could remember, and whom everyone in the house referred to as 'Chao Khun'.

Ned shook his mother's arm with excitement that he was seeing his father for the first time.

"Mother, Father's here...Don't you remember him?"

The stranger's eyes rested on Ned with an expression that he had never seen in anyone's eyes before. Instinctively, he sensed his father's love and, although he was too young to explain it, he recognized his own flesh and blood.

Phraya Wisetsingnart patted the arm of the chair and called to him, his voice shaking.

"Ned, come and see me."

Ned looked at his mother as if to ask for permission and, when she nodded and stroked his back, he slid down from her lap without any shyness and went to his father for the first time.

His eyes were bright and penetrating, his little head was covered with shiny black hair, and he walked with a straight back.

Being a soldier was in his blood, Nart thought, and knew it was his son.

"Pay respect to your father," Gade instructed him when she saw him standing and staring up at his father.

Ned knew how to prostrate himself, since his mother had taught him to do it at the temple when he paid respect to the monks, and also from when he went to see Khun Chom, whom he was allowed to call 'Aunt'.

He knelt down on the floor and bowed, and when he raised his head, he found his father's hand reaching out to lift him onto his lap and hug him so tightly that he almost couldn't breathe.

Originally, Colonel Phraya Wisetsingnart had gone to his wife's house in Bang Pho simply to check on them, since he was responsible for their welfare as a husband and father.

He told himself that he didn't expect anything more than to see that Gade was safe and well, and that there was no other man harassing her. More importantly he wanted to see his son in the flesh.

Once he had Ned in his arms and heard him call him 'Father', he was filled with a new emotion that he had never felt before. That emotion was more than gladness. It was the gladness, joy and pride, mixed with intense love that parents feel towards their children when holding them in their arms.

"Ned," Phraya Wisetsingnart said happily, "What do you want to be when you grow up?"

Ned showed no signs of shyness, since he was so used to hearing about 'Chao Khun' from everyone in the house. Man, in particular, never ceased telling him stories about 'Chao Khun', and Ned had been desperately wanting to meet him. He answered immediately, "I want to be a soldier, like you."

Phraya Wisetsingnart laughed, delighted with everything his son said.

"So you know I'm a soldier, do you? Do you know my rank?"

"You're a Chao Khun."

"Very good. I'm a colonel. Remember that. When you're older, you can join the Army Academy and wear a uniform like mine. Have you learned to read yet?"

"The monk at the temple taught me."

"When you're old enough, I'll send you to Suan Kulap School. How old are you now?"

"Ten," he answered, holding up ten fingers, and trying, unsuccessfully, to count them.

"What? How can you be ten? Gade, how old is he?"

Gade glared at him reproachfully. How could he not even know how old his son was?

"He's four, but he likes to tell everyone he's ten. You can't believe everything he says. Ned, come back here."

The little boy looked disappointed when his mother called him, so he came up with an excuse.

"I want to look at Father's shirt."

Since Nart was wearing his uniform, there were lots of exciting looking badges on his shirt, and Ned was interested.

"Ned," Gade repeated more sternly. "Did you hear what I said?"

"Let him be, Gade," Nart protested. "He can look if he wants to. I don't mind. Which one do you want to look at? I see you want to look at my rank. You've never seen it before, have you?"

By this time, not only did Nart not want to let Ned down from his lap, but he also wanted to carry him back to Khorat with him.

Finally, Gade ended their meeting abruptly when she saw that father and son had been enjoying each other's company for long enough.

"It's very late. It's way past your bedtime, Ned. It's time you went to bed, or you'll be cranky in the morning."

Phraya Wisetsingnart was dismayed. He looked pleadingly at his wife but she ignored him, so there was nothing else he could do except let his son go to his mother.

Gade called the nanny to take her son to bed, after she had him prostrate himself before his father once more before leaving the room, but he turned back to look at his father fondly.

"I want to see my father," he told the nanny and his voice could be heard from outside the room.

"Come to bed, or your mother will be cross."

Nart peeled his eyes away from the door and turned to his wife.

"Gade, is there anyone else living here with you apart from your relatives?"

The long question received a short answer.

"No, just my relatives."

"Aren't there any men here?"

"Well, there's Bun Khlong…" she replied in more detail. "He's the youngest son of my Uncle Muen. He's just turned thirteen. Klai sent him here to go to school."

So since Man had gone to live with his wife, there were no grown men in the house. If there was an emergency, how would the women and children protect themselves?

Phraya Wisetsingnart left his wife's house and walked across the wooden bridge to Man's house. He had left both the commissioned and non-commissioned officers who were under his command there because he wasn't sure how Gade would respond to him and wanted to avoid embarrassment. Now he felt both relieved and anxious. He was relieved that Gade hadn't changed and was still as calm and collected as always, but he was worried about many things.

"Man…" he said glumly as they were walking back, Man leading the way with a lantern. "I asked you to stay in Bang Pho to keep an eye on Khunying and my son, but you went and found yourself a wife."

"Yes, sir," Man replied, not knowing what else to say.

"If you'd found a wife and continued living in the house, I wouldn't have minded, but you're living in your wife's house, which is far away. What if robbers break in? Who will they call for help? There are only women and children there."

In truth, Khunying had been living there for almost a year, and all the neighbours knew her husband lived in Khorat. If robbers had wanted to break it, surely, they would not have waited this long. There was no need to worry about that anymore.After considering his words for a moment, Man sought to reassure him.

"There are no robbers in Bang Pho, sir. They're good people here, and almost everyone's related in some way."

"How do you know? You're not from around here."

"Everyone around here's related to Juan, sir. There are a lot of families…" he coughed proudly, "and all her relatives respect me. Khunying's my boss, and everyone respects her. No one would dream of harming her. In fact, everyone looks out for her."

When he noticed that his boss was listening intently, Man realized he'd been right in guessing that he was worried about his wife and son, so he continued in earnest, "Ever since she came to live here, Khunying's behaviour has been faultless. She helps people, and she's not at all arrogant. All her relatives who've come to live with her are well behaved, and everyone respects her. Ned knows everyone. He walks all over the place and people invite him in for fruit or sweets. Khunying won't let him be snobbish."

"Wait a minute, Man," Phraya Wisetsingnart interrupted. "What did you say? Gade lets her son walk all over the place like a farmer's son?"

Man swallowed, seeing that his boss was becoming irritated again.

"How can a child of his age be left to walk around by himself? The furrows are as deep as canals. Who will see him if he falls in? There's no one about, and he's wearing gold bracelets. What if he meets gangsters? How can he protect himself?"

Chao Khun was worried about his son alright, thought Man. His mother was a lot more relaxed, and that was why he wasn't shy of strangers and everyone loved him.

"I've never seen any, sir."

"Are you going to wait until you see some? That's it. If anything happens, you're dead."

"He's never alone, sir. If he isn't with Suk, he's with me, or at least Bun Khlong. When he comes home from school, he takes him to pick fruit."

"He's just a child himself. How can you rely on him? I should have known I couldn't trust you to keep an eye on him."

"From now on, you're not to let Ned out of your sight. Do you hear, Man?"

"Yes, sir," Man replied as politely as before.

The dogs under Man's house barked as they reached the courtyard, and Nart took advantage of the opportunity to ask about the other matter that was troubling him.

"Man, has anyone from Khun Chom Amphan's house been to see Gade?"

He didn't specify 'Khun Chom's brother' because he didn't want his servant to know that he was worried. Man didn't suspect anything and answered sincerely, "Khun Chom moved to Phetchaburi ages ago. Khunying only goes into the city occasionally, but her relatives from Phetchaburi come every month. Rern will be coming in two-or three-days' time. She loves her sister and visits often."

Nart let out a sigh of relief. That was one less thing to worry about.

Gade was behaving with propriety, and wasn't leading on any other man while he was away. Nevertheless, she seemed out of his reach, and this prevented him from feeling truly content.

❋❋❋❋❋

The house that Phraya Wisetsingnart brought Nuathong to stay in while he was in Bangkok on business was the home of his police colonel cousin, Phra Prabribupai, who lived with his widowed mother, who was in her sixties. When Nart gave money to his cousin to pass on to Gade, she took advantage of the opportunity to visit his mother, since she was her husband's aunt and it was a way of introducing herself to her husband's family in accordance with Chao Chom Amphan's advice. Since Gade held Chao Chom Amphan in high esteem, she swallowed her pride and went to introduce herself to Phra Prabribupai's mother, Lamai, depending on her talkative young son to break the ice.

Lamai was smitten with Ned at once, and sympathized with Gade as a woman. In addition, when she had met Nuathong, she had taken an instant dislike to her, so she was very much on Gade's side.

When her nephew came to stay with her this time on his return from Khorat, after they had prostrated themselves before her and had barely lifted their faces, she began to scold him.

"You've been gone for almost a year. I've missed you. And now you're back, have you been to see Gade yet?"

Nart was dumbfounded and glanced at Nuathong. She looked very displeased, but there was nothing else he could do except answer quietly, "Not yet, Aunt."

"Have you seen your son yet, Nart? Everyone says he's the spitting image of his mother, but I think he's a lot like you. It's a shame I can't find any photos of you when you were a boy, or we'd be able to compare the two of you."

These questions made Nart want to see his son, so he decided to go to Bang Pho the very next day.

As soon as her husband had left the house that morning, Nuathong hurried to the gambling table that she had so desperately missed. She did not have the prudence to foresee how her actions would damage her, since Nart's aunt was keeping a close eye on her every move. When Lamai found out, she naturally told her son and other relatives and, since it was her house that they were staying in, she was not embarrassed to ask Nuathong where she had been in front of her husband.

"Where do you go, Nuathong? You go out every day."

Nuathong frowned and replied, "I go to see my friends. I haven't seen them for so long. If I don't go and see them, they'll say I'm mean."

Lamai smiled knowingly.

"Oh, I sympathize. I play with my relatives when I'm bored, but I never go to gambling houses. It would embarrass my son."

Nart knew that Nuathong had come with him from Nakhon Ratchasima, partly because she was possessive over him, but mostly because she wanted to gamble, and this made their relationship more and more awkward. Once they were inside the bedroom, she vented her anger.

"Why doesn't the old fool just mind her own business, instead of poking her nose into other people's affairs? I've no respect for her."

"Don't say that!" Nart warned angrily. "We're staying in her house."

"You don't have to remind me," she complained. "You're a grown man and you still can't find a house of your own."

"We don't even live in Bangkok. Why would I buy a house here when we're only staying a few days? Of course, we have to stay with a relative."

"If you'd have done what your friends did, we wouldn't be in this mess. All your friends have been promoted. You only have to say the word and Chao Khun Thep will help you. I don't know why you have to be so stubborn."

They had had countless arguments over the matter and this time, Phraya Wisetsingnart was so annoyed that he left the house at once without saying another word to her. Nart was also anxious about something else that he couldn't tell anyone about, even though he guessed that a police officer like his cousin, Phra Prab, knew all about it.

The reason he was concerned was that he had been called to Bangkok on business. It was significant that, less than a year later, the second political change was carried out in the same manner as the first time.

Just as he had expected, soon after Phraya Mano had resigned as Prime Minister, Colonel Phraya Si Sitthisongkhram was asked to resign from his position as Director of Army Training Command and Deputy Commander of Army Operations immediately.

When he arrived at the Ministry of Defence, he found out that his friend was behind the order. Colonel Phraya Thepakanee did not beat around the bush when they met after almost a year.

"I asked the ministry to call you because I don't want you to be involved with the rebellion that I've heard rumours of."

Although his blood ran cold, he feigned confusion.

"I don't know what you mean."

"Don't try to pull the wool over my eyes. I haven't forgotten what you said to me at Ananta Samakhom Throne Hall last year."

Nart took time to weigh up his words, but his heart was heavy.

Det had been his best friend and they had once trusted each other so much that they would have laid down their lives for each other, but now there was a crack in their relationship that seemed impossible to fix.

The tension continued as no one knew the way out, and caused Nart to hesitate before responding because he did not know what the outcome would be.

"I asked them to call you from Khorat to the Ministry. It's nothing important. You know that, don't you?"

Phraya Thepakanee continued speaking, keeping his eyes fixed on his friend scrutinizingly.

"I don't want you getting involved with certain people because certain matters will get you in trouble."

"Tell me who you mean," Phraya Wisetsingnart retorted, also not wanting to beat around the bush.

Phraya Thepakanee gave him a direct answer.

"Prince Boworadet and Chao Khun Si Sitthisongkhram."

Nart showed no sign of alarm.

"I'm not close to him, and I haven't seen Din since he returned from Khorat."

"Good. Stay away from them, and if anything happens, there won't be a coup."

Nart held his gaze steadily, even though his blood was boiling because of his friend's words.

"I don't believe that anyone in the land would betray the king. If there is someone, it's not me for sure."

Phraya Thepakanee slammed his fist on the table in irritation.

"Don't try to be clever. I know what you're thinking. I'll get to the point, so we don't have to argue. And don't go back to Khorat, yet. Stay here in Bangkok until you're told to return. That's an order."

He spoke sternly as if he was talking to someone under his command.

"Whose order?" Nart asked quietly, without aggression, but not submissively.

"My order, but if you want it signed by someone higher, tell me and I'll get it."

Nart put his hat on and saluted his old friend, who had now become his 'boss'.

"Yes, sir."

He did not turn around as he walked towards the door, even when he heard his friend say, "A friend like you deserves to be cursed. I don't know why I keep helping you."

*****

Colonel Phraya Wisetsingnart realized that he was getting closer and closer to a raging political whirlpool.

Nart wanted to meet and sound out various individuals, but he was frustrated to find that if he went to see one person, they would be on 'this side', and if he went to see the other side, they would become 'that side'. He didn't want to be caught in the middle, but he had no choice when an officer close to Luang Phibun Songkhram came to his residence with a letter of invitation.

By now, Phibun had come closer to the throne of power than any of his peers, since he had been in the group who had ousted Phraya Mano's government. Even though the leader had been Phraya Pahonphonphayuhesena, many people realized where the real power lay.

Nart was relieved to find that Luang Phibun Songkhram still treated him politely, without the aggression of Phraya Thepakanee, but he could not tell what he was thinking about him. The fact that they were able to talk together alone, without a third-party eased the tension considerably.

Nart again made his position clear.

"I won't betray the king. If you're asking, that's all I'll say."

Luang Phibun Songkhram smiled enigmatically.

"You haven't changed. You still think and act the same."

"And how do you want me to change?"

"I don't," he answered and was silent for a moment, before continuing, "You're fine the way you are, but I'm asking...because I'm concerned about you. Don't do anything that might lead to misunderstandings. Your every move, and those of all the officers of your rank, is being watched by Luang Adun. That's all I can tell you."

Both Nart's cousin, Phra Prab, and Nart himself were well aware that Luang Adundetcharat was monitoring anyone who showed any signs of 'movement' that was antagonistic towards the government.

Nart couldn't help thinking about the situation in France after the bloody revolution of 1789. Even after Louis XVI and Marie Antoinette had been removed, the country was not peaceful and the hoped for equality did not materialize. Instead, there was a bloodbath for years after.

He glanced out of the window at the setting sun, and told his host, "I should go."

Luang Phibun Songkhram put his hand on his arm, saying sincerely, "Please stay for dinner, Nart. My wife has already prepared a meal."

Nart smiled gratefully, but was adamant.

"I'll stay another time, but today I want to see my son. I haven't seen him for days."

10
The Battle

"Mother, I'm not going to sleep, yet."

Gade unfolded the blanket and covered Ned with it. The October weather was changing from humid to cool, and she was afraid he would catch a cold, but he pushed the blanket away unhappily.

"Go to sleep. It's time to sleep. If you stay up late, you'll be grumpy tomorrow."

"But...Father hasn't come yet."

Gade stopped stroking his hair for a moment and tried to think of a response.

Usually, her husband came to see their son every day, but it had been two days since he had last visited. In contrast to the calm and composed demeanour that she adopted as Khunying Wisetsingnart in order to maintain the respect of her relatives and servants, Gade had not felt calm since she had first set eyes on Nart again. He could not have known that after the first night he appeared she did not sleep until morning.

She stood holding onto the window frame and looked up at the stars, remembering that he had sworn by the stars to love her and never leave or forsake her; she couldn't help smiling bitterly. Even the stars moved in orbit and did not remain in the same place, so how could one man's words remain unchanged? His promise that if he was unfaithful, he would not be successful had also not come true. They were the empty words of a man trying to win a young girl's heart because her parents did not want her to marry him.

Gade still could not find an answer to the question of what would become of their relationship. Until recently, as Nart had gradually becoming more distant from them, she thought she had an answer. She sighed and bent down to kiss her son.

"Go to sleep. Your father isn't coming."

"Where is he?" Ned persisted.

"Your father's far away. Sometimes he can come and sometimes he can't. Don't wait up, darling. Go to sleep...and tomorrow, I'll let Aunt Khlong take you to Uncle Man's house."

"I don't want to go to Uncle Man's house."

"Then what do you want to do?"

"I want you to sing…"

"Again?"

"Again…" Ned said brightly, imitating his mother's voice. "Again…"

Gade felt touched and bent down to kiss his cheek. Ned put his arms around her neck and hugged her so tightly that she lost her balance and fell onto the bed. Afraid of squashing him, she cried out, "Hey! Be careful!"

The sound of mother and son's squeals of laughter rang out as someone stopped outside the open door of the bedroom. His serious face broke into a smile when he heard their bright laughter from inside the room. Gade released her son's arms to lie him back down again and almost dropped him when she suddenly heard a deep voice as he entered the room.

"What are you two playing?"

Gade froze while Ned leapt up and wrenched back the mosquito net, jumping down from the bed and running to his father.

"Father...Father's here!"

His father scooped him up in his arms and Ned hugged him as tightly as he had hugged his mother, overjoyed as he turned to her and cried, "You see, Mother? Father's here!"

As if that wasn't enough, he tattled on her cheerfully.

"Mother said you weren't coming. I knew you'd come."

The boy's delight moved his father – more than he could understand, and Nart asked for affirmation.

"Were you waiting for me, Ned?"

"I was waiting for you," he answered brightly.

Gade slowly pulled back the mosquito net, masking her inner turmoil with difficulty.

"I want to sleep with Father. Can you sleep with me, Father?"

Nart held his son in his arms, hiding a smile as he bent down to press his head against his shoulder. Incredibly, his son had helped to make everything easier.

"Of course, I can. I'll sleep here tonight."

Gade felt cold all over.

The servant girl put down a mat and covered it with a white cloth for the meal, while another brought a small round bamboo table with a tray of food neatly laid out and a bowl of water for handwashing sprinkled with fragrant jasmine. Even though his arrival had been unexpected, Gade had managed to arrange everything effortlessly. And it was also true that, since Gade had stepped out of the bedroom and left him to play with Ned until he led him by the hand to have dinner with him, he had not seen her again.

Only her younger sister sat on the floor politely, leaving some distance between them because she was conscious of his high status, but chatting away as she had always done.

Gade forced herself to tuck the sheet tightly around the mattress and chased a mosquito out of the net with a horse tail whip before putting the net back in place. If Chao Khun was going to stay the night, only this room was fitting for a man of his rank, but he could not expect Gade to share the room with him. Rern's room was big enough for both of them, and there was still room for Ned. Confident that she had found a way out of the awkward situation between the two of them, she breathed a sigh of relief.

Rern sat hugging her knees inside the mosquito net on the wide mattress that was placed on a mat in the middle of her room. She looked at her sister, who was lying on her side with her back to her, with a mixture of weariness and pity. The idea of keeping her thoughts to herself did not enter her mind.

"Oh, Gade! Chao Khun made the effort to make up with you and asked to stay the night, and you're sleeping in my room! He'll lose face! You're not a couple of teenagers anymore. Can't you stop sulking?"

Gade continued lying with her back to her sister and said irritably, "I'm going to sleep. If you want to talk, go and find Suk or someone else to talk to. Don't bother me."

"If you keep on sulking, Chao Khun will go back to that woman and she'll be the one laughing, while you'll be without a husband. What good will that do?"

Now Gade turned to looked at Rern and said firmly, "Do you really think Chao Khun has finished with that woman? I know he hasn't. He's brought her with him from Khorat. In a few days, when his business is finished, they'll be going back, and what about me, Rern? I'll stay here in Bang Pho like before. Have you ever seen him take me to live with him as his wife, even when I'm his rightful wife? No, never."

Rern was speechless.

"If he comes on business again, he'll show up once more, and then he'll go back again. I'll be his minor wife, and someone else will be his principal wife, or is that not true?"

"It's true, but..."

"If Chao Khun really cares about me, he has to sort it out. It's not that he doesn't know. He knows why I'm angry. If he doesn't sort it out, and he just comes here when he feels like it, he can sleep in that room alone. Even though I've never laid a word of blame on him, I haven't forgotten how he hurt me."

Rern's lips, which had parted to argue, closed when she heard the last sentence, and Gade reminded her, "Like I told you before, it's hard enough with one child. I don't want to have a second and a third child longing for their father. No matter how much I love him, if I can't trust him, I can't go back to him again."

Once again, Rern had been silenced, and she crawled out of the mosquito net and sat outside it, hugging her knees as she turned to her sister who had lain back down to go to sleep.

The sound of his son's voice rang out beside him as he chatted about Uncle Man, Suk, Aunt Khlong and the villagers. Ned seemed to know everyone.

Almost every sentence contained the word 'Mother', and ended with a question addressed to 'Father'.

"Mother's taking me to the temple to see the monks. Will you come too, Father?"

"Mother's taking me to see Grandma. Will you come, Father?"

Mother this and Mother that. His mother was on his mind with every breath he took. Nart sighed softly as he nodded to his son, although his mind was on his own affairs.

Gradually Ned's voice grew softer, his eyes closed, and a moment later he had fallen asleep in the middle of the story he was telling. Nart covered his son with the blanket, adjusted his pillow and pulled another blanket over himself. The fresh blanket was infused with the delicate scent of jasmine, which mixed with the fragrance of the nocturnal blossoms that were carried in through the window on the breeze. The house in the Bang Pho plantation was silent apart from the sound of nocturnal birds chirping and fish flipping on the surface of the water in the furrows.

There was no sign of Gade coming back into the bedroom. She had prepared a meal and a bed for him and disappeared. There were so many people in the house that he couldn't just go looking to see which room she was sleeping in. He supposed she was sleeping in her sister's room and was using her sister as a shield to prevent him from talking to her.

He knew that she still loved him. The fact that she had not shown him animosity or made the servants turn against him proved that behind his back she still felt a connection with him and wanted her son to be close to him. It was clear that she still accepted him as her son's father. The only thing that concerned him was that she did not accept him as her husband.

"Let's see if Chao Khun comes today," Rern said to Gade.

Gade ignored her as usual. That was the best thing to do, she decided, in order to nip the topic in the bud. But Rern persisted. Even if her sister remained silent, she would do the talking.

"I think he'll come. When he left the house this morning, he was smiling, and he said the rice soup was nice and hot. I asked him what he wanted for dinner, and he said something bland. He's been eating spicy food for several days in succession, and it upsets his stomach."

She lowered her voice and chuckled as she asked without expecting an answer, "When he goes home today, he's bound to get a scolding after being gone all night! Who would believe he was sleeping with his son and not his wife?"

Gade walked away in irritation and spent the rest of the day busying herself with her work with extra diligence, making sure that she was not left alone with her sister, because she was afraid she would mention her brother-in-law again. Despite her resolve, that afternoon, when it was time to begin preparations for dinner, Gade could not resist ordering the servants to make several dishes that were not spicy, telling herself, 'Even if he doesn't come, we can still eat them ourselves.'

Although she spoke to her sister with determination, as if her decision was final, only she knew that it was just a fortress she had built to protect her broken heart.

The fortress was fragile and easy to destroy, and if Gade yielded, even a little, and let Nart come close, they would soon be talking as they had done in the past. There might be remonstrations from her, and after that, Nart would only have to hold her in his arms, and she would be unable to resist, even though she knew she would be hurt again, even worse than before because, added to the pain, would be the knowledge that she had not learned her lesson.

For that reason, Gade had decided to close the door from the start. On the other hand, why did it have to end in disappointment? Couldn't it end with her and Nart making up and living together happily as Rern hoped? It could not, because the other woman still remained, and her husband showed no sign of leaving her.

Besides this, how many times had Nart walked out of Gade's life, without caring if he hurt the very woman he had promised to love forever? Gade wanted to ask him how anyone, after being hurt many times, would not be afraid of a repeat performance. Or, if he had been in her situation, would he not have been scared of such a thing happening again?

Despite knowing this, however, she could not escape the truth that she had been unable to stop loving the man who had hurt her so badly.

If only she could hate him, or just be indifferent to him, as he was to her, there would be no need for her to build this fortress. She would be able to act naturally around him, would be able to face him calmly and tell him it was over between them. She would be the one to walk out of his life with as much indifference as he had shown her. If she could do that, she would not have to hide her anxious feelings in the evenings as she waited to see if he would come, her heart would not sink into the depths of despair when he did not, and when she saw the first star twinkling in the night sky, the tears would not roll down her cheeks again.

That evening, the time passed slowly as it always did. Gade glanced at the clock on the wall several times, trying not to let Rern see that she was waiting for Nart, as she sat doing her work under the house surrounded by people selecting fruit to give to traders.

Ned was the first to ask, "Why isn't Father coming?"

"He'll be here soon," his aunt told him, and added, "Go and have a wash and be powdered, so you won't smell bad when your father picks you up. He likes people to be clean and to smell nice."

He stood up obediently without argument, which made Rern smile, and she told her sister, "Look at him! As soon as I mention his father, he'll do anything!"

Gade did not answer and continued to weave the garland she was making as if she hadn't heard, or wasn't interested. A moment later, her heart quickened when someone arrived in front of the house. Man walked in carrying a trunk, followed by Nart and a soldier who, after taking an order, saluted him and turned to Gade to pay respect to her before leaving.

Gade put off standing up to greet her husband by asking Man, "What's this?"

"This belongs to Chao Khun, madam. He asked me to bring it here."

Nart stood in front of the bamboo table, and answered with a smile, even though Gade had not asked him, "These are my clothes and my things. It's a hassle to have to go back to my aunt's house to change.

Oh! My aunt gave me these sweets for Ned. She asked you to take him to see her sometime. She misses him."

When he spoke to her so amiably and mentioned his relative, it would have been rude of her to ignore him, so she answered politely, "Yes, I will. I'll take him to thank her. Is she well?"

"Yes, she's as fit as ever. She mentioned you. You used to go and see her every month, but you haven't been this month, so she misses you."

"This month, I haven't been able to find a good time. Not since the beginning of the month."

He knew she meant it was not a good time because Nuathong was there. Gade was subtle enough not to say it directly.

"Since I arrived from Khorat."

"Yes."

"I suppose you'll wait until I've gone back to Khorat before you go and see her," he said with a hint of sarcasm.

"Yes, I will," she replied with indifference and not a hint of sarcasm.

I shouldn't have said that, Nart thought to himself, so he did not mention it again. Just then, Suk brought Ned in, so he turned to the boy running towards him, full of joy.

"Father's here! Father's here!"

Nart scooped him up in his arms, teasing as he put him down, "Did you fall in a basket of powder? My uniform's all white! Look!"

Gade watched her son and his father go up inside the house. The lamps began to glow, and tonight the atmosphere in the house seemed strangely cosy, even though nothing had changed except for the presence of one man.

The one who hugged his father's knees and chatted away was his son. When Suk crawled inside to take Ned downstairs because she was afraid he would disturb Chao Khun, Nart raised his hand to stop her.

"There's no need to take him. Leave him chatting here."

Rern followed her sister inside the room and with feigned innocence told her, "Man's brought Chao Khun's things in. Can you go and arrange his clothes for him? He's going to have a wash and change his clothes. It wouldn't be proper for me to do it."

"Where's Man? Why isn't he attending to him?"

"Oh…" Rern said, sounding surprised, "Man's gone home to have dinner with his family. He's not Chao Khun's servant anymore. He never interferes here. It would make Suk uncomfortable."

Gade ended the conversation by walking out of the room without speaking, opening the door to the bedroom and going over to the small rattan chest that Man had carried in. As she was unpacking, she felt a pang in her chest as pictures from the past came back to her.

When they were together, only Gade could touch his clothes. She would fold them neatly and choose each of his outfits according to the occasion, making her feel connected to him as if they were one. Gade was so preoccupied with the task in hand that she did not hear footsteps, since Nart had deliberately walked into the room without making a sound and opened the door so quietly that Gade did not hear. He stopped and stood behind her as she knelt in front of the rattan chest, taking out his clothes and folding them.

Nart stared at her without her knowing and the picture he saw was no different from years ago in Phetchaburi when his life had been peaceful and carefree unlike today. Gade suddenly turned around and was so startled when she caught her husband staring at her that the linen shirt slipped out of her hands.

Nart changed his expression as soon as he saw her alarm, and, smiling as if nothing was bothering him, he said, "Thanks for arranging my clothes. I'll go and bathe now. Oh! Tomorrow, I'll be back late. I'm going to see a friend. Just have some rice soup ready for me."

That night, Nart slept alone in his room. Ned did not sleep with him because he fell asleep in the evening, so Gade had Suk carry him into Rern's room to sleep with her and Rern. Gade ignored her sister's comments.

"Oh! This room's so small. It's so hot being squashed together. Poor Ned! I'm going to sleep outside the mosquito net!"

When Rern pulled back the mosquito net, Gade ignored her and let her sleep outside it.

In actual fact, Rern slept with a silk blanket over her head and went to sleep contentedly because the dried orange peel which they had lit kept the mosquitoes away. Instead, it was Gade who lay awake tossing and turning all night long.

Gade did not know that across the hallway, Nart was lying on the large bed with his arm across his forehead, depressed about both his work and his personal life, which were like a large pile of ropes tangled together. If he pulled one rope this way, another would stick, and if he pulled it there, it would get tighter here. There was no way out.

The sound of Nuathong's screams and sobs when he had gone home that morning still rang in his ears.

"Where have you been? Don't lie to me! You've been to see your old wife, haven't you? There are people trying to split us up. The old woman's got a nerve!"

The last sentence was directed at Nart's aunt, so he scolded her, "You leave my aunt out of it!"

"I won't! Why should I?"

Lamai was astute enough not to join in, but instead ordered a servant to go into Nart's room, put his clothes in a chest, and bring it downstairs without Nuathong seeing. Even though Tieng saw, she could do nothing about it. Lamai then ordered Nart's subordinate to put the chest in the car and whispered, "I've had enough! Tell Nart to stay somewhere else because I'm sick of their arguments in my house. Here are some sweets for my nephew. Tell Khunying Gade to bring him to see me. I miss him."

When he heard what his aunt had said, Nart did not waste any more time arguing. When Nuathong ran upstairs crying and went into the bedroom, hoping he would make up with her in bed as usual, he turned and walked out of the house with no intention of making up with her again.

The problem of Nuathong was nothing compared with the anxiety he felt about some of his friends, which had increased until he was almost at breaking point. Nart felt he was truly stuck between a rock and a hard place. He felt certain that, within the next few days, military forces from Nakhon Ratchasima would be surrounding Bangkok in order to overthrow the government once more.

Democracy, where the power to govern came from the people, had now disappeared far from reach. Just over a year after the revolution.

Despite the warning, or to be correct, the order that Phraya Thepakanee had given him, Nart found it impossible to stay alone quietly in Bangkok and pretend not to notice the mounting tension, or meet any of his friends, just because he wanted to survive the current that was getting stronger on both sides. If he did that, he would not be Colonel Phraya Wisetsingnart. He could not do it. They could order him to leave Nakhon Ratchasima to come to Bangkok, so that he would remain within the confines of the capital, but they could not force him not to meet his old friends.

He had met General Phraya Sena Songkhram only two days before, and yesterday he had met Colonel Phraya Si Sitthisongkhram and two or three other officers, but they had talked about the news in general, nothing specific.

The thing that alarmed Nart was that opposition to the government was sure to lead to violence. He did not believe that it would end peacefully as it had on 24th of June the previous year. Those who thought the government would negotiate were mistaken. He remembered Phraya Thepakanee's obstinate remarks and could not help thinking that it reflected the attitude of many of those in power.

Wasn't there anyone – there was no one that Nart could not think of – who would follow in the footsteps of the king, who had calmed the situation down before it got out of hand in order to spare the lives of his fellow Thais?

Gade woke up before dawn in order to get everything ready for her husband. She did not miss anything, from the clean water she filled to the brim of the metal basin in the bathroom to his uniform and his breakfast. The only thing missing was herself and she did not come out for him to see her, but sent her sister and her son's nanny to greet him instead.

Nart did not say anything and did not ask about his wife, but ate his breakfast, got dressed and left the house, saying only, "Rern, tonight I'm going to see a friend. I won't be back for dinner."

And with that he left, not forgetting to pat his son on the head to bid him farewell.

Rern stood watching her brother-in-law until he had disappeared out of sight amid the green plantations before hurrying to find her sister, who was in the kitchen behind the house.

Before Rern could say anything, Gade forestalled her.

"Don't say you're going back to Phetchaburi. I won't let you go back, yet."

"Well, I've been here for days. If I go back today, Klai won't need to come and fetch me."

"Klai won't mind coming up to Bangkok. He'll be able to buy medicine for his parents. Oh! The rice is almost gone. When the Chinese merchant comes by in his boat, go and buy some. I'm going to the temple this morning."

In this way, Gade had steered the conversation to another topic, so that Rern did not have an opportunity to mention her brother-in-law.

It was almost dark and the lamps in the house had been lit, but tonight it was quiet and the courtyard was not full of people as it usually was.

Tonight, there was a fair at Soi Thong Temple, so Gade had allowed the young people in the house to go and see the theatre and the puppet shows, warning them, "Go with the people from Man's house. Don't go by yourselves. You're all girls alone. It's dangerous."

The only servant left in the house was Suk, who was resting having complained of aches and pains. Rern stayed in the house doing light work, while chatting to her sister as Ned rolled about close by. The sound of a dog barking told them that a stranger had arrived, and Gade thought of her husband at once.

"It might be Chao Khun. Tell Suk to go and see," Gade told her sister, thereby revealing that she had been waiting for him.

Rern suppressed a smile and hastily stood up, going downstairs herself to meet her brother-in-law. Ned went after her.

"I'm coming to see Father."

"Oh, alright! Let's go together."

Rern held a lamp in one hand and Ned's hand in the other as they walked across the courtyard to the gate, chasing the dogs back under the house. When she saw who had pushed inside the gate, she shouted "Hey!" and stood frozen to the spot.

Nuathong walked inside, followed by her old servant, her face as hard as leather, looking hesitant. Behind her was Nart's subordinate, a first lieutenant, with an anxious expression and another servant.

Nuathong looked Rern up and down and said tartly, "I'm here to see Chao Khun. I know he's here."

Rern's animosity overrode her alarm when she realized who it was, and she countered at once, "Who said you could come in? Get out!"

Nuathong screamed back, "So they're in the house, are they? Meeting in secret! In that case, I'll go in there myself!"

She attempted to storm past Rern to go inside, but Rern was too quick for her, pushing her with such force that she was almost knocked to the ground.

"You can't go in. This is my sister's house!" she screamed back.

Gade heard the commotion and opened the window to look. When she saw who it was, her heart sank, and her face went numb with embarrassment when she heard the screams and curse words pouring out of Nuathong's mouth. Concern for Ned outweighed her anger and she went downstairs in order to bring him inside, but she had to compete with Nuathong's screaming.

As soon as Ned saw his mother, he ran to her and held on to her.

"Mother...I'm afraid!"

Gade held onto her son tightly and when she saw him trembling, she tried to comfort him.

"Chao Khun's not here," she told the other woman firmly, but calmly. "Leave this house right now!"

But Nuathong's anger was uncontrollable. She was used to getting her own way, and had forgotten that this was Gade's house, and that Gade was Nart's legal and rightful wife, not her. She lunged for Gade in order to strike her, pushing Suk out of the way, but instead met Rern who had jumped in front of her to protect her sister, shouting out to Gade, "Gade! Take Ned in the house! Quick! Don't worry about me."

Gade was not as concerned for herself as she was for her son and, seeing that Nuathong had lost control and might harm him, picked him up and turned to go inside the house. As she reached the stairs, Nuathong broke free from Rern's grasp, and approaching Gade yanked her arm so that Ned slipped to the ground. He let out a cry, more out of shock than of pain.

The sound of her son's cries pierced Gade's heart.

She didn't know where her strength came from, but she pushed Nuathong out of the way and picked up Ned from the ground as he held onto her tightly and sobbed even louder than before.

"Don't cry. There's no need to be afraid," she told him shakily. "I'm here."

Suddenly the commotion stopped at the sound of a deep voice from the direction of the gate.

"What's going on?"

It was as if an unseen hand had come and put a stop to the uproar. Suk and Rern, who were each holding onto one of Nuathong's arms, let go of her, while Tieng came to help her mistress by pushing Suk out of the way.

Phraya Wisetsingnart looked tense as he looked from face to face as if he could not believe what he had seen.

The only sound was of Ned's sobs, which had still not subsided. Gade and the others were silent, not knowing what to do.

Nuathong was the first to come to her senses, knowing from experience exactly what to do in such situations, so she ran to her husband and flung her arms around him, sobbing, "I came to see you and they attacked me! Please help me!"

He pushed her away a little, but still held her loosely, before he looked at her and then at Gade, asking, "What happened?"

The casual question, not addressed to anyone in particular, made everyone avoid his gaze and nobody dared to answer. Even Rern, who was itching to speak, kept quiet, realizing that it was not her place to explain.

Nuathong was the first to answer, sobbing, "I came to see you...I was so worried about you, I couldn't eat or sleep. I was going into the house to find you and they dragged me away and wouldn't let me in. It's lucky you came just in time..."

Gade was sickened by her guile and the sight of them in each other's arms right in front of her cut through her heart like a knife and the wound that she thought was healing began to throb again. She turned to go, not wanting the two of them to see her tears, and picked up her son to carry him upstairs inside the house.

But the sound of her husband's voice made her stop.

"Nuathong. I didn't give you permission to come here. Go home."

"Nart!" Nuathong cried.

With a grave expression, her husband, who had always given in to her, said tersely, "I heard only you shouting. I could hear you from the pier. I don't want you coming here bothering Gade. Go home this minute! Do you hear?"

She was too shocked to speak for a moment before screaming angrily, "How can you throw me out? I won't stand for it! And what about her? She came to my house. Why didn't you say anything then?"

Gade looked her husband full in the face, her eyes filled with tears and her voice shook with all the suppressed pain and anger that now reached the surface.

"This is my house. Please don't let your wife come here again. Don't you think I've been through enough?"

He turned to his subordinate and ordered, "Tiwon, take Nuathong home. Don't come here again."

The first lieutenant who had been looking on in alarm hurried to follow the order, while Nuathong pulled away from her husband in anger and disappointment.

"If your wife had any respect for you, she'd let me stay here. I'm your wife as well, after all. I've been with you longer than she has."

Ned stood shaking as he clung onto his mother and despite his innocence, he knew instinctively that the strange and intimidating woman in front of him had hurt his mother, had not listened to his father, and was coming to live in his house.

"I won't let her! I won't let her!"

Then, letting go of his mother's hand, he ran to the other person he loved and instinctively depended on, putting himself between Nuathong and his father and clinging onto his father's leg, sobbing, "Father...Father, I won't let her. Go! Go!"

If that wasn't enough, he turned to Nauthong and started punching and pinching the woman who had taken away his father, so that she could not touch him again.

Nuathong was only slightly hurt, but she directed her anger and hostility towards Gade's son and pushed him hard, screaming, "You insolent boy!"

Ned lost his balance, but before he fell to the ground, his father caught him just in time and enfolded him in his arms. Nart's initial irritation turned to anger, more intense than he had ever felt before, even more than when the picture of his son was ripped, and he thundered at his second wife, "Nuathong! Enough!"

His voice was so harsh that her face became ashen, and the other women in the courtyard stopped dead, except for Gade who strode over to collect her son from his father feeling that she could not stand it a minute longer.

"I…I…" Nuathong stammered, her lips quivering. Realizing she had gone way too far she attempted to excuse herself, "I didn't mean to...Nart...I'm sorry...Your son's like my son."

Gade tried to free Ned from his father's arms, but Ned held onto him tightly, refusing to let go.

"I want Father!"

Nart finally put an end to the scene by heading towards the house, shaking off Nuathong who was trying to cling onto him until she had to let go. He strode up the stairs, ignoring everyone except his son, telling him, "Don't cry. I'm staying with you."

Gade sat on the bedroom floor wearily, her heart still racing as if she had been doing something strenuous. Ned's sobs had subsided and he was half sitting and half lying on the bed. Although the tears still stained his cheeks, he was chatting away as cheerily as before.

"Father, when I grow up, I want to be a soldier...I'll shoot...I won't let anyone in...if they hurt Mother...I'll help her."

He spoke clearly, and even though his words were disjointed, his parents understood him. Gade's eyes brimmed with tears, touched by her son's loyalty. His father stroked his hair gently and sighed to himself before glancing at his wife who was sitting on the floor in front of the bed.

Ned continued to gaze at his father as if searching for the truth. Nart saw his quizzical expression was exactly like his mother's.

"I won't let her in," he repeated.

Both his mother and father knew who he meant by 'her'. Gade shifted to a kneeling position in order to pull her son from the bed.

"You're all hot and sticky. Come and have another wash before you go to bed, so you'll sleep better. I'll wash you."

Ned resisted.

"Has Father had dinner?"

"Not yet. Go and have a wash and then you can come and sit next to me and we'll have dinner together. How does that sound?"

The atmosphere of tension from earlier that night melted away and became bright and clear once more.

But there was still a dark shadow in Gade's heart.

It was the fear of someone who had been grievously wounded many times. Even though she had been reassured that there was nothing to be afraid of, and that nothing could hurt her again, she was not fully convinced.

Rern busied herself helping Suk prepare rice soup as a late-night supper for her brother-in-law and headed for her bedroom, telling Ned's nanny with a grave expression, "I'm going to bed now, Suk. Tell my sister I'm exhausted, so I'm going to have an early night."

Suk assumed an innocent expression.

"I feel like I have a fever coming on. I'll go to bed as soon as I've finished washing the dishes. I'll leave the girls to lock up tonight when they come back from the temple."

Rern went inside her bedroom, not forgetting to pull the latch across before going to sleep inside her mosquito net without making a sound as if she was fast asleep. She heard someone trying to open the door and knew that it was Gade as Chao Khun was sleeping in her bedroom, but Rern pretended to be sound asleep.

A mat with a sheet over it was placed in front of the bed with a pillow inside a clean white pillow case and a thin blanket, and Gade sat down on it with as much nonchalance as she could muster.

She heard a voice from inside the mosquito net on the bed say, "You don't have a mosquito net, Gade. The mosquitoes on the plantation are big. If they bite, it will hurt you."

"I'm used to it."

He wondered more in amusement than in despair if she meant she was used to the mosquitoes, or used to being hurt.

"Come and sleep on the bed. Ned's asleep. I'm not so cruel that I would let you get bitten, while I sleep inside the mosquito net."

Gade glanced at him through the mosquito net and her dark eyes met his and stirred his heart.

"This isn't cruel."

He was silent and for the first time found that the more he tried to make up with her, the more he opened her old wound. What could he do? He was the one who had hurt her in the first place. He had no idea how he could make up for what he had done.

Nart decided to pull back the mosquito net and lower himself onto the mat in front of the bed, ignoring that Gade moved away from him.

"Gade."

He said her name softly.

"What happened was karma. Don't think so much."

"I can put up with anything."

She heard the sound of her voice, cold and bitter.

"But if it's my son, I can't. I'd rather die than see my son get pushed and slapped around. I'm his mother, and I've never done that to him. You can blame karma, but I blame a person!"

Nart was silent again.

He had no justification. He knew full well who she meant by 'a person', but if he admitted it and brought Nuathong into it, he would have no way to justify himself, so he evaded the topic.

"You must mean me. What father would harm his own child?"

Gade was so angry that she blurted out, "Don't make excuses for your wife. Why would I blame my husband and Ned's father?"

"I'm glad you haven't forgotten I'm your husband."

At that moment, she was torn between love and the fear that had been caused by her suffering, and she was scared that, if she gave in to Nart, everything that had happened five years ago would happen again. She knew she did not have the strength to relive the pain for a second time.

"I've never forgotten that you're my husband, but I haven't forgotten that I'm not your only wife, either."

By this time, they were not "Chao Khun" and "Khunying", but simply Nart and Gade as they had been five years ago before her husband's fortune had brought suffering to Gade.

"If you're not prepared to finish with her, then don't keep coming back. Ned and I are doing fine by ourselves."

"Why are you so angry with me? I threw Nuathong out, didn't I? I won't let her come here and bother you again. Isn't that enough?"

"And what if she comes again?"

"If she comes again, I'll throw her out again. This is your house. I won't let her come here."

"But if you go back to Khorat, you won't let me go there either, will you? That's your other wife's house."

Nart's head was spinning with various possible scenarios. He realized full well that if he let Nuathong stay in Bangkok as she wished to, she would keep spending more and more money, which would be disastrous for him. If he took her back to Khorat, it would solve that problem, but then his life would continue to be entangled with her and there would be no way out.

At the same time he felt he could not just abandon her. After all, she was also his wife and had made him happy for several years. If he were to finish with her, he would have to do it in a way that was not too cruel. He would give her some money and let her keep all the jewellery he had given her. It would be enough for her to live comfortably after they split up. He could not stand her behaviour and her actions anymore. Her charms, that she thought were her trump card, had worked in the past, but could not keep him anymore when other qualities were absent.

"Don't jump to conclusions, Gade. I got into this mess, so I'll get out of it."

Any glimmers of hope Gade had felt now began to dim. Nart had not convinced her at all that he was going to remove that woman from his life.

Gade knew that as long as she considered herself his wife, she would not leave Gade and her son in peace.

"I can't put up with you having two wives."

She had not intended to say it, but the words just slipped out. As she heard herself speak, she shifted away from her husband.

"Until now, I still don't know if I'm your principal wife or your minor wife. Everyone calls me Khunying, but you've never acknowledged me in public, and when you go back to Khorat, I'll have to stay here in Bang Pho. If you don't want to finish with your other wife, then please…"

Her eyes were brimming with tears, but out of pride she managed to hold them back.

"Don't make me bring another child into the world who has to look for their father. I've been humiliated enough!"

"You talk as if I abandoned you!"

His voice became harsher and his cheerful mood began to fade.

"I still send you money. I've never abandoned you and I gave you the money for this house, didn't I?"

He got up and walked over to the window, looking out angrily.

Gade did not answer and gazed at him coolly as she tried to suppress her emotions and ignore the voice in her head that told her, 'Don't be so proud that you push him away. You won't be happy without him. If you were over him, it would be fine, but you're not over him, so why are you doing this?'

But Gade had made up her mind she would not yield to her husband until he gave her a definite answer concerning that woman.

"I've never forgotten your generosity in giving me money to buy land to build a house on, but like I said…"

He laughed bitterly and finished the sentence without turning around.

"You don't trust me, so you can't tell if you're my principal wife or my minor wife."

"Isn't it because I trusted you that I'm in this mess? Because I believed your promise...when you swore by the stars...that you would love me and never forsake me...or you'd suffer...well, it wasn't true. If I'd listened to my parents instead of listening to you..."

Nart spun around. His wife's words had hit him where it hurt.

When Gade reminded him of his broken promise, he had no defence.

"Yes. You should have listened to your parents instead of me, and by now you'd be fine. You'd have a rich husband in Phetchaburi, or the good fortune to be Khun Chom's sister-in-law! You wouldn't have married the wrong man!"

He raised his hand to stop her when she began to argue.

"Enough! I've seen your true feelings tonight. This will be the last night I stay with my son. I won't bother you again."

It was the first time they had slept in the same bedroom without speaking a word to each other. Gade lay on the mat in front of the bed as before. She did not know if Nart slept. She heard him turn over from time to time, but she herself did not sleep a wink.

Love was like a stream that could not run backwards. Their relationship had ended without her being prepared for it.

Many times, she thought of getting up from the mat and asking Nart to turn around and talk to her before walking away, but when she thought of the dark path that stretched out in front of her, she felt defeated and dared not face it.

Gade finally drifted off to sleep in the early hours of the morning because she was so exhausted, and she had not been asleep for long when she was suddenly awakened by the sound of a dog barking, indicating that a stranger had entered the house.

Then she heard Man's voice shouting in alarm.

"Suk! Suk! Is Chao Khun awake?"

Her thoughts turned to Nuathong and she feared she had intruded for a second time, refusing to leave her in peace. She pulled up the cloth around her which had slipped down.

At that moment, Nart pulled back the mosquito net, looking as if he had not slept all night either.

He went to the window at the head of the bed, which looked out onto the courtyard. Silver rays were beginning to streak the sky and he could see the peaceful green orchards that surrounded the house. There was only the sound of birds flying out of their nests and the dogs had quietened down because Man had chased them away.

"What's happening, Man?"

Man was standing next to Lieutenant Thiwon, Nart's subordinate. Both of them looked alarmed. When he saw his boss look out of the window, he put his heels together and saluted, before reporting with speed and clarity.

"There's an urgent matter, sir. The Ayutthaya Engineer Battalion has taken over the railway station. There's news that forces from up country are on their way to seize Bangkok. There's been an order for all soldiers to report for duty, sir. "

In the early hours of the 11th of June 1933 General Phraya Si Sitthisongkhram (Din Tharap) led the two battalions of the Ayutthaya Engineer Battalion into action as the first unit, took over Ayutthaya Train Station, and another two divisions took control of Ban Phachi Railway Station.

That evening, the Third Army Area Command from Nakhon Ratchasima moved their troops to Bangkok, using the slogan, the 'National Salvation Group', and were made up of cavalry, infantry, and artillery men from three regiments led by General Prince Boworadet, while the 21st Infantry Regiment from Ubon Ratchathani followed the next day.

The 'National Salvation Group' assigned Navy Captain Phra Saeng Sitthikarn as their representative to take their letter to the government to get an answer by midday. The contents of the letter were as follows:

1. Siam must always have a constitutional monarchy.

2. There must be a genuine constitution and the government must be elected by majority vote, not established by force, and must be lawful.

3. Both military and civilian government personnel must stay out of politics, except for those who have a direct responsibility in politics, but they will not have any legal political rights taken away, and they must not use their authority or position to support their own political interests, or to directly or indirectly force or threaten others to agree with their political interests.

The military must not interfere in politics.

4. The appointment of individuals to government positions must depend on the individual's qualifications and abilities, not their political connections.

5. The second type of representatives must be chosen by the king.

6. The army must have mixed units, and weapons must be distributed evenly, so that the majority of weapons are not in one place.

Colonel Phraya Wisetsingnart looked up from the letter after reading the last sentence, at the person who had handed it to him and did not ask any questions. None were necessary. The fact that he had been called to Colonel Phraya Thepakanee's office urgently amid the chaos and confusion of the army and the government today was an answer in itself. He had been called to be given an order, not to ask questions.

"Nart, I can only come out of the meeting for ten minutes at the most. I suggested you in the meeting as a mediator with the rebels. Tell Chao Khun Si Sitthisongkhram that the government will never listen to their threats. Right now, the government has their representative, Phra Saeng Sitthikarn hostage. If they surrender, there will be no bloodshed. Otherwise...if they don't give up, don't expect it to end easily. There will be a bloodbath this time. Those are my words. You can tell him."

Nart held his breath for a moment.

If he had been chosen as the government's representative after the opposition's representative had been taken hostage, his fate would probably not be much different. He calculated that he had been chosen as the government's representative because they were probably suspicious of him and reckoned there were more advantages in sending him than disadvantages. If he was successful, the government would benefit and he would survive, but if he joined Phraya Si Sitthisongkhram, he would be called a traitor without a doubt, and if the government won, he would be executed.

Praya Thepakanee's move showed that he was confident that the government would win the conflict. Nart concealed his anxiety and asked calmly in order to find out more, "Aren't you going to negotiate with them first so you can reach a peaceful agreement? Their propositions aren't difficult and they're consistent with democratic principles after all."

"Only those who surrender will compromise with their rivals. We're no cowards!"

"But still, it's better not to have bloodshed. On the 24th of June last year, there was no bloodshed. If it happens this time, it will be a blemish on our history."

Phraya Thepakanee slammed his fist on the table.

"Exactly. That's what you have to tell Phraya Si Sitthisongkhram. Let him know that Luang Phibun Songkhram has been made Commander-in-Chief…"

Nart listened intently, hiding his anger at his old friend's aggression.

"He's been made what?"

"Head of the army. He's already sent troops to the front line. There'll be a bloodbath for sure. It's unavoidable. We're not thinking of avoiding it."

The minute hand was marching on, and after ten minutes, Phraya Thepakanee stood up from behind his desk and concluded, "I have to go back in the meeting. You go ahead. It's a secret. No one outside knows. Don't tell anyone."

"Wait!"

Phraya Thepakanee turned around, his face tense.

"What if they ask about democracy that people are willing to die for? What will you tell them?"

He looked at his questioner with blazing eyes.

"Tell them that's the stupidest question they could ask. This is war. It has nothing to do with democracy."

11
The End of the Light

"Nart!"

The sound of a voice calling him from behind made Phraya Wisetsingnart, who was walking hurriedly towards the stairs behind the Ministry of Defence building to the waiting car, turn around.

He saw his cousin, Police Lieutenant Colonel Phra Prabribupai panting as he approached him, speaking quickly and gasping for breath as if he knew he shouldn't delay him when the situation was so critical that no one could predict what would happen in the next hour or day, and whether or not things would get worse.

"Forgive me, I know you're in a hurry. I'm here with the Assistant Chief of Police for a meeting. I…"

"What is it? Tell me, Nop."

After being prompted, he told him at once.

"Last night, I don't know what your wife was angry about, but when she came home, she started shouting and throwing things. It disturbed my mother, so she told her to stop and then they got into a big argument…"

Nart raised his hand to stop him. He had heard enough.

"Go and tell Nuathong to move her things out of the house. Tell her I have to go away on business and I don't know when I'll be back…"

He took all the money he had out of his wallet, and gave it to his cousin.

"Let her find somewhere else to live. Don't let her disturb you again. Please tell my aunt I'm sorry for the trouble I've caused. Tell Nuathong I don't want any more to do with her. That's my final word."

The younger man took the money and looked as if he was going to ask a question, but seeing that his older cousin was tense, decided against it, and answered, "Alright, I'll do as you say."

"Thanks. I'll be off then."

Phraya Wisetsingnart strode hastily away from his cousin towards the back stairs until he was out of sight.

Phra Prabribupai gazed after him and bent his head to look at the banknotes in his hand before tucking them away inside his wallet and hastily walking in the opposite direction.

Nuathong lay on the bed with her arm across her forehead, her mind racing. She had heard the sound of Lamai's voice that morning, but refused to come out of the room. The previous night, she had had a big argument with Nart's aunt who was the first to retreat into her room because she was about to faint. Nuathong had gone back inside her room and locked the door, so that no one could enter.

Only Tieng was there for her to vent to.

"How long have I been his wife, damn it? He can't just abandon me. Just watch me, Tieng! He hasn't seen anything yet!"

When Lamai told her to leave, she retorted without flinching, "I'm not going! You can't throw me out! I'm staying! My husband brought me here! I didn't want to come here!"

Lamai was shaking with fury.

"You've no shame!"

"You've no shame trying to break up a husband and wife!"

Then she went back inside her room, slamming the door in Lamai's face and venting her anger by throwing things around.

Nuathong sat up, forgetting her fatigue and becoming suddenly sprightly. She pulled out the key that was tucked into her waistband and slid off the bed to open the wardrobe and unlock a drawer inside it before picking up a small metal box that she had brought with her from Nakhon Ratchasima.

Inside were several items of jewellery that she had pleaded with her husband to buy her on different occasions. In fact, there would have been more if she had not lost them at the gambling table, but there were still several beautiful pieces left.

Nuathong tightly wrapped all the jewellery in a handkerchief and scooped all the money that was in the box into a small cloth bag before placing everything inside the leather handbag that she habitually carried.

She was interrupted by the sound of a loud knocking on the door, and shouted, "Go away! Leave me alone!"

A man's voice, which she recognized as her husband's cousin's, called out clearly, "Nart has left you some money. If you don't want it, it's up to you."

"And where is he?"

"He's away on business."

"You're lying!"

The young man almost lost patience with her because of the harshness in her voice, and replied more severely, "Don't believe me then. Don't take the money."

Nuathong hesitated before nodding towards Tieng for her to go over to the door.

"Leave the money outside the door. I'm not opening it. I don't trust you."

Phra Prabribupai let out an angry laugh.

"Who could defeat someone as shameless as you? You're still hiding in this house even when the owner's told you to get out."

Nuathong was not so thick-skinned that she didn't care. It was just that she had not yet decided what to do, so she had to remain so as to have a roof over her head until she had a plan. She had become accustomed to living in comfort and, even though she was not the principal wife, she had been able to claim that status more than his real wife. She refused to slink away defeated and return to her former state in humiliation.

There was the sound of footsteps walking away from the door and Tieng carefully unlocked the door and peered outside, but she cried out in alarm when the person waiting outside pushed the door open and shoved Tieng out of the way before stepping inside the room. There was the sound of footsteps returning and Phra Prabinbupai's servant stood beside him poised to carry out his orders.

The police officer spoke with finality, "Pack your things and get out. Otherwise, I'll have you dragged out. If you don't believe me, try me!"

Nuathong stood in shock and, realizing she was beaten, screamed at the top of her lungs.

Colonel Wisetsingnart stood before the man he had taken his leave from not long before. This was his senior officer whom he loved and respected, and whom he had always talked to as a friend. This was the first time that he was facing him in a different capacity. Nart was a mediator for the government, a role he wasn't entirely comfortable about, while the other man was a leader of the "National Salvation Group", Phraya Si Sitthisongkhram.

The Engineer Battalion had advanced to Tung Bang Khen, and Nart was able to get inside the barracks because he had come alone as a government representative.

Both men were silent for a moment before Phraya Si Sitthisongkhram spoke.

"We're not going to surrender. The only thing I want to know is will the government compromise with us or not?"

"No. They refused every proposal."

"I thought so."

There was another pause. Phraya Wisetsingnart said, "Din, Luang Phibun Songkhram is Commander-in-Chief on the government's side. The government has to be firm. If there's fighting, there'll be division. I don't want a Civil War."

"No one wants it, but we can't allow the situation to get worse. We hope to put a stop to it without more bloodshed than necessary. Several battalions in Bangkok have agreed to join us. I don't think the government will continue to resist us for long."

Nart shook his head.

"When I left the ministry, the last I heard was that opinion was wavering in Bangkok because the government announced that the counter revolutionaries are planning to bring the aristocracy back to rule Siam."

The expression on Phraya Si Sitthisongkhram's face did not change.

"We stated clearly in the letter that Phra Saeng Sitthikarn handed to the government that we don't intend to take Siam backwards to how it was before, but right now, a lot of things are not right. The people haven't gained the rights that they were promised, and parliament is full of those who've been appointed. Anyone with backers fills it with their partisans, and changes in power are carried out by force."

"And you think that using force will put things right?"

"We've pledged to do it for the right end."

The young officer who was also present looked agitated, as if he wanted to speak, but his junior rank prevented him. Phraya Si Sitthisongkhram realized this and gave him permission to speak.

"Tell Chao Khun what we pledged, Tuan."

A deep voice answered at once.

"If I may, sir. The pledge that the National Salvation Group has made has three points. One: We will not accept members that have a personal vendetta against the government. We will only accept those who can really help, not just increase our numbers. Two: We will not accept anyone who wishes to join for financial gain. Three: Military officers will not accept any positions, or seize positions from subordinates."

Although Nart felt discouraged that his negotiations would be fruitless, that fact did not sadden him as much as the fact that the hopes of the National Salvation Group might never be realized.

The main thing he tried to warn them about, despite them seeming too confident in themselves to listen, was that the result of fighting would be far more severe than they imagined.

Phraya Si Sitthisongkhram was a good and able man, but although many in the army respected him and fully supported him, the weakness of the counter revolution was that the leader was Prince Boworadet. This fact had created suspicion among the battalions that had joined them that they were bringing the absolute monarchy back to Siam.

Any concerns that Luang Pradit Manutham, who had returned to politics, was going to spread communist ideology in Siam did not overly worry Nart for he believed that it was a matter of opinion. Furthermore, it was not nearly as urgent as the problem in front of him, which was that the National Salvation Group thought that the government was weak, lacked coordination between units, was disorganized and would easily falter.

"Din, the government wants an answer by two o'clock this afternoon. It's already…"

Before he could finish his sentence with two o'clock, they heard a sound like thunder loud enough to make the ground tremble.

Someone shouted, "They've started firing at us in the city!"

The plains of Tung Bang Khen in the month of October were flooded with water, which hampered the government's attempt to use tanks to suppress the counter revolutionaries. For this reason, Luang Phibun Songkram, Commander-in-Chief on the government's side, decided to fire a bullet from the Vickers-Armstrong machine gun from the battlefront in Bang Sue as a warning at two o'clock on the 12th of October, 1933.

Amidst all the confusion, Phraya Wisetsingnart heard a resolute voice say, "Nart. You must stay here. You can't go back now."

All the windows of the house in Bang Pho were shut. Everyone in the house had packed their belongings ready to evacuate. All the valuables were wrapped up in cloth bundles, and other items had been locked away inside each room.

Gade changed position to relieve her stiffness, and looked down at her son who was asleep on her lap in blissful ignorance. She heard the bullets from the machine guns at the battlefront in Bang Sue and started every time a loud rumble reached her ears.

Gade was so agitated with concern for Nart, and for the other lives in her home that she was responsible for, that she could hardly sit still. Rern was equally anxious and prayed that the fighting would not reach Phetchaburi, for she feared Klai would be in danger.

Man came panting up the stairs before sitting down and saying with urgency, "The boat's ready, madam. I've brought a small boat up to the pier."

Ned woke up as he was being carried out of the house and asked sleepily, "Mother? Where are we going?"

Gade forced herself to speak calmly, so as not to alarm him.

"We're going to see Grandmother and Grandfather. We haven't

been to see them for a while. Keep still. We're about to get in the boat."

12th of October, 1933.

King Prajadhipok was staying at Klai Kangwon Palace when he received a telegram from the government.

Your Majesty,

Yesterday evening, the Ayutthaya Engineer Battalion advanced to Bangkhen, and the Nakhon Ratchasima Battalion advanced to Don Muang just after two o'clock this afternoon. Phra Saeng Sitthikarn presented General Phraya Si Sitthisongkhram's letter, which stated that this cabinet had humiliated Your Majesty, and brought Luang Pradit Manotham back to create a Communist state, and asked for our resignation within an hour. Otherwise, they would use force to seize power temporarily until Your Majesty appointed a new government without military officers. These two accusations are not true. The government has brought a charge of Lèse-majesté and ensured that Luang Pradit Manotham will not be a Communist, and this cabinet has carried out a policy of strictly observing the Constitution and being loyal to Your Majesty as I pledged. Therefore, as Commander-in-Chief of the Army, I believe that it is necessary to declare a curfew according to Clause 4 of the Curfew Act of 1932 to be in effect from 1.45am.

The government will return the situation to normal thereafter.

The decision is yours.

General Phraya Pahonphonphayuhasena

Prime Minister

Although the railway line between Phetchaburi and Bangkok had been paralyzed during the fighting, the boat route was still operating. Rice barges sailed unhurriedly along the Chao Phraya River and the Tha Chin River to the Mae Klong River without anyone noticing that there were more people on the boats than usual.

Gade sat in the end of the boat, watching the waves, and heard Rern ask about food, but she was not in the mood to answer. The strong breeze from the river was cool and Gade took a shawl out of one of the bundles and wrapped it around her shoulders. She began to feel cold.

She sat with a heavy heart, sick with worry for her husband.

She didn't know where he was, near or far, or what he was doing. All she prayed was that he would be safe.

When Gade arrived home, she sensed more distress than when the system of government had changed the previous year.

Although Ban Tha Hin was outside the town, it was close enough for its residents to be aware of the tension among the soldiers in the city. Klai, her brother-in-law, had been called for duty and had not been home for days. All her relatives were anxiously waiting for news, not knowing if there would be bloodshed or not.

Gade decided to go and see Chao Chom Amphan the day after she arrived home, taking her son and his nanny along. Khun Chom had built a new house in the town, not far from the governor's residence and close to her relatives. It was a wooden two-storey house with a hip roof, much smaller than her former abode, but it still looked imposing with a large front lawn shaded by the fully grown trees that had been there since before it was built.

When Khun Chom saw them, she greeted them happily.

"Oh, look who it is! I was just saying I was worried about you. Are you alright, Khunying?"

When Gade saw the older lady, whom she respected and knew that she could share her feelings with, her eyes filled with tears and she told her through sobs, "I'm alright, but I don't know what's happened to Chao Khun. Khun Phra Prab told me to evacuate to Phetchaburi by boat."

When she saw Gade's distress, Chao Chom Amphan hid her anxiety and tried to comfort her, stroking her back kindly.

"Don't cry. It's bad luck. If anything had happened to Chao Khun, I'm sure I would have heard by now, but I haven't heard anything. Your Chao Khun is important. Nobody would dare to harm him. Trust me."

Even though she knew Khun Chom was just trying to comfort her, Gade felt better, and Khun Chom continued, "The king is staying at

Klai Kangwon. I'm so worried about him. I don't know if he's safe or not. I know he wouldn't want any fighting."

Gade stopped crying and listened to Khun Chom until she felt better. At least, she was back in the warm bosom of her family and near to Chao Chom Amphan, whom she had depended on for emotional support during her darkest moments. There was nowhere better than coming home.

Gade said goodbye to Chao Chom Amphan and went home to wait anxiously for news from both the town and from the capital. The news that everyone had heard was that General Luang Sornsitthi Yanukarn was still fighting, had sent troops to control the railway, and had stopped the carriage transporting the troops on the afternoon of the 14th of October, with only six hundred soldiers.

"They say…"

Gade's elder brother-in-law lowered his voice to a whisper and looked grave, even though he was among his close relatives.

"Khun Luang sent a telegraph to the king telling him that the Phetchaburi soldiers are loyal to him and would lay down their lives for him."

Sergeant Reng Ngan Rop asked at once, "And did His Majesty answer?"

No one could answer that question until the next day when the same relative brought more news.

"The king will not take sides. He doesn't want Thais to fight each other."

"Lord above!" cried Gade's father, Mee, pressing his palms together above his head and facing south, in the direction of Klai Kangwon Palace in Hua Hin. "I don't want to see that either. It's like my relatives are fighting each other."

"And how long will they continue fighting?" asked Eaem to herself, without expecting an answer.

All eyes turned to Gade, and although no one dared say anything out of deference to 'Khunying Gade', the expressions on their faces showed their concern for the young woman.

Gade wandered aimlessly to the edge of the compound, and finally found herself on the old bridge. The evening breeze gently blew the leaves and the crows returned to their nests, cawing in the large trees a little further away, interspersed with the sound of cicadas rubbing their wings together in the twilight.

The first star began to twinkle in the dark sky turning Gade's thoughts to Nart. Her heart sank when she thought of him far from home and possibly involved in the fighting. Gade could not imagine what his fate would be.

She reassured herself that the fighting would be over quickly and that there would be no loss of life, as on the 24th of June the previous year, and she would soon be able to return to her house at Bang Pho. Perhaps, she hoped wildly, Nart might be waiting for her at Bang Pho, even if it was just to say goodbye before he left for Khorat. That would be better than him just taking his other wife back without giving her a second thought.

But when she recalled the last night that they had spent together in the same room, her heart sank again.

If only she had known it was their last night together. She would not have caused a rift between them, because Nart had tried to make up with her, but she had been too stubborn, until they had both turned their backs on each other out of pride, even though she was sure that neither of them had wanted it to end that way.

She heard shouts coming from inside the house, and, after a moment, turned to look.

Rern was running down the steps behind the house in alarm, and even in the dim light, Gade could see that her face was white and she was scared.

Rern opened her mouth to speak and closed it as if she was trying to find the right words. She hesitated before blurting out, "The rebels have lost! They say some soldiers with the rank of Phraya...were killed in the fighting."

Gade knew nothing except that everything around her went dark and the ground began to sway before floating up to engulf her. When Gade came to, her parents comforted her.

“Don’t be alarmed. They’re saying it was soldiers from Khorat, not your Chao Khun...We don’t know which Phraya it was.”

That night, Gade was ravaged by a fever and was confined to bed the next day, slipping in and out of consciousness. The following day, her fever began to let up and she heard her mother sobbing, and Ned’s voice crying, “Mummy! Please don’t die!”

Her son’s clear and woeful voice was a powerful thread that gave her courage and pulled her back to consciousness. She told herself that she could not die and that, even if Nart was not coming back, he had left someone in his place, whom Gade was responsible for as long as she was still alive. Otherwise, she would not be able to face him in the next life.

“Gade,” Eeam called her daughter and shook her gently as if to wake her. “Khun Chom’s brother, Chat, came this morning, and he told us that Nart’s not dead. Did you hear? Ned’s father is still alive.”

Her words were like water on dry cracked earth, and Gade almost stood up in shock, but she became so dizzy that she had to sink back on the pillow as before.

“Where’s Chat, Mother?” Gade asked hoarsely. “I want to see him.”

Although Gade had not seen Khun Chom’s brother for almost a year, she did not expect him to have changed so much.

When they met again, if she had not been so worried about Nart, she would have exclaimed in alarm, but as it was, all she said was, “Haven’t you been well, Chat?”

Chat had been a handsome man full of vigour, but now, he had grown thin and appeared hard and coarse. There were dark circles under his eyes and fine crows’ feet had appeared. His mouth, that used to smile, was shut tight and there were lines at the corners as if he had been under stress.

But when Chat smiled at Gade, the sparkle in his eyes returned.

“That’s what everyone says. There’s nothing the matter. I just don’t eat or sleep at regular times.”

As if sensing her anxiety, he did not waste any more time talking about himself, but got straight to the point.

"The Phraya that lost his life...it's such a shame...was Phraya Si Sitthisongkhram."

Gade's heart sank. Even though she had not known him personally, she had heard his name and knew that Nart had been close to him.

"May he rest in peace."

Chat sighed and his face darkened.

"At first, I didn't know how serious it would get. I realized when Prince Boworadet retreated from Don Muang on the 15th. Chao Khun Si Sitthi was on guard at the back. He fought to the end and died like a true soldier. I'm still grieving."

Gade was silent. The sincerity in his voice told her that he had been shaken. If she remembered correctly, he had agreed with the People's Party's revolution and should have been on the government's side, but now, his face showed his sadness.

"And…" she asked hoarsely, "What about my Chao Khun? Which side is he on? How is he?"

Chat looked her in the eye, and his awkwardness was written all over his face.

"At first, they say the government sent him to be a mediator with the rebels, but once the fighting began, things got complicated. All I know is that when the soldiers on Prince Boworadet's side were captured Chao Khun wasn't there…"

A sense of foreboding spread an icy chill through her veins.

"I don't follow you, Chat. Where is Chao Khun?"

The young man shook his head slowly.

"So far, nobody's seen him."

"Nobody's seen him," Gade repeated in confusion. She did not understand.

"If the fighting was over, how could nobody have seen him? He has to be somewhere."

"It's hard to tell," Chat said, swallowing with difficulty. "Many have scattered and nobody knows who's who or who's died. I don't know if the latest rumour is true…"

Gade began to grow impatient.

"Chat, would you please tell me…"

"I'm about to tell you. The latest rumour is that Prince Boworadet has left the country. Some people are saying Chao Khun Wisetsing's gone with him. They say Chao Khun joined the rebels when he went to negotiate with them, and when they lost, he left the country. I'm trying my best to find out...Don't be alarmed just yet."

He stopped when he saw that Gade's face had turned as white as a sheet.

Chat realized that she still had strong feelings for her husband and she was as far out of his reach as she had ever been.

Although the sun still came up each morning, the sunshine in Gade's heart was gone.

Klai was given permission to return home. He was not a high-ranking soldier and so he was not affected by the situation. Nevertheless, the young man struggled to hide his concern for Phraya Wisetsingnart, and warned Rern not to mention the subject while Gade was home.

"And how come you haven't heard any news about Chao Khun. It isn't as if he's not important. How could he just disappear?"

Rern continued to press her husband, for one thing, because she knew he loved her and for another, because she was concerned about her brother-in-law on Gade's behalf.

"I've heard news alright, but I don't know if it's true or not," Klai answered glumly. "But if I tell Gade, I'm afraid she'll be sick again. Some say Chao Khun died along with Chao Khun Si Sitthi, and others say he escaped to Indo-China because the government said he was on the rebel side."

"And what really happened? I'm about to burst," Rern cried, shaking her husband's arm.

"I don't know! Chat's been trying to find out. His friends are reporters. They'll know more than I do. Also, don't forget Khun Phra Phrab hasn't sent any news, yet."

Rern let out several long sighs before reassuring herself.

"If anything bad had happened, Khun Phra Phrab would have let us know, so it can't be so terrible. We'll probably find out soon."

Rern relayed the news to her sister with all the words of comfort that she could think of until Gade told her with a sad smile, "Don't be afraid I'll die. I have to be here to take care of Ned until he's grown up."

Rern breathed a sigh of relief.

Chat travelled back and forth between Phetchaburi and Bangkok until the middle of November 1933. Although the rebellion had been quashed, the grave consequences were only just beginning. News that shook him to the core when he arrived at his office on the 5th of November was relayed to him in alarm by his colleagues.

"Have you heard the news? Your friend, Luang Maha Sitthivoharn, has been accused of treason!"

"You mean Sor?" he cried, his heart sinking in disbelief.

Sor Sethabutr, as Chat called him, or Luang Maha Sitthivoharn as he had been titled, was, in his opinion, one of the most learned young men that he knew, and none of the other reporters could deny it. After he graduated from England with an honour's degree in Geology and Mining Engineering at the age of only twenty-three, he worked for the government for five years before having the title of Luang Maha Sitthivoharn bestowed on him by the king.

Their friendship had begun when Chat was a student in France and had got to know other Thai students while visiting England, and they had quickly become close, remaining in regular contact after they returned to their homeland.

Chat remembered that he and Luang Maha Sitthivoharn had once had a disagreement after the revolution the previous year. Chat had agreed with the People's Party wholeheartedly, but his friend had been adamantly opposed to it. But their difference of opinion had not caused a rift between them and they had remained friends. Even though their work had sometimes kept them apart, they had always kept in touch. Chat was well aware that his friend was determined, confident in what he thought was right, and would not allow fear of the People's Party's power to dilute his beliefs. He was, therefore, not surprised that he had left his government job after the revolution and gone to work for Boonrawd Breweries, as well as regularly writing newspaper articles.

"What was Sor accused of?" Chat asked after collecting himself for a moment.

"Collaborating with the rebels by translating their declaration into English. Actually, we heard on the 19th of October that all the reporters for the *Daily Mail* were arrested. You were in Phetchaburi, so you don't know what chaos it was."

"And where's Sor now?" he asked with urgency.

"We think he's being held at the Ministry of Defence. He probably won't be sent to Bang Kwang Prison like the others. A ton of them are in there."

Chat temporarily forgot all about Phraya Wisetsingnart and grabbed his hat from the hook before rushing down the stairs to find a way to meet his friend, even though he had only a glimmer of hope.

A colleague called after him.

"Hey! Aren't you going to ask about Chao Khun Wiset? I've got news."

Chat stopped halfway down the stairs and ran back up.

"He's dead."

"Dead?" Chat exclaimed, grabbing hold of the banister to steady himself. "Who told you?"

"From the Ministry of Defence. It's top secret. Chao Khun was hit by a bullet from which side, I don't know, while the rebels were retreating. He died before he reached Bangkok, but even if he wasn't dead, he'd have had to do time in Bang Kwang Prison. The government had prepared a case against him."

The house at Bang Pho returned to its former state when the lady of the house returned from Phetchaburi with her relatives and servants. Only Rern was missing because she was suffering from morning sickness, so Gade had told her not to visit until she had given birth, fearing that the long journey would do her harm.

Gade had only been back a day when a group of military officers came to her house to investigate evidence pertaining to Phraya Wisetsingnart. She led them into the bedroom to show them his uniform and clothing, which were hanging up neatly.

"This is all there is."

"And what about his other things? Documents and things to do with his work."

"He didn't bring anything. They're in Khorat. He was only here for two or three days."

Police Lieutenant Colonel Phra Prabribupai arrived less than half an hour later. His face was taut and dark.

He said to the group of officers, "Chao Khun Wisetsingnart has lived in Khorat for the past few years. This house belongs to Khunying. Chao Khun and Khunying don't live together. He just came here to visit his son."

The group of officers nodded, and after asking a few more questions, took their leave without touching anything in the house.

"I had to tell them that so as not to cause trouble for you."

"Trouble? What do you mean?"

"You might be called to the military court…" he replied, and when he noticed her alarm quickly continued, "Don't worry. Just tell the truth and don't hide anything. Tell them you haven't lived with Nart for the past few years, and that he lived with his other wife. It might be uncomfortable for you, but it's for your own good. Then they won't ask you too many questions. There are plenty of people who can verify that it's true."

Gade was still confused.

"And...and what's it about? I don't know anything. Why do they have to…?"

"They don't believe Nart's really dead because they haven't found a body. All they have is his uniform with his rank on it, found by the villagers. A lot of other soldiers disappeared after the fighting. It's only natural for them to investigate those connected with them."

He unrolled the newspaper he had brought with the picture of General Phraya Si Sitthisongkhram, and explained, "One of the soldiers saw Chao Khun Si Sitthi with Nart at Hin Lap, which makes it look like he was cooperating with him, but he couldn't confirm it. Some of the officers say Nart didn't join the rebels, but he couldn't come back because of the fighting."

Gade's heart sank with despair.

"Please tell me straight, Khun Phra. Do you think Chao Khun is still alive? That's all I hope for."

It didn't matter to her which side he was on. All she cared about was that he was still alive. Even if he was accused of treason and would face punishment, she was comforted by the hope that she would see his face again.

The month of October came and went. November and December passed by slowly.

The cold wind this year was no different from previous ones, but in the orchards of Bang Pho, Gade felt that the cold pierced her to her very core, especially when she woke before sunrise and looked out at the mist that enveloped the treetops, and had to get out of bed and go down to the kitchen by lamplight.

Gade prepared the same food that Nart had eaten on his last two days to give to the monks in order to make merit for him. Her hope that he was still alive had disappeared. Even though nobody had been found, there was no news that he had left the country. Gade started to feel certain that if he were still alive, he would not have disappeared for this long. Even if he did not care for Gade, he would not have abandoned his son without a word. Nart loved his son, Gade could tell, and he would have been concerned about him.

Gade's one comfort was that her life had not been affected at all, except for once when she had been called to the special military court. Gade told the truth as Phra Prabribupai had instructed her and after that, everything was quiet and she was not called a second time.

Life in Bang Pho returned to its normal pattern. The name of Khunying Wisetsingnart continued to be respected amongst the villagers and on the surface, it seemed that the fighting had not touched them.

But beneath the surface tranquillity, many had friends or relatives who had been sent to Bang Kwang Prison for treason. Everyone swallowed their pain, speaking of it only amongst themselves as they struggled to find a way to visit those in prison.

Man was one of the people who brought these people together as a group, so that they could assist each other, and when Gade found out, she gave her support in empathy.

"We're all in the same boat," she told Man. "I can't imagine how I'd feel if Chao Khun was in prison."

But only Gade knew that nothing could cause her more suffering than this.

"Bun Khlong!"

Gade walked down the stairs to the courtyard and called her relative, who was nowhere to be seen. The light from the lanterns was beginning to glow in the courtyard, and the girls in the house were busy sorting fruits. The atmosphere was as warm and cosy as before. Suk shouted a reply from under the house. She had just finished arranging the best fruits ready for the traders to collect.

"Bun Khlong's taken Ned to see Man. They're not back yet."

"I thought so. Those two are always going off together. It's the cool season now and it gets dark early. I don't want them coming home late."

No sooner had she finished speaking when a teenage boy came ambling through the door carrying a small figure on his back. Gade sighed with relief and bent down to pick up her son who had come down from the young man's back and was running towards her.

"Mother... Mother...I'm hungry!"

Ned, who was almost five, had figured out a way to distract his mother before she scolded him for coming home late. Gade hugged her son and scolded him, but did not sound angry.

"Where have you been? I've been worried about you. Bun Khlong, just lately you've been going to see Man a lot. What for?"

Bun Klong frowned and answered hesitatingly, "Ned didn't want to come back."

Ned held out his hand to show her something small. Gade looked and saw it was a cage made out of a coconut shell with a cricket inside.

"I got this, too, Mother!" Ned beamed.

There were all sorts of things to play with in the garden, such as banana stalks, coconut shells cut in two and tied to the feet like clogs, and clay that could be shaped into animals, so Gade didn't think the cage with the cricket in it was anything out of the ordinary. She guessed he had got it from one of the local children.

"No wonder. You got a new toy. Man knows how to entice children!"

"It wasn't Uncle Man. It was Uncle Poon."

Bun Khlong tugged on his arm as if to stop him, but his mother had already heard and was puzzled.

"Who? I've never heard of him."

Bun Khlong replied stiffly, "He guards Man's garden. He likes to play with children."

When she heard it was one of Man's neighbours, she was relieved, knowing that he sometimes hired someone to guard his garden, especially during the durian season or at times when fruit was expensive as he was afraid of thieves.

Ned said, "Uncle Poon walked us home."

He turned to look at the gate. In the lamplight, the arched entrance entwined with vines was visible and just past it, no one noticed a figure hiding in the shadows of the coconut palms.

Gade lost interest and led her son into the house, while Bun Khlong sheepishly went to join the others to finish selecting fruit. Nobody saw the pair of eyes that were quietly watching the illuminated courtyard where the girls were chatting as they worked and joked.

The peaceful atmosphere was warm and comforting, in contrast to the cold darkness outside, which was full of emptiness and loneliness.

The person outside stood there for an hour without moving, looking at the light in the front bedroom until it was turned out, indicating that the little boy had gone to bed. A moment later, the owner of the house came down the stairs to help the others select fruit.

He gazed at the pretty young woman with the smooth fair skin as if he was looking at a star twinkling in the night sky. All he could do was gaze, but she was out of his reach.

12
The Promise

The sight of the towering concrete fence of Bang Kwang Prison, which was also enclosed with sharp electric wire all around, chilled Chat to the bone every time he came to visit on Wednesdays, especially the watchtower where guards with machine guns stood to attention in all four directions.

Luang Maha Sitthivoharn, or Sor Sethabutra, his old friend, was being held in Area Six, and Chat was relieved to see that his expression was still as resolute as always with no sign of despondency at his fate. They met in a long single-storey room divided by metal bars down its length with long benches for visitors who came to visit the suspects.

"The living conditions here are quite comfortable. There's no need to worry," he said, guessing how Chat was feeling. "Area Six is wide and clean. We're political prisoners, not criminals."

"I'm sure you'll be released before long," Chat reassured him.

He did not answer, but Luang Maha Sitthivoharn's determined expression did not falter, and he changed the subject.

"There are several of us here. We're all like-minded. Oh, yes, Nart! I remember now, last time you were asking about Chao Khun Wisetsingnart. I heard this from an officer, but I can't tell you his name."

Chat moved closer at once to listen and Luang Maha Sitthivoharn lowered his voice.

"I don't believe he's dead...but he had to escape because...he's being persecuted."

This was something Chat had not expected to hear. He stared in shock at Luang Maha Sitthivoharn, who nodded slowly.

"The government won't admit that they sent him as a mediator with the rebels. They're saying he went of his own accord and joined them."

Chat hid his alarm in case others noticed, and he did not want to make things worse.

He whispered, "Who's involved?"

"Chao Khun Thepakanee."

Chat remembered that he had been a close friend of Phraya Wisetsingnart and had been at his housewarming party. He also remembered they had become suspicious of one another after Phraya Thepakanee joined the People's Party, but Phraya Wisetsingnart refused to join. Indeed, it was for that reason that the latter had been moved to Nakhon Ratchasima, while the former had been promoted in the capital.

Chat changed the subject and talked about other matters before taking his leave. Even after he had left Bang Kwang, his head was spinning with the things he had heard. Chat did not know Phraya Wisetsingnart well enough to judge the truth of what he had heard. If it were true, he would be charged with treason without a doubt.

But if it were not?.

If it were not true, it meant that Chao Khun had become a pawn in someone else's game. He might have found out just in time, but with no way to prove his innocence, escaping was his only option. Perhaps he might come back when he was sure he could prove his innocence, but if he could not, there was no point in coming back to fight with individuals who had absolute power.

There was sufficient reason for Chat's next visit to the house at the Bang Pho plantation for Gade to welcome him without embarrassment. He brought news about the political situation and showed no romantic inclinations. He could tell that Gade was anxious for news of her husband, and even though he did not have anything concrete, it was better than nothing.

"I believe Chao Khun's still alive, but he had to escape, because if he stayed, he'd be accused of treason. He might not have sided with Prince Boworadet, but..."

He chose his words carefully so as to cause her the least distress.

"It's politics," he concluded as vaguely as possible with a sigh.

The expression on Gade's face showed that she did not understand, but she was more concerned about her husband than anything else.

"And have they caught Chao Khun?"

"They're looking for him. The last I heard was that he was seen close to the Mekong River."

Given that Nart had lived in Udon before moving to Khorat, Gade thought he might have had friends who could help take him across the Mekong River.

"Heaven, please let it be true!" Gade gasped, forgetting herself. "Until now, I'd lost all hope!"

Chat glanced out of the window and said, "It's getting late. I'd better be going. If I hear anything about Chao Khun, I'll come again. In the meantime, if anything happens, send someone to let me know. Please don't be afraid of imposing."

Gade thanked him sincerely, but she did not keep him, or even invite him to have dinner with her. Their relationship had become one of friendship, but Gade did not forget that, as a widow, she was an easy target for gossip, even in the eyes of those who had always been full of respect for her. The nights in the cool season were drawing in, and the mornings were cloudy and dark because of the unseasonal rain. By five o'clock, it was getting too dark to see clearly as if it were evening, and the girls came down to sit and work in the courtyard where they lit lamps. Gade showed Chat the courtesy of walking him to the stairs, but she did not see him off at the gate, sending Man, to escort him to the bridge instead.

"Man, please walk Chat to the bridge."

The plantation beyond the gate was so dark that it was impossible to see from the courtyard into the shadows of the coconut palms. Gade and Chat did not know that they were being watched by someone who was hiding in the darkest corner. He saw her gentle manner when she pressed her palms together to say goodbye, and the polite way that he returned the gesture. They said a few words to each other, which he guessed were words of farewell, or the assurance that they would see each other again soon, before Chat put his hat on and walked out of the gate.

The young woman stood watching her guest before she turned and walked back up the stairs. The person watching clenched his fists tightly without being aware of it. A strange pain stabbed at his chest in waves until he could hardly stand upright and he had to restrain himself from running into the courtyard to reveal himself right there. But if he did, he would bring trouble, not only on himself, but on all the people in the house.

He turned back and walked away silently along the shortcut to the hut at the end of the plantation, looking back every now and then at the lamplight in the windows of the house until it was out of sight. There was a sound of barking from the dog that Man had given him as a guard dog, alerting him to someone's arrival, before it stopped as if it remembered its old master's voice. Someone came closer without the light of a lamp because he was familiar with the place.

Phraya Wisetsingnart asked, "Man?"

"Yes, sir. I've brought you dinner."

The faithful servant carefully walked around the bamboo table into the hut, lighting a lamp and arranging the rice and fish that he had sneaked out of his house, feeling sorry that his old boss was hungry as well as uncomfortable.

"Don't bring anymore. Your wife will be suspicious."

"She won't, sir," Man answered confidently, reassuring his old boss, "Today I got it from Suk. I told her it was for Juan, and when Ned heard, he slipped in some fried fish as well. Do you want to eat now, sir?"

As soon as he heard his son's name, his mood brightened.

"Ned hasn't been for days."

Man carefully arranged the food on the bamboo table and sat down on the floor to attend to his boss and keep him company.

"Khunying won't let him come. Now it's dark, she won't let him out of the house. I was there this evening, and Ned was talking about you. He asked if Uncle Poon had made him another cricket cage."

A smile appeared for the first time behind the beard that hid his face.

"My boy certainly likes crickets! I don't know when he'll come and see me again. Man, bring him to see me once more. I don't know when I'll have to leave here."

Man's heart sank, and he hurriedly answered, "Stay here. Nobody suspects anything."

"Bang Pho's right next to Bang Sue. I'm standing right on the tiger's nose here."

"All my people are on the lookout," Man assured him, indirectly boasting of his influence. "If one policeman or soldier sets foot here, all the villagers will spread the word. I've instructed them. Nobody knows who you are, not even Juan."

"Even so, I can't be too careful. If needs be, I'll have to leave...The only thing I'm worried about is my son."

"Has anyone seen Ned, or has Bun Khlong taken him out again?"

Gade walked down the stairs into the courtyard after searching all over the house for them. Suk had gone out and had not yet returned, and only the girls were left in the house as they had returned from school, washed and changed, and were helping out in the house.

No sooner had she finished speaking when Bun Khlong appeared from under the house carrying a bundle of logs.

"I'm here!"

"Oh!" Gade cried in surprise. "And where's Ned? He hasn't gone with Suk. Has anyone seen him?"

This time, everyone who heard looked at each other in alarm, and some went out to look for him until one girl cried out, remembering, "Aunt, I think he went out by himself."

"Oh, no!" Gade cried in shock. "Where did he go?"

"He said he was going to catch crickets. I thought he meant around here."

Gade spun around to look at Bun Khlong, and her heart sank as she realized where he had gone to 'catch crickets'. The teenage boy dropped the logs at once and spluttered, "I'll go to get him at Uncle Poon's."

Gade could not contain her agitation and told the others to look for Ned outside the fence in case he was playing there, while she hurried after the teenager because it was already dark. Once they had cleared the house grounds, the plantations were enveloped in pitch darkness.

Usually, Gade would have walked there without nervousness because she was used to it, but when her heart was racing with anxiety for her son, the dark shadows appeared foreboding. Bun Khlong was agitated and felt guilty for letting the young boy out of the house, so he hurried across the bridges over the furrows, or jumped over them, until Gade could hardly keep up.

A small hut in the shadows of two large coconut palms was hidden in the darkness.

"Yoo-hoo! Uncle Poon! Yoo-hoo!" Bun Khlong called. "Is Ned here? Uncle!"

A dog barked in reply, but there was no answer, so Bun Khlong ran inside, and when the dog rushed inside, he hit it with the stick he was holding until it whimpered.

"What's going on?" a deep voice called from behind the hut.

A figure walked around the side of the hut holding a young boy's hand, so Bun Khlong ran towards them, while Gade stood still, becoming wary when she saw it was a tall man with a beard, wearing dark cotton pants that reached halfway down his shins with a cloth tied around his waist and a ragged old shirt.

Ned left the man and ran past the teenager to his mother, holding a branch in one hand and a cage made of coconut palms, bigger than the cricket cage, in the other with a green insect inside.

"Mother! Mother! I've got a beetle! It's a beetle!"

Gade bent down to hug her son tightly, feeling so relieved her legs almost gave way. Her racing heart slowed, but her voice still trembled.

"Ned! Why did you go out alone? I've been worried. Don't do it again. If you do it again, I'll have to spank you. It was very naughty, you know."

"I wasn't alone. I was with Uncle Poon," he argued.

As if to prove his innocence, Ned pulled his mother by the hand towards the tall man who had been standing motionless in the shadows of the coconut palms.

"Here he is, mother. Uncle Poon caught a beetle for me."

Gade grew inexplicably uncomfortable when she felt the man with the beard staring at her. Even in the darkness, she could see his penetrating eyes and he did not lower his gaze in deference as the other villagers did when they saw Khunying Wisetsingnart.

But Gade was too dignified to show that she was shaken, so she simply said, “Mr. Poon, you shouldn’t have brought my son here without anyone knowing. We’ve all been worried about him.”

“Forgive me,” he answered in a deep voice. “I missed him. I haven’t seen him for days.”

There was something about his voice that made the hairs on the back of her neck stand up, although she didn’t know why, so she told him firmly, “You shouldn’t have brought him here. I don’t know who you are, or where you come from. I’m afraid I can’t let you bring my son to play with you like this.”

“I’d never harm Ned, I promise. I’d lay down my life for him.”

This time, Gade felt as cold as ice from head to toe and began to sway as if she was going to faint, so she had to take several deep breaths in order to compose herself.

“Aunt,” said Bun Khlong. “Let’s go home.”

He felt uncomfortable about their exchange and began to worry because Uncle Poon was large and muscular, while Gade was young and pretty, and there was no one else about. He was not sure if he would be able to protect Gade, especially as Ned was also there.

Her nephew’s voice brought her to her senses, so she replied, “Yes, let’s go.”

Bun Khlong hurriedly crouched down, so that Ned could climb on his back because it was completely dark and he could only find his way back because he knew the way. Gade turned back after walking away and noticed that the figure was still standing there watching her every move.

When the three figures disappeared into the shadows of the coconut palms, the man who was watching them sank down onto the bamboo table as if his legs had turned to jelly and the darkness that engulfed him was darker than the night.

The light in Nart’s heart was extinguished when she disappeared out of sight, having shown no sign of remembering him. He could not blame her, since it was his doing, from the moment she had found him in the capital and he had ignored her to be with another woman. By the time he had come to his senses, Gade was no longer waiting.

Her remonstrations on the last night they were together still rang in his ears.

"You swore by the moon and the stars, but it wasn't true."

Yes, he had broken the promise that he made to the lovely young girl on the bridge. At the time, he had meant it, that he would love her and never abandon her, and never meant to deceive her, but infatuation had caused him to stray and forget her in favour of another woman who was more enticing, closer, and had ensnared him. Although he tried to make excuses to assuage his guilt, a promise was a promise without exception, and he could not help but wonder if that was the reason he now found himself destitute.

How much longer could he stand his condition now that Gade had slipped away from him?

The three of them walked for a while without speaking until they came to the junction where the paths divided between the way to Man's house and the way to Gade's. Gade decided to instruct the teenager, "Khlong, take Ned home. I need to see Man."

Gade didn't normally go to see Man herself, and if she needed to see him, she would send for him, so Bun Khlong looked puzzled and said, "I can go and fetch him."

"There's no need. I need to talk to him right now."

Unable to argue, Bun Khlong was obliged to take Ned home, but he kept looking back anxiously until she was out of sight.

When Gade felt sure that he had gone far enough not to come back, Gade changed direction and hurried back to the hut, arriving a few moments later.

It was pitch dark with not even the light of a lantern as there ought to have been. Gade slowly went inside the hut and stopped in the middle of the dirt floor, listening for the sound of a dog barking. Everything was silent except for wind rustling the coconut palms.

Her instinct made her turn around and she almost bumped into the person who had silently approached her. She gasped and took a step back.

"It's me," a deep voice said. "Please don't be scared, Khunying."

Gade stared at the face that she could just make out in the darkness, just a step away, and answered shakily, "I'm not scared. I wanted to be sure..."

"Sure of what?"

"Sure that…" Gade took a deep breath and forced herself to sound normal. "Sure that you didn't mean any harm…"

His voice changed from husky to loud and clear.

"I promised you I'd lay down my life for Ned, so how could I harm him?"

"That's why I'm afraid…"

With her fists clenched, Gade blurted out shakily, *"Don't you remember you once promised someone that you'd love her forever?"*

At Gade's words he fell silent and became as still as a statue.

Although they were surrounded by darkness, a light began to shine in their hearts, brighter than the stars that were beginning to appear and the moon that shone through the coconut palms and was reflected in the water in the furrows.

"Gade."

His voice was hoarse as he spoke the words that came straight from his heart.

"I'm so sorry I hurt you."

Gade could no longer control herself ; a sob escaped from her throat and the tears rolled down her cheeks as she fell into her husband's outstretched arms.

Nart held his wife tightly to his chest and rested his face on her soft hair as if he no longer had the strength to pretend to be a stranger.

Gade glanced up at her husband. Her tears had dried and she could feel his chin on her forehead and his warm hands gently caressing her back. Gade tried to speak, but words escaped her. Nart understood and knew that, in that moment, they might forget their worries for the time being, so he whispered with a chuckle, "It's me, your husband. I'm not an imposter trying to hug you."

Gade managed to laugh through her sobs.

"I thought I'd never see you again."

"I refuse to die when Ned's still a child, and you're still young. I had to come back to you."

"You missed us?"

Nart brushed his lips against her forehead and answered firmly, "From the day I left your house until today, I couldn't think of anyone except you and Ned. I thought of you every day and every night with every breath I took. If it wasn't true, why would I have risked coming back?"

"And why were you so cruel, not coming to see me, and hiding in the orchard? If I hadn't found you, you would have left me crying even longer."

He kissed her gently again, and even though his wife's words hurt him, he felt happier than he'd ever felt before.

"Don't say that. I missed you more than anything. I could see you and our son, but I couldn't go to you. I was afraid of bringing trouble. Even when Ned came to play here, I couldn't tell him who I was...I had to pretend to be someone else. It was torture."

Gade leaned her cheek against his chest and could hear his heart beating under his warm skin. It was the most welcome sound she had heard, ever since she had first heard it five years before. The years that they had been apart melted away as if nothing had ever come between them since they had first got married in Phetchaburi.

Nart asked gently, "How did you know it was me?"

"I recognized your voice, even though you tried to change it, I knew it was you."

"I thought so. I wanted to test you."

Gade looked up at him, puzzled.

"Why did you have to test me?"

He was silent until Gade repeated the question, so he answered, "I wanted to know if you would recognize me. Even Ned and Bun Khlong didn't know me. I walked past officers in Bang Sue and they didn't know me."

Gade smiled, not knowing if she was sad or happy.

"What wife wouldn't recognize her own husband? Nart, let's go home."

Go home...Gade did not know how sweet those words sounded to his ears, and with a heavy heart, he answered, "I can't let anyone know I'm hiding here. Nobody knows apart from Man and you. Did you tell Bun Khlong?"

"No. No one knows. You can hide in the house. No one in the house will tell anyone."

"I can't, Gade. It's too risky. If they catch me, you'll be in trouble, too."

"Bu…But…" Gade stammered, her voice trembling again as she held onto his arm. "But I can't let you stay in this hut. It's intolerable!"

"I'm used to sleeping rough. It's not intolerable as long as I'm close to you and Ned."

Gade wanted to lay her head on his shoulder and cry. That Nart had escaped death was the best thing that had ever happened to her, but how could she bear for him to be so close and yet so far, since he could not come and live with her and Ned as he ought.

Gade made up her mind without hesitation.

"You can't stay here. If I keep bringing Ned to see you, people will notice and they'll find you. Let's go to Phetchaburi. We can work in the orchards and no one will know."

Nart sighed and clasped Gade's hand.

"If I go to Phetchaburi, the soldiers there will catch me for sure, but they'll never guess I'm here right on the tiger's nose. Bang Pho's safer because no one will guess, but I'll have to hide here for now."

Gade felt as if she couldn't breathe and slowly moved away to face him, not letting go of his hand.

"What will happen if they catch you?"

"At first, they'll send me to Bang Kwang, and if they find me guilty, I'll be sent to prison."

Gade held her breath and tried to dispel her fear.

"In that case, I'll wait for you until you're released, and you can come back to live with me...and Ned. I can wait."

Nart felt a lump in his throat and was silent for a moment before pulling Gade into his embrace once more.

"Thank you, Gade. I should have known you would."

They remained motionless for a moment before Nart said cheerfully, "If I'm lucky, it won't come to that. I can't turn myself in before I'm accused."

"I don't understand."

"I didn't join the rebels, but I couldn't let my friends die. It was bad. I didn't know until it was over that I'd have to confess. If I'd have stayed, I'd be in Bang Kwang by now."

"Chat told me you escaped across the Mekong. Is it true?"

When she mentioned Chat's name, the tension in the atmosphere was palpable, and Gade could see his eyes probing her feelings in the moonlight.

"Yes. My cousin helped me."

He paused before returning to the other matter.

"Khun Chom's brother comes to see you often, doesn't he?"

The question did not require an answer, but was intended to let her know that she could not hide anything from him. Gade looked into his eyes innocently.

"He came three or four times. He was bringing news about you. If I hadn't wanted to hear news about you, I wouldn't have let him come again."

"Why?"

Gade's silence made him realize he had offended her. If he continued to be jealous of Chat, it would turn into something bigger and drive them apart.

"Are you angry with me?" he finally asked.

"Why would I be angry with you?" she asked.

"Because I was jealous of Khun Chom's younger brother," he admitted. "When I should have accepted it. If I have to stay in prison for years, you should have someone to protect you."

Gade brushed his lips with the tip of her finger, a gesture she had never done before. She realized that their time together was running out and, not knowing when they would be together again, she did not want anything to come between them.

"Please, don't talk about it."

Gade rested her head against his shoulder again and felt his arms hold her tightly as if he was thinking the same thing, namely how many more days, or hours, did they have until they would be separated?

"Ned's father is the only man for me."

When Gade was newly married, she was so happy that there was no room for sadness, and when Nart left, only sadness remained. She never imagined that the next stage of her life would have both happiness and sadness simultaneously. Such were the feelings she was experiencing as she came out of her house the next evening. So as not to arouse suspicion, she said, "Suk, I'm going to see Mae Chee Yuen. I heard she's not well."

The old nun lived behind Soi Thong Temple and Gade regularly supported her with food and essential items, so it was nothing out of the ordinary, but if anyone had asked why Khunying Wisetsingnart was going to visit her alone after dark, she would have been hard pressed to explain.

"Don't you want Bun Khlong to go with you, madam?"

"That won't be necessary."

Gade carried a bowl of food with a lid on it, leading Suk to believe that it was for the nun, when it was actually for Nart, since she could not bear to see her husband eating scraps.

At first, she had wanted to take Ned along, but Nart had forbidden her, telling her, "Let Bun Khlong bring him here to play instead. That way no one will be suspicious because everyone knows he likes to play in the orchards, but if you bring him, they'll all wonder why you brought him to visit the guard at his hut."

The happiness she felt at the prospect of seeing her husband was enough to nullify any anxiety she had and she quickened her pace as she approached the hut. The dog barked as a signal and Gade stopped until she saw Nart emerge to greet her.

"Come in. I've been waiting for you."

The happiness in his voice indicated that unlike her he was not distressed by his living conditions, but Gade swallowed a lump in her throat before forcing herself to sound cheerful.

"I've brought you salted crab. Have you cooked some rice?"

"Great! I'm starving! Man brought me some rice wrapped in banana leaves. He brought enough for three meals!"

If she ignored the impoverished surroundings and Nart's shabby condition, it was just like old times, when there had been just the two of them at the army base in Phetchaburi.

Gade had buried such memories deep in her heart and had not thought she would revive them but they arose easily and naturally. Even in the pitch darkness, the orchard seemed bright to her. Nart asked her about ordinary things such as a husband would do after returning from work, and Gade answered cheerfully.

"Hasn't Rern come to visit you this month?"

"She's heavily pregnant, so she can't come. The baby's due in June. I want to take Ned to see her, but I'm worried about leaving the house with only the girls."

"Go if you want to. Will you be gone for long?"

"But then again, I don't really want to go."

Gade did not explain why, but Nart understood. He continued eating quietly until he was full, and Gade pushed a bowl of water towards him for him to drink. Then his voice became serious.

"Gade, I didn't want to tell you yet, but I have to. If I can't stay here, I'll have to escape. If there's any trouble here, you can go and see my cousin. My aunt's very fond of you, and she'd be happy to help you."

Gade's hands began to tremble, but her voice remained steady.

"If you go, I'll go with you."

"Gade..." he cried. "How can you go with me?"

"Why not?"

"What about Ned, and your house and orchards that you've worked so hard to build up? And there's your relatives from Phetchaburi, too..."

Gade slowly shook her head and her eyes sparkled in the darkness like the stars that flickered in the night sky. Her voice was determined.

"I'll take Ned with us. I can let my relatives from Phetchaburi take turns to look after the house. I don't care about anything else, as long as we're together. Even if we're poor, it's better than being apart."

Nart was still before he got up from the floor to sit next to her on the bamboo table and pulled her into his arms again. He could not speak, for there was a lump in his throat and all he could do was gaze at her, mesmerized by her bravery.

At that moment, Colonel Phraya Wisetsingnart told himself that he must take action. If he procrastinated any longer, his present condition would not be any good for either of them, and he would put his wife and child in danger.

Gade pulled the blanket over her son because the night air was getting colder. She heard the sound of water droplets clearly in the silence of the orchards, and every so often, there was the sound of fish splashing in the furrows and birds singing in the boughs of the nearby trees. Everything was normal. A dog barked in front of the house and, a moment later, was quiet. Then she heard the sound of a small stone hitting the roof of the house and she sat up at once.

When she heard it a second time, she pulled open the mosquito net and went to the window as she noticed someone hanging onto the window frame before pulling himself up and climbing quickly and quietly inside.

It was Nart, but not in the form of the shabby and bearded Uncle Poom who guarded the orchard. It was Colonel Wisetsingnart, looking dignified in his uniform, no different from how she had seen him on the last night he had stayed at the house.

"Gade," he said softly. "I have to go tonight."

Gade fell into her husband's arms again and her heart sank as he hugged her tightly as if could not bear to lose her.

"Nart...take me and Ned with you. Don't leave us."

Nart bent his head to kiss her, and when she looked up at him, he said firmly, "I'm not running away. It's time for me to turn myself in to the government. My cousin sent news this evening. He sent my clothes to me. I don't have much time to talk."

Gade held onto her husband's arms tightly. Although she felt a little better after finding out that he would not have to go abroad, she was still shaken to the core.

"And...and what will happen to you?"

"I don't know. I might have to go to the military court like the others, or maybe not. Let's hope I won't have to. Let me tell you the whole story."

Nart's eyes gleamed in the darkness and his voice was low, but clear.

"I was betrayed by my friend. Det...Phraya Thepakanee. He

informed me that the government wanted me to act as a mediator with Prince Boworadet, but he told the government I volunteered. It's not the same. Do you understand, Gade? Now, it looks like I joined the rebels and volunteered to mediate, in order to defect. That's why I had to run away until I could find someone who believed me before I turned myself in to fight the charges against me."

Gade couldn't believe her ears. Even though she had never met Phraya Thepakanee, she knew he was a close friend of her husband and that they had known each other since they were young. Aware of the fact that she was a country woman on her own, whose husband had abandoned her, Gade had never asked for help from any of Nart's important friends, but had stood on her own two feet.

"And why did Chao Khun Thep betray you?"

"He's been against me for a while, ever since I disagreed with him about the People's Party. I opposed his ideas all along. It's about power. Once some people get power, they get drunk on it. They see other people as thorns in their sides that they must get rid of. I want you to know that...whatever happens, you must never trust Det. Don't trust anyone except my cousin, and take care of Ned..."

Nart turned to look at his son who was fast asleep on the bed. He bent down and gently stroked his hair, being careful not to wake him.

"Goodbye, Ned. Take care of your mother for me."

He turned back to her, and before he could take hold of her hands, she placed her palms together.

"No matter what happens, I'll wait for you until you come back, or I'll go to you. May the gods protect you and keep you from harm."

Nart enfolded Gade in his arms for the last time and kissed her cheek with more feeling than ever before.

"Don't be afraid. I won't abandon you again."

A moment later, Nart climbed out the window and landed on the ground beneath before he disappeared into the darkness.

Gade held onto the window frame tightly and a cool breeze brushed her skin. No matter how cold it was, Gade continued standing there for hours, staring into the darkness that had swallowed Nart's figure from her sight.

“What? Is this news about Phraya Wisetsingnart true?” Chat called when he read the headline in the newly printed newspaper that had not yet left the printers.

His colleague nodded, his face drawn from staying up all night to write the article.

“He’s not dead. He turned himself in to fight the charges against him. I expect we’ll know the outcome in a few days.”

Chat read the details with shaking hands.

“And where is he now? Bang Kwang?”

“He’s being held at the Ministry of Defence. Hey, where are you going?”

He asked because he saw the young man pick up the newspaper and run down the stairs, calling behind him, “Bang Pho.”

Chat did not meet the house owner as he had intended. Gade’s house was quiet as if no one was home and only Suk came out to greet him.

“Khunying’s not home, sir. She’s gone to stay with Chao Khun’s relatives. She won’t be back for several days.”

He had to leave disappointed, unaware that, after he had gone, Gade came out of her room and asked her son’s nanny quietly, “What did Chat say?”

“He left this newspaper for you, madam. There’s news about Chao Khun.”

Gade took the newspaper, scanning the headline before she folded it up again with a sigh.

“Remember, Suk. Apart from Khun Phra Prab, I won’t see anyone.”

“Yes, madam. I’ll tell everyone you’re not home. Like just now.”

Gade could only nod before going back inside her room.

She was sorry she couldn’t see Chat when he had been so consistently kind to her in her time of need, but what could she do? She knew that both herself and Nart were on a knife edge, and that whoever she talked to and whatever she said might put herself or her husband in grave danger.

The light work that she did each day did not help her to focus, and in the end, she went inside the altar room and tried to clear her mind of confusion, telling herself, "Nart will be safe."

Police Lieutenant Colonel Phra Prabribupai came to see Gade the next day and told her in a low whisper, "There's news that Nart won't have to go to Bang Kwang like the other political suspects, but he's being investigated for high treason at the Ministry of Defence."

Gade squeezed her hands together tightly and she felt an indescribable sense of relief.

"And where's Chao Khun now?"

"He's at the Ministry of Defence."

"Can I visit him, Khun Phra?" Gade asked, hiding her anxiety.

"I don't think it would be appropriate at the moment, but as soon as it is, I'll come and collect you and take you there myself."

The police officer continued, as if guessing she was disappointed, "Don't worry. As far as I can see, if Khun Luang Phibun Songkhram believes Nart, it will be an advantage for us."

"I'll pray he believes him."

"I'll pray, too," he smiled encouragingly at her. "He's known Nart for several years, and he knows Nart's honest and not deceptive. And for another thing, I've noticed that he and Phraya Thepekanee don't always see eye to eye."

Gade looked at him questioningly, and he explained only, "Some people are saying that, as a result of quashing this rebellion, Khun Luang Phibun Songkhram will get promoted too fast, and some people aren't happy about it. If you ask me, Chao Khun Thep's one of them."

This was a complicated matter that was hard to understand, and Gade did not think any more about it, except for being concerned about her husband. Nor did Police Lieutenant Colonel Phra Prabribupai disclose any further details, so as not to alarm Gade further.

He was relieved that his cousin had not yet had to go to a special tribunal because he knew that in such cases the Minister of Defence had absolute authority to appoint the judge, jury, prosecutor, and bailiff, and more importantly, that the defendant did not have the right to a defence lawyer. Therefore, the verdict was based entirely on the prosecution's evidence, and the verdict was final with no right of appeal. In the case of his cousin, Phra Prapribupai could see that the bottom line was, would the government believe his cousin's testimony, or Phraya Thepakanee's?

Colonel Phraya Wisetsingnart was not taken to the special tribunal like other political suspects, where Major General Phraya Prasert Songkhram, the Minister of Defence, was judge. Instead the Minister of Defence had appointed a special inside jury to determine the matter, as it was a case unlike any of the others because Phraya Wisetsingnart had been sent to negotiate with the rebels on behalf of the government.

An important point to be taken into consideration and recorded in his testimony was whether he had volunteered to negotiate or had been ordered by someone to do so. If this matter was cleared up, the next question was whether he had intended to join General Phraya Si Sitthisongkhram from the start.

In the meantime, Nart was held in the Ministry of Defence and was not sent to Bang Kwang as he had first expected. His relative, Phra Prapribupai, had been given permission to visit him, but Nart had instructed him not to bring his wife and Ned until the investigation was over.

"I don't want them to see me like this. They would be upset. Please tell them I'm fine and they don't need to worry about me."

He could not write her a letter or note because if he was caught, he would be in even more trouble. His cousin understood.

Nart told himself that even though it would be hard to fight his case, it was better than staying in hiding.

He comforted himself with the fact that there was nothing that now stood between him and Gade. If he was acquitted, they would be able to start their life together as they should have done from the beginning, five years earlier.

Nart stepped inside the room, which had once been the Ministry of Defence meeting room. The yellow rays of the afternoon sun shone onto the stern faces of the jury sitting lined up inside.

Nart scanned their faces. Each one was familiar to him from being in the army together. They were his juniors and his seniors whom he had seen since they were cadets and every face was imprinted in his memory. His gaze came to rest on the handsome face of Lieutenant Colonel Luang Phibun Songkram, who was acting as the judge. Khun Luang sat upright with his shoulders squared as Nart had always seen him. The only change was that his taut face had no trace of his former smile.

Then his eyes turned to the face of a man who had become a complete stranger to him – Colonel Phraya Thepakanee!

His former best friend looked at him coldly, his face as expressionless as a statue. Nart searched his face for a hint of derision, but found none. Nor was there any sign of friendship or concern, but in his eyes, Nart thought he saw a gleam of triumph. His eyes told him that they were no longer friends, that he had him in the palm of his hand and that if he squeezed him, he'd die. And today he would squeeze him to death!

Det was both jury and an important witness. Nart did not know the exact words he would say, but he could guess what his testimony would be. When Nart was called to give evidence he was alone, not like in a court when he would have had the opportunity to hear the testimony of others, but whatever happened, Nart was ready to accept the harshest consequences.

The judge handed the verdict for the secretary of the jury to stand up and read, so Nart stood to listen to the words that would decide his fate.

The beginning of the statement referred to the fighting that had taken place before coming to the conclusion and the final verdict.

"From investigating the witness and the evidence, and after considering the statements, we have reached the conclusion that Colonel Phraya Wisetsingnart did his duty on behalf of the government to persuade Din Tharap (Phraya Si Sitthisongkhram) to give up the rebellion against the government of Siam as assigned by the government.

There was no evidence from the witness or the circumstances to indicate that, on the 17th of August 1933 or thereafter, Colonel Phraya Wisetsingnart collaborated with the rebels in opposition to the government.

For this reason, the jury has reached the conclusion that Colonel Phraya

Wisetsingnart is not guilty. It will not be necessary to send evidence to a special prosecutor for a special tribunal trial. This is the jury's verdict."

When the reading was finished, the room was so silent that you could have heard a pin drop. Suddenly, Colonel Thepakanee stood up and shouted, "How can this be?"

All eyes turned towards him. Lieutenant Colonel Luang Phibun Songkhram shifted for the first time after sitting still throughout the proceedings, and said politely, but resolutely, "Please respect the court."

Colonel Phraya Thepaknee held onto the table until his knuckles were white and the blood rushed to his face.

"I object to the jury's resolution. This is not what we agreed to."

"Objection overruled," Luang Phibun replied as coldly as before. "You did not vote, and the result is a secret. It's only revealed when it's read out."

"The reason I didn't vote is because I was called as a witness, so I thought it only proper not to vote, but as far as I understand, it isn't…"

The jury looked at each other uncomfortably before one of them spoke out.

"We gave our votes to the judge. The result is final."

Another added, "As you know this isn't a court of law. This jury has been set up as a special case."

"I'm well aware of that!" Phraya Thepakanee replied angrily. "But I object! This isn't over yet!"

The impetuous and cocksure Det had manifested in front of Colonel Phraya Wisetsingnart once more. As with many times in the past, Det's impulsiveness had backfired.

Lieutenant Colonel Phibun Songkhram was much calmer and showed no sign of anger towards the other man, although Nart told himself that he saw a glimmer of triumph in Khun Luang's eyes when he saw Phraya Thepakanee's fury.

"This is just my temporary office," Luang Phibun said to ease the tension between them. The smile had reappeared as had his manners and he was as friendly as he had been before.

"Please have a seat, Nart. It's just the two of us. Let's get rid of all pretence. I've been wanting to meet you as we did before, but because of that business, I couldn't speak to you."

Nart knew well that Luang Phibun Songkhram was softly spoken in contrast to his determination in battle and that he was a more profound thinker than the hot-headed Det.

It did not surprise him that the two of them had become enemies, and that his friend had been defeated with no way out. The incident just a moment ago was a clear example.

Nart sat down and replied, "I'm very grateful to you."

"Oh, come on. You're still my senior and I'm still your junior. Nothing's changed."

"Thanks," Nart answered and asked him, "Will I be going back to Khorat, or will the chief move me to another post?"

"Er, I haven't heard him say anything, but I expect you'll have to stay in the Ministry for now, as the order that Chao Khun Prasert signed said. Would you prefer to stay in Bangkok, or go upcountry?"

It all sounded reasonable, but Phraya Wisetsingnart could see that underneath his calm voice he was confident in his answer. He was not surprised by Luang Phibun Songkram's current prominent role, and when he thought about it, he could see that many of the officers who had played an important role in the revolution last year had faded in importance.

One of them was Colonel Phraya Rit Akanae. And Colonel Phraya Thepakanee was his right-hand man.

It was a well-known saying that several tigers could not stay in the same cave, and this young tiger was rising to prominence with energy and intelligence, while being careful to protect himself.

Det had been determined to bring down his old friend, so that he would not be a thorn in his side after irritating him for more than a year, but he had failed to realize that someone with more power was standing in another corner and was not going to let the future of one of his senior officers be destroyed without stepping in. In this way, besides earning Phraya Wisetsingnart's loyalty, he would also curtail Phraya Thepakanee's power.

Between himself and Phraya Thepakanee, if Luang Phibun had to choose which man he would trust not to be a danger to him in the future, Nart was sure he would choose him.

"If I have a say, I would choose to stay in Bangkok," he answered without hesitation.

A thin smile on the lips of the other man indicated his satisfaction with his answer.

"Very well. I wish you all the best. With your knowledge and experience, you'll be useful wherever you are. Anyway, I expect you want to go home and rest. I won't take any more of your time."

He stood up and held out his hand before shaking the other man's hand warmly.

"I'd like to congratulate you sincerely, Nart."

"And I thank you...sincerely as well."

He did not mention the incident in the meeting room, Phraya Thepakanee, or even Phaya Khamphang.

Nart's thoughts returned to the jury's verdict. There had been no mention of him going into hiding after the fighting had ended, and all that had been said was, 'There was no evidence that he was opposed to the government.'

Phraya Thepaknee's reaction showed that there must have been a change in the verdict. Clearly a prior decision had been agreed upon, which was then altered. Det had seemed so confident that the jury would decide to send Phraya Wisetsingnart to a prosecutor in a special tribunal. Nart's friend felt he had him in the palm of his hand and was sure he could squeeze him to death. The gleam of triumph in his eyes betrayed as much, as if to say, 'I've let you get away with your impudence for long enough. It's time you learned your lesson. You can't obstruct the world any longer.'

Luang Phibun Songkhram had likely given Det no hint that the verdict would be different. He had allowed Det to gloat that the other members of the jury agreed with him, and by the time he found out to the contrary, it was too late. Luang Phibun Songkhram knew that Nart wasn't the kind of man to overly display his gratitude, but neither would he gloat over his rivals.

13
The End of Sorrow

Colonel Phraya Wisetsingnart walked into the bedroom wearing silk trousers and a cotton shirt, as he usually did at home. His face was clean and smooth, since he had just bathed and shaved, and he looked happy and relaxed.

Gade turned from the bed, on which she had just put clean white sheets that were fragrant with jasmine, its scent mingling with that of the flower garland hanging on the bedhead. The mosquito net swayed gently in the breeze that blew in through the open window.

Nart loved this room, which he felt epitomised Gade. She knew how to create an atmosphere that was calm and tranquil, just like herself, far from the turmoil and stress that he had just come from.

He smiled at his wife and when he didn't see his son asked, "Where's Ned?"

"He's asleep in my room."

"Which room is yours?" he asked, puzzled. "You sleep in this room every night, don't you?"

"The room Rern stayed in," she answered softly. "It's empty now. Rern won't be coming again until next year, so I've arranged my things in it."

"Why do you have to find another room? Stay here."

"You can have this room," she replied, turning away from him and busying herself folding the silk blanket at the foot of the bed.

Her husband's hands reached out to touch the tops of her arms, and the resolute voice she'd practised disappeared in her throat.

Nart turned her around by her shoulders and gazed at her, from her lovely face to her shoulders and bosom. Tonight, Gade was dressed comfortably, as she was every night after bathing, with a simple cloth wrapped around her chest and a *jongkraben*, instead of a blouse and sarong like she wore in the daytime. The pale pink cloth around her chest made her skin look radiant and when Nart saw her figure, that was still as shapely as that of a young girl, he felt sorry yet again that he had been away from her for so long.

"I've been sleeping alone for I don't know how many months. Now I'm back in your house, are you going to be so cruel as to make me sleep alone again?"

If it had been before, Gade would have answered coldly or scornfully, but by now, she knew her true feelings, since the day she thought that Nart was gone and would never come back. She knew she could not be happy without him. Life was short, and she did not know when fate would take Nart away from her again. If they did not have much time together, they should spend it happily rather than fighting.

"Since when have I been the cruel one?"

There was no anger in her voice, and Nart laughed out loud for the first time, his voice full of happiness. He enfolded her in his arms and, although she resisted at first, she soon became still when she heard his soft voice as he rested his chin on her forehead.

"Yes, you are cruel. You don't know how much I've missed you and Ned. I missed you so much I couldn't let you visit me at the ministry. I was afraid you'd see me and be worried, and I wouldn't be able to stand the thought of you worrying. I've never missed anyone so much before. I didn't know how strong a husband and father's love could be."

Gade rested her head on his broad shoulders and breathed out softly in response. She was glad that he had realized the power of love, so that he would know how much she had suffered, and think twice before doing the same thing again.

As if guessing what she was thinking, he said earnestly, "Our sorrow has ended at last. The past is over. I've come back to you and Ned. I'll never go anywhere else again."

"You won't go anywhere..." Gade repeated, looking up at him. "Aren't you going back to Khorat?"

"My position in Khorat has gone to someone else. I've been moved to an inactive post in the Ministry of Defence. I'll be staying in Bangkok until I'm ordered to go upcountry, but if I go, I'll take you and Ned with me."

Gade inadvertently squeezed her husband's arms. She didn't care about his position, or where he would be posted. All she cared about was that Nart had promised never to leave her again. This was enough to lighten her heart.

"Nart, I'm...I'm so happy we'll all be together at last."

He caressed her comfortingly as if he understood her feelings for the first time. At that moment, he realized that, for them fully to begin their lives together again, he would have to get rid of the thorn in his side first.

"Yes, we'll all be together, without anyone else."

Gade held her breath before asking hesitantly, "And...what if that woman asks you to make up with her?"

Now she knew that Nart was still alive, she might try to rekindle the old flame. Gade was well aware of how she had used all her feminine wiles to ensnare her husband.

"I finished with her ages ago, Gade. Ever since I came to Bangkok that time."

"You never told me."

"Can't you tell I want to be with you and Ned? That's why I kept coming to see you. Nuathong knew. That's why she came here. You don't need to worry I'll go back to her. We're finished."

Gade felt as if a heavy weight had been lifted off her shoulders, and she looked up at him and smiled. She had not smiled such a bright and happy smile for years. Her eyes sparkled with tears like the sky outside twinkled with stars. Nart gazed at his wife for a moment with a lump in his throat that was hard to explain before kissing her on the forehead and hugging her close as if he would never allow her to be separated from him again.

Colonel Phraya Wisetsingnart did not have a car of his own, since the house at Bang Pho did not yet have a road that reached it. He travelled to the ministry from Bang Pho by boat and alighted at Chang Wang Luang Pier, where Phra Prabribupai was kind enough to pick him up in his car and take him to the ministry each day.

Nart held a position in the Ministry of Defence and did not move back to Nakhon Ratchasima. Although his position was not higher than the one he had had in Nakhon Ratchasima, it was not any lower.

Several of his friends had told him he was lucky and congratulated him, but Phraya Wisetsingnart had answered grimly, "If there had not been a reason for me to hold this position, I would be happier."

Everyone was silent because they knew what he was referring to.

The special court's decision after the Boworadet Rebellion had affected both military and civilian civil servants like never before in Siam.

Over a thousand civil servants from the rank of Phraya to Khun, from intendants to clerks, had been dismissed, and over five hundred suspected rebels had been imprisoned in Bang Kwang Prison.

Even though many months had passed and they had already entered a new year, the tension remained. Transfers and dismissals continued unabated, and political prisoners were given harsher and longer sentences than they had ever imagined, even those soldiers who had been following the orders of their commanders.

Nart was uncomfortable about it, but he could not mention it to anyone. He had learned that nobody trusted anyone anymore, and Det had made him realize that ambition and hunger for power could destroy even the closest friendship. Nart had seen how the lust for power had driven a wedge between the leaders after the revolution of 1932, and now it seemed to be happening again after the Boworadet Rebellion. Many soldiers of the same rank as him felt that it was difficult to remain in the middle.

In the end, you had to pick a side, and if you were not on one side it meant you were on the other. You could not remain neutral unless you were of such low rank and so unimportant that nobody cared which side you were on.

Tonight, Phra Prabribupai waited in his car in front of the Ministry of Defence. Nart had invited him to have dinner with him as since the beginning of the month they had barely seen each other for a proper conversation.

At dinner, there was only Nart and his cousin at the table, and

Khunying Wisetsingnart did not join them.

All she said was, "Please have dinner, Khun Phra. I'm not hungry. I won't eat until eight or nine o'clock."

"Gade's lost her appetite," Phraya Wisetsingnart told his cousin. "She doesn't want to eat anything. Let's eat just the two of us."

Gade had not told her husband that whatever she ate made her feel nauseous until she had to throw up. Some meals, especially breakfast, she skipped all together and could only eat sour fruits that chased the sickness away. Gade had experienced these symptoms before, so she knew what it was and decided to tell her husband at the first opportunity as she thought he'd be happy. She had planned to tell him that evening, but when Phra Prabribupai came for dinner, she decided to wait until after he'd gone.

There was nobody listening to their conversation, so the two men were able to talk freely to each other.

"I want to go to Saraburi," Nart said, "To Hin Lap to pay my respects to Din. Gade wants to go, too. He was from Phetchaburi as well."

General Phraya Si Sitthisongkram's last stronghold was close to the Hin Lap in Saraburi province. It was there that Nart's friend and senior died bravely.

Phra Prabribupai chose his words carefully.

"You're not unimportant, Nart. If Phraya Thepakanee finds out, he'll be suspicious again. It'll cause trouble."

"I'm planning to go quietly. I want to pay my last respects. If anyone has a problem with that, too bad."

Although the Boworadet Rebellion was over, the losses that resulted were irreplaceable. Nor had the peace that followed made the political situation stable. For Nart, it felt like the calm before the storm. He disagreed with completely eliminating those people who had been powerful before to prevent more trouble, although he understood the reasons for doing so because the present government was riding on a tiger's back. They could not get down, and had to run the country at the same time, but the result was an unavoidable conflict over policy with King Prajadhipok.

Since Nart was a high-ranking officer, even though he was not directly involved in politics, he knew as much inside information as many prominent individuals, and he had seen the letter that the king had sent to the government while he was receiving medical treatment in England. It asked the government to revise some clauses of the constitution in order to give genuine rights and freedoms to the people. Nart remembered everything it said:

...For this reason, when the coup perpetrators asked me to be a constitutional monarch, I accepted immediately without any objections, but when I arrived in Bangkok and saw the first constitution that Luang Pradit gave me to sign, I realized immediately that the coup perpetrators' principles and my principles differed because the coup perpetrators did not aim to give complete political freedom, but to have a single political party...

A seizure of power does not increase political freedom. It becomes a bitter pill to swallow because absolute power has not ended. Only the leaders have changed and freedom has even decreased because dissenters must be captured and silenced...

Nart's thoughts turned to the eleven newspapers that had had their licenses revoked in 1933. During his time on the run after the Boworadet rebellion, he had heard that one newspaper had had its license revoked indefinitely simply for printing news about the rebellion.

But clauses five, six and eight of the king's letter concerned him more than anything else, and he could not see how the king's wishes could be fulfilled.

Whether I am asking for a pardon or for clemency for suspected rebels, I ask that civil servants who have been dismissed because they are suspected of 'political wrongdoing' or 'slandering the government' receive their rightful pensions, and that the arrest of civil servants suspected of being connected to the rebellion ceases.

His thoughts were interrupted by Phra Prabribupai.

"Do you think the same as I do? I thought from the start that the government wouldn't yield easily, but I don't know how it will end."

"With division," Phraya Wisetsongnart replied tersely.

"What kind of division? Another coup or rebellion?" the police officer asked at once.

"I mean there won't be any more compromise. I don't think there'll be another rebellion because the government's moved all its forces. Nowadays it's become that if you're not on the government's side, you're on the other side for sure. You can't be neutral."

Phra Prabribupai was silent for a moment.

"Nart, we're moving towards the 'Great Fear' like after the French Revolution."

He hoped Nart would refute him, but the only reply he heard was, "I hope it doesn't come to that."

Phra Prabribupai took his leave just after nine o'clock.

When Nart did not see his wife come out as usual, he asked Suk, "Where's Khunying?"

"She's in the bedroom, sir. She's not feeling well."

"Oh! What's the matter?"

Without waiting for an answer, he hurried into the bedroom and found Gate sitting on the floor in front of the bed lifting smelling salts to her nose, her face pale.

Phraya Wisetsingnart sat down next to her and stroked her back in alarm.

"Gade, shall I call a doctor? Or I can take you to see a doctor right away."

Even though she was exhausted from vomiting, and felt dizzy, Gade forced a smile for her husband.

"It's nothing. I'm just nauseous."

"Don't soldier on. You look pale. I'll tell Bun Khlong to fetch a doctor."

Gade clutched his hand in time, smiling in amusement at his overreaction.

"No! I said it's nothing. I've been like this before. I'll be better in a couple of months."

"What? A couple of months before you're better? What's wrong?"

Gade looked at her husband, in both shyness and gladness, before telling him, "It's like the first time I was pregnant."

Phraya Wisetsingnart's shocked expression gradually broke into a smile all over his face, and he held onto her arms.

"I'm so happy!" he said. "I haven't been this happy in a very long time."

He bent down to look at his wife's stomach as if to search for a sign of the tiny life beginning to grow, but he couldn't notice any change, before suddenly asking, "Are you very sick? What should you do? Should you see a doctor?"

"There's no need. It will soon pass," Gade smiled at her husband so as not to worry him, and asked shyly, "Do you want a boy or a girl?"'

Nart put his arms around her tenderly and whispered, "This time I want a girl. The more like you she is the better. And when you have your third pregnancy, I'll tell you if I want a boy or a girl next."

The good news from his wife made Phraya Wisetsingnart so happy that he forgot all about his anxiety about the political situation until King Prajadhipok's letter to the government was discussed in parliament on the 31st of January 1934.

The resolution of the Thai parliament was that ninety-six voted against it and only eight voted in favour, since parliament disagreed with many of the details in the letter.

On the 2nd of March 1934 King Prajadhipok, who was staying in England, sent his private secretary to the government with this message for the people of Siam:

"...Since those who brought about the change in the system of government did not give rise to complete political freedom and did not listen to the true voice of the people, and from both constitutions, it can be seen that the power to implement policies is solely in the hands of the perpetrators and those who support them, not the representatives chosen by the people...

Since the perpetrators did not bring real political freedom, and the people did not have the opportunity to vote before important policies were implemented, there was a rebellion, which led to Thais fighting and killing each other.

When I asked for the constitution to be revised in keeping with real democracy in order to satisfy the people, the government and those who have now seized absolute power refused, and even when important matters, such as my requests, were discussed in parliament, the members of parliament did not have an opportunity to consider them carefully because they were pressured to vote in one meeting. Furthermore, the government made laws to suppress individuals accused of political wrongdoing, in contradiction to international justice. That is, they did not have an opportunity to take it to court and there were secret payments by the jury, which are methods that I never used when absolute power was in my hands, and when I asked for these methods to cease, they refused.

In my view, the government and its cronies have used methods that are not in keeping with the principles of individual freedom and justice as I understand and hold them. I cannot continue to allow any individual or group to use such methods of governing in my name. I am willing to surrender the powers I formerly exercised to the people as a whole, but I am not willing to turn them over to any specific individual or group to use in an autocratic manner without heeding the voice of the people.

I now see that my wish to truly give the people a voice in the country's policies has not been realized, and since I now feel that I no longer have any way to help or protect the people, I hereby abdicate from this day forth.

On the evening of Wednesday the 6th of March 1934 Colonel Phraya Wisetsingnart left his office in the Ministry of Defence and walked along the long corridor open on one side to reach his car to go home as usual. The passageway was empty except for someone who opened the door of the last room along and came walking the other way. Both men had to stop.

It was the first time in several months, since the jury had voted that Nart was not guilty, that he had come face to face with his erstwhile best friend. Colonel Phraya Thepakanee looked at him frostily.

"You've heard about the king's abdication, have you?"

"Yes," Colonel Wisetsingnart replied coldly. "Why do you ask?"

Phraya Thepakanee chuckled vindictively.

"Because today the Prime Minister is going to announce it in parliament. What do you say? Are you still harping on about democracy like before? Not anymore, I expect. A good civil servant has to follow whatever direction the government decrees."

Nart was not angry, and he did not need to suppress his feelings. He looked at the other man and saw the shadow of the same impetuous young man as before standing in front of him.

"That's for sure. Now the king has abdicated, Siam has lost a gentleman of politics and a fighter for true democracy...and I'll tell you as a friend for the last time, Det…"

His last word was said with such sincerity that the smile disappeared from the other man's face.

"I believe that democracy will come to Siam, if not today, in the future, and those who hunger for power, without intelligence or sincerity, will eventually lose everything!"

From 1934 to 1938, there were no violent political incidents, and the government of Phraya Pahonphonphayuhasena implemented its policies smoothly until it lost the vote in parliament on the 11th of September 1938.

The leader that stepped up to take the premiership was Colonel Luang Phibun Songkhram, and he also took over the positions of Minister of Defence and Interior Minister.

One month and ten days after he took over, the government arrested several people on charge of treason, even when they had not done anything wrong. Other individuals who had been involved in the revolution were Phraya Song Suradet, who went into exile in Indochina until his death, and Phraya Ritakanae, who was sent to Malaya. General Thepakanee accompanied Phraya Ritakanae to Malaya where he lived until his death without returning to his homeland.

General Phraya Wisetsingnart continued to work in the Ministry of Defence and was not involved in politics until he retired.

Epilogue
The Apple of Their Eyes

It was almost ten o'clock at night. A medium-sized car moved slowly along the road that ran alongside Khlong Lot, and had almost reached Phraeng Sappasat.

The driver was dressed in a sergeant's uniform. A boy of eleven wearing a shirt and shorts with shoes and socks sat next to him to make room on the backseat for his younger sister to sit with their parents without being squashed.

In the back was a tall man in a general's uniform and a lady dressed in a purple lace blouse and an ankle length brocade sarong of the same colour with a matching set of earrings and a necklace. Their dress indicated that they were on their way back from an important event.

In between them was a fresh-faced five-year-old girl with round cheeks wearing a white organza dress with white leather shoes and socks, holding a red balloon on a string and jerking it up and down excitedly.

"Hold it still, dear," her mother scolded. "Sit nicely."

General Phraya Wisetsingnart fondly stroked her hair that was braided into two plaits tied with white organza ribbon.

"She's excited with it. Leave her, Gade."

No sooner had he spoken than a gust of wind came in through the car window and blew the string attached to the balloon out of her small hand. A moment later, the balloon had floated out the window and into the air.

"Oh! It's gone!" her father cried.

The little girl looked on in surprise, and when she realized that her balloon was gone her eyes filled with tears which rolled down her face. She opened her mouth to cry.

"Stop crying," Khunying Wisetsingnart told her. "I told you to hold it still, but you didn't listen."

"Don't cry. I'll buy you a new one," her father comforted her.

"Turn the car around. I expect the seller's still there."

"You're spoiling her," Gade cautioned, but she knew it was no use.

Everyone knew that Khunying was strict with her children. She thought the world of them, but she did not spoil them. However much she loved her son, she loved her daughter no less.

"Ned! Don't lean your head out the window. It's dangerous!" Gade scolded her son, who was becoming more active with every passing year.

At that moment, the excited young boy craned his neck out of the window and shouted, "Mother, it's got stuck in that tree. Sergeant Nien, stop the car!"

The sergeant braked. He was so used to the comings and goings of this family that he knew that if the balloon was not retrieved, he would have to turn the car around to go and buy another one, since Chao Khun wasn't someone to let his daughter cry all the way home without giving in to her.

He pulled over, and Phraya Wisetsingnart's son opened the door and jumped out, ignoring his mother's warnings to be careful as he made a beeline for the large tree standing by the roadside.

The red balloon was stuck in a branch halfway up the tree and was wobbling in the wind ready to drop down at any moment. Ned looked left and right, and seeing that there was no low branch on which to hold onto, decided to take off his shoes and shimmy up to the lowest branch.

Sergeant Jamnien ran after him shouting, "Ned, come down! I'll climb up there myself!"

"I can climb quicker!" he called, climbing up to the bough.

Phraya Wisetsingnart opened the car door and went after him. He looked up and was relieved to see that Ned was adroitly holding onto a branch with one hand, his legs wrapped tightly around it, and deftly reaching for the string attached to the balloon with the other.

Khunying Gade followed with her daughter and looked on in a mixture of amusement and irritation, but she said nothing, gladdened by Ned's love for his sister and Chao Khun's love for his children.

Their youngest child had stayed at home with his nanny. What kind of commotion would there have been if he had come too, Gade wondered? Ned climbed down from the tree and passed the balloon to his sister, who smiled in return, showing her little teeth as white as jasmine, her tears on her cheeks now dry.

Gade pulled the balloon string from her daughter's hand and gave it to her son, telling him firmly.

"You hold it tight, Ned. Give it to your sister when we get home, or it'll float away again."

The little girl dared not argue with her mother, feeling happy that she had got her balloon back, and allowed her mother to take her back to the car where she rested her head on her knee, indicating that she was getting sleepy. Ned tied the balloon string to his wrist so that it would not float away, and sat down to put on his shoes. He looked around him curiosly and his eyes rested on a small terraced house deep inside the adjacent street on the other side of the road. It was dimly lit and several people walked out, in contrast to the other houses which were all dark, or at least had dim lights shining through the vents, and whose inhabitants had gone to bed.

"Father, is there a party going on there?"

Several women sat outside in a row, wearing brightly coloured blouses and calling out to the men who walked past. Phraya Wisetsingnart looked away and told his son, "It's nothing. Let's go home."

He had forgotten such sights existed. Over ten years ago, he had sat in a horse-drawn carriage with a woman and passed through this area. His path after that night had taken a wrong turn, but luckily, he had returned to his former path in the end.

The sound of loud arguing came out of a small roadside house, not far from the busy one. An angry woman was letting out a stream of swear words, followed by a man's voice yelling abuse at her in return. She pushed the door open and the light from inside illuminated her frame in a brightly coloured sarong and a villager's loose sleeveless blouse. She turned to the man swaying drunkenly behind her. The light shone on her face, which had a trace of beauty, but was prematurely haggard, as was her figure.

Phraya Wisetsingnart started when he heard the loud voice, as drunken and slurred as the man's, and his hand holding onto his son's shoulder, jerked a little.

"Don't be insolent to me. I'm not common like you...I'm posh. I used to be somebody, you know."

"Oh! If you're so important, get out of my house, you slut!"

The man who was waving his finger at her was wearing nothing but a loincloth. He was skinny with tattoos all over his sunburned arms and chest, and was clearly drunk.

Ned looked on in alarm, having never seen a husband and wife in such a heated argument, and asked his father, "What are they arguing about?"

"Don't look at them," his father told him firmly.

The couple walked back inside the house but the sound of their arguing continued. The neighbours must have been used to it.

Phraya Wisetsingnart held his son by the arm and hurried back to the car. When he sat down, he was relieved to see that his wife was busy with their daughter and had not been looking out of the car window. He did not want Gade to see what he had just witnessed, afraid that it would bring back bad memories from the past. Even though she never mentioned it, he knew that she had not forgotten.

He moved over a little to make room for his wife and their daughter to sit comfortably and leaned forward to pat his son, who was sitting in front, on the shoulder.

"Well done! I'll reward you when we get home."

The young boy turned around and smiled at his father.

Nart glanced at his wife, who was shifting her daughter so that she could rest her head on her chest comfortably, and the streetlamps shone in on the purple stones in her earrings and her lovely face. Gade's figure had filled out after having three children, but at thirty years old, she was still radiant and beautiful.

"Is she asleep?" he asked.

"Yes, she went to sleep quickly," she answered softly.

Phraya Wisetsingnart gently stroked his daughter's hair before placing his hand on his wife's, which rested on the girl's shoulder, a show of affection that nobody else in the car could see except the two of them. Gade smiled at him, as she always did when he showed her tenderness, her eyes shining with contentment.

The car pulled out into Ratchadamnoen Avenue, taking its owners and their children back to their house in Bang Pho.

Background

This novel was inspired by the memorial book for the funeral of Khunying Wisetsingnart (Geng Chulanon) who died in 1947.

The record of her early life until she had a family was penned by her eldest son, who wrote with as much eloquence and tenderness as any son could have towards his mother.

I was given a photocopy of the book, along with historical documents from her son's early life, by Khunying Wisetsingnart's granddaughter, Ajarn Puangkaew (Olarnsombat) Laphirattanakun, who is both my student and my colleague.

After reading it, I asked for her permission to use it as a framework for a novel because Khunying Wisetsingnart's life is an inspiring example of a Thai woman who both 'rocked the cradle and wielded a dagger'. Even though she never actually went to war, she fought battles in her own life and came through them gracefully in the end, reflecting that good mothers are vital in the development of good families in society.

Before reading this book, I had intended to write a novel set in the reign of Rama VII, but had not found main characters or a plot that were suitable for that era, but after reading this book, I was able to combine these two things by shifting the real-life events by about twenty years. The events in the real lives of Phraya and Khunying Wisetsingnart took place at the end of King Chulalongkorn's reign and during King Vajiravudh's reign.

General Phraya Wisetsingnart did not have the opportunity to witness the events of 1932 and 1934 because he died in 1925. (If the title of Phraya Wisetsingnart appears in 1932, or after that time, it refers to another individual with a different name and surname.) Khunying lived until old age, and some of her descendants are still living in the house at Bang Pho until this day.

When I began to plan this novel, I did not realize that it would be as difficult as writing the novel itself because the framework from the memorial book for Khunying Wisetsingnart's funeral made the task easier for me, since I did not have to think of a framework. Moreover, this novel was published in instalments in *'Kulasatree',* which as its name indicates is a woman's magazine, and the letters I received from readers indicated that most readers like to read novels as novels, not to learn about either recent or past politics. Therefore, I did not delve into the history of Rama VII's era any more than was necessary in referring to the social setting, in line with my purpose to write a novel set in this era.

On the contrary, when I actually began to write, I had to pore over book after book before I was able to come up with the setting for the 24th of June 1932 which was the day of the revolution, and even more difficult was the 11th of October 1933 which was the start of the fighting, which later became known as the 'Boworadet Rebellion'. If I had passed over it with only a brief mention, the protagonist's fate would not have been apparent, so more research was necessary than I had originally planned.

Although the People's Party was successful in creating a new form of government, in practice, democracy was not fully realized, and the Boworadet Rebellion, which took place just over a year later, was not a separate event, but a continuation of the former. I agree with the ideas of Professor Dr Chayanan Samuthawinich, who wrote the following in *'Kana Rasadorn kab Kabot Boworadet'* ('The People's Party and the Boworadet Rebellion'):

I have noticed the following things, which have led to my personal conclusion about the Boworadet Rebellion of October 1933:

'The Boworadet Rebellion' and the elimination of individuals between 1933 and 1939 was part of the Revolution of 1932, which did not end completely on the 24th of June 1932.

Dr Chayanan also posed the following question in addition to the aforementioned idea:

Recent history books in both Thai and English tend to say that the Revolution of 1932 was a smooth transition, which did not result in loss of life like in other countries and was a bloodless revolution.

Students of the Revolution of 1932 should not stop at the events of the 24th of June 1932 but should research the People's Party, or the perpetrators, who claimed to be the people's vanguards in order to bring about more freedom and equality than the system of absolute monarchy had allowed. The Revolution of 1932 was not bloodless. The elimination of both individuals who opposed the perpetrators and the perpetrators themselves continued between 1933 and 1939.

Fair-minded individuals should also research whether any of the perpetrators, who made ten promises, were ever true vanguards of the people once they gained power.

It is an interesting question for outsiders with a passing or serious interest in history, and although *A Night Full of Stars* does not answer it, since it is outside the scope of the novel, it is not a question that can be ignored, so I decided to weave it into some chapters of the novel.

When Major General M.R. Kukrit Pramoj wrote *Four Reigns*, he probably did not expect that his accuracy in relating the details behind historical events would become a blueprint for Thai historical novels, which I have abided by.

I have no one to blame for this novel but myself.

In actual fact, writing a historical novel was awkward for someone like myself, without a strong background in history, for the following reasons:

1. Since the evidence for past events is contradictory, it was necessary for the writer to choose one version, and it was difficult to know which to choose.

A clear example when I was researching was the 11th of October, 1933, when the government decided to open fire on the 'National Salvation Group' troops at Thung Bang Khen. It is stated in the book *'Chao Fa Prachadhipok rachan phu nirat'* by 'Nai Hon Huay' that the rebels fired back immediately, but a letter from Captain Khun Rerng Ronachai, one of the rebels, to Phraya Pahonphonphayuhasena, the Prime Minister, states clearly that General Prince Boworadet, the leader of the rebels, ordered his troops not to use force in return, and that the provincial soldiers on the frontline withstood government fire for one day and one night, and only resorted to fighting when the government refused to negotiate.

'Nai Hon Huay's' book provided a great deal of detail about the past and was a good source of historical background, which several chapters of my novel refer to. However, when I found contradictory evidence, it took me some time to decide to trust Khun Rerng Ronnachai's letter more, because if it were untrue, I do not believe he would have been bold enough to tell the Prime Minister otherwise, since opening fire is not something that can be done in secret with only a few people knowing about it. Phraya Pahon must have known the truth, but King Prajadhipok wrote about it in 1949, sixteen years after the event, so some of the details may have been inaccurate. [he was dead in 1941]

2. Sensitivity to the feelings of those involved was required.

Although those involved in the events of 1932-33 are no longer here, some of their children are still alive (although very few), and many of their grandchildren are living.

When I was writing my first draft, I received a telephone call from General Phraya Si Sitthisongkhram's daughter. Her love for her father was evident in her voice, and I realized that she had some reservations with regard to me writing about her father and was concerned that I had information that would be detrimental to her children and grandchildren's feelings, so I could only answer that I would be careful not to refer to him in a bad light. Therefore, it was unavoidable for the characters in the novel who are based on real people, such as Luang Phibun Songkhram and General Phraya Si Sitthisongkhram, to say very little and have only minor roles, since the more I wrote about them, the more likely I would be to make a mistake. Even if some things really happened, it would not have been appropriate to write about them if it would have caused offense to those involved, and if I had written about them blindly, I would have had to revise what I had written later.

Even the main characters of Chao Khun and Khunying Wisetsingnart, whom I have stated are only fifty-percent based on real life, caused me some awkwardness when writing about them because, even though their grandchildren were happy for me to write about them and provided me with additional information, there were some grandchildren from whom I was not able to ask permission and I did not know whether they would like it or not. Therefore, I had to be careful not to damage their reputations in any way.

If Gade sometimes appears to be a 'superwoman', it was for that reason, but I must insist that basing 'Gade's' character in the novel on Khunying Wisetsingnart was no exaggeration. She was a beautiful woman (as is evident in her granddaughter's photograph of herself when she was a student, whom her father said looked identical to her grandmother when she was the same age), and Khun Pisawong Saiyen, her eighty-year-old niece from Phetchaburi, who was born in time to see Chao Khun and Khunying, confirmed to me that "Khunying was more beautiful and elegant than any of the other villagers."

Moreover, Khunying's life was not exaggerated in Gade's life and may indeed have been even more difficult, since she was separated from her husband for eight years (not four years like in the novel) and she lived alone with her child in Ban Tha Hin, not with her parents and sisters. She also had to travel from Phetchaburi to look for her husband in the capital several times for a whole year before she found him, and it was no less difficult for them to reach a mutual understanding.

Her descendants, who were born in time to see Khunying Wisetsingnart, confirmed that she was kind, diligent, frugal and upright, as well as loyal towards her husband. As I was writing this novel, I felt as though I had come to know 'Gade' more and more as if she had been a real person and it was this feeling that was instrumental in enabling me to see the novel through to the finish.

The character of the male protagonist, Nart, or Phraya Wisetsingnart, was even more difficult to write than that of 'Gade'. In the sixty or so novels that I have written, I have never created a male protagonist that has this kind of conflict with the female protagonist.

It must be remembered that, in Thai society in the past, it was not illegal for Thai men to have several wives and was considered normal. Even if the practice caused some problems, it was considered a private matter, not an act of wrongdoing that affected others. However, when writing the novel in 1998, in an era when women stood shoulder to shoulder with men, I felt that it was difficult to persuade readers to support the protagonists making up with each other, rather than supporting the female protagonist to marry another man, which she could have done if the same thing were to happen today.

The real Phraya Wisetsingnart's character was a mystery to me because he died before any of his grandchildren were born, so I didn't have an opportunity to ask anyone. I was told briefly by Khun Pisawong Saiyen that "Chao Khun was a calm man", but she did not see him until he was close to the end of his life.

Ajarn Puangkaew shared that her mother had told her that Chao Khun was a kind father whose children were the apple of his eye. One night, when they had been on their way back from an important event, his daughter had let go of the balloon that he had bought for her, and he had had the car turn back, so he could buy her a new one. Therefore, I believe he must have been gentle with his children.

The other inferences made about his character are entirely my own, and if they are inaccurate or inappropriate, I take full responsibility because I imagined 'Nart' to be like that and that is why the story ends happily. I might add that, during the period when this story was published in instalments in *'Kulasatree'* magazine, there were no readers who disapproved of 'Nart' and most of them supported the protagonists in making up.

Chao Chom Amphan is also based on a real person who was one of the five favourite consorts of King Chulalongkorn. She was someone whom Khunying Wisetsingnart highly esteemed and they were very close. Khunying's granddaughter told me that Khun Chom had given her a set of gold buttons inscribed with her name along with a photograph of herself when she was young.

All the other characters in this novel are fictional, such as Ned, Phraya Thepakanee, Man, Surai and Malai. If they bear any resemblance to real people, it is pure coincidence.

Another individual whom I must thank for his kindness is Honorary Professor Dr Thermsuk Numnon, one of the country's historical experts. Besides his book, *'Lakorn karn muang'* (or its previous title, *'Pathiwat 2475')*, which provides a clear picture of the events of the 24th of June 1932 he also kindly enlightened me each time I bothered him with my questions about the history of Rama VII's reign and was never impatient, no matter how trivial my questions.

Finally, I would like to give all the credit for readers' enjoyment of this novel to General Phraya Wisetsingnart and Khunying Wisetsingnart, and I take sole responsibility for any mistakes or inaccuracies, no matter how significant or insignificant they may be.

Bibliography

Books about political events from 1932-1939:

Chayanan Samuthawonich, Professor Dr
Kana Rasadorn kap Kabot Boworadet (The People's Party and the Boworadet Rebellion)

'Na Petch Phoom' (pseudonym)
Kamsaruan Phraya Si (Mourning Phraya Si)

Thermsuk Numnon, Honorary Professor, Dr
Lakorn karn muang (Political Theatre)

'Nai Hon Huay' (pseudonym)
Chao Fa Prajadhipok rachan phu nirat (Prince Prajadhipok, King of Poetry)

Pimwan Sethabutr
Sor Sethabutr (prawat chiwit) (Sor Sethabutr: A Bibliography)

Phunpisamai Disakul, Mom Chao Ying
Sing thi khapachao pop hen (The Things I Have Seen)
(Published for the funeral of Mom Chao Ying Phunpisamai Disakul)

Acharaporn Kumutphisamai
Panha pai nai sangkom Thai korn karn pathiwat song phan ha roi jet sip ha:phap sathorn jaak ngan khien thang nang sua pim (Problems in Thai Society before the Revolution of 1932: Reflections from Newspaper Articles)
(Published by the Institute for Thai Case Studies, Thammasat University)

Books about Past Thai Society

Kanchanakphan (pseudonym)
Krungthep mue paed sip pi korn (Bangkok Eighty Years Ago)
Dek khlong bang luang (A Child from Khlong Bang Luang)

Kaemkarn Supawan (pseudonym)
Kep wai nai kwam song cham (Keep the Memories)

Chula Chakrabongse, Prachao Worawong Ther Pra Ong Chao
Chao Chiwit (Lords of Life)

Jintana Isarangkul Na Ayutthaya
Wan warn thi parn pai (Past Days)

Thipawanee Sanithawong
Mue khun ta khun yai yang dek (When my Grandparents were Young)

Thep Chu Thap Tong
Krungthep nai adid (Bangkok in the Past)

M.L. Nueang Nilrat
Chiwit nai wang (Life in the Palace) Books 1 and 2

Pramoj Thasanasuwan
Rattanakosin ro so song roi (Two-hundred Years of Rattanakosin)

Lawan Chotamaru
Morodok Thai (Thai Heritage)

Suwicha (pseudonym)
Wan warn thi parn ma (Past Days)

Anek Nawikamul
Raek mi nai siam (The First in Siam) Books 1-4
Prapheni chiwit Thai (Thai Life and Customs)
Tamnarn hang ran Siam (A History of Siamese Stores)

About Khunying Vinita (Vinicchayakul) Diteeyont

Khunying Vinita Diteeyont, the National Artist of 2004, is an author, academic, critic and translator under the pen names V. Vinicchayakul and Kaewkao.

Educational Background

Alumnus of 35th class of Mater Dei College

Alumnus of 26th class of Triam Udom Suksa School

Bachelor degree from the Faculty of Language Arts, Chulalongkorn University, 34th class

EdD in Curriculum and Instruction (Literature) from the University of Northern Colorado, USA

Professional Background

She was a lecturer in the Faculty of Language Arts, Silpakorn University from 1970-1995 for 25 years. The year before retiring, she held the position_of Level 9 Associate Professor.

She was a part time lecturer in Translation for graduate students of the Language Research Institute, Mahidol University from 1995-2010.

She has been in charge of the website www.reurnthai.com since 1999 until the present, proliferating knowledge of language, culture, literature, history and general knowledge under the name "Tao Chompoo" after the colour of the Faculty of Language Arts, Chulalongkorn University.

She has received 12 other honorary awards, namely:

1. The Thai National Heritage Preservation Award in 1994
2. The Thai National Culture Award in 1997

3. The Prakaew Thong Kam Award for Outstanding Alumni of the Faculty of Language Arts, Chulalongkorn University in 2001
4. The Angela Award of the Inter-Ursuline Student Community (Thailand) as an alumnus of Mater Dei College for Service to Society in 2004
5. The National Artist Award for Literature in 2004
6. The Democratic Family Example (The 'Diteeyont' family Sompan-Khunying Vinita Diteeyont) in 2005 from the National Identity Committee
7. She was the first foreigner to receive the Doctor of Humane Letters from the University of Northern Colorado in 2005 because her work received numerous national awards and she brought prestige to the university.
8. Outstanding Mother of Bangkok in 2007 for promoting Thai Arts and Culture and Performance
9. The Surintaracha Award for Outstanding Senior Translators in 2008 from the The Translator and Interpreter Association of Thailand
10. Honoured Alumna of the University of Northern Colorado in 2009
11. The Patokta Silpa Bhirasri Award in 2014 and the Silpa Bhirasri Medal of Honour
12. The Honorary Award for Literature of Bangkok Districts for her novels *"Song Fang Khlong"* (Khlongsarn District), *"Jak Fan Su Nirandorn"* (Ladprao District), and "Burapha" (Thonburi District) in 2014

She has received 24 awards for writing from both the government and private sectors, including awards for *Rattanakosin, Song Fang Khlong, Niramit, Ratri Pradap Dao, Burapha, Malai Sam Chai*, and others.

Of these, the novel, *"Rattanakosin"* has been acclaimed as national literature. She is a composer for the Suntaraporn Band. Most of her work was writing the lyrics for royal songs and songs for Suntaraporn concerts, such as *Tawaisaja* and *Dangsaifon*.

Examples of Past Work

1. Arbitrator for the Institute of the Department of Intellectual Property
2. President of the Board of Judges for the SEA Write Award Fiction Category
3. Subcommittee for Child and Youth Affairs of the Social Commission, National Legislative Assembly

Current Work

1. She is an advisor to the Suntaraporn Foundation.
2. She is on the subcommittee for publications in honour of His Majesty King Maha Vajiralongkorn in the field of sports of the Sports Authority of Thailand.
3. She is a member of the National Identity Foundation committee.
4. She is a member of the National Identity committee.

She has been awarded the following decorations of honour:

1. The Most Exalted Order of the White Elephant in 1991
2. The Knight Grand Cross (First Class) of the Most Noble Order of the Crown of Thailand in 1995
3. The Most Illustrious Order of Chulachomklao (Fourth Class) in 1998
4. The Most Illustrious Order of Chulachomklao (Third Class) in 2001
5. Companion (Fourth Class) of the Most Admirable Order of the Direkgunabhorn in 2006

ราตรี
ประดับดาว

ราตรี
ประดับดาว

ราตรีประดับดาว

ราตรี
ประดับดาว